THE STATION

NIKKI PEOPLES

The Station

For information about this title or to order other books and/or electronic media, contact the publisher:

Black Kat Books
P. O. Box 24462
Knoxville, TN 37933-4462
www.blackkatbooks.com
publisher@blackkatbooks.com

Library of Congress Control Number: 2019918350

ISBN: 978-1-7341826-0-6 (Hardcover)
       978-1-7341826-1-3 (Softcover)
       978-1-7341826-2-0 (eBook)

Printed in the United States of America

Cover and Interior design: 1106 Design

To Mom and Dad,
This first one is for you. Your never-ending
love, support, personal sacrifices, and faith in me
means more than you can possibly fathom.

Acknowledgements

Roger, thanks for being my partner in crime both in life and in the writing world. Your enthusiasm about writing inspires me.

Phaedra, big sis, you always have my back . . . no matter what . . . even when I don't deserve it.

Kip, you're the one who encouraged me to study the craft of writing and make it a priority in my life. For that, I am profoundly grateful.

Peter Duvall, thank you for guiding me with a gentle but firm hand. Your advice was always invaluable.

Thank you to Jodi Lisberger, Rachel Harper, Sam Zalutsky, Eleanor Morse, and Phil Deaver, my other mentors from Spalding University, who played a huge part in making this novel possible. I'd like to give additional thanks to the staff and faculty at Spalding University. All of you have been generous with your help and have given me a plethora of gems regarding the craft of writing.

My fellow classmates at Spalding University: thank you for the support and shared experience of being newbies in the writing world.

My good friends: Ziad, Jennifer W., Jennifer R., Emily, thank you for the positive yet honest feedback.

Leah, thanks for understanding the struggle and for your willingness to give advice whenever I needed it.

Spyder and Dao, you were my faithful companions throughout this journey. Spyder, for well over a decade, you were always beside me, peacefully curled up next to my keyboard and a stack of books. Dao, my spiritual guide, you kept my feet warm and my soul full during the ups and downs. I love and miss you both so much.

1

Mining Station #0517212 (Station Tengelei)
Biotech Research Laboratories Dumpster

I know how to find trouble.

Or rather, it knows how to find me like a heat-seeking missile. Life has always been that way for me, though, a continuous onslaught of near misses and close calls. This time, I wonder if I'll make it through intact.

I had five years of obligated Navy service which I wanted to complete as quickly and hassle free as possible, but it turns out the universe had other things in mind. When I was informed that my first ship assignment was the *USSS Midway,* I was livid. I'd heard rumors of an excessive number of scandals and mishaps on the floating city of three thousand. Despite my best efforts to be assigned to a different ship, it would be my home for the next two years. I resolved to mind my own business and get the tour over with as soon as possible. But I'm the legal officer, and I've been thrust, front and center, face-to-face with danger, the kind of danger that can get you killed. People have died.

What I'm about to tell you involves *things* I never imagined could exist: wild, diabolical, super-human things. I'll save you the embellishments and exaggerations. Just the facts are all that's required. I wouldn't even know what to call them except for being told they are called ACs. What's an AC, you might ask? An animated corpse. So a zombie? No, not exactly. *Zombie* implies: mindless, dawdling corpse in tattered rags, a creature in limbo, not quite living but not quite dead, either. ACs are in limbo, too, but they think, sense and strategize. They hunt. A zombie doesn't hunt. It moves with the urgency of a sloth. I'd hardly say they elicit any measure of fear. Maybe if you're pathetic enough to stumble at the right moment while being chased, a gaggle of them will dog-pile you in hungry desperation. But let those two little letters, *A* and *C,* trickle from a person's lips, and *that* will evoke terror. ACs are pure evil, the calculating, impervious-to-pain, lightning-fast mother-fucking kind of evil. They're meat puppets controlled by the nasty little slugs.

And they're about to find me.

If they do, they'll rip me to pieces with ruthless efficiency and maybe eat my brains out, unless I can get out of this laboratory dumpster unnoticed.

2

One week earlier

August 2398
United States Spaceship Midway (LHD-61), Eris Class, Multi-sphere Assault Ship, Flagship
Interplanetary Space Interdiction Company Three (ISIC 3), approximately 848 light years from Earth and 1000.78 miles from Station Tengelei.

Life began to deteriorate on a Monday. Two shitty things happened that day. First, I witnessed my boyfriend flirting with the gorgeous, newly reported Marine geologist. Second, I received news of my senior chief's murder. Now, I had no great love for Senior Chief McGinn, but the thought of a murder happening onboard the *Midway* was an unsettling thought.

It was Monday afternoon, and I was late for yoga. I rushed to get changed. I slipped on a pair of tight yoga pants over a curvy figure. I don't have the ideal yoga body. I'm not tall, rail thin or bendy. I'm built more like a sprinter, tight and compact with narrow hips, and a protruding but well-defined rear end. I've got boobs too. They're not enormous, but I'm not flat-chested, either. There's enough there for them to meet my thighs during a forward fold.

I took one last glance into the mirror. My hair needed to be put up, so I smoothed the kinky cloud away from my face and gathered the unruly curls into a tight bun. I smeared a touch of burgundy-colored lip gloss on to my full lips. I was blessed with soft, smooth dark skin, so I don't need a ton of makeup. Foundation is out of the question. If I sweat it'll drip right off, and if there's a stain to be had on a pair of dress whites or even my khakis, I'll manage it. It certainly doesn't do much to cover the scar across my cheekbone, a souvenir from one of my father's ruthless training sessions in the woods. My eyes, a prominent feature on my face, are the only feature about myself that I appreciate. Their espresso-colored irises twinkle yet hold a certain intensity, and they sweep upward, giving me a somewhat feline-like appearance. Today my eyes looked tired. I used an extra layer of mascara along my lashes to draw attention away from the bags that hugged the bottom lids. Satisfied with my appearance, I snatched up my yoga mat and left my stateroom.

I hurried long the catwalk, determined not to be late for the class. Self-conscious of my appearance, I didn't want to endure any scrutiny or the sanctimonious gazes reserved for latecomers. I put some turbo into my step.

Despite running late, I stopped and peered over the catwalk railing. A lump formed in the back of my throat. Marine Captain Eric Hunt was getting touchy-feely with the new Marine Corps geologist who'd reported onboard two weeks ago. She was wearing *my* ring, the one he'd given me. I grimaced.

This was the same Monday that Afloat Training Group was conducting an inspection of the ship. Gridlock and delays popped up everywhere onboard, especially the well deck. I avoided my usual trek through the belly of the ship and decided to take an alternate route. The catwalk was a narrow walkway, a metal, grated platform suspended forty feet up above the well deck and ran its perimeter.

The catwalk would give me the shortcut I needed to circumvent the chaos below and get me to class on time.

The well deck was packed to maximum capacity, its congestion level now at its peak. If the *Midway* didn't get its well deck certification, the ship wouldn't deploy. It only took one division failure for the entire ship to fail inspection, and there were approximately 120 divisions onboard. A failed ATG deployment certification inspection would be bad for everyone. Word would get around to the space stations, and the commodore's career would lose its upward trajectory. No one wanted a grumpy commodore on deck. A grumpy commodore meant pissed-off department heads, which meant torture for the division officers. No one wanted their individual units to be the reason for a failed inspection. So all of the department heads and division officers hunkered down and had their people occupied all week at a relentless pace. Loading robots, Marines, and Sailors worked side by side in assembly-line fashion to pack vehicles and spacecraft with essential equipment.

The ATG inspectors observed the efficiency of the Zippers as they glided across the well deck to deliver equipment parts, electronic documents, holographic images and messages to eager recipients. Essentials moved back and forth from forward to aft, port to starboard at high speeds along the rail system that spread its web across the well deck floor. Skeeters followed suit, except in the air, whizzing about with similar urgency. Assault and cargo vehicles were staged, loaded, and rotated around on the well deck turntable to be made ready for extraction into space from the ship's bowels. Force reconnaissance and special warfare equipment was strewn everywhere. Boxes of x-ray and night vision eyewear, handheld laser shields, first aid canisters, meals-ready-to-eat, several large ammo pallets and various Marine assault equipment peppered the edges of the well deck floor. The belly of the *Midway* was a virtual hive of activity to conduct all loading and repositioning operations. Like its waterborne predecessors, the big deck amphibious surface ships, the *Midway* was a space-craft carrier that extracted spacecraft out of its well and across its stern gate instead of watercraft.

To my relief, my division had passed its part of the inspection early. I told my senior chief to let the guys take the rest of the day off. I decided to use the extra time to work out and de-stress.

I watched the distraction below. A current of jealousy pulsed through me as Sherri's fingers rested lightly on Eric's abdomen while she leaned in to whisper something into his ear. A ritual of whispering, laughing and touching each other unfolded before me. It was all so casual. No one around them seemed to notice.

I noticed, though. Eric used to be like that with me.

This confirmed that Eric and I were done. The end of our relationship had never been vocalized, but I'd felt a shift a couple of weeks back. He'd always had an eye for women with European features (i.e., lighter skin and bone-straight hair). I'd been biding my time, waiting for him to move on to lighter pastures. Two months ago, he started to pull away, after *it* arrived. *It* was Indian, which was perfect for him. His mother had made it clear: *Don't bring home any white girls.* But 2nd Lieutenant Sherri Kolar wasn't white. She wasn't black, either. She had enough melanin in her skin not to totally offend his mother, who would put up a mild protest.

Eric's calls became infrequent and his visits even more so. A week ago, he announced that we should "take some time to think" . . . whatever that meant. Now, *it* was wearing *my* HyFiT ring, the one he'd given me.

That prick.

We'd dated for two years. The first time he offered me his old HyFiT ring, I politely refused. It was too lavish a gift. Hydrostatic Field Technology was high tech and pricey. Compact, mobile and capable of providing 360-degree protection from almost anything, including bullets, they were an exclusive item in high demand. Only the elite of the elite special forces were issued HyFiT rings, and only the wealthy could afford them. I didn't go out in the field all that much. Most of my workday was spent inside ammo magazine spaces and missile control rooms. So, I didn't understand his insistence on me having one, plus I felt it would be put to better use if he gave it to a fellow Marine. Eric liked to flaunt his status, though, and I declined his offer three times before he finally mentioned that it was some sort of a romantic gesture. Guiltily, I accepted it and cherished it, until now. Seeing it on Sherri's dainty hand felt like a kick in the face. I shouldn't have left it in his stateroom during our last quarrel. Now it adorned Sherri Kolar's slender, perfectly manicured finger—the same perfectly manicured finger that traced a line along Eric's velvety, brown bicep.

A vein strained against the hem of his olive-green t-shirt sleeve. His arms looked bigger. He'd been working out. For her, probably. He rested an elbow on the same ammunition pallet Sherri was leaning against. He grinned at her as he passed an inventory wand back and forth across the pallet. There was a beep. A blue holograph of the SKU number flashed briefly before disappearing. Sherri leaned in close to whisper something again. *Did she have to whisper every damn thing she said to him?* Eric's eyes dropped to her lips. I could feel my stomach roll. Then he said something, and she laughed like it was the funniest thing she'd ever heard. I knew for a fact that Eric wasn't *that* funny. He flashed another bright white smile. She flashed an even whiter one in return.

I could feel a lump form in the back of my throat. We'd been in love, or maybe only *I* had been in love. Suddenly he'd wanted to take a break. Now, he was crazy for some girl he just met. Was I so easily forgotten? Of course, she was part of the reason he'd moved on, but had our relationship begun to fall apart before or after her arrival? These thoughts tinkered around in my head until I found myself staring down at Sherri, who squinted up at me from below. Momentary recognition flashed in her eyes just before I clutched my yoga mat to my chest and ducked into a small alcove nearby. I waited. Then I heard laughing. Were they laughing at me? Their laughter floated up above the noise caused by the pandemonium below. I refused to leave with them watching me. I waited. Time passed painfully slow. It felt like eons, but only a couple of minutes had passed. I could still get to yoga in time. I waited a little bit longer until finally I didn't care. I left the alcove and decided to ditch yoga. Yoga wouldn't cut it. I needed a fight.

3

I turned to head for the fight simulator and ran into someone's chest. A man's. Massive. Chiseled. My hands came up to steady myself. My fingers gripped chords of pectoral muscles that streamed across a broad torso. Whoever he was, he was tall and fit. The tip of my nose reached his collarbone. He smelled *good*.

"Uh. Excuse me. I'm sorry," I said.

"No problem. So are you always this unaware?" There was a note of amusement in his voice.

"I was distracted and didn't know you were behind me." I sounded more defensive than I'd intended.

"I know." He smirked.

My heart sped up a little. I looked down and toyed with the tassel on my yoga mat, searching for something witty to say—something along the lines of "if you saw me, why didn't you move?" But, of course, I didn't say that. He lifted my chin with his finger.

Inappropriate for a stranger and arrogant, I thought. Though he didn't strike me as the type of guy who cared about propriety. Being honest with myself, I didn't exactly mind, either.

At first glance, his eyes were brown. Then I noticed the green. I shifted my chin away, ever so slightly.

"You're Ensign Amelia Brown, right?"

How did he know that?

"Uh, yeah." He seemed to wait for me to ask who he was, so I did. "Who are you?"

"I'm Gerard LaSalle." He smirked and extended his hand. "Nice to meet you."

"Nice to meet you too."

We stood regarding each other while our hands were locked. I pulled away first, but his fingers lingered a bit before all contact was broken. Then it got awkward. I looked away. His gaze went to the well deck.

"The Marine captain over there . . . what's his name?" He tilted his head toward Eric, who was momentarily looking at Sherri like she was grilled steak.

"That's Eric Hunt."

"Well, Eric's an idiot."

"You know him?"

"No." He shrugged.

I didn't know what to say, so I looked away.

"I take it you were together?" LaSalle took a step closer to me. "How did *that* happen?"

"That's really none of your business." I felt my face heat up. The words spilled out like a container of razor blades. He'd obviously watched me watch them.

I opened my mouth to qualify my statement, but he held up his hand. "I was only curious, but you're right. It's none of my business. You seem too good for him, though."

He thought I was too good for Eric. That made me feel all tingly inside and a little guilty. I wanted to take it back, but I didn't say anything. I didn't trust him. My spidey senses said: *Be careful with this one.* Besides, I was still waiting for him to say something stupid like: *You're pretty for a black girl.*

His eyes scanned my entire body. *Rude or cocky? Definitely cocky.* He stared at me until I squirmed a bit. Could he tell that I felt guilty for being so bitchy?

"You're the ship's legal officer, right? Is that a collateral duty?"

"Yes. It is. My primary duty is as the ship's Weapons Officer."

"Ah, you got to spend some time at JJOI. How long?"

JJOI (pronounced "joy") stood for Joint Junior Officer Instruction, the place where newly commissioned officers went to study their expertise.

"Three years. Two years for Legal Officer Training. One year for Weapons Officer Training."

"Holy hell. Your collateral duties take up more time than your primary duties. Typical Navy."

"You were at JJOI?"

"Yep, and there was nothing *joyful* about it, except the chow."

I agreed. The entire compound was one color: gray. It looked like a World War II communist bloc city. No recreation, no civilians and no nightlife. Mail, supplies and personnel were delivered or sent only twice a week because it was isolated. Life there felt like a prison camp.

"How did you end up there?"

"I was there for Basic Underwater Demolition Training. Then I had four more months after BUD/S for SQT. Couldn't wait to get out of there."

"You're a SEAL?"

"Was a SEAL. Now I work for Biotech, one of the government contractors."

I felt my shields go up. His credentials and how he carried himself—like someone accustomed to wealth—made me think *arrogant, entitled douchebag.* Yet, I was impressed. Becoming a SEAL, especially in recent times, was no small feat. Ever since space travel and the discovery of "other beings," SEALS were required to push beyond the limits of the human body and mind. Fighting other species and beings with attributes that often surpassed the capabilities of humans required a special kind of soldier. No wonder he was so ripped. I was curious about the work he did for Biotech, but I'd save those questions for later. I didn't want to seem eager.

He raised his eyebrows at me, as if he knew I had questions I didn't ask. He didn't say anything, though. He just stared, perfectly comfortable with the silence. He passed a hand through his sandy-colored hair. He had strong hands and an angular jaw. He was tall but not freakishly so. He was probably around six foot two or three, holding 200 pounds of solid muscle. Mounds of quadricepral greatness bulged from the hem of his mid-thigh length, black PT shorts. Two columns and eight rows of hard granite abs strained against his black t-shirt. An emblem stitched in neon green shimmered with the words: "A.F.I.B. ~ BIOTECH" on his left pectoral muscle. His arms bulged and popped with veins that ran like treacherous highways down to his wrists. He was handsome, not in a *GQ*-way but in an *I've-seen-some-serious-shit-in-my-life* kind of way. He oozed confidence and reeked of danger, which I found oddly intoxicating.

He watched me look at him. He looked at me back, daring me not to look away, but I did. My nerves were firing like pistons.

"Well, I need to get moving," I said.

"Where are you going?"

He's audacious.

"Vinyasa Flow Yoga class."

"I like yoga. Mind if I join you?"

"It's an advanced class."

"I'm sure I can handle it."

I'm sure you can too.

Despite his muscles, I had the feeling he was still pretty limber. Thank goodness for my dark skin. I could feel my face heat up at the thought of his body.

"It's too late anyway. I'll probably just duck out of it. The class has already started."

"Why don't you join me then?"

Panic. He wasn't giving up. "Thanks, but I think I'll wait for the evening class."

It wasn't a total lie. I planned to go later in the evening as long as I wasn't too worn out from the combat simulator. I needed contact, but I didn't want him knowing that. Being a SEAL and all, he'd try to go with me. That simulator was one of the best-kept secrets on the ship. I wanted to keep it that way.

He eyed me for a moment. My skin tingled as his eyes traveled up and down my body before he smiled and said, "Okay. Sure. Some other time perhaps."

He left. I exhaled as I watched his retreating form. Relieved, I glanced back down at the well deck. Both Eric and Sherri were watching me.

Funny how I didn't care.

4

The simulator was tucked away in the back room of the Anchor Windlass, a shipboard bar frequented mostly by civilian contractors. Military personnel (except for the occasional officer) rarely went there because the drinks were more expensive. Thankfully it afforded some privacy and little wait on the days I needed a good workout. It was the only hand-to-hand combat game onboard that was outfitted with "full immersion software." Each simulation, therefore, felt like a real fight. The consequences of a missed block or landed punch translated to actual pain.

I arrived at the Windlass and tossed my yoga mat to the midshipman on duty, a new kid in training I'd never seen before. He managed to look miserable and bored all at once.

"Think fast."

He snatched it in the air and shoved it behind the bar. "Can I help you, ma'am?"

"Unless you want to fight me, no."

His eyes lit up, and he stood. The petty officer who managed the bar nodded to me but shook his head "no" at the midshipman. The midshipman slumped back down onto his stool and sulked.

The Windlass was generally empty during working hours, unlike the Flying Spinnaker, an enlisted dive bar which stayed busy at all hours due to varying port and starboard shift schedules. While the Flying Spinnaker offered more up-to-date recreational games like HALO XXIII and Drag Racer V, I preferred the Windlass. It was the largest bar on the *Midway*. The décor was basic. The layout and design of the tables and chairs was plain yet functional. The carpet was clean but cheap. Faux wood paneling graced the walls. Cocktails were served in mason jars, and beers were served out of the bottle or in plastic mugs. It was a place that valued practicality over luxury. The highest piece of art was a mounted license plate collage cut out of each state arranged in the shape of the United States.

What the Windlass lacked in decor, it made up for in fun, though. It offered old-school classics like pool tables, dart boards, foosball and air hockey. The only contemporary game in the Windlass was the personal combat simulator: Gladiator 4-D. I'd been playing it since I was a plebe at the Naval Academy, seven years ago. It was a great workout, and it propelled my self-defense skills set to the next level. The only other self-defense training I'd had were the grueling sessions my father made me endure.

When I arrived at the simulator, I was surprised to see people waiting to play. My division's Leading Petty Officer, Elena Martinez, several of my gunners mates and fire control technicians, along with a gaggle of other sailors and Marines, stood in line.

Just great. So much for my alone time.

"I thought you all were headed out for drinks," I said, trying to suppress my irritation.

"This is the only bar that has Gladiator 4D," said Martinez. "We usually come here in the evenings, but Senior Chief let us leave early."

She gave me a cautious look, hoping I wouldn't override Senior Chief McGinn, who hadn't even given the order. Senior Chief was my division chief, but he was my polar opposite: an older, conservative male from a small town who believed in respecting institutions (unless they didn't align with his way of thinking). We were constantly at odds, and like wary children of divorces, the people in my division were usually caught in the middle.

"Yeah. The decision to let you off early was mine, not Senior Chief's." I was being petty. I wanted him to know what it felt like to be undermined for once.

Her shoulders relaxed a little. "So this is where you typically sneak off to for your morning workout."

Bitch, don't keep tabs on me. Martinez wasn't generally a nosy person. So I chose to ignore the comment. "I thought I was the only person who used this game."

"No way, ma'am. We use it whenever we can. And we've been trying forever to get the MWR officer to order another two stations."

"Fantastic." I feigned enthusiasm. I didn't want a new simulator replacing this one.

"Ma'am, have you played anyone good lately?"

"Well, I usually just link my A.I. advisor, Shakespeare, to the game's mainframe. I don't like him, but he's a ruthless adversary and much smarter than the game's computer."

"Wait. You have an A.I. advisor?"

"Yes."

"But you don't like him?"

"No, I don't like any forms of artificial intelligence."

"Why not?"

"I don't trust it. Shakespeare has helped me improve a lot, so I allow him to train me."

She just looked at me. I could tell that she thought I was spoiled. Only senior officers had A.I. advisors. None of the other junior officers or enlisted personnel had A.I. technology. I was lucky enough to room with a technology whiz who gave me access. Shakespeare was our personal information butler, and in the past eight months, his workouts had sharpened my combat skills. I'd advanced to Segundus Palus—Second Sword.

"It looks like there are a lot of people waiting to play," I said, keeping my tone even. I didn't want to wait, but I couldn't leave; it'd look like I was throwing a silent tantrum. I wasn't going to throw my rank around, either, to advance in line. I hated senior officers who did that to me. "I guess I'll just watch."

I looked past Martinez to see Petty Officer Corbel and Marine Corporal Harrison slipping into black skintight, morph suits. A colored seam traveled the length of their suits from foot to fingertips, all the way up to the crown of their heads, identifying each player. As they stepped up to their individual platforms, the lights dimmed, and the seams of their suits illuminated—Corbel in orange and Harrison in neon green. Their eyes were covered with game goggles that matched their respective colors. They bounced up and down, lifting their legs as high as possible, stretching, tilting their heads forwards, backwards, sideways.

I understood the feeling, the nerves that preceded a good fight. The game felt so real. Suspended above them was a hologram of a scoreboard that floated in between the two platforms. Each player stood at the center of their own separate sizable, shiny black platforms that were each about twenty feet in diameter. At three equidistant points along the perimeter of each platform were canisters which held an assortment of long and short game weapons, the deadly ends formed by laser light imaging and holographs. Each platform was wirelessly linked to a long rectangular black box that rested between the platforms. The box processed data from the signals transmitted by the sensors which were stitched within the morph suits. The data produced live video images. The players by themselves looked ridiculous, simulating rapid punches, kicks and a bevy of acrobatic martial arts moves on the platform with no visible opponent. But once the fighting began, we didn't watch the players, our gazes traveled up. Each player's name flashed in their respective colors above before three-dimensional life-sized images, in full color, materialized above the box between them. The images included everything from the players' fighting stances and facial expressions to their chosen landscape for the fight (in this case, desert).

In the 3D images, the players also appeared in "outfits" rather than the morph suits they were actually playing in. This was more for showmanship rather than having any real functionality. Some people donned Shogun apparel; others went for Roman gladiator gear or something along the lines of Viking war outfits. I generally chose a post-apocalyptic, Mad Max–type of garb. All gray and brown, distressed leather. I couldn't quite get into the theatrical even though the choice of outfit in no way hampered my movements, since I'd actually be wearing a simulator morph suit. Competitor outfit choices were solely for the benefit of onlookers, who watched the fights as though enjoying a cinematic experience. This was all made possible through intense transcutaneous laser neuromuscular stimulation. The hand-to-hand combat in this game looked real, sounded real and felt real. Some of my best workouts came from this game, and the authenticity behind it gave one an incentive to get really good at self-protection.

Two petty officers were suited up and ready to go. I watched as each player shook hands (of course, they shook air). From the player's perspective, the game not only felt real, but the visual perception felt real too. Being in the simulator felt like being in an actual cage or a gladiator's arena or whatever environment the players pre-programmed into the simulator. Even though each player moved on separate platforms, the players' perceptions were that their opponents were directly in front of them. They could feel their opponent touching them even though they were far apart. Whether a tap on the shoulder or a punch to the midsection, it was all perceived as real.

After the two petty officers shook hands, the countdown to their fight began, provided by a suitably British computer voice. Heads raised to the floating images above as the fighters faced off. A hush fell across the onlookers. Images of a desert-like landscape began to fill the air above the platforms. Sharp, thorny cactus materialized into view. Sand whipped up into the air and spiraled around the fighters—Petty Officer Corbel in a long black trench coat and black shiny leather and Petty Officer Harrison in Spartan apparel. All were eager to witness the impending violence that was about to take place. Only those who were waiting to fight next ignored the images, both out of nervousness and a desire to focus on their own upcoming fight. They warmed up, unsure if the fight between the petty officers would be drawn out or quick.

Petty Officer Corbel's trench coat billowed out behind him as a tendril of sand swirled around him. He advanced to throw the first punch, but Corporal Harrison deflected it with a leather-plated forearm. My gaze dropped from the images above to focus on the competitors . . . I liked to watch the morph suits light up once contact was made. Lights pulsed through Harrison's morph suit as he deflected Corbel's strike. A bold green neon starburst flashed on his along the blade of Harrison's forearm to indicate the location of contact. He answered Corbel's punch with one of his own. A green light pulsed from his shoulder blade and radiated down his arm to his knuckles as he sent his fist flying towards Corbel's jaw. The scoreboard lit up and the computer voice announced: *Gladiator in Orange. 40% damage. Trauma. Left jaw.* All fighters were called "gladiator" by the computer, even though Corbel was dressed like a character in a science fiction film.

Corbel staggered back but recovered quick enough to defend a kick to his left temple. Then he peppered Harrison in the face with a three-punch combination.

Gladiator in Green: 53% damage. Trauma. Right eye. Orbit bone.

Motivated by the damage he caused, Corbel advanced forward with unchecked fervor. He sent wild punches Harrison's way, but Harrison kept his composure. The corporal covered up his face, waiting for his moment. Corbel got too close, and Harrison capitalized on it. He clenched his hands behind Corbel's neck and drove his knee straight into Corbel's liver. Corbel froze for a moment, as if suspended in time, and suddenly crumpled to the canvas floor of his platform, silently clutching his midsection.

"Unhook his suit," someone said. "Hurry!"

Another petty officer rushed to Corbel's side and knelt, unstrapping the wires connected to his suit as fast as possible. Once the wires were unhooked, Corbel recomposed himself. No longer clutching his midsection, he sat up and took a deep breath. He began the task of peeling off his game suit in short, jerky motions.

Lance Corporal Harrison walked over to Corbel's platform and extended a hand. "Good game, man. Are you okay?"

Corbel slapped his hand away and stormed off.

"He's pissed as hell," Martinez said. "What a sore-fucking loser."

"You ever been kicked in the liver?" I asked.

"No."

"It hurts like a son-of-a-bitch."

"I'm sure it does, but not as much as having an arm lopped off, I'll bet."

"Get the hell out," I said with a look of disbelief.

Her face was hard as steel. "I'm serious. By a broadsword. I can't even describe it. At first you don't feel anything, and then the pain sets in."

My stomach was doing somersaults. Shakespeare had never taken my arm, or any limb for that matter, but he had taken my eye once and my ear the first time we ever fought. Those are moments you never forget. Sheer agony. Even after over a hundred simulations, I always got nervous before a fight. While the blows didn't cause actual physical harm, the pain was real. I'd even thought of quitting for good, but there was something about real pain that made me keep coming back. I felt *alive.*

I looked over at Petty Officer Martinez. "Are you any good?"

"Why?" she asked, grinning. "Do you want to find out, ma'am?"

I shrugged. "I'm game if you are."

"You're on. You should know that I won't hold back just because you're my division officer."

"I certainly wouldn't want you to. And I won't hold back, either."

I had to win. I appeared nonchalant, but I was dreading this. *Why did you have to open your mouth, Mel?* She'd thrown the gauntlet down, and I couldn't back out. I'd appear weak. Regardless of the outcome, no one would ever question Martinez' toughness. If I lost, I'd lose a little of the respect of my division.

The minute Petty Officer Martinez and I suited up, people started forming a crowd around the simulator. A few new people showed up, too, including some senior officers. People were so eager to see us fight, that when the last two fighters stepped off of their platforms, we were skipped to the front of the line. Someone announced: Ensign Brown and Petty Officer Martinez get next!

As we donned our game suits, I thought of all the jokes I'd have to endure if I lost: *Officers are too soft. Baby ensign got a dose of the real world. Academy grads are snobs; they can't lead—or fight.* So, I'd play dirty. I would *not* lose. First, I'd get inside her head.

"I've been playing since I was a youngster at the Academy. I'm a Second Sword."

"Well, I've been playing since A-school. Primus Palus—First Sword."

Shit. That backfired. I felt a surge of panic but ignored it. Anything could happen. It all boiled down to who performed better that day. Martinez had the advantage of experience, stamina

21

and reach. She was fit with long limbs. If the fight lasted too long, she'd obliterate me, but I had the advantage of speed, power and her underestimation of me. I knew she'd assume I'd fight fair. I was a green, junior officer who was new to the ship and somewhat quiet, which people often confused with timidity. She'd assume that I'd "set the example" by playing fair, but I intended on using every trick at my disposal.

I tried to guess what type of fighting style she'd use. By the looks of her long, lean build and her stamina, I knew she was more of a striker—Muay Tai or perhaps Karate. She wouldn't want to be on the ground, but that's exactly where I intended to take her. I was more of a grappler. I wanted to get inside and fight close. I'd dirty box her and wrestle her to the ground. Definitely some Jiu Jitsu. She caught me looking at her.

"What?" she said grinning. "You sizing me up?"

"No, sweetie. I've already got you figured out," I said in a deadly tone, but I winked at her.

She snorted but grinned back.

"Weapons?" I asked, hoping that would unsettle her. Most people hadn't gone far enough in this game to have any proficiency with weapons.

She shrugged. "Sure. Let's give these guys a show."

Damn. My eyes followed her as she strutted toward the computer box. After issuing a few voice commands, the canisters lit up with blue light. What looked like empty handles lit up with blue lasers of varying shape. Short, long, thin, wide, curved and jagged blades, as well as many other forms of cutlery lit up in the empty handles. There were even a couple of maces and two meteor hammers, each held by a long chain.

Once we finished suiting up and had our eyewear in place, we stepped onto the platforms. The voice from the simulator spoke. As usual, it was a high society British voice. This one, female: "Fighters, please tap your respective levers when you're ready to proceed."

We both pressed down with our toes on the large colored levers that jutted out from the edges our platforms. My lever was red, and my suit was black with red stitching along the seams. Martinez's suit was the same but in yellow, as was her lever.

After we pressed the levers, the computer said, "Fighters, take your positions." We both stood at the center of our platforms and waited. Clear fiberglass walls slid upwards from the base of the platforms, forming see-through cages around our respective platforms. As soon as we were both enclosed, we heard, "Prepare to begin in five seconds. Initiating countdown. 5 . . . 4 . . . 3 . . . 2 . . . 1 . . . Fight!"

Martinez advanced on me like an Aztec goddess. She threw the first punch and followed it with a series of punches. Her punches were were quick. Shocking. Fast. Precise. Jab to the face. Jab to the side of the head. Jab to the face. *Jab, jab, jab.* Then a few to the body, a relentless assault. I tried to get in close, but her jabs landed and kept me back. I backed her up with a few low leg kicks, and she responded with a few of her own. They hurt. She tagged me at will, exploiting anything that was exposed. *One, two. One, two. One, one, two.* I tried to get in and grab her leg but ate a knee on the way in. That dazed me a bit, and then she was on me like a hungry jackal.

She seemed to have eight arms and legs. I covered up as much as I could. Some of her strikes grazed and a lot landed. I saw prisms of light in my peripherals. Out of desperation, I caught her last kick and swept her other leg out from under her. *Finally.* She was on her back. I dropped onto her and rained down as many punches as I could manage. I could see the panic begin to set in her eyes. Her nose was bleeding. Some of my elbows were getting through too. With one great heave she managed to buck me off of her and slither her way out from beneath my mount. She was on her feet. We faced each other. She took some deep breaths, but I was breathing much harder. I could already tell that I would gas out well before her. I'd either have to knock her out or disable her quickly.

She came at me again but this time with a left roundhouse kick to my right side. The top side of her left foot blasted my right flank. *Pain.* Not the liver, thank goodness, but I wondered if I'd cracked a rib. Then the computer confirmed it for me: Gladiator in red: 23% damage. Right flank–fractured rib cage. I clutched at my ribs involuntarily. *Shouldn't have done that.* Now she was after my rib again. Before I could back away, she followed up with another left kick. I did an oblique crunch and blocked with my arm to absorb some of the blow. It helped block the kick, but my rib was on fire. I winced. She smirked. Then she followed with another jab and a left hook to my right temple, but I'd anticipated it. I blocked it with my right forearm.

I knew from the last series of assaults that she liked to follow up her punches, so I moved in close, fast. I clinched the back of her neck and tried to control her a bit. I had my left arm wrapped around her right arm. Then as fast as I could manage, I turned into her body, pivoting my right hip toward her, and yanked her arm over my shoulder. I jutted my hip into her pelvis and lifted her off the ground, judo flipping her over my right shoulder. I put as much force into the throw as I could muster. She landed on her back with a loud thud, but she didn't wait. She sat up. I dropped to my knees and took her back as fast as I could. I laid all of my weight onto her. I wrapped one arm around her neck and proceeded to choke her unconscious. She reared forward and then back, headbutting my face. *Crack!*

My nose felt like it broke. I teetered back. Tiny spots clouded my vision. My eyes watered. I could hear her chuckle, but it was far away. I expected her to pounce on me, but she had other things in mind. I blinked, trying to clear my vision and noticed that she decided to go for a weapon. So, in turn, I staggered over to the opposite canister. My vision was still a bit blurred, but I saw what she was up to. She grabbed a broadsword and jetted toward me leaping into the air like a cat. I had to do a blind grab, snatching at the first thing that met my hand, just to deflect her attack. I'd gotten a Khukuri, a long inwardly curved Nepalese blade, a weapon with which I was familiar. Lucky me, but how would it fare against a damned broadsword? On her ascent she'd brought her sword up in a high arc. The end of her descent would be a heavy blow aimed at slicing me down the middle from the top of my head.

I thrust the Khukuri as hard as I could up above my head and met the sword with my blade. I'd deflected her sword enough to step to the right and sent my right fist into her kidneys three times like a piston. She winced. I heard a gust of air leave her mouth. I'd hurt her. Kidney punches suck. I would've kept going, but she slashed at my head again. I couldn't believe her resilience. The Judo throw alone would've secured a win for me with most people, but not Martinez. She had grit. The scoreboard showed that her life meter had dropped significantly from those kidney punches, but she was still in the green, a hair above yellow. My life meter was dangerously low. I hadn't hit red yet, but all of my green bars were gone. Her earlier jabs, the rib kick and the headbutt, drained me. I could still recover some ground, though.

She slung her sword toward my neck and would've taken off my head, but I ducked in time. Ducking turned into a full-on monkey roll. I lost hold of the Khukuri after the somersault-like maneuver but scrambled back to it in time to deflect another blow intended for the crown of my head. I was on my knees now. I wasn't sure how long I could survive in that position. She kept beating down on me with the sword like she was chopping wood. I knew that I couldn't defend the steady onslaught for too long. I was getting tired, and she seemed to be getting more energy. She was impatient, ready to end me. She seemed frenzied, annoyed that I wasn't going down so easily. I'd use her impatience against her.

While she focused on hacking me down, I thought of something dirty to do. It was a gamble as I was still on my knees, but it was my only option. As she raised her sword, I launched my body forward into a prone position, and rolled like a log to the right. Quick as a cobra, I shot my blade around in a wide arc and slashed the tendons across her ankle. I'd timed it perfectly.

She cried out. This was all simulation, but she felt the pain all the same. She staggered back. I'd crippled her. I was in pain too. Adrenaline was wearing off, and my face started to ache from the jabs and headbutt to my face. My head felt heavier than a sack of bricks, but I knew the ankle cut was worse. It would impair her speed, which I desperately needed. I hoped it would be enough to make her drop her sword, but she fought through it. If I had thought she was pissed before . . . It started to feel personal. She managed to knee my face and knock the Khukuri blade out of my hand with her sword. I scampered away from her to get some footing. She came at me again with the sword, slashing out at me several times. But her attempts were slower now . . . sloppy. She telegraphed her movements as she limped and swung with the sword. I jumped out of harm's way each time. It bought me enough time to get to my feet by this point, but she still had a huge advantage with the sword.

She only needed to connect once.

To get it out of her hands, I realized that I'd have to tackle her before she could swipe again. I ran at her, aiming for her midsection like a battering ram. When my shoulder met with her midsection, it was enough force to push her backwards. She dropped the sword to catch her fall. I could hear the sound of a metal clink, a simulation of it skidding across the platform. Then I realized my mistake. I had an advantage standing while her ankle was injured. Now, on the ground, the ankle injury held little relevance.

Stupid.

With shocking speed, she rolled over and put me into a bulldog choke. Clutching on to me like a nimble monkey. The boniest part of her forearm, the radial bone, sank into my throat. The choke was tight. It would only be seconds before I was out. I strained and pulled down on her arm with both hands, but she was strong.

We were both still kneeling, with her right arm firmly around my neck. My windpipe felt like it would burst. My carotid was being pinched off. I was getting light-headed. I had to do something quickly. She chuckled lightly into my ear and whispered, "You're done, Ensign. Give it up. Tap out."

Give up? Screw her. My mind slowed. Things were becoming foggy. I started to see the world go black. But I would—not—quit. What was her Achilles heel? Then it hit me. Her *Achilles heel.* I was certain I could reach it. So I sunk my fingers into the area where I'd wounded her. That was enough to loosen her grip *just enough* around my neck. I used the opening to wrench out of it and bring my left elbow up into an uppercut motion. It landed right on her chin. Her head snapped back, and I knew I'd won. She fell onto her back. The simulator voice announced: "Ensign Brown—Wins. Victor."

This knockout, of course, was simulated. Martinez' goggles went black, and she was a little disoriented at first, but then she stood up from her platform. She ripped her suit off with abrupt movements. None of the people in my division said anything. I heard some murmuring and a few expletives. I felt everyone's eyes on me. I even saw some money secretly exchange hands. No one bothered Martinez as she finished disrobing. When she was done, she walked directly toward me.

"Great fight, Ensign." She stuck out her hand.

I shook it. "Thanks. You too."

"You got lucky with that ankle cut. Kind of dirty, wouldn't you say?"

"It's a fight. It's all dirty." I looked at her warily.

"I should've said 'screw the sword' and finished you off after the headbutt."

I winced but smiled at her. "Yeah, you should've. I could barely see after that."

"Ensigns," she grumbled, shaking her head. "Always giving them some slack."

Someone clapped. We both turned to find Gerard, the SEAL I'd met earlier, standing at the edge of the crowd. He clapped slowly and deliberately.

"What's his problem?"

"Who knows? He's odd," I said, but secretly I felt a momentary sense of glee. Then I realized that I'd been caught in my earlier lie.

He smirked at me for a moment and then left. I wondered what he was thinking.

5

After the fight, everyone decided to hang out and drink. I stuck around for one and then left. I knew some of the men (and women) were waiting for me to leave. They'd patron some of the "human services" contractors the minute I left. Who was I to get in the way of a good lay?

I was in a high mood. I planned to go out to a shipboard bar for the evening, and I knew my roommate, Heather, would be all in. A hot shower, fresh coveralls and a premium-cut steak were in my future. Maybe even some French fries.

That all changed, however, when Shakespeare delivered the bad news: My senior chief had been brutally murdered.

Before I get into the details surrounding Senior Chief's murder, you should know that this entire shit show began with two important scientists: Dr. Kasim Tengelei of Kenya and Dr. Heinrich Gerg from Austria. The former, a pioneer. The latter, an innovator. Both dead. Both previous employees of Biotech. The details surrounding their deaths were unclear, until Senior Chief Lark McGinn found a journal. Turns out it belonged to Dr. Gerg. The good doctor's journal recordings had been highly classified since his death. In fact, no one knew it even existed, except for a few. I'd find out later that LaSalle was one of those few. The only others who knew were a few government officials, some very senior Navy officers, and the most senior executives of a bank called A.F.I.B. A.F.I.B owns Biotech. As A.F.I.B's subsidiary, Biotech had significant financial backing, and therefore the means to win a government contract. All biomedical research, drilling operations and slug excavations at the mining station were overseen by Biotech. Senior Chief had been to the station several times for work. I believe he found the journal there.

Once I learned of Gerg's private recordings, I requested access to them but was denied several times, even with my top-secret clearance. The hand that pulled the strings on Biotech's clandestine operations ensured those files were locked away for good.

Until I stole them.

But we'll get to that in due time.

6

Monday. 10 August 2398
Time: 2045 hrs.

stripped down and shoved my dirty clothes into a metal bin. I stepped into a rectangular enclave and closed the shower door behind me. Immediately a steady mist of steam shot from all directions, wetting me down. Then a mist of anti-bacterial soap sprayed from every direction. Then steam again. Then steady gusts of air. Finally, an antimicrobial blue light illuminated the entire inside of the shower. My body glowed blue for about five seconds before shutting off. The entire process took under a minute. I stepped from the shower totally dry and sprayed my armpits with deodorant. Then I gave instructions to the CMS.

"Shakespeare: Dry clean."

"As you wish, Miss Brown," he said, in a perfectly refined British accent. *Shakespeare*. Every time I said the computer's name aloud, I felt like a fool. My roommate, Lieutenant Junior Grade Heather Jordan, had a penchant for anything British: Their literature. Their accents. Their men. So, it wasn't a shock that we had a British A.I. advisor or that she liked my department head, Lieutenant Rivera, who spent part of his time growing up in the UK. As the ship's communications officer, Heather took full advantage of her position. She linked Shakespeare's system to the ship's internal CMS, giving him access to practically all data that passed in and out of the *Midway*. We had our own digital butler. He went with us everywhere. We were the only ones on the entire ship who had access to our CMS *outside* of our staterooms and pretty much anywhere we went via our wrist devices. He was our personal concierge. Even the commodore didn't have this. It wasn't exactly on the up and up. Heather was brilliant, and she managed to (sort of illegally) perform a "shadow patch." Shakespeare surveilled and connected to several station mainframes, located within a 10,000-mile radius of the ship, without anyone knowing.

"Dry cleaning commenced as you've requested, ma'am. Based on my readings, you appear to have some trepidations. Is this related to Lieutenant Rivera's sudden arrival at your stateroom door? Perhaps I can help."

"I doubt it." I hated when Shakespeare took unauthorized readings on me. Occasionally he'd access my wrist device to deduce my mood. "If I need something, I'll let you know. I don't even know why he's here."

"I suspect it might have something to do with the—" Shakespeare paused.

"With the what?"

"Oh, my—" Shakespeare laughed nervously. "How embarrassing. It occurred to me that I might not be authorized to share this new development."

"Christ. Tell me, will you?"

"Well, I suppose it would be of no consequence. A body was found in the ship's well deck."

"A body? Do you mean *a dead body?*"

"That is correct, Miss Brown." Shakespeare's tone was reminiscent of two people discussing the weather. "A human head was detached from its owner's body, and the body was surreptitiously placed in the center of the well deck."

"Lovely." I tried to sound unmoved, but deep down I could feel the tentacles of my fear stretch up from my belly to the surface.

"Your coveralls are ready for use, Miss Brown." Sometimes Shakespeare's abrupt change in subject or his lack of emotions regarding serious matters unnerved me.

I donned a clean white t-shirt and a pair of Navy working suit that rested in the metal bin that Shakespeare ejected from the stateroom deck.

"Open the hatch."

"Certainly, Miss Brown."

stopped walking and let the information settle in. "Wait—it's *Senior Chief's* body down there?"

Rivera briefed me while we made our way down a few levels to the ship's well deck. I hadn't even realized it until we arrived at the hatch to the well. He was prepared to console me, but I was composed. I was more shocked than anything. Rivera waited by the door. His hand hovered over the access display that opened the hatch. His hand shook as he paused to touch the screen.

"Why are you manually entering the access code? Use the voice module."

"Do you want me to wake up the entire ship?" Rivera tossed me a disapproving glance. He was always irritated with me. "We need to keep this under wraps until we know the who, what, when, where and why. Got it?"

"Okay, jeez." I held my hands up. "Am I to understand that only his body is in there?"

"Yes. No one has found his head yet."

I could already smell a pungent, coppery odor drift from the other side of the hatch. I'd seen a dead body before but not one without its head. The idea of seeing it now made me anxious. My

breath caught. I started to feel claustrophobic. I took short, perforated breaths. Something about this ship made everything close
in on me. I still had four years and four months left on a five-year
contract. At the moment, four *weeks* seemed like a life sentence.
I kept my face neutral. I didn't want Rivera to see me freak out.

"You look like you're in bad shape." Rivera's eyebrows were
raised.

"Yeah, well you don't look great, either."

"I know, but you look green, and you're black. Weird. I've
never seen a black person look green."

"It's called nausea. Still got the space bugs."

"Still? You should have your space legs by now."

"Well I don't, and I probably never will."

"I thought you might be upset over your senior chief."

"You might think I'm a cold-hearted bitch for saying this, but
good riddance."

"Wow, Mel."

"Oh c'mon, sir. Whether you want to admit it or not, he made
everyone miserable. His being dead doesn't change that."

Rivera didn't say anything. By the look on his face I could
tell he agreed. Karma had finally done its work, in my opinion.
I hadn't liked Senior Chief McGinn from the moment I spotted his
big square head and beady little eyes. He'd been a source of misery
since my first day onboard the *Midway*. We were polar opposites.
He was a product of the old Navy where respect was based on social
hierarchies, and much of it went to the men in leadership positions,
irrespective of their capabilities. Information was disseminated via
antiquated technologies, on digital libraries contained in oversized
electronic devices. I was a product of the new Navy. Respect had to
be earned. Gender and race held little significance in the amount
of respect one was afforded. This was mainly due to the degree of
danger involved with space travel and exploration. The environment of the new Navy was one of constant danger. People didn't

have time to make distinctions amongst fellow humans, because there were just too many threats to humanity that existed. In the new Navy, information was shared through advanced technologies like virtual and holographic information sharing systems, accessed through devices that could fit in your pocket and gadgets that could slip under your fingernail.

McGinn grew up on a farm in one of the few small towns left over that reminded one of the antebellum South. I grew up in a wooded suburb near a sprawling metropolis. After high school he enlisted and went to Navy boot camp in Great Lakes, Michigan, followed by A-school. After high school, I went to the Naval Academy in Annapolis, Maryland, an academic institution with all the trappings of an Ivy league education and military boarding school put together.

He hated academy grads, and he hated reporting to a woman. "Idiot, zero military experience and cunt" were the words I over-heard him use once. To me, he was an entitled, male chauvinist bigot approaching a mid-life crisis.

His constant undermining of my authority was finally over. I accepted his death with ease. I doubted he'd afford me any sympathies, either, if our roles had been reversed. I reasoned that at least I wouldn't crack open a beer at his eulogy (which I shamefully considered).

"I suppose he won't *totally* be missed." Rivera lowered his hand from the hatch access display to cup his nose and mouth. "Maybe you should grab your bio-hazard suit first. It's pretty rank in there."

I opened the hatch anyway and then closed it with frantic movements. The intensity of the smell had tripled. I shook my head at Rivera. "You're right. It's disgusting. I thought you said you just got the call. It shouldn't smell *that* bad already, especially with part of the body missing."

"I did just get the call," said Rivera. "I don't know. Maybe he's been dead for a while, and they just now decided to call."

"Who is *they?*"

"Don't know. It was anonymous and we couldn't get an ID."

"That would be stupid. I bet he's been lying there for a while, and they just found him," I said. "I'll know more once I finish the sweep. Bet you his head is tucked away somewhere in there too."

He turned to leave.

"Wait," I said, grabbing his shoulder. "Where are you going?"

"Back on watch. I'm not going in there. I can't handle gruesome sights."

"Seriously?"

"Dead serious." He already looked a few shades lighter, almost white. He swallowed. "You're gonna need to gather all the DNA and get some good prints before reveille. The Marines are moving their vehicles first thing. Be quick about it."

"I like how you're dictating to me how I need to hurry up, but you're unwilling to go in there yourself."

"I left the Junior Officer of the Deck alone in the pilot house. I'm the OOD. I shouldn't even be down here as it is."

"Okay. I've got it, sir."

"Get it done quickly but keep it confidential. Get Captain Hunt to help you."

"No way."

"That wasn't a request. I know it's a Navy issue, but the Marines are well trained in forensics. They're efficient." Rivera could tell I was nervous, and he knew I was too prideful to ask Eric for help. *Ordering* me to get Captain Hunt to assist was his weird way of being helpful. "They can provide security. You never know what can happen at a crime scene."

Wait—what? I felt the back of my neck tingle. I didn't even want to know what he meant by that. I knew deep down that something was coming, and I'd be in the middle of it. I recalled a conversation I'd overheard my first month onboard. Two sailors gossiped about unexplained disappearances, self-mutilations and all sorts of other violent freak accidents. I wondered if any other ships were dealing with similar incidents. Would I become a victim of this ship too? The *Midway* was unlucky, and I wanted off.

The commodore was getting annoyed with me lately for not having answers. Rivera started to get annoyed with me, too, at first, but eventually he knew something was off. What really weirded him out was the fact that no one was doing anything about it. The incidents had been reported up the chain of command all the way to the admiral, but everything was swept away like yesterday's dust.

I didn't want to investigate Senior Chief's death. I wanted to call my forensics team and have them stuff Senior Chief's body into a vacuum sealed bag while I made my way back to my stateroom. Instead, I changed into my bio-hazardous waste protection suit and made a call.

"Shakespeare, get Petty Officer Martinez for me."

"Calling Petty Officer Martinez now."

The CMS display on the bulkhead of my stateroom lit up, and I heard an old fashioned telephone ring echo throughout the room. The display showed a drawing of an old fashioned phone vibrating, until finally a face appeared on the screen. She was sharing a berthing space with nine other senior female petty officers. The sailor who answered the call was squinting, pinching the bridge of her nose. She had that look on her face: *fucking officers wake us up for stupid shit.*

"Put Martinez on," I said with a tone. Not totally mean, but it said: *this is important, so I won't be tolerating your shit today.*

"Yes, ma'am," said the sailor.

Martinez approached the console, rubbing sleep from her eyes. Her face filled the screen. She had big eyes, thick black, long curls that were frizzy from having slept hard and a heart-shaped face like a Japanese anime character.

"Martinez, put a sound curtain on. I need to tell you something confidential."

She pushed a button on the console and a message in the upper corner of the screen flashed: Conversation Muted. "Yes, ma'am?"

"Senior Chief is dead. Grab one other sailor, someone who is pistol qualified, can do sweeps and who can also keep their mouth shut. Take a sidearm yourself. Don't tell anyone or let anyone on the turntable. I don't care if it's an ATG inspector or even the commodore himself. . . ."

I continued to rattle off several more instructions, and her eyes opened wider and wider. She looked concerned. Maybe scared? *Good. She'll be extra careful.*

". . . I'll meet you down there. The Marines have several landing craft and assault buggies they have to turn and deploy in about three hours. So, we need to be done before reveille."

"Yes, ma'am. I understand."

". . . and if anyone asks what you're doing—lie."

"Yes, ma'am."

"Oh, and one more thing. Congratulations. You just made chief."

8

With all of the associated dangers of traveling through space, spot promotions are common and even necessary. In this instance, I was grateful the Navy had brought them back. Of course, one must be selective about them. There are certain rules and limitations, and, of course, Martinez would still be required to undergo all of the traditions and ceremonies that would indoctrinate her into the chief's mess. They'd probably favor her presence in the goat locker over McGinn's anyway. Promoting Petty Officer Martinez to chief was my one last "screw you" to Senior Chief McGinn. She was already doing the lion's share of his job, and she was more respected by the other sailors than McGinn ever was.

After I hung up with Martinez, I called Eric, but he didn't answer. No surprise there since Eric slept like the dead. As the "Commander of Troops" of the Marine combat engineering battalion attached to the *Midway* (a fact he readily advertised), Eric resided in close proximity to the well deck, so I headed to his stateroom.

I hesitated at his door, wondering how he'd respond to my presence so late at night. Unfortunately, the smug look on his face when he opened the hatch said it all: *she wants sex.*

That was typical, arrogant Eric. He believed I'd actually proposition him for sex at 3:45 in the morning.

"Hey beautiful," he said, leaning in the door frame. He wore only camouflage pants and no shirt. His perfectly sculpted, brown pecks twitched a little. *He's doing it on purpose.* His pants rode a little too low, revealing chiseled abs and a faint happy trail that trickled far enough down to elicit certain thoughts. I ignored the warm feeling that started to spread in my groin. I knew Eric too well to succumb to his charms. I'd be damned before letting myself go there. I shifted my gaze up, to rest on the top of his perfectly groomed head. He had a fade that had been shaped with thoughtful precision.

"Who is it, baby?" A female voice drifted to the door from the back of his stateroom. I detected a mild accent, barely, but it was there.

"Go back to sleep, sweetie," he said over his shoulder.

Sweetie? Since when does he use pet names?

"Okay, but hurry back," she said in a sultry voice.

I wanted to gag.

"What do you want, Mel?" His tone was serious and impatient this time. Was he irritated by my refusal to look at him?

"Sorry to wake you. Rivera ordered me up here. I didn't want to come."

He sighed. "And?"

"I need you to put up a sound curtain."

He frowned but voiced the necessary commands. "Okay. What is it?"

"There's been a murder . . ."

I explained everything I knew, and he agreed to come down to the well deck. He shut the hatch, and, for a brief moment, I thought I heard arguing. I wasn't sure.

41

By the time everyone gathered, Eric, Chief Martinez, Petty Officer Mackie, a gunner's mate from my division and three Marines stood outside the well deck ready to conduct the forensics testing and cleanup. It was almost four in the morning, and we had under two hours to complete the sweep before reveille sounded.

Before I opened the hatch, I turned to everyone. "Look, I'm not sure what it's going to look like on the other side, but no matter what, let's stay calm and remain professional. If anyone feels like they need to gag—"

At that point, my wrist display lit up. It was Shakespeare. "Miss Brown, if you would like, I can monitor everyone's digestive tract activity. Surveil the pH levels in their gastric fluids as well as notify you of any probable digestive mishap—"

"Thanks, but we're good," I said, shaking my head. I rolled my eyes at Eric's amused look. He knew how much Shakespeare annoyed me.

As each one of us stepped through the hatch, we gasped. Despite knowing what we would see, it was still an appalling sight: a body lying in the prone position with no head attached. Would I find the head tucked away in some obscure corner of the ship? Oddly, his feet were pointed toward the door. Part of his foot was missing with the shoe still on it, and there was a deep bite mark in his leg along his inner thigh. Blood poured from his leg but was beginning to congeal on the well deck. A substantial portion of his tricep had been ripped at, too, and exposed some bone. The area where his neck and head were supposed to meet was just a tattered mess. The fleshy edges of his neck curled jaggedly upwards where the tearing had occurred. Something or someone had ripped his head right out of his body, as it wasn't a clean cut. The edges were serrated, and all manner of tendons, nerve tissue, veins, arteries, bone and ligaments trailed in a blood-soaked wake from his neck like jellyfish tentacles.

My gunner's mate, Petty Officer Mackie, stepped closer and bent over Senior Chief's body to have a closer look. As he stared at it, a lance corporal nudged him jokingly, as if to knock him over onto the mess. He stumbled a bit. A couple of Eric's Marines snickered.

"Quit it," I snapped. "You mess up my crime scene, I'll have your ass."

They forced the grins off their faces, and Eric scowled at them for their antics. He walked over to me while he considered the body and leaned in. "What do you think?"

I knew that he was asking me this more to confirm his own suspicions. Eric never wanted anyone's opinion. He was cocky enough to think he had the answers to everything. We both knew the only explanation for such a display would look preposterous to anyone who wasn't there at the scene.

"I think something ripped Senior Chief's head from his body. Had to be something pretty strong to do that." I was trying to appear unaffected, but I could feel the bile rise in my throat.

"That's impossible. Only something non-human could do this. I'm the force protection officer, and I know for a fact there aren't any interplanetary foreigners or exotic organisms on the ship's manifest."

He sounded unsure.

"Well, what other explanation is there?"

"If I may, Ensign Brown," Shakespeare crooned, "Captain Hunt is correct. According to my data, all life forms onboard the *Midway* are human, and the quarantine cells are free of any extra-terrestrial or extra-planetary organisms. The perpetrator of this crime must indeed be human . . . after a fashion."

"What's that mean?" Eric said.

"Who knows?" I said, shrugging. "He's always running his mouth when he should be quiet."

"My apologies, ma'am," said Shakespeare. "Would you prefer that I only provide information upon request?"

"That would be dandy," I said, circling my finger in the air. "All right, enough of this. Let's get what we need and get the hell out of here."

Petty Officer Mackie, Chief Martinez and I peeled of all of the video stickers from the well deck, while Eric's crew cleaned up the headless body and any other lingering DNA.

"I can't believe they don't have sanitroids onboard. We don't get paid enough for this shit," said a Marine private. The private picked up a handsaw with a rotating laser blade and sectioned off a piece of Senior Chief's torso into a smaller, more manageable chunk. He dropped the section of dripping flesh into a large orange medical waste container. "It's going to take forever to sanitize everything."

Eric's face turned a shade whiter, and he stood as still as an iron post, overseeing the task. I saw him quietly swallow, his Adam's apple shifted ever so slightly as the private packed the lump of Senior Chief's flesh down into the container.

Chief Martinez closed her eyes briefly and swallowed too. Then she commenced scanning the space for prints. She was handling this much better than I was. I couldn't look anymore. So I preoccupied myself with the video stickers.

I was certain that I gathered all of them, I would know exactly what happened to Senior Chief. I unfolded my Mobile Computer Board and laid it flat on the deck. I knelt down over the picture board-like display and started typing commands on the touch screen keyboard. Then I actually peeled the first sticker from the bulkhead wall and smoothed it over the screen of my MCB. I was disappointed. Holographic footage shot out from the MCB, but I couldn't make sense of any of the events that transpired. To make matters worse, the footage was cut off before I could ascertain any real leads.

Video stickers were very durable. Virtually indestructible. Most spaces onboard had a five by five-inch video sticker mounted on its bulkhead to provide full coverage of any events that transpired. They were made of military-grade material, basically an organic polymer light-emitting diode enhanced by fiberglass. They were durable, yet the polymeric material of the sticker was quite flexible with a strong adhesive backing allowing it to be mounted anywhere with a flat surface. We generally positioned them along the bulkheads of the ship, but they could also be mounted on ceilings and along the decks. The sticker contained a paper-thin camera with an ionic battery that allowed for continuous filming and very little maintenance. Once mounted, they were impossible to remove without a special access optical scanner. The only two people onboard who had special access scanners to unlock video stickers were myself and the commodore; but once we started gathering them, we discovered that they were all corrupted. Video stickers couldn't be destroyed unless removed.

Someone removed them first. It couldn't have been the commodore. So who?

Whoever removed them didn't know the location of the stealth sticker I'd secretly installed myself. Part of our legal officer training was to learn how to mount stealth stickers, and we were issued a confidential number of them to install in high traffic areas and spaces that held highly sensitive information and weapons ordnance. We were also under strict orders not to tell anyone we had them and especially not where they were mounted. Even the commodore himself wasn't privy to this information. Stealth stickers contained "cloaking" technology. Even if someone knew there was one in the space, the cloaking made them invisible to the eye, much less access. This was to ensure that even the most senior of leadership wasn't above military law, and there were others that *I* didn't know about. This was to ensure that legal officers weren't immune to legal prosecution, either.

I instructed everyone on the forensics team to exit the well deck and to not let anyone back in. Eric didn't want to leave at first. He seemed suspicious, but finally it dawned on him what I was about to do, and he shuttled everyone from the space.

After Eric closed the hatch behind him, I passed the special optical scanner over the inside of my wrist. The scanner beeped three times once it locked on to my barcode tattoo. I looked up to the ceiling where I remembered installing it a long time ago. Suddenly, a ten by ten-inch sticker materialized into visibility. I rolled the portable lift to the center of the well deck and touched the display screen. I stepped on, and the lift elevated me to the ceiling. I touched the display screen again until my head was an inch from the ceiling. I tilted my chin up to align, my left eye with the stealth sticker's tiny optic scanner. Once it caught my optical signature, the screen illuminated blue. I peeled the sticker effortlessly from the ceiling. It would turn out to be the only sticker that would provide any helpful footage of what had occurred in the well deck.

My stomach tumbled over several times as I descended back down to the floor. If anything happened to me, access to the sticker's video footage would not be available until a new legal officer was identified and available for assignment to the *Midway*. That could be as much as two years from now. Fear coiled itself within me. Why did that thought even cross my mind? The fact that my life might be in danger rushed to the forefront of my mind.

I wanted out of there. Holding the stealth sticker in my hand suddenly felt like holding a ticking time bomb. Whoever destroyed those other stickers would certainly want to destroy the only sticker that contained any real footage. Then it occurred to me: The same person who vandalized the stickers on the well deck bulkhead was the same person who'd killed Senior Chief.

Shakespeare seemed to sense my concerns. "Ensign Brown, might I recommend that you allow me to download the information from the sticker as soon as humanly possible to your hard drive and a secure backup information cache—"

"Uh, yes. Good idea."

"It's quite possible that the individual who destroyed the sticker is the same indiv—"

"Yes, I know, Shakespeare. Begin backup protocols and keep quiet. I need to sleep."

"As you wish, Miss Brown. I'm glad that I could help."

"Great."

"Would you like me to schedule a wake-up call?"

"Oh, for Pete's sake. Yes. Now be quiet."

I called the others back into the well deck to finish the remainder of the forensics sweep. The entire sweep only took about fifty minutes, but it took another forty minutes to remove all evidence of Senior Chief's body from the well deck.

9

After we finished, I headed back to my stateroom to shower again and change into a fresh uniform. Even though my coveralls had been covered in the cleanup suits, and I hadn't really touched anything, I felt disgusting. I donned the coveralls I had dry cleaned before I left.

Heather wasn't there and had already left for her workspaces in the satellite sector. I was grateful. With her, I would've had to come up with some sort of bullshit explanation. I decided to stay in my stateroom and compile the rest of my report rather than go to my office. I wasn't ready to deal with any inquiries about Senior Chief's whereabouts. Rivera wanted the news to remain confidential at least until we finished briefing the commodore.

I powered on the forensic scanner, a small black cube which resembled an engagement ring box, but was really a handheld portable 3D laser device that could hold up to 5 terabytes of images. It was also outfitted with a thumbnail-sized projector that emitted holographic images capable of being viewed from several directions. I linked the device to Shakespeare's mainframe, and a tiny blue light began to blink. I immediately placed everything in manual mode. There would be certain bits of forensics information I would need him to analyze, but I only wanted to feed him that information bit by bit. I wanted to put the brief together myself. In other words, while I compiled the brief manually, Shakespeare wouldn't have access. Only Heather and I had direct access to Shakespeare's server, but he could share information requested by A.I. advisors who belonged to people with higher clearances. "Miss Brown, are you sure you don't want me to compile everything for you? It would save you a considerable amount of time."

I was tempted to hand everything over to him, but something in my gut told me that I should compile my brief before anyone else could access it. "No. I'm good. I've got this."

"But Miss Brown, I should remind you that my capabilities allow me to—"

"What the—Ugh. Go to sleep."

"My apologies, Miss Brown. Powering down to sleep mode now."

I pushed a tiny button on the scanner to power on the projector. Another blue light blinked at the corner of the device. Then the first image floated above the cube right before me. It was a three-dimensional depiction of Senior Chief's head, lying motionless on the well deck floor. I pulled the black stylus glove from the top drawer of my desk and slipped it over my hand. With my gloved hand, I wrapped my stylus-tipped fingers around the image of Senior Chief and dropped it into the report on my MCB. I scrolled through all of the images, sliding my finger from right to left, spinning them around and flipping them upside down. I examined them with all of the motions of symphony conductor until I was either satisfied and dropped them into my report or into the virtual wastebasket image that floated above the images. I de-cluttered and alphabetized them before I looked at the footage from the stealth sticker. It took me an hour. I dictated the summary of the events, from the phone call to Lieutenant Rivera reporting the death all the way up to our own actual discovery of the head. I spoke in low tones as I dictated the entire succession of events into my wrist device. When I was finished, I told Shakespeare to: *Compile, analyze, look for any discrepancies and make an evaluation.* Based on the data I fed him, he came up with some useful conclusions.

"Senior Chief McGinn expired on the well deck at approximately 2:17 a.m. The initial cause of his death is inconclusive; however, the tears along his neck would suggest that decapitation was the source of his unfortunate demise. Without access to the rest of his body, one may only formulate theories as to the cause of his death. Based on your findings and other forensic analysis which I've run, I postulate there to be a 63 percent probability that Mr. McGinn died when his head was removed from his body. I've uploaded images of the fingerprints found around Senior Chief McGinn's neck to several databases. Based on my findings, it's safe to infer that a struggle did, in fact, ensue between Mr. McGinn and the owner of said fingerprints."

"Who do the fingerprints belong to?" I asked.

"I'm afraid I can't tell you that, Miss Brown."

"*Can't* or *won't?*"

"Ahem. Due to the size of the fingerprints in relation to Mr. McGinn's physical makeup, his murderer was of a considerably smaller frame. My calculations reveal that his attacker was petite, probably anywhere from five-foot-four to five-foot-five inches in height and no more than approximately 135 pounds. However, his assailant was quite powerful and had a surprisingly vast advantage in terms of strength, speed and reactiveness. My predictions would indicate that the struggle could not have lasted more than mere seconds and that Senior Chief McGinn's death was quite fast."

Someone much smaller than Senior Chief ripped his head off and tossed it somewhere? Who the hell could that be?

"You don't have an ID on the prints?"

"I am unable to identify the assailant at this time."

I don't buy it.

Shakespeare wasn't telling me everything. Had someone already accessed his finding? Pressing him was of no use, but a feeling in my gut also told me that I shouldn't press him, that I should play the ignorant legal officer who is simply putting her brief together. I decided to review the footage provided by the one good remaining video sticker that I retrieved from the ceiling of the well deck. I looked for people with small frames, but I didn't notice anyone fitting that description. In fact, I didn't notice anything strange at all. At first. People came in and out, playing one-on-one, two-on-two and three-on-three basketball using a hoop which ejected in and out from one of the bulkheads. Some leaned against the walls and smoked, flicking their butts into the metal cylinder which mechanically retracted from the bulkhead wall upon command. They even made a game of it, seeing who could flick their butt into the can with the least amount of opening. Others rolled dice.

Then a slick-looking gentleman stepped into the well deck wearing the trademark all blue jumpsuit that most civilian contractors wore. The patch of a human hand with an eye in the middle, stitched to his sleeve and breast pocket, distinguished him as a "human services" contractor. A couple of sailors who'd been lingering there for a while seemed to brighten at his presence. They cast aside their cigarette butts and surrounded him. He had a metal case clutched beneath his arm and held it out, placing his finger on the tiny screen located near the top. The case slid open to reveal several rows of various joints and small baggies. He distributed various items to each of the sailors. Then they outstretched their wrists. He pulled a small, black cylindrical object from his pocket that emitted a blue light and passed it over each of their wrists. Then he left, and the sailors went back to their conversations. A couple of them lit the joints they'd purchased, and one pulled a flask, surely containing alcohol, from his cargo pocket.

The footage alone would've been enough to bring them all to Captain's mast and have the human services contractor fired.

There were strict rules aboard ship. All consumption of alcohol and all human services exchanges were to be conducted inside the pubs onboard, as each pub was outfitted with sobriety scanners at every exit, ensuring nobody worked under the influence. But I didn't care about their shady dealings. I simply wanted clues, any that would give me a lead regarding Senior Chief's death.

I scanned through the footage several times, hoping to maybe even get sight of Senior Chief. Finally, I had to scroll back through three days of footage before I could get any sighting of him.

Once I spotted him, I paused the video and slowed everything down. He walked into the well deck alone with a journal in one hand and a pack of cigarettes in the other. I remembered being surprised at seeing the journal, a leather-bound book with old paper. It looked like something from the twenty-first century. Most people kept diaries (if they kept one at all) via a personal MCB or their wrist device. Then again, I wasn't surprised. As I'd mentioned before, Senior Chief was old-school and liked old-school things. Why wouldn't he keep a handwritten diary? But what was weird was that he kept a diary at all. He didn't seem like the journal-keeping type.

He lit a cigarette, and I noticed his hands trembled as he placed the cigarette into the corner of his mouth and opened the journal. I'd never seen him this rattled before. With the lit cigarette hanging loosely from the corner of his mouth, he read through the journal at a feverish pace. He read it as if he was reading it for the second time, eagerly flipping through the pages to get to the best parts. His eyes widened at moments which said a lot, considering that he was not a man who succumbed to surprises. He was an old, salty dog who'd seen everything.

I wanted to get my hands on the journal.

If I found his body, would I find the journal? Did Senior Chief's murderer have it? After Senior Chief flipped through the pages, he scanned the contents of the journal with his wrist device. This at least gave me some sort of lead. The fact that he scanned and uploaded images of the journal to a database somewhere proved that it wasn't his. I probably even had a good chance of getting access to its contents since my security clearance was higher than his. If I couldn't, Heather could. I continued watching the footage with reluctant curiosity. Something had his attention. My heart sped up when I saw him look up from the journal. At first, I thought I might witness his gruesome death. He was looking at someone. His eyes were wide, shocked. For a moment, I thought I'd see his murderer, but then it occurred to me that his death happened hours before, not three days ago, which was how old the footage was. He continued to stare, but the stare was vacant, as if he was considering what to say. Then one of the Marines from Eric's combat engineering battalion came into view. The Marine was holding paperwork for some ordnance we had to store for them. Senior Chief tucked the journal beneath his arm and followed the Marine out of the well deck.

I decided to again look at the most recent footage. I scrolled all the way to the end of the file. The well deck was empty until I saw a light filter into the well deck from the opening of a hatch. Once again, I thought I was about to get a visual of the murderer. But because the stealth sticker was mounted on the ceiling, I was only able to catch a glimpse of a shadow stretch out onto the well deck turntable. Then the video went completely dark.

By the time I was finished looking at all of the footage, I was tired. All I could think of was sleep, but I knew I would have to summarize my findings for Rivera before we briefed the commodore. I prayed that I could snatch a couple hours of sleep after the brief. I only had four hours before I was supposed to stand watch.

"Shakespeare, any guesses as to where the rest of his body might be?"

"Unfortunately, no, Miss Brown. The fact that there are no other traces of blood, other than where you found his body, would indicate that either the head was removed and hidden or consumed."

"*Consumed?* What the hell—"

"According to Merriam-Webster, *consume* means: to use, to destroy, to eat—"

"I know what consume means. I was asking what you were implying by that statement."

"Should we find that Senior Chief McGinn's head was not hidden or removed, based on my data, there is a high probability that it was, in fact, consumed."

"Okay, I don't like where this is going, and you make some pretty big leaps with your theories and *your data*. Only a superhuman life form or a wild animal is capable of such a feat, and there are no known alien-like cannibals in the galaxy, much less onboard. Wild animals either."

"That we know of, Ensign Brown."

"What the hell are you saying, Shakespeare?"

"I'm simply suggesting that we don't know all of the variables and machinations of the universe."

A cold chill swept through my body. I didn't like Shakespeare's mysterious explanations, but I had to abandon my line of questioning and finish my brief. Reveille was approaching, and I'd be in real trouble if I didn't finish before then.

"I took the liberty of running an additional optic scan across a significant portion of the well deck, and there are no other traces of blood or DNA," Shakespeare said. "Of the remaining DNA I was able to detect, I analyzed and discovered that their respective ages and compositions are exact matches to the people who showed up on your video footage prior to the late Senior Chief's death."

I began to go through the footage again. I reviewed the twenty-four hours leading up to finding Senior Chief's body. A visual documentation of Senior Chief's actual death would've turned this into the proverbial open-and-shut case, but I didn't have that luxury. I watched footage of various people going in and out of the well deck all day. I ran facial recognition programs, fingerprint and DNA tests for each and every person. It took forever, but as Shakespeare concluded, none turned out to be legitimate suspects.

I was kind of relieved not to find out who murdered my senior chief. I wouldn't be exposed to the gory footage of his murder. I did, however, search for the images of the journal that Senior Chief had scanned to his wrist device. I couldn't find anything. I went through his files three more times with no luck. At this point I was beyond exhaustion and considered laying down for five or ten minutes when I spotted a file with a skull and crossbones icon across it that said: *Keep Out.* I clicked on it and promptly received an *Access Denied.*

"Shakespeare, get me access to this file."

"I can't do that, Miss Brown."

"The hell you can't."

"Miss Brown, you don't have the clearance."

"I have one of the highest clearances on this ship."

"You don't have *elite secret* clearance; it's required for this particular set of data."

"Hey, asshat. What the hell good are you if you can't get me the information that I need?"

"While I have extensive file-sharing capabilities, there are certain—"

"Just fucking do it."

"My apologies, Miss Brown. The tone in your voice, your word choice and the dramatic shift in your respiratory and cardiovascular functions would indicate that I've somehow distressed you. Has my performance fallen below par?"

I forced myself to calm down. I felt a twinge of guilt even. I tried to think of other ways to access the file. "Never mind. Who do I need to speak to about getting access?"

"That, too, is classified, Miss Brown."

"Oh, for shit's sake," I said under my breath. In the meantime, I decided that I wasn't going to hurl insults at Shakespeare anymore. I had to remind myself that although I wasn't a huge fan of A.I., it wasn't personal. Shakespeare was really a great A.I. advisor, and my distaste of artificial intelligence technology didn't give me the right to verbally abuse him.

It was the only file I couldn't open. In tiny lettering there were two names that had access to the file, but they were redacted. The file was saved on a classified shared network. It required "elite secret" clearance, a level of clearance that was way beyond my "top secret" clearance. There were only 150 people in the U.S. whom I knew of who held "elite secret" clearances, and only ten of those came from the U.S. Navy. I wondered what possibly could be contained in those files, scanned by a U.S Navy senior chief, to be vetted and evaluated so quickly amongst the upper echelons of government. For a file to be deemed "elite secret," it had to be filtered pretty far up the chain of command and quickly. Why hadn't I seen any investigators onboard? Surely, I would've been notified as the legal officer. A trickle of fear wormed its way up my spine.

Why would he save it to a classified shared network that he didn't even have access to? Why did only two other people, not including myself, have access to it? Who were these people? I had one of the highest clearances onboard. I could feel myself getting heated. How and where did Senior Chief get his hands on a journal that has now been deemed classified? Did someone give it to him? Was this another instance of Senior Chief circumventing me? The little voice in my head told me: *No way. He got ahold of something he wasn't supposed to see. That's why he's dead now.* I kept wracking my brain, wondering who might have access? *The commodore, I bet.* I resolved to get access to the files from him directly, but then a tiny voice said: *don't tell him.* For some inexplicable reason, I sensed that I shouldn't tell a soul about the journal-file. I needed access, but not through the commodore and not through the other person who had access. Maybe Heather would be able to help me. I'd wait until the time was right.

After I'd given up on the file, I finished putting together my comprehensive forty-five-minute report which included a time-line of events, photos, DNA scan results, lab test results and video. I had to construct a holographic simulation of the events around Senior Chief McGinn's death since the video was incomplete. The simulation would be a hypothetical reenactment of his death based on what little I had. It would give Lieutenant Rivera somewhat of an idea of what had occurred, but it wouldn't be 100 percent. Wouldn't even be 70 percent.

After I processed all of the data I gathered, I clicked *Run Simulation*. Satisfied, I was ready to debrief Lieutenant Rivera and the commodore.

10

aptain Wyatt T. Radcliff was unpredictable. One minute tyran-
nical, the next amenable. When he wasn't a functional, flirta-
tious drunk (which was often), he was socially awkward. In either
capacity, most people didn't like him.

As the Commodore of Interplanetary Space Interdiction
Squadron Three (ISIC 3), Captain Radcliff was responsible for
a squadron of three large vessels: the USSS Midway, dubbed the
"command ship," the USSS Annapolis and the USSS Newport.
USSS Midway was the largest of the three, and it was also where
the commodore lived. The commodore orchestrated all squadron
operations and exercises from the Midway as well as held important
meetings and briefings.

The commodore didn't handle the stress of running an entire
squadron very well. There was speculation amongst the crew that
he was on a cocktail of anxiety meds and that he was having marital
problems at home. Regardless, he was a powder keg of emotions,
which is why I generally gave him a wide berth.

I could feel a slight smile threaten my face as the snoring
sounds which erupted from the commodore's stateroom door stayed
Lieutenant Rivera's fist. Rivera was scared of the commodore,

and this amused me. To buy some time, Rivera leaned against the bulkhead outside the stateroom door and took a deep breath.

"Probably shouldn't wake him yet. Let's go over the brief again," he said. "I want to make sure I've got all the details."

This was the third time I would debrief him. Once I was finished repeating the information to Rivera, he let out a long exhale. Then he smoothed out the front of his coveralls, pushing himself away from the bulkhead. He closed his eyes for a couple of moments, figuring out how to frame his words.

As the *Midway's* operations department head, Rivera had essentially become the commodore's bitch. I remembered once seeing Rivera scurry through the passageway with a McDonald's happy meal bag toward the commodore's stateroom. His coveralls were wrinkled, which meant he'd probably been fast asleep in his rack when the commodore called. Oddly, Rivera accepted this treatment when most other department heads would've told Captain Radcliff to "get fucked." I wondered when the day would come when Rivera snapped. His subservience reminded me of a sleeping lion being poked.

Rivera was overly cautious and indecisive. As my boss, the energy he put into perfecting everything trickled down to me in the form of unnecessary busywork. CMS calls in the early morning hours weren't unusual, and they usually precipitated a mad dash to fix things that didn't need to be fixed. Last-minute operational changes were the norm. Rivera was constantly trying to anticipate what the commodore would want, and he consistently failed in his predictions. So, I wasn't surprised when Rivera left the commodore's stateroom and informed me that I'd be conducting the brief myself.

The commodore liked me. I didn't speak much. I worked well under pressure, letting my instincts take hold. I knew how to fall into a routine when things got hairy. And I knew when to keep my mouth shut. He was still an unbelievable dick to me as he was to everyone else, but if given the choice between a briefing from Rivera or a debrief from me, he'd choose me. I wondered how many times he'd ogle me during the brief.

Before going back into the commodore's stateroom, Rivera pulled me farther down the passageway and had me wait a moment.

"Listen, Mel. Keep it brief. I'll be in there with you. Follow my lead."

"Yes, sir." *Uh no. Following your lead will get us bitched out.*

"Don't say anything about the fingerprints. Not until we find out more about who they belong to."

I raised my eyebrows. "Okay."

"All I'm saying is be careful what you say and what you agree to, all right?"

I wanted to ask what he meant, but he was already knocking on Captain Radcliffe's door.

⋙

"Request permission to come aboard, sir?" Rivera said as he knocked on the commodore's door.

"Permission granted." The commodore's voice boomed through the door down the passageway.

I walked in behind Rivera and noticed a man in an expensive suit. I couldn't see his face because he was in my peripheral vision, but I could see that he was sitting in a corner in one of the commodore's plush red chairs. Legs crossed. Leaned back. Silent. Something about his demeanor screamed *powerful* and *dangerous*. I wanted to steal a look, but I couldn't. Whoever he was, he was watching me.

The commodore didn't make any effort to introduce him and wasn't even looking at him, which seemed odd, but Rivera was, even though the commodore had us both standing at attention.

Rivera's eyes were trained on the man whom he obviously knew well because his olive skin turned pale. He sent an accusatory glance towards the man. "When did you get back?" His tone was quiet yet threatening. *Lion indeed.*

"This morning." The man in the suit's voice was neutral.

"What shit-storm did you bring with you this time, LaSalle?" Rivera crossed his arms.

"That's enough, Rivera," the commodore barked.

Rivera looked like he wanted to say something else, but instead he clamped his mouth shut. His jaw bulged from clenched teeth. Finally, standing at attention, Rivera averted his eyes and ignored the man.

I, however, took a quick glance in his direction. *Crap. That's the hot ex-Navy SEAL that I met on my way to yoga.*

My mind raced. Why is he here in the commodore's stateroom? Is he staying for my brief? Why does Rivera despise him? What's his job description? It almost seemed like this LaSalle was reading my mind. I could feel him watching me, and I barely detected a smirk from the corner of my eye.

Captain Radcliff bent over his bathroom sink, splashing water on his face. He patted his face dry with a small hand towel before ordering a scotch from his CMS computer. The computer issued a brushed nickel decanter with a finger of scotch from the wall. The commodore threw it back and placed the empty decanter in the holder before the computer issued another. He grabbed it and extended it to LaSalle, who waved it away. The commodore shrugged and plopped down in the scarlet leather cushioned chair behind his desk—one of the few luxuries onboard a U.S. Naval spaceship. He lit a cigarette and blew out a puff of smoke while surveying Rivera.

He extended the decanter of scotch to me with one hand, while his cigarette burned between the first two fingers of his other. "A drink?"

"No. Thank you, sir," I said, trying to sound neutral even though I thought he was being a rude jackass by offering me the scotch first instead of my department head.

He pointed it at Rivera. "Rivera?"

"No, thank you, sir. I'm on watch."

"Hmm. Well, then, who's watching the pilot house? Why are you even here?"

"Lieutenant Bay said he'd cover me while we debriefed you. My watch is about to end anyway."

Captain Radcliff grunted. "You left Bay in charge of the pilot house? That clown? If any meteors crash us, Rivera, you're done for good." He turned back to me. "So, where's the rest of your team?"

My team. Oh shit. I hadn't thought of that. "Sir?"

"Okay, I'll repeat myself, which you know I love so much. The forensics team? Why aren't they here?"

"I sent them back to their racks, sir," I said, while my eyes stayed trained on the painting behind him.

"Well, that wasn't your call to make, Ensign. I want them in here," he said, snapping his fingers impatiently. "C'mon. Let's go. I don't have all day."

Actually, you do. You're the commodore. You don't do shit all day except issue orders and abuse Rivera.

"Aye, sir."

I touched the display on my wrist and sent a CMS high priority announcement to Chief Martinez. In the meantime, the commodore motioned for Rivera to look at some papers on his desk.

"Ops, get over here. I need you to explain to me why you're submitting all of these CASREPs on the navigation system. This is a newly commissioned ship."

"Sir, to upgrade some of the basic software and prove it's obsolete, a CASREP is required, as per the instruction . . ."

Rivera and the commodore went back and forth about casualty reports and the navigation system as well as a few other major systems' suites that were ready to undergo repair. I was so glad to be out of that conversation. Getting the commodore to sign casualty reports was like slinging steel beams, one-handed.

I waited at parade rest. It was nerve-racking because I could feel LaSalle quietly assess me. I stole a quick peek at him, and he was indeed watching me. I couldn't help but squirm a little. I decided to concentrate on the painting again directly ahead on the bulkhead, above the commodore's chair. There were other paintings along the bulkhead in my field of vision, but the one directly in front was strangely alluring.

"Kush," he said. He was suddenly standing close. I flinched. I hadn't even heard him approach. Rivera, who was still reviewing casualty reports with the commodore, managed to look up for a second and frown. I simply nodded and looked back at the print. LaSalle continued on as if unaware of the awkwardness that hovered in the room. "Vladimir Kush was a Russian painter from the twenty-first century. The print you're looking at is *City by the Sea*. The other ones along the bulkhead are Salvador Dali prints. As you can see, Kush's art is majorly influenced by Dali."

My stomach flipped. I could almost feel his breath on my neck. What would Rivera and the commodore think if they were paying attention? This had to look bad, LaSalle in my personal space. Luckily, Rivera and the commodore were preoccupied with the reports. LaSalle waited for my reaction to the painting. All of his attention was on me. I didn't like it. Or did I? He definitely made me nervous. I couldn't continue to ignore him, so I said the first word that came to mind. "Pretty."

Luckily, Chief Martinez, Eric and the rest of the forensics team all filed in at that moment. I was relieved. I inched away from LaSalle as fast as I could.

The commodore looked up from the reports and raised his eyebrows at me expectantly.

"Well, what are you waiting for?" said the commodore. He flicked his hand impatiently. "Begin."

"Sir, don't you want the XO and Lieutenant Commander Cox present for this?" I said.

"No. I don't. Now start before I lose my patience." His tone clipped. I wanted to tee off on him, but instead, like a dutiful ensign, I began my brief.

My presentation took about forty-five minutes. As I neared the end, I powered up my MCB and clicked on the file that held the footage. Then I clicked: Holographic Video Simulation—Conference. A three-dimensional holographic image of Senior Chief's body (without head) projected from my MCB. His mutilated body shuffled onto the well deck and collapsed to its knees before completely toppling over.

As ghastly as it was, everyone was glued to the holographic video in complete silence—well, most everyone. LaSalle was the only one not watching. He seemed . . . disappointed . . . almost vexed by the whole scene. He was antsy, tapping his foot impatiently. Arms crossed. Somewhat irritated. He wanted to say something, but his mouth fastened in a hard line.

Rivera stepped forward. "Sir, you should also know that Ensign Brown found some unknown fingerprints on the body, with the hand scanner. They don't belong to anyone from the ship's manifest, and—"

"And what?" The commodore stood up from his chair.

Rivera laughed nervously but continued, "and they're not totally human. I know it sounds crazy, but the results of the fingerprint analysis and the DNA scan indicate that the fingerprints belong to something or someone unknown."

Then Rivera glared at LaSalle.

First Rivera tells me to hush about the fingerprints, and then he blurts it all out? I don't get it.

Captain Radcliff threw his head back, slipping the remainder of the second scotch down his throat.

"Well, what the hell is that supposed to mean?"

"Based on the computer's assessment, it looks like the prints were once human but have evolved in some way," Rivera said. He stole another glance at the man in the chair before continuing. "They've—mutated—you know?"

"No. I don't know, Lieutenant." The commodore's voice trembled a bit.

Space travel made almost anything believable, but even the notion of a mutating human would normally be laughable. At the moment, no one was laughing.

Rivera continued. "Sir, we don't know yet, but, in my opinion, whatever it is, it's hostile."

"No shit, Rivera." The commodore's voice grew louder. "I think it's safe to say that since Senior Chief is missing his head, the killer is indeed hostile."

The commodore stood over his desk as everyone let his last statement sink in. No one said anything. We waited for him to speak until an announcement on the 1MC echoed throughout his stateroom, giving indication that everyone on the ship was waking up and starting their days: *"Reveille, reveille. All hands heave out and trice up. It is now reveille."*

The sound of people moving briskly to their workspaces echoed in from the passageway outside. Still we waited for the commodore to say something. I considered breaking the silence when finally he spoke.

"First of all, I want to know if any of you has breathed a word of this to anyone," he said, "particularly Lieutenant Commander Cox. He may be Admiral Willard's liaison, but I run things on the *Midway.*"

Silence again. Even if anyone had told Cox, I doubt they'd have admitted it now. Everyone knew that the commodore hated Travis Cox. And to be honest, I wasn't a fan either.

Cox really was a bastard. As operations liaison officer to Admiral John Willard, he was unapologetically arrogant. Admiral Willard was the Commander of ISG 3, and as such, he depended on Lieutenant Commander Cox to have eyes on ISIC 3, the third of six subordinate commands that the admiral governed. Admiral Willard used Cox's leadership and expertise to ensure that Captain Radcliff's efforts were in keeping with his vision of how ISG 3 would meet its mission objectives. While Captain Radcliff was the commodore of ISIC 3 and the skipper of the *Midway,* a significant amount of power lay with Lieutenant Commander Cox as the admiral's liaison. Cox used a measure of his power over the commodore and his staff at every opportunity. The entire crew of the *Midway* knew this but kept up the pretense that Captain Radcliff was completely in charge. Easier to justify following the commodore's orders to Cox rather than the other way around.

After surveying the room, I looked backed to the commodore and reassured him. "No, sir. None of us has told Lieutenant Commander Cox or anyone else for that matter."

To drive the point home, I added, "and none of us will."

I gave them all the *I'll strangle you* look if they said otherwise. They all nodded to signify they wouldn't say anything. The commodore plopped back into his chair, pleased. LaSalle smirked.

Radcliff poured another decanter of scotch and gestured to LaSalle who was now standing next to him. "Everyone, in case you don't know already, the gentleman to my right is Dr. Gerard LaSalle. Dr. LaSalle is the operations director and head of security for Biotech's mining operations on Station #0517212. He handles all scheduling, port arrangements, operations planning and security regarding any drilling or mining activities at the station. He's also a prior Navy SEAL, so he speaks Navy. You won't have to dumb anything down for him."

"What business does he have with all of this? We're conducting a murder investigation onboard, not at the mines," I asked without looking at LaSalle. I knew I was being rude. I didn't care. If Rivera didn't trust him, neither did I, and if the commodore trusted LaSalle, I especially didn't trust him.

The commodore looked irritated but ignored my insubordination. "Au contraire. You're going to the mining station to do a forensics sweep of Senior Chief's last-seen whereabouts, and Dr. LaSalle is going with you."

"Why?"

"Because I said so, Ensign. That's why."

"But—"

"As I said before, he's the head of Biotech security."

I gestured to Eric. "I thought Captain Hunt provided shipboard security."

The commodore slammed his scotch down. "Yes. *Shipboard* security. Not station and mining security, Ensign Brown. Not to mention he's highly trained and knowledgeable about the station's resources. He's going with you."

The commodore has a man-crush on Eric . . . and LaSalle—the Marine and the Navy SEAL. He wants to be part of the "badass boys club," but he doesn't even come close. Pathetic.

"That doesn't make sense," I said. "Wouldn't it make sense for us to search the ship for the rest of Senior's remains? Who said anything about him being at the mines?"

"I did," said Eric, stepping forward. "That's where I saw him last. I meant to tell you, but I didn't get a chance."

Didn't get a chance? Son of a bitch. We spent almost three hours investigating Senior Chief's crime scene together, and he didn't get a chance? Since when did Eric meet up with Senior Chief without me knowing about it anyway? And more importantly, how did the commodore know? Obviously, Eric reported those little details to the commodore while I wasn't paying attention. It would certainly explain LaSalle's presence.

I glared at Eric. *Apparently, fucking someone doesn't guarantee future loyalty.*

"We need to see where he was last seen alive," LaSalle said, gesturing at Eric. "According to the Marine captain here, Senior Chief McGinn was at the mines a week ago."

"No," I said. "He was at Port Juliette visiting his brother. He didn't have any business in the actually cave mines. I have a signed copy of his leave papers."

"I'm sure you do." Eric looked smug.

"His plan was to return a few days ago."

"Well, that's probably what he told you," said Eric.

Rivera was seething. He was as surprised by this development as me. Eric was sneaky. The more I got to know him, the more I was unimpressed. I was certain that Rivera would rip him a new one later for throwing us both under the bus.

I refused to back down. "Either way, I'm certain his death occurred onboard."

"Are you?" the commodore asked. "Did he check in with you when he got back?"

He would never "check" in with me because he was a sexist jerk off.

"Well, no, but—"

"Captain Hunt informed me that Senior Chief McGinn wasn't on any of the manifests documenting return trips that the *Pegasus* made this past week. What truly concerns me is that you don't know that, Legal Officer," said the commodore as he slipped yet another scotch down his throat.

I'm gonna kill Eric.

"Well, sir, I was worried about—oh gee—I don't know—a forensic brief.

"Don't get smart with me, Ensign."

"But—"

"Has anyone from your division reported seeing him?"

"Well I haven't had a chance to talk to my div—"

"So you don't have any clue where he was murdered."

"No, sir. But there's video that suggests he came back—"

"Didn't you say that all of the video stickers were destroyed?"

"Yes, but I have some footage which I was able to extract from the stealth sticker I installed."

"And where was that?"

"You know I can't tell you that, sir." A shadow crossed the commodore's face for a moment. LaSalle was grinning. I ignored him but looked over at Rivera, who nodded at me. I continued on as though I hadn't just put a full-bird Navy captain in check. "The video shows—"

"That video is inconclusive," the commodore said, his face a deep shade of scarlet. Glaring at me, he rose from his chair with his hands on his hips.

I bit my lip. *The commodore has girl hips.*

His voice grew louder. "One sticker couldn't possibly supply us with all of the information we need. You still can't tell me where the rest of his body is."

My own anger bubbled to the surface. I could hear the volume in my own voice rising. "Yes, but, you can still see that he—"

"You're going to the station. That's final." The commodore leaned forward across his desk. He pointed at me, his finger hovering in front of my face. It stayed there for a beat. I thought about biting it off. Finally, he lowered his hand and turned to pour another finger of scotch.

Amazing this asshole isn't drunk yet. How many scotches is that?

"I'll go to the station with her, sir," Rivera offered.

"No, Rivera, I need you here."

The commodore's logic was absurd. I could tell by the way Rivera shifted his body that he didn't agree, either. I stole a look at LaSalle. Now he wouldn't look at me. *Weird.*

Normally I would've been thrilled about a trip away from the *Midway,* but I'd heard from others that the mining station was too wild and uncivilized, like the Wild West and the Amazon all mixed in one.

I made one last attempt with the commodore. "Sir, I'm sure Senior Chief checked in with someone in my division. Let me just talk to my division—"

"How could he have checked in if he wasn't on any of this past week's return launches?" Eric said.

Damn him. Why was he chiming in? The only interaction that he generally had with Senior Chief was regarding the inventory and management of the combat engineer battalion's small arms ammunition and demolitions. Their magazine spaces belonged to the *Midway,* so any ammunition or demolitions that the Marines had to store had to be inventoried by my division. Any requisitioning of ammo had to be done through me.

"And why, pray tell, did you and Senior Chief have a conversation at the mines when he was supposed to be on leave at the port?" I asked.

He shrugged. "We were running low on demolitions. So, he and a couple of gunner's mates visited the station and offloaded some of our munitions."

"What munitions?" I asked. "Nothing came through me."

Eric squirmed a bit. "Well, it was kind of last-minute. He was headed on leave and offered to bring stuff with him. We were running low on ammo, so I asked him to bring a carton of hydraulic grenades and blasting caps."

Son of a bitch. Eric knew how I felt about Senior Chief's constant undermining of me, and yet he still conducted business with him without notifying me. Even in death, Senior Chief managed to have the last laugh.

"Wait a minute. You accepted ammo that hadn't been properly requisitioned and signed for?" I asked. Surely the commodore would have something to say to Eric about this. If he wanted to play "Back-Stabby" Stanley, then I could too.

The commodore had one agenda, though. "Ensign Brown, I'm tired of this. I've made my decision. This discussion is over," he said, slipping more scotch down his throat. He pulled a cigar from a cherry walnut case on his desk and began to light it—his famous dismissive gesture. "One more word on this, and I'll take you to mast. Now, you're going to the station. Dr. LaSalle and his team will accompany you. Captain Hunt, can you make the trip as well?"

Well fuck me sideways. I'm ordered to go, and he gets a polite request?

"Yes, sir. If you don't mind, I'd like to bring Lance Corporal Jones and Lieutenant Kolar with me."

Ah, I see. He's bringing his new fuck buddy. Sherri Fucking Kolar.

"That's fine," said the commodore.

The commodore announced that we'd leave at the end of the week. We went over a couple of minor details, and then he dismissed us all from the cabin. I considered bringing up the journal-file, but again, that weird feeling told me not to. I left the commodore's stateroom without uttering a word about it.

11

"What did I tell you?" Rivera grabbed me after we stepped outside of the commodore's stateroom into the passageway. "I told you to be careful about what you agree to."

I yanked my arm away. "In case you hadn't noticed, I didn't have a choice. And you didn't exactly help me back there."

"I tried to go with you."

"Yeah, well it didn't work. What's the big deal anyway? The station can't be *that* bad."

"Well it is."

"You were willing to go."

"Only to help you."

"Does it totally suck?"

"Well, it's not a trip to the day spa."

"Cute. Seriously, is it that bad?"

"I'll put it this way: It'll suck for you."

I rolled my eyes. "Whatever. Stop trying to spin me up."

"I'm not trying to spin you up. You're going to the mines. I'll bet my next paycheck that's where the majority of your investigation will be."

"So what?"

"Well, if you were going to the actual station, where the tavern, stores and other everyday conveniences are, then you might be all right. Maybe. But you won't be going there. You'll be heading out to the actual cave mines."

"And?"

"Have you reviewed any of the station files, Mel?"

"Pfft. Why would I do that? I don't go there."

"Your people—you know, your division? The people you're in charge of? Your gunner's mates go there all the time to deliver ammunition."

I looked at him, and he looked back at me incredulously. "You're a piece of work, Mel."

"I haven't had time! I've been knee-deep in ATG certifications and now this investigation."

Rivera sighed and raked his fingers through his thick, black mane. "Look. Going to the mines means a full expedition. You'll have to traipse through blankets of humidity and heat, dense wilderness, contend with wildlife and possibly deal with the lowlifes that work at the port. Not to mention the crap you'll have to get through to navigate the mines. It's a real blast."

"Sounds awesome."

Rivera ignored my sarcasm. "That's not all. There's a swim involved."

WHAT?!? Current technology offered swimming solutions for "non-swimmers" like myself, but I didn't like the idea of water at all. I remembered almost drowning as a young girl. A young boy grabbed me and lifted me out of the pool. I haven't swam since. I willingly put my life in the hands of assisted swimming technology, and I'm okay with that.

Rivera placed a comforting hand on my shoulder. "Don't worry," he said. "I wasn't trying to scare you. I mean . . . I was a little. I just want you to be prepared. Besides, as much as I'm not a fan of LaSalle's, he's—"

On cue, LaSalle exited the commodore's stateroom door. He looked conflicted. He turned to go back into the commodore's stateroom, but then changed his mind and left.

Rivera ended our conversation abruptly and left me to catch up with LaSalle. I decided to head the other direction to catch up with Eric, who'd already left the briefing. I took one look back at Rivera and LaSalle, who were in a heated conversation. Rivera's face was red. He was pointing his finger at LaSalle. LaSalle's arms were crossed, like he contemplated knocking Rivera out. *Let them work it out, Amelia. Time to deal with that sneaky little shit, Eric.*

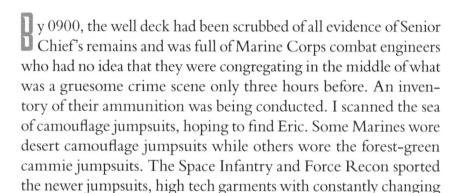

12

By 0900, the well deck had been scrubbed of all evidence of Senior Chief's remains and was full of Marine Corps combat engineers who had no idea that they were congregating in the middle of what was a gruesome crime scene only three hours before. An inventory of their ammunition was being conducted. I scanned the sea of camouflage jumpsuits, hoping to find Eric. Some Marines wore desert camouflage jumpsuits while others wore the forest-green cammie jumpsuits. The Space Infantry and Force Recon sported the newer jumpsuits, high tech garments with constantly changing patterns to match one's surroundings. I watched with amazement as one Marine walked over to a section of the bulkhead with the Marine Corps emblem. He leaned against it, and his suit blended in exactly with the eagle, globe and anchor.

I scanned the faces until finally I spotted Eric. His muscular physique was easy to spot. His sparkly brown eyes were directed at some female Marine who'd brought him an electronic clipboard to sign. The king of irresistible charm, he passed his wrist over the clipboard's laser scanner while he winked at her. She rewarded him with a demure smile and nodded, before heading back to the pallet of ammunition she was inventorying. I wanted to scream.

I could feel my blood boil as I walked up. I wasn't jealous. I was just annoyed that his manipulative, fake charm won him so many admirers. I managed to calm myself. Even now, as pissed as I was, I was still somewhat attracted to him, which made me almost hate myself. I noticed the muscles in his arms bulge from his camouflage jumpsuit.

"Hey," I said, trying to interject some friendliness in my voice. I didn't want him to know how pissed I was, or worse, have him think I was jealous. I did want a goddamn apology for doing back-alley arrangements with my dead senior chief, though.

"Hey," he said, his demeanor nonchalant.

"What's going on?"

"Not much."

He was acting the same way he did a week after our return from JJOI: detached and distant. I recalled how the regularity of our sexual encounters waned from every day to once a week (and I was mostly initiating them). Then a month passed, and I noticed we weren't having sex at all. One day I saw Sherri at yoga, and before I'd even seen her with him, I just knew. It was an inexplicable feeling of certainty. He'd seen her and fallen head over heels. I'd bet my life on it.

Admittedly, Sherri was a bombshell. An exotic beauty. She had flawless, tan skin. Her complexion was a honey, butternut shade. She was tall and slender, with sleek feminine lines, like a ballet dancer. Her best features were her dark eyes and her long, dark, charcoal-colored hair. In uniform, she pulled her hair up into a tight bun, which only accented her high cheekbones and large brown eyes. Her features were dramatic enough that she could pull off the "natural look." She had the clean-cut, put together look of a female Marine that you'd see on a recruiting poster. I expected her to be somewhat of a snob, but she was friendly. Almost a little too friendly. I wondered if she was genuine or vicious beneath her polished veneer. She couldn't possibly have known that Eric and I had been together, though. So, I decided on the former.

I resolved to get down to brass tacks with him. "You threw me under the bus back there."

Preoccupied, he passed a wand over several pallets of ammunition, looking for defects. Neon red words hovered above the wand: "Moisture exposure. Corroded rounds. SKUs #973797-897." He placed a red sticker on the defected pallet.

"I don't know what you're talking about," he said.

"Look, it may not have been intentional, but you did throw me under the bus. It would've helped to know that Senior Chief met with you. You knew how I felt about him going behind my back."

He set the wand on a pallet and crossed his arms. "I didn't throw you under the bus. You threw yourself under the bus."

"How do you figure?"

"By not having control of your people. I was doing my job. We were under a time crunch. I didn't have time to get your approval, so I got Senior Chief to help me."

"That makes it okay to ignore procedure and do whatever you wanted?"

"You would've done the same thing in my position."

"No. I wouldn't have, Eric."

"Well, I don't report to you or answer to you, Mel." He let out a long-exasperated sigh. "I don't know why I'm having this discussion with you. The commodore was fine with it." He picked up the wand again and continued with his ammo inspection.

It annoyed me that he wouldn't even make eye contact. "Oh. I forgot that you're his new golden boy now. You told him about Senior Chief not being on the manifest and about the results of the investigation before either myself or Rivera could debrief him. Why would you do that when you were specifically told not to?" My voice was obviously getting too loud. People were starting to look at us.

"The commodore needed to know. You're the fork calling the spoon silverware. Everyone knows the commodore gets a boner every time you're in a room with him. How convenient he made *you* his legal officer."

"I was given that assignment before I even reported, dimwit. And—you know what? The fact of the matter is that everyone knows you're a little, fucking weasel. You totally bilged me in there." Now everyone *was* watching.

"I'm done with this. I don't owe you any explanation because, again, I don't report to you. In fact, I outrank you, so you might want to watch your tone with me."

"So, it's gonna be like that?"

"Yeah, it's like that." He was looking at me now. "Honestly, I think you're pissed that McGinn respected me more than he respected you. Maybe if you'd show up to actually *lead* your division, you'd have had more visibility on what your NCO was up to."

So, we're going below the belt.

"Hey idiot. No one takes you seriously. You're a pretty boy in a Marine costume. That's all." It wasn't clever, but I knew that Eric had insecurities about being taken seriously.

His face was as hard as steel. I'd struck a nerve. *Yaaaay.* He struck back. "As usual, Mel, you keep running your mouth when you should keep it shut. It's why you can't keep a man."

Yikes. That hurt. I swallowed, pushing back the emotions that welled up. I wanted to kick Eric in the face. Instead, I had one last thing to stay. "Stay away from my division. You need something, you come through me. Otherwise, stay out of my way, shit stain."

I shoved my way past him and walked off. I was embarrassed that people overheard our conversation. Had I gone too far? Would he write me up for blatant disrespect?

I doubted it. As always, though, he got in the last word. "Yeah—well—this has been great. Really. Do me a favor? Next time don't come all the way down here when you can simply message me, *Ensign* Brown."

My face heated up from his emphasis on my rank. To make
matters worse, LaSalle had arrived at the worse possible moment,
witnessing the end of our exchange. He leaned against a bulkhead in
my periphery. I pretended not to see him as I stalked out of the space.

⌁

After my exchange with Eric, I shuffled toward my stateroom
in a daze. The pain of our separation fully sunk in. I sifted through
snatches of conversations to see where it all went wrong. I recalled
an argument we had around the time he and Sherri had begun
cozying up. I called him on it; he snapped at me:

"I don't think I'm gonna make it to dinner tonight. I have a lot
to do now," I said, hoping he'd change his mind about her and come
back to me. Apologize. Admit he'd fucked up, but it never came.

"That's fine," he said. "I've got other plans anyway."

I wasn't a "crier", but in that moment, I wasn't so sure. Stunned.
All could think to say was, "I bet you do."

As I approached my stateroom door, I ran into the only other
person on the *Midway* that I didn't want to run into: Lieutenant
Commander Travis Cox.

Jeez. Is it Asshole Day today?

Ever since the commodore had been investigated for a UCMJ
violation I'd witnessed, I'd been avoiding Cox altogether.

Travis Cox was meticulous to a fault, ruthlessly straightforward,
and unwavering with regard to rules and regulations. Everyone
called him a "self-righteous tool." In my estimation, he was a control freak. If he didn't like someone's behavior, he'd either control
it or correct it. That became clear after he'd openly posed accusations against the commodore regarding ungentlemanly, drunken

behavior during an international ball. I had the misfortune to witness the entire event along with two others. The commodore groped a female officer from the Chilean fleet. Unfortunately, the boyfriend of said female officer saw Captain Radcliff's hand make its way to the woman's ass. Her boyfriend went berserk. Within seconds, the command master chief was dragging Captain Radcliff (who was yelling obscenities at any male Chilean officer within sight) out of the ball in a full nelson. Yet when Admiral Willard's JAG officer began his investigation, I was the one he called to corroborate Lieutenant Cox's account of that evening.

The JAG officer didn't push very hard. He was no fool. He knew of Admiral Willard's longstanding friendship with Captain Radcliff. Having been classmates at the Citadel, an international scandal with the commodore would've put Admiral Willard in an awkward position—an outcome that would've put the JAG in a *shoot-the-messenger* situation. The JAG officer questioned everyone who'd been at the ball up until the point he'd questioned me. No one said a word. I was the only witness left to question. Cox gave my name to the JAG because he saw me at the ball. I played stupid, though, making Cox's credibility appear questionable. In turn, the investigation was immediately closed by the JAG officer, a decision he eagerly made without much follow-up. In the end, I'd made an ally of the commodore and an inadvertent enemy of Cox.

"So, if it isn't the commodore's new pet," said Cox. His eyes narrowed.

"Sir, it's been a long day. I'm really tired."

"Oh, really? What a coincidence. I don't care."

"What do you want?" I dropped the *Sir*.

"I want you to show me some fucking respect," he said, taking a step closer into my personal space.

I knew I'd overstepped, but I'd dealt with Senior Chief (even though he was dead), Eric, Captain Radcliffe, then Eric again, all on less than a half-hour of sleep. Now Cox was in my face. I was beat.

"Sir, I just finished a briefing with the commodore. My department head said that I could get a couple of hours in the rack before I—"

"What briefing?"

Shitballs. Thanks, Sleep Deprivation. "What?"

"Don't *what* me. You said you just finished a briefing with the commodore."

The commodore expressly told us not to say anything, and I already opened my big mouth.

"Sir, I—"

"Was it regarding your murder investigation?"

Looks like I'm not the only one with loose lips.

"I'm really not at liberty to say. Next time you report to the commodore, maybe you can ask him."

"I don't report to the commodore. I report to the admiral. Don't forget that."

"Yeah. You've made that clear . . . to everyone onboard."

He was a little too close. He looked directly into my eyes. I didn't like it, but I wasn't going to let him know I was intimidated. I stared back.

"You know you lied about that ball. You made me look like an idiot."

"I didn't have to try very hard," I blurted. A blatantly disrespectful comment like that would've gotten me in trouble with any other outranking officer, but I knew that the commodore wouldn't entertain any complaints from Cox about me. I also knew that he wouldn't go to the admiral over something so petty, especially since his previous accusations against the commodore were now in question.

His face went from red to ghost white. "By lying you've violated the Uniform Code of Military Justice. One day your mouth is going to get you in serious trouble, Ensign Brown."

"Yeah, that seems to be the today's theme," I muttered.

"What?"

"Nothing, sir."

He surveyed me a moment longer. I used every ounce of restraint not to look away.

Finally, he turned and left. I exhaled.

13

Senior Chief's murder, the briefing, the argument with Eric and then the run-in with Cox all happened early Tuesday morning. The rest of Tuesday flew by. So did Wednesday. By Thursday, I had finished preps for the trip to the mining station and decided it would be a good time to speak to my division. I held quarters and addressed any questions they had regarding Senior's absence. I hated to lie, but I lied. I told them that Senior Chief had to leave due to a family emergency. I told them he'd been administratively separated from the Navy and transferred off the ship due to personal reasons. Many took this to mean that he had mental health issues, which wasn't totally far from the truth. This was the best solution I could come up with in order to avoid any haranguing by them. I looked at the two gunner's mates in my division who had assisted with the forensics sweep, and I made sure they knew beforehand that I'd nail their ass to a wall if they leaked any of the facts about Senior Chief's death.

Oddly enough, they seemed content with keep up the pretense, and no one seemed too upset by McGinn's death. In fact, it seemed that his absence lifted a heavy mental weight from the division. We accomplished more work that day than any other. Spirits seemed unusually high. People took pride in their work. They didn't settle for the bare minimums anymore. Some of the guys even cracked jokes. The maintenance that needed to be done on the gun mounts was completed ahead of schedule. The additional ammunition, recently delivered for the combat engineering battalion, had been safely loaded into their magazine. All of my division's work was completed well before the workday was over. For the first time in a long time I was finally enjoying work and spending time with my division. I chose to let everyone off early again.

I showered and decided on a nice quiet dinner at my other favorite shipboard bar, the Scuttlebutt. The Scuttlebutt was unofficially known to be frequented by civilian contractors, engineers as well as "other" miscellaneous non–military personnel. It was tucked away on the engineering level, in the bowels of the *Midway,* where few, if any, military personnel were willing to venture. It was my best option for a delicious meal with peace and quiet. I'd bury myself in a few cocktails, quietly celebrate my win over Chief Martinez on Monday while I simultaneously wallowed in self-loathing over my failure with men.

I hadn't talked to Eric since our conversation after the briefing. I called him on Wednesday for work-related issues, but he ignored me. I assumed that a call through the ship's ICS would indicate that my intentions were of a professional nature, but his failure to call me back was like another unanticipated blow. If he wouldn't speak with me directly, I decided I didn't want to see his face anyhow. I sent Petty Officer Mackie, one of my gunner's mates, to Eric's sector to handle the business I had with him in my stead. When he tried to call me back, I refused his calls. He called again. I refused again. Then he showed up at my workspace, but I left through a rear hatch before he could gain access.

My division began to suspect something was up. I'm sure they pieced together the fact that we'd been in a relationship, but I didn't care. *I'd* be avoiding *him* now.

The Scuttlebutt was open twenty-four hours, and because most of the engineers worked around the clock, it hadn't suffered from much wear and tear. The fabric on the chairs and booths hadn't faded yet. The dark wood along the bar and walls remained a shiny, dark mahogany color. The floors remained unscratched. Even better, it wasn't Eric's scene. It was too quiet, too mature, and, frankly, not a great place to show off his new dime piece. He was most likely showing her off at the Marine officer hangout, Leathernecks.

Inside, I spotted a human services contractor, a scantily clad Sirens Inc. woman sitting at the bar having a drink. Her outfit was conservative by comparison to the table of other Sirens Inc. girls chatting in a corner booth. She sat alone at the bar, and she wasn't trying to wrangle any customers. She was a loner, and I liked that she looked like she wouldn't talk my ear off. Initially, I considered sitting alone, but then I realized I didn't want to be alone. I headed for an empty seat next to hers.

"Do you mind if I sit here?"

"Not at all." The tone of her voice suggested that she was surprised a female military officer would want to sit next to her.

Then her face changed. "I should let you know that I'm off the clock, and I don't do women. A lot of the other girls do, though." She pointed at the corner table with the other Sirens whose clothes were even racier than hers.

"Uh. No. I'm good. I don't do women, either," I chuckled. "I want a couple of quiet drinks and good conversation. That's all."

I held out my hand. "Mel."

Her face relaxed. "Lauralie," she said, shaking my hand.

"Lauralie," I said. "Wow. That's an old-school name . . . but pretty."

"Thanks. I think," she said with a smirk. "So, how 'bout I buy *you* a drink? You look like you could use one."

"I look that bad, huh?"

"Frankly, you're the first woman officer on this goddamn ship who has been friendly to me, except for the ones who want to get into my pants. They're real nice too."

I laughed. "I'm not one to turn down a free drink, and I don't really care what you do for living. A living's a living. I'll take a mojito."

She smiled and then turned back to the bar where, in front of her, was a small, brightly lit console inlaid on the bar's surface. She leaned over the console, and the blue light enveloped her face. I could see her features clearly now. She wasn't as old as she initially appeared to be. The makeup and crap she wore on her face made her look like a fit forty-eight-year-old, but the blue light from the console revealed a face in its late thirties. She tapped a couple of buttons on the touch screen console. They glowed like starbursts with every touch of her finger, painted in bright candy-apple red.

Within a minute, a young midshipman, an officer-in-training, appeared. He looked like a male model with thick, wavy brown hair that looked like it had been carefully punked up into organized chaos. He set two drinks in front of us.

"One mojito. One whiskey neat. Anything else?" He waited, arms crossed. Somewhat bored but interested enough and cocky enough to openly stare at Lauralie's rack. Me? I was invisible as far as he was concerned.

"No, we're good," she said.

"Then that'll be twelve earthnotes." The midshipman's voice took on a seductive note. It sounded comical to me.

Lauralie leaned over to place her wrist over the console. The midshipman's eyes were welded to the tops of her breasts which swelled up from her snuggly fitted lace top. The supervising petty officer, a second class, watched, too, as the milky white peaks rose toward them. He blinked several times then caught himself. He slapped the midshipman upside the head and pushed him along.

"Get back into the kitchen. There's dishes that need doing."

The midshipman said something smart under his breath and then shoved his way through the kitchen door, slamming it against the bulkhead, before coming back with a tray of clean beer glasses. I knew he wasn't thrilled about his tavern duties, especially under the tutelage of a petty officer not much older than him. He looked tired. I felt bad for him but not too bad. He had it easy.

All midshipmen (a.k.a. middies) were officers-to-be, which meant that they had summer training requirements to meet before they were allowed to commission. This included working onboard Navy vessels as bartenders/busboys (or girls), mess cooks, dishwashers, etc., during the summers between the school years. Poseidon's was where most of the senior officers and senior contractors drank, and Wings was known to be an aviator bar. As bars went, Poseidon's and Wings were considered to be the cushiest assignments for midshipmen, along with the Scuttlebutt.

The NCO hangouts, however, were to be avoided at all costs. Senior NCOs—not so much the master chiefs and sergeant majors (most had been in the military too long to care)—loved to mess with junior officers and officers-in-training. If you pulled a bar like the Quartermaster, you were in "Shitsville." Even an officer couldn't protect you once you were in. The Rifleman, the Marine Corps version of the Quartermaster, was even worse. The midshipmen were outright hazed by both their supervising petty officers and staff sergeants, along with any chiefs, senior chiefs, gunnery sergeants or first sergeants present at the bar, and rightly so. Many midshipmen (particularly the "legacies") reported to training arrogant and untrainable, especially their final summer. Some could already envision the possibility of retribution against those NCOs who'd harassed them every summer for the past two years. They might soon be leading and managing the very same people, a fact they openly advertised. In response, the NCOs resented the soon-to-be officers' sense of entitlement, apathy and lack of subject matter expertise. Newly commissioned officers often depended on their chief or gunny's years of experience and needed to be reminded that their careers could be made or destroyed by an NCO.

So, naturally, there was a lot of friction in the NCO bars and, as a result, constant fighting. Midshipmen and NCOs walked around with black eyes. Hazing and fighting was prohibited by the UCMJ, but it still happened daily. The middies fought to defend themselves, and the NCOs fought because it was fun. Bets were even made. It was actually what prompted me to formally learn to fight. I'd pulled an NCO bar my first summer training assignment. One female chief had taken particular interest in me when her long-time crush, another chief, made a comment about my eyes. As soon as the words floated from his mouth, I shut my eyes in silent despair. I knew it would be a long summer of catching shit from her. And she did, in fact, ride me all summer long. I walked away with more black eyes, bumps and bruises than I'd ever had in my entire life. It was also the first time I'd ever popped anyone in the face.

That's when I started to secretly play Gladiator 4D. I played every free moment I had. After I got pretty good, and after a few fights, the NCOs started to leave me alone. They still yelled, of course, but none of them laid hands on me. There were two camps of middies that survived summer training: those that could fight and those that routinely got their asses kicked. Regardless, there were always more NCOs than midshipmen, which meant that every midshipman got their ass kicked and was forced to navigate the six stages of summer misery: shock, denial, acceptance, apathy, rage and productivity. By the time most middies finished the last of their three summer training rotations, they were hardened, jaded misanthropes ready to lead.

The midshipman who served us at the Scuttlebutt was clearly entering the rage stage and exiting apathy. There was only one NCO running him, but the petty officer never let up on him. Insults were hurled every couple of minutes or so. Unnecessary shoving, pinching and occasional slaps seemed to be commonplace, but I could see this middie had grit. While he had a fresh shiner not more than a day or two old, so did the petty officer. The midshipman glanced over at Lauralie again. This time it was her ass that had him captured. She had raised up from the bar stool to head to the restroom. This time the supervising junior petty officer pinched his arm and shoved him toward the kitchen. The midshipman stood there for a second, considering retaliation, but then thought better of it. His shiner looked worse than the petty officer's and still tender.

Lauralie returned and held her wrist over the console, ignoring the midshipman and petty officer, as if she'd seen it all before. Finally, a thin red laser beam appeared in the corner of the screen. The console beeped, and she removed her wrist. I got a glimpse of the barcode that had been tattooed on her wrist. It was precise. Small. Subtle.

"Where did you get your barcode done?" I asked. Mine was big and blotchy compared to hers and sometimes didn't work. "Yours was expensive. I can tell."

"My brother did it. He's a tattoo artist. He used to be a contractor during the Barcode Summonings. He insisted on doing mine instead of allowing some hack to do it."

In some respects, I was grateful for a crappy barcode tattoo. The quality of it suggested that I wasn't too wealthy. When the Summonings first began, the idea of being *required* to get a barcode tattoo was appalling for most, but after a decrease in identity thefts, the protests fell away to sporadic rumblings. Then, the nature of theft changed. The incidents were of a much more violent nature, a fact concealed by those who enjoyed socioeconomics. If you were rich, you could afford privatized health care, which might cover alternative therapies like clone technology and stem cell regeneration. In other words, if someone lopped off your arm to access your barcode, you could essentially pay to grow a new limb. The rest of the public had to settle for a stump or a prosthesis.

"So is your name really Mel? I thought that was a guy's name."

"It's short for Amelia. My brother started calling me that when we were little, and it sort of stuck."

Lauralie looked at me curiously. I didn't expect what she would ask next. "You like to drink, don't you, Mel?" I looked away, then glanced back up to find her unwavering gaze considering me. "I've seen you in here before. You drink *a lot*."

"I suppose now you're going to tell me I have a drinking problem," I said defensively.

"Do you?" she asked genuinely. She wasn't being a smart-ass. She was frank.

"No, I—" I paused, not knowing what to say without sounding overly sensitive, "I like a drink from time to time is all. A lot of Navy officers do. I'm a little bummed right now and need an escape from my problems." I wanted good conversation. I hadn't bargained for this.

"Problems?" Her question was sincere but direct. I chalked it up to her profession, which I supposed accompanied a certain measure of candidness. "You seem to have a lot going for you. What problems could you possibly have?"

As if on cue, Eric walked into the tavern with Sherri and a few other Marines.

14

Seriously?

A pit formed in the back of my throat. Eric was trying to upset me. On purpose. It was working.

Lauralie followed the direction of my gaze. She watched Eric for a couple of moments. He had his arm draped around Sherri. He knew I liked to sneak away to the Scuttlebutt when I wanted to avoid other military people. To make matters worse, he'd brought an entire group. I felt alone.

I worried that Lauralie's staring would attract Eric's attention. I pinched her. She flinched, looking back at me like I was crazy. "What?"

"Don't stare. He'll see you, and that's the last thing I want," I said shamefully.

"*He's* your problem?" she asked. She shrugged. She didn't seem impressed by Eric. "I wouldn't worry about it. That one's easy: Ignore the shit out of him. Find some idiot. Make sure he's tall and hot (you're pretty enough) and flirt with him in front of—"

"—Eric," I whispered.

"Eric. Right. Flirt with some hottie in front of him, and it'll irritate the shit out of him."

"He'll know I'm trying to make him jealous."

"Won't matter," she said before lifting her whiskey neat to her lips and tilting her head back to empty it. "He needs to be the center of attention. It's obvious. Take that away from him, and he'll freak."

"Wow. You should be a psychologist."

She shrugged. "I basically am. People always tell me their problems. They'll trust a hooker over a doctor with private information."

"I wonder why."

"Because I don't judge. I'd be a hypocrite if I did. Plus, I know what people need and when they need it . . . men especially. I wouldn't be good at my job if I didn't."

I took a sip of my mojito as I pondered that. I supposed she was right. She certainly had Eric figured out in under a minute.

She looked back over at Eric and shook her head. "I don't get it. What's so great about him besides his body?"

"I don't know. Why is anyone attracted to anyone?"

"Fair point," she said. "Look, don't stop ignoring him even if he starts to come around. Be ruthless. Until he throws a tantrum. At that point, you can decide to keep him or toss him back. Honestly, you're better off on your own. Now, *that's* a man," she said, gesturing toward the end of the bar.

I looked toward the end of the bar. LaSalle. I hadn't even seen him come in.

"Gerard LaSalle?" I asked. I felt a flash of panic. For some reason, I didn't want her to know that I was attracted to him, so I played him down. "I don't know about that. He's got a nice body and all, but he's arrogant. Besides, look how tight he wears his t-shirt. What a douche."

Lauralie shook her head. "No. Not the guy in the t-shirt. The guy next to him. In uniform."

I looked past LaSalle. A tall, muscular dark-skinned black man sat on a stainless, steel-colored stool next to him. He was

in his early forties but in pristine shape. First a track star at the
academy, then an alternate for the Olympics in the 200-meter
dash, he could run his ass off. Since I'd known him, he was always
mindful of his physique. It showed. He also had advanced degrees
in sports science and nutrition, a non-traditional course of study
for an O-5 in the Navy. I'd thought the commodore was fit for
his age, but Commander Yuri Jefferson made Captain Radcliff
look soft. He also made Eric and LaSalle look like amateurs in the
physique department. Even still, I couldn't help my face curling
up in disgust.

Commander Yuri Jefferson was the ship's executive officer.
As the XO, he was second in command on the *Midway*. He would
eventually fleet up to be the commanding officer as well as assume
the mantel of Commodore of ISIC 3, if Captain Radcliff ever
retired. Commander Jefferson was also my brother, a fact no one
knew but the commodore.

"Who, *Yuri*? Are you high?" My voice resonated louder than
I'd planned.

"Why not? Smooth dark skin. A bangin' body. Plus, he's really
sweet." She ran her fingers through her long dark hair as she stared
off dreamily.

Gag.

"Really?" I frowned and then stared at my drink. "You know
each other that well?"

"What's it to you?" She appeared hurt.

I tried to wipe the judgment from my face. They knew each
other. That was clear. I wondered if he'd ever "hired" her. The
thought made me ill—more the thought of Yuri having sex than
the fact that he might've paid for it. Truthfully, I didn't really care
who Yuri slept with. He was the son of my adoptive parents, but
he was also a grown man capable of making decisions for himself.

I tried to reassure her. "Nothing. I—"

"I don't need this, you know. If you want to sit here and act like you're better than me, then I'm going to leave." She made every effort to keep up the pretense of being unaffected. So like a cornered, wounded animal, she attacked. A flicker of jealously slithered into her voice. "Since when are you on a first-name basis with the executive officer of the ship, anyway?"

"Chill, Lauralie. Yuri is my brother." I looked over at him. He was watching us intently. I'm sure he was dying to know what we were talking about. "I'm sorry, but thinking of Yuri having sex with *anyone* grossed me out for a sec."

"Oh," she muttered, staring back into her drink. "You two don't look anything alike, and you have different last names."

"I'm adopted. My parents died in an accident. My father knew my biological parents and decided to let me keep my name," I said, fingering the pendant necklace around my neck. It was a habit. Anytime I thought of my family, including my deceased parents, I grabbed it. "I guess he was really close to them."

"I'm sorry," she said. She lifted the pendant from my neck and examined it. "It's pretty. I like the compass with the globe setting. What did they do?"

"It's cool. I don't know. I don't remember anything or know much about them."

Lauralie hesitated. "Don't you want to know more? Aren't you curious?"

I shrugged. "My father doesn't talk much about them. And he won't. I've tried."

"That sucks."

"It used to bother me when I was a teenager. I'd scream at him, but he wouldn't say a word. He's ridiculously stoic."

I watched Lauralie watch me. She seemed to be reading me. Her silent gaze compelled me to want to break the silence.

"I don't care anymore about that. I had a great childhood growing up." I smiled, hoping to lighten things up. "Uh—can you not repeat this though? I don't want anyone to know."

Her face softened. She nodded respectfully. "I'll have to file that away in my mental folder of ship's secrets," she said with a slight grin. "How did you get stationed on the same ship though? Aren't there rules against that kind of thing?"

"Well, sort of. It's not an ideal situation. The assignment detailers try to prevent it, but sometimes it happens." I shrugged. "He showed up a month after me. If he'd been here before me, he probably would've made sure I'd been issued a new set of orders."

"I'm surprised he didn't do that anyway after he took over as the XO."

"Yeah, I think he'd planned to, but my dad found out and insisted that we look out for each other. This ship has a bad rap. Too many mishaps over the past couple of years."

"Yeah, no shit," she said. "You ever hear about the Sirens girl who was murdered onboard . . . or at least we think she was murdered, on account of the condition her body was in. Happened a year ago. It'll raise the hairs on the back of your neck."

I took another sip of my mojito. "Uh . . . I think I'd like to table that discussion for now. I can't swallow any more doom and gloom right now."

The fact that Lauralie confirmed the *Midway's* bad luck did nothing to brighten my mood.

Several drinks later, and I was almost drunk. Lauralie was kind of sloppy, too, but she held her liquor much better than I did. We were both at the point where everything was funny.

"So. A pig walks into a bar and—"

Before she could finish, I sputtered my drink, laughing so hard I could barely breathe. I clutched at my gut, bent over into a giggle fit.

"I haven't even finished the joke yet, and you're already laughing," she said, chuckling.

"I'm sorry . . . but your jokes are . . ."

She laughed then stopped. Her attention was directed at someone behind me. I spun around on my barstool to find Yuri standing there. I laughed some more.

"Ensign Brown." His nod was curt and professional. "What is it that you all find so funny?"

"Hey, bro," I said. I popped to standing position in mock attention and formed a wobbly salute. Then I lifted my drink to him. "Whatsup?" I knew my lack of military formality irritated him. That made me laugh more, which only made Lauralie laugh again.

He frowned. "Be professional, Mel, especially in front of other people." He stole a hesitant glance toward Lauralie. "Either call me 'XO' or 'Commander Jefferson' or 'Sir.' This isn't the first time we've discussed this."

"You know what?" My voice went up an octave. My voice seemed to always get higher when I was drunk. "Your head is—really large." I broke out into another laughing fit. Lauralie joined me.

Yuri brushed my arm off his shoulder and waited for us to settle down. "So, she told you that we're related?"

Lauralie nodded.

He scowled while I made every effort to keep a straight face. "I'm going to the head. When I get back, I'm going to measure the circumference of your head, sir."

Lauralie bit her lip, trying not to laugh again. I gave up my seat to him and teetered toward the restrooms. I pointed at the midshipman and yelled. "Barkeep. I'm gonna need a laser measure . . . got some craniums to measure."

It wasn't that funny, but we were both drunk, so everything was funny. She clutched her stomach again and laughed. The midshipman rolled his eyes, shaking his head as he walked back into the kitchen. I was embarrassing myself, and I knew it. I didn't care because the impending trip to the station weighed on me. I had about 97 million other things to worry about. Being tipsy in public was the least of my concerns.

15

decided to take the roundabout way, away from LaSalle. I looked over to where he'd been sitting, but I noticed he was gone. I had to go by Eric's table, though, which sucked. There was no way around it. His table almost blocked the only path to the restroom. I would've gone back to my stateroom instead, but it was too far, and I wasn't quite ready to leave the Scuttlebutt yet. I made it to the restroom undisturbed, but after I emerged, Sherri intercepted me outside the restroom door. I gave her a dismissive "hey," encouraging her to move on, but she blocked my path like an offensive lineman.

I was glad that Eric was nowhere in sight, but I wasn't in the mood for Sherri either. I wanted to hate her, or at the very least, politely maintain my distance from her. It wasn't fair that I should have to suffer both Eric's rejection and her innocent congeniality. Sherri was persistent, though. Annoyingly so. Her reason for wanting to be friends with me so badly was bewildering. I wondered if she actually knew about my dalliances with Eric. I considered that maybe she was pulling the old "keep-your-friends-close-and-your-enemies-closer" maneuver. Whatever she was doing, I didn't like it, but I endured it with grace.

She flicked her hair behind her shoulder in that way that women do when they want to appear more confident than they actually are.

"Hey, sweetie," she said.

My teeth clenched. The "hey sweetie" made it easier to dislike her. So condescending. A cheap way of attempting to gain the upper hand. I might've been projecting. Conjuring a subtle belittling that wasn't there. But if that syrupy, sweet word rolled off her tongue again, I'd turn ghetto real quick.

"Hey, Sherri," I smiled graciously. My courteous veneer, a burkha to my ever-growing impatience. "Whatsup?"

"Eric and I and few others are going out for dinner tomorrow night after work, and I wanted to see if you'd like to join us?" she said.

"Oh, well that's so kind of you," I replied with counterfeit enthusiasm. "But I'm headed to the mines tomorrow. I'll be there all day, and I probably won't be back until late."

"No. You misunderstand," she said with an expectant smile. "We're going too. Eric advised me to come along to take some rock readings at the mines. We're having dinner at the station after you've done your investigation."

Everything she said after that was fuzzy. All I could think was: *Are you fucking kidding me?*

I didn't say anything.

She filled the uncomfortable space. "You know that's what I do here, right?"

I was still orbiting planet Are-You-Fucking-Kidding-Me, but I forced myself back. "What?"

"I'm a geologist. That's my M.O.S. in the Marine Corps."

Great—I almost forgot. Sherri the Geologist is going. Hale-fucking-leuiah. All I could manage was, "Oh, well, I've never met a Marine Corps geologist."

She jumped on that, giving me a dissertation about all the inner workings of geology and the study of rocks, a subject I could really give a shit about. I drifted off into a trance. I imagined snapping her neck in a round of Gladiator 4D as she rambled on: "Most of my work entails hydrocarbon exploration, mineral excavations, some limited study of organisms and inorganic specimens. Also, there's the engineering piece. I mean, how can you excavate or drill if you don't understand soil mechanics or hydrology or natural gases, even? Then there is the natural habitat you're working with and the" on and on she went, "and minerals are so complex." I wondered if she could see me swaying back and forth. The room was starting to spin.

I thought about the silliness of it all. Then it clicked. I'd found Sherri's secret. She was a catch, for guys like Eric, because she'd mastered the trifecta. The unrealistic combination of three traits to have insecure, young men licking your feet: beauty, approachability and controllability. She was a nerd. Remnants of a gangly, bespectacled girl pushed its way to the surface as she rambled on about rock formations and elemental chemistry. She was smart, too, but Eric didn't want her for her mind. I knew that because Eric, while smart, wasn't what I would call "an intellectual." Sherri was a beautiful, exotic armpiece who was far too impressionable and compliant. Nothing more.

I wondered how long it'd take before he grew bored with her, or better yet, before he became threatened by her. She was young, riddled with the same personal insecurities that most women our age battled. To my dating detriment, I'd caught on fast and rid myself of any codependency or approval-seeking behaviors. Perhaps she'd make the same discovery. Oddly, this gave me a measure of gratification.

I decided to cut her off. She'd have me there all day. I scrambled frantically for a believable response. "Uh, Sherri. I have some errands to run after the investigation. So, I don't think I can go—"

"Oh c'mon!" she pressed. "You've gotta eat, right? Besides, I was telling Eric the other day how we need to take a trip to Amsterdam.

He said you've vacationed there. He told me we should invite you to dinner with us."

"Yeah, Mel. It'll be fun to catch up." Eric popped up unexpectedly from behind us. I'd forgotten that the men's restroom was still behind us. He rested his elbow casually on my shoulder, as if we had been lifelong buddies.

Dick. I couldn't believe he would suggest such a thing. I guess he really could be cruel.

"Yeah. We should catch up," I said. Sarcasm dripped from my voice, "because it's been so long."

Eric ignored my smart remark. I'd never seen him so sure of himself. "We're all going to the mines together. We'll be done together. We'll have dinner together."

"That's not gonna work," said an unexpected voice from behind.

LaSalle. Again. Out of nowhere. This time to the rescue. *Thank God.*

He walked up and slipped his arm cool-like around my shoulder, effectively brushing Eric's elbow aside. "She's having dinner with me tomorrow night, guys."

Sherri raised her eyebrows. She was grinning, but I caught a spark of envy flare across her face briefly. Eric's face was priceless. A chameleon of emotions: Shock. Panic. Irritation. Jealousy.

Vindication after all. I wished I could've soaked in the moment, but LaSalle didn't give any of us an opportunity to react. After a brief nod, he shuttled me away, arm still around my shoulders. I wanted so badly to look back, to see their faces, but I resisted. LaSalle steered us toward the area of the bar where Yuri and Lauralie were engrossed in what looked like an intimate conversation.

16

We headed back to the bar where Yuri and Lauralie sat. It was weird to walk so close to someone I barely knew. His arm had dropped from around my shoulders to around my waist. We moved as if we were lovers. He was considerably taller than me, so I could feel wisps of air from his breath tickle my scalp. My face warmed. I was glad he was tall. He wouldn't be able to see my sudden onset of bashfulness.

As we neared the bar, he pointed at Yuri and Lauralie who were talking closely. "So, what's up with those two?"

"I'm not sure, but I think she really likes him. I mean, I don't think she considers him a customer."

"It's hard to know," he said quietly.

"What do you mean?" I asked, looking up at him for the first time.

He looked down at me. "It's hard to know how much a woman genuinely likes you based on only a few looks. We all wear masks. Me personally, I wouldn't let her off the hook until I knew for sure."

I could feel my nerves fray. I got an inkling that there was a double reference there. I shifted slightly, putting some space between his body and mine. In response, he let go completely. He stopped and faced me directly.

My heart sped up.

"That guy, Eric . . . Captain Hunt," he said, gesturing with a thumb back to Eric, who still watched us stonily from the opposite corner of the bar. "He's a coward. He rejected you because he knows you're smarter than him, and that terrifies him."

"Well, I guess I should dumb it down in the future," I said.

LaSalle shrugged. "No. He's not the right guy for you." His gaze didn't waver. His eyes bore into mine. "The right guy would appreciate you."

I wanted to ask, *And who would be the right guy?* But I couldn't. I noticed the intensity that seemed to always be captured on LaSalle's face. He was a serious guy who could be charming when it suited him. This constantly kept me on edge. I wasn't afraid of him, but he was the type of guy who forced you to see things as they are.

LaSalle was right, though. Eric was a coward. His game playing wasn't clever at all. Why hadn't I noticed before?

LaSalle watched me, waiting for a response. A sense of unease slid through me. I could detect a faint smirk. Arrogant and somewhat predatory. His eyes searched mine, almost like he could read my thoughts. Panicked, I spoke. "LaSalle, thanks for—"

"Gerard," he said, taking a step closer. Real close. Close enough to lean in and kiss me, but instead he clasped my hand and shook it. "Use my first name."

The maneuver wasn't quite as formal as a first-time greeting. Instead it felt intimate.

"Okay, Gerard," I smiled politely and returned the handshake. I pulled my hand to let go, but his held mine firmly. His hand was warm.

He winked and then led me the rest of the way to where Yuri and Lauralie sat, my hand still in his. As we approached, Yuri looked down at our hands. I gave him a look. *Don't start with me, and I won't start with you.*

Lauralie, however, wasn't as discreet. "Are you guys a couple now?" she asked giggling.

"Well—"

LaSalle cut me off. "No," he said a little too quickly. He let go of my hand and glanced past me.

I turned to find Rivera standing beside me. He was still in uniform, in obvious work mode. "What're you guys talking about?"

"Nothing." LaSalle said. He turned to Lauralie. "We're not a couple. I was helping a friend out. That's all."

Ouch. I hadn't even considered LaSalle as a potential love interest, but for some reason his hasty response came like a bucket of ice in my face. *Two rejections in one month. Must be a record.*

Rivera looked confused. Yuri and Lauralie looked embarrassed. For me.

"Yeah," I said. I turned away from him. "He was only helping me out."

"Helping you out with what?" asked Rivera.

"Nothing," I didn't bother to mask the irritation in my tone. "I'm really tired. I'm heading to my rack. I leave in the morning for the station. I need sleep."

"I need to speak you," Rivera announced.

"Mind if I speak to her first?" LaSalle said as he gave me a contrite look. He moved to grab my arm, but I shook him off.

"I'm tired, and I need to speak to my department head. Goodnight everyone." I left them and followed Rivera to the other side of the bar.

~~~

Rivera looked unhappy with my compromised state. With Senior Chief's recent death and me having to go to the mines, he'd been giving me a lot of slack the past week.

"I've been looking all over for you," he said.

"Yeah, well you should've come here first." I leaned over the bar console and put my wrist over the red beam until it beeped. I put one finger up. The midshipman was still there, leaning against a bulkhead, looking miserable. He pushed away from the bulkhead to prepare my order.

"Here," he said, shoving a thumbnail-sized, square silver case into the palm of my hand. I could see the outline of a tiny round disk inside. Nano-drives were so tiny, you had to pick them up with tweezer magnets. "There's information on it about the mining station you need to review. Do it tonight."

"You could've transferred the file to me from your smart-wrist to mine," I said.

"Actually, that's not safe. The information needed to be burned to an external source that couldn't be tracked. You can't tell anyone."

"Why not?"

"Because Heather put some extra stuff on there. Classified stuff even you don't have access to. If anyone found out that she gave it to you, well . . ."

"How does she get this stuff without getting caught?" I whispered, more to myself than to Rivera. I held up the disc in the air like it was a winning lottery ticket and examined it with obvious fascination.

"Put that thing away. What're you, crazy?" He slapped my hand down. The tone in his voice made me nervous, so I discreetly slipped the tiny disc into my pocket. His tone softened. "She's always been smarter than she lets on. That's her talent, getting people to underestimate her. She's clever as hell."

"I know. That's why we all love her and tolerate her bullshit."

"I suppose." There was pride in his voice.

The midshipman slid me a mojito. I started to sip on it.

"Mel, you have a long trip tomorrow. You shouldn't be drinking."

"I shouldn't be going to a mining station to investigate the death of an asshole who died onboard, but it is what it is."

"Well, you need to be ready. Look at the station files tonight."

"I'm tired. I'll look at them in the morning."

"They're important. They may even be lifesaving."

Lifesaving? "What the hell?"

"Everyone is all excited about going to the station, but they probably don't know what they're getting into."

"You already told me. It's going to be a sucky camping excursion basically."

"There's more to it than that. Historically, mining stations have had bad raps."

"You're really scaring me now."

"Good."

Rivera's worrying worried me. But like always when he did this, I forced myself to apply reason and logic. "I'm sure it'll be safe. LaSalle is bringing an army with him."

"Don't you think that's odd?"

I did think it was odd, but I didn't want to hear it. "I've heard that LaSalle always travels with an entourage of guards. They're all boys with guns who love what they do a little too much. They're probably all gung-ho to play toy soldier. This is only routine, I'm sure."

"Sometimes I think you like to have your head in the sand, Mel."

"Maybe, but you're my department head. You should've found a way to convince the commodore for me to not go."

"Wouldn't make a bit of difference," he said. "The commodore never changes his mind. Circuitous methods are the only way to change his mind, and we just don't have time for that." He frowned but pulled a silver cylindrical object from his coveralls breast pocket. It looked like a tube of lipstick. "Here."

"Another gift? You're going to make Heather jealous." I grinned devilishly and poked him in the ribs.

"Cute," he said, shoving my hand away, "but you'll thank me tomorrow morning."

"Only if you promise to make me breakfast in bed," I said as he turned to leave. Rivera was so easily embarrassed. And like Yuri, he hated when I circumvented military etiquette. He shook his head and walked out.

I decided for once that I'd listen to Rivera and call it quits, but I was determined to get food. Suddenly, I was starving. The midshipman-bartender was leaning with one elbow on the bar, openly staring. He was annoyed.

"What's your problem?"

"Nothing ma'am. I love my life," he said with the enthusiasm of someone scrubbing a toilet.

"Just wrap up this mojito and give me a chicken burrito, to go."

"Ma'am, it's against policy to let alcohol out of the bar, and the kitchen is closed." It wasn't unusual for a midshipman to get smart with an ensign.

"What's your name, Midshipman?"

"Whitaker, ma'am," he said. He appeared detached, but there was still some hesitancy in his voice. "Midshipman First Class Chase Whitaker."

I glanced in both directions to make sure no one was watching. LaSalle was, but I didn't care. I grabbed Whitaker's collar and snatched him across the bar. "Listen, turd," I spoke in low tones. "There's two things that I want right now: my mojito to go and food. I don't care if you have to go in the goddam kitchen and make it yourself. And don't even *think* of doing anything to my food. I have OFE software on my wrist device—one of the perks of being legal officer."

"What's that?" he snorted, openly bored.

"Optical Forensics Examination software. If I find any saliva, evidence of any other bodily fluids or more than the usual levels of bacteria on my food, you'll be in a whirlwind of shit." I let go of his collar and shoved him back behind the bar. In a much softer tone, I added, "I'll get you a seat on tomorrow's launch. In fact, every time I head to the mining station, I'll get you out of your bartending and kitchen duties. Deal?"

I knew I'd get whatever I wanted at that point. Having manhandled the shit out of him didn't matter. A trip to the mining station, for a midshipman, was like a trip to Vegas. I could already see his eyes sparkling. He was wringing his hands together. "I can't let you leave with the mojito. Seriously. The chiefs have been on my ass about letting alcohol leave the bar, but I'll deliver a sprite and a burrito to your stateroom, personally, ma'am, when I get my next break which is in about ten minutes."

It would do. I nodded.

"Cool. Let Commander Jefferson know that you'll be going as a guest of my division but that your function will be to assist him as he sees fit," I said, motioning to Yuri, who was at the other end of the bar sending me sidelong glances of disapproval in between moments of overt physical flirtations with Lauralie. The commodore wouldn't give up any of his yeomen. He wanted a team of specialists available at all times. Providing Yuri with his own personal assistant for the trip would be a good way to win some brownie points with him. "If you face any problems with the mess chiefs, tell them that you will be on loan to the XO."

"Yes, ma'am," said Whitaker, grinning. "Thank you. I'll get you your food soon."

I stole a quick glance back to the end of the bar. LaSalle was watching us. He scowled.

I nodded to Whitaker and walked out of the bar without looking back, but I could feel LaSalle's eyes on me.

12

thought about everything Rivera said. About needing to review the files—the potentially lifesaving files—and that things weren't as safe as they seemed. Thoughts of the mining station made me worry about the trip itself. Most people took for granted the fact that space travel is dangerous. Traveling at speeds greater than the speed of light guaranteed the possibility of accidents on a catastrophic level. No one walked away from a space collision alive. And if you didn't collide with something, the loss of a major component could bring on all sorts of problems. Loss of oxygen, you could drift in space, die of starvation or freezing temperatures once all of your heating sources ceased to operate.

I thought of the *Odysseus. The Midway's* other transport launch. I'd heard her story only a day after having been onboard. Barely winged by a stray asteroid, the *Odysseus* tumbled into an uncontrollable spin. Her main positioning system destroyed by the impact, she, along with her crew, went missing. Communication was lost instantly, and the crew was never heard from again. Even after almost a year, still, no one knows if her thirteen-person crew survived.

I caught myself. I wasn't going to let Rivera's worry-windfall possess me too. He could get a room full of corpses revved up with all of the worrying he did.

I'd review the station files later. The trip to the station was eight hours. I'd review the files then.

Besides, it wasn't like I could get out of it if I didn't like what I saw. No sense in being worried all night long.

Besides, there were other things I was interested in. I was curious about LaSalle. He was dangerous. I could tell. That made me interested in him. After he defended me at the bar, my interest was peaked. Granted, I was still mad at him, but he had me fixated. The heady feeling of being around him was like a pure adrenaline rush. Scary to tap into the sensation, but addictive nonetheless. That, combined with the tipsy sensation of alcohol in my system, and I wondered what it would be like to have sex with him. The thought of his hands all over me made me burn with anticipation. I knew I could find out if I really wanted to, but it would require some discretion.

I sat up on the edge of my rack and started digging. I accessed the virtual library and found his personal record. His photo and icons of other associated files floated around me in holographic glory. To access his record, one had to send an "access request." Luckily, I had access with my clearances. I could navigate his record as much as I wanted to without him knowing. But to connect to his profile link on the Physiological Capabilities Program would be much riskier. The PCP had strict protocols that required any curious visitors to ask the owner of the profile for access. While access gave one the physical capabilities of a profilee, just asking would be an obvious indication of my sexual interest. I couldn't use the old *"I just wanted see what it would be like to arm wrestle you"* excuse. It was two o'clock in the morning.

I set aside the thought as absurd and began to get ready for bed. As I brushed my teeth, a thought came to me. The idea was crazy. I was alone, bored, and despite being somewhat drunk, I was wide awake. I really wanted to know what it'd be like with LaSalle.

I touched the display screen to my private safe and pulled out a round black canister, a sensory transmitter connected to a set of electrodes. I unsnapped my coveralls and slipped them off completely. I took off my shirt. I sat down at the edge of my bed in just my bra and panties. Then I carefully placed the electrodes all over my body—against my temples, the area beneath my jawline along my neck, just above my collarbone, my chest, my lower abdomen and my inner thighs. I decided that I would try to access LaSalle's profile on the PCP anonymously, through a generic request portal. It was a risky move. He'd know someone had accessed his record, but only if he checked. And why would he even check? It wasn't uncommon for people to go months, years even, without checking (I don't remember the last time I checked mine). By the time he figured out someone had accessed it, he'd have forgotten all about me. But, on the other hand, he'd see that someone with my clearance level had accessed his record. My name wouldn't be attached, but how many female officers onboard had my level of access? None. He'd most likely know it was me, but he wouldn't be 100 percent sure. But would he even check? He was probably already asleep.

Fuck it. So what if he finds out. He should be flattered.

I gave Shakespeare a couple of commands and logged in anonymously to pull up his record again. Once it was up, I asked Shakespeare to link me—anonymously—to his PCP profile.

"I'm afraid I can't do *that* anonymously, Ensign Brown."

"Why not?"

"Mr. LaSalle has set up parameters enabling him to identify whomever accesses his PCP profile. You should also know that even if I were able to access his profile anonymously, he would still be alerted that the request was made."

"Damn." I ran my fingers through my hair. An alert at this time of night? *Hell no.* I wouldn't take that chance. But then another idea came. "Locate Lieutenant Junior Grade Heather Jordan."

After several moments of hearing Shakespeare think, there were a few quiet beeps. "Located. Would you like me to alert her?"

"Yes. Call her." Heather was a night owl, so I wasn't worried about waking her.

After a couple of beeps, a-more-than-normal disheveled Heather's face appeared on the CMS display. I was thankful she had her mobile portal with her. "What?" she asked. I could tell she was irritated that I'd interrupted what was probably a make-out session with Rivera. There was lipstick smeared all over her face. I couldn't see that it was Rivera with her, but I was certain it was him. A finger kept appearing on the screen, poking her in the ribs, making her laugh unwillingly. I recognized the voice trying to stifle giggles in the background.

I took an impatient breath. "Could you please go to privacy mode?"

A finger tickled her ear lobe. She slapped it away, turning back to him, "Stop it. I'm trying to talk to my roommate." She turned back to me. "Hold on a sec." Her gaze redirected to the top corner of the screen, and she touched a couple of buttons. I saw a message blink across the top part of the screen: *Sound Curtain—On.* Then she redirected her gaze back to me. "Okay. What? You're on the clock."

"Is it on?"

"Yes. Watch." She shifted slightly to yell over her shoulder as she watched the screen. "Hey, babe?"

He said nothing. I could hear Rivera pouring himself a glass of water, but he didn't talk. I relaxed a bit.

"Okay. I need a quick favor," I said. I looked down. I knew the minute I asked what I was about to, Heather would make a big deal about it. Even in privacy mode, I leaned into the display anyway and whispered, "and you have to promise not to tell Rivera or anyone else for that manner."

"Okay. I won't."

"I mean it."

"I swear. Jeez. Cross my heart and hope to die."

I took a deep breath. "Can you give me access to someone's PCP profile without them knowing it's me or without them even being alerted?"

I could feel myself boring holes into the screen as I stared at her. She waited a couple beats before responding. I was worried she'd say "no," but this was Heather. She was one of the most uninhibited people I knew. After considering me for a moment, she made a couple of *tsk* sounds. A devious grin stretched across her face. "Oooh. You dirty little whore. Nothing like a virtual interactive booty call on a Friday night. And who's going to be your lucky little unknowing sex slave tonight?"

"Jesus, Heather. For once, can you just do me a favor without being annoying about it?" I looked away from the screen. I could feel my face heat up. "And it's not like that."

"Oh c'mon. Don't bullshit me. I don't know what you're so ashamed of anyway. Everyone does it. Besides, can't you just let me enjoy this moment? Miss holier-than-thou-Amelia Brown never tells me anything juicy."

"I'm telling you now. And I don't act holier than thou—"

"Oh, yes you do. Just because you're clearly drunk doesn't mean you can just forget how you really are when you're sober."

"Whatever," I said, exasperated. "Can you do it or not?"

"Wow. You're really testy about it. And you've been awfully short lately. A good lay will do you good. Now are you gonna tell me his name or not?"

"I'm about to tell you. But before I do, I need to know if you can actually do it."

"Well, I can do anything. But no one can do this one 100 percent. This will be one of my best hacks if I can pull it off. I don't care how good you are . . . this one is a dice roll. You've got a fifty-fifty chance of him finding out."

"Fifty-fifty? Those aren't very good odds."

"They're great odds. I doubt anyone else could get you even that. An average hack might guarantee you one in five odds if you're lucky. I'm getting you much more. Now, who is the lucky gent?"

"Gerard LaSalle."

"LaSalle! He's a hottie." She smirked as she entered in a few commands. "Although he does seem like he has a lot of secrets."

Rivera's hand grabbed at her elbow from the corner of the screen. He was trying to get her to end our conversation.

"Just a minute, baby," she said, looking behind her. She sucked on her finger for effect. Rivera couldn't hear her, but the movement was exaggerated. Cat-like. It sent a clear message. I heard Rivera clear his throat.

Oh, Jeez. I might throw up.

I rubbed my temples, realizing what I was about to do. "I'm not sure this is ethical."

"Oh relax. You don't think he'd do the same if he could get away with it?"

I thought about that for a moment. I didn't know LaSalle very well, but I got the impression that he was a man who lived beyond rules. Constantly testing boundaries. Breaking institutional structures. And I believed that he wouldn't stew too long on the moral implications of accessing someone's PCP profile. If he wanted something, he took it . . . without regret.

"I suppose." I chewed on my finger a bit. I was drunk making unwise decisions I knew I'd regret later. "I change my mind. Let's forget this."

"Sorry, sweetie, You can't back out now. It's already done."

"Did it work?"

"Of course, it worked. You have access."

"I mean without him knowing."

"That I can't tell you, babe. There is no way of knowing. If he acts weird around you tomorrow, you'll have your answer. Now I need to get my freak on. Nite, hon."

She ended the transmission.

For fuck's sake, Heather. I knew there was a chance she'd tell Rivera about what she did, but I wasn't really worried. He wouldn't say anything to LaSalle. It was clear—they weren't friends.

18

Several minutes passed before I had access to LaSalle's PCP profile. She assured me that he wouldn't be able to trace *who* accessed his profile. And she sequestered the alert. There was just a 50 percent chance that he would know someone accessed his profile, *if* he checked.

Heather was a great hacker. I trusted her. Yet it did nothing to lessen my uneasiness. My curiosity about LaSalle was so great, though, that I knew I would go all the way through with it. But I wondered if I should do it. I wavered. I almost felt like I was about to take something that wasn't mine to take. *Most guys would be flattered, wouldn't they? Or would they consider this an invasion of privacy—a form of virtual rape?* I realized that there wasn't just one answer. That every guy was different. Some would be pissed. Some would be overjoyed. I wondered what LaSalle's reaction would be if he found out. *Would he?* Finally, my curiosity took over. I opened LaSalle's profile and waited. I managed to convince myself that he wouldn't find out, but deep down something niggled at me. I pushed aside the thought that his discovery of my intrusion was a very real possibility.

The moments ticked by in slow motion, like a robot moving underwater. Just when I was about to cancel the request, an army of sensations flooded my body. I was breathless. I closed my eyes and relaxed, allowing the onslaught of sensations to radiate throughout my body. Then images floated in and out of my mind. His hand was on my neck. Then his mouth was there. His mouth was everywhere, licking, biting and sucking. His hands, smooth and velvety, explored the areas where his mouth wasn't. His movements were slow but deliberate. Taunting, tingling, and warm all at once, he sent goosebumps all over my body. Then I became overwhelmed by the collage of emotions I felt. First shock. Then excitement turned to eagerness. A delightful burn spread throughout my groin. I would have asked him to do whatever he wanted at that point, but I'd been consigned to passive participant in this virtual fantasy. I could only feel. Not do. Wait patiently while I was trapped in sensory voyeurism. Once it was finished, I wanted to savor the experience for a few moments, but a voice interrupted my thoughts.

"I take it you're satisfied with the session, Miss Brown?"

"What the—I—" My breath caught in my throat. "Damnit, Shakespeare. Don't you know what privacy is?"

"My apologies, ma'am. But you did ask for my assistance in accessing Mr. LaSalle's file. If you wanted privacy, perhaps you should have temporarily shut down my server."

I raised both of my middle fingers to the speakers above in silent rebuke.

"May I ask you a question?" he asked, ignoring my insult. Shakespeare might have been A.I., but he could see the movements of everyone he monitored.

"You've got some nerve." Incredulous, I shook my head.

"It's quite innocent. I assure you."

"Innocent? You just barged in on me—"

"I have just one question for you."

"Sure. Whatever," I said, throwing my hands up in the air. "What?"

"What is it like?"

"What's what like?"

"Intercourse."

My face felt hot. I couldn't believe he was asking me this. I considered shutting him down, but there was no point. He'd just ask me again after I powered him back up. He was getting more and more curious these days (I'd have to ask Heather about that). I couldn't believe I was about to give the "birds and the bees talk" to an A.I. computer. "Why do you want to know? I mean, you should know this stuff."

"I'm well versed in all manner of practices that constitute human sexual interaction. And I am aware of the mechanisms that engender the various modes of sensory processing during sexual intercourse. But as you are the one human I've conversed with the most—independent of Lieutenant Jordan, of course—I am curious to know your perceptions of sex. I want *you* to tell me what it *feels* like."

"Oh good gawd."

"Please. Humor me."

"Well, it's . . . kind of—" I sucked in my breath as I thought of what LaSalle did to me in this virtual fantasy, but then I thought about how good it felt too. I exhaled. "Kind of dirty . . . but . . . divine."

"I don't understand."

"You're not supposed to."

"That seems a contradiction."

"Dirty in a good way."

"I don't understand."

"Sometimes getting dirty feels good. I don't know . . . it's hard to explain. What do you care anyway? You're a computer."

There was silence from Shakespeare for once. Not the silence of thinking but of disappointment. I waited and said nothing. I didn't know what else to say, and I was curious about what he'd say next.

"Perhaps I should implement a temporary shutdown while you finish?"

Hmm. Is he agitated? Is that even possible?

"Yeah. That'd be nice," I said. "All the way off. Not sleep mode."

I laid down on my side and stretched across my rack. I planned to take a shower before bed, but so many thoughts entered my head. I'd been caught by a computer. I was ashamed, but it was worth it. If the simulation was accurate, LaSalle would be an amazing lover, and I'd only had a sampling. Of course, the sensations I felt were all formulations of sensory data based on predictions and hypothesis. The PCP used LaSalle's medical examination records and psychological profile to implement the simulation. It was all theoretical, but it felt accurate. I believed it. I wanted to believe it. I could always tell if a guy would be good in bed by the way he moved. The virtual escapade only proved that I'd been right about LaSalle.

Sleep pulled at me, but just before my eyes closed, I had a fleeting moment of panic. *What if LaSalle finds out about me accessing his PCP file?* A fifty-fifty chance. What had I been thinking, accepting those odds? A spark of anxiety niggled at me. Something told me he'd find out. Then what would I do? Would he think I was an awful person? Maybe a slut even? My heart fluttered. I rolled over onto my back and stared up at the ceiling, fervently wishing I'd just gone to bed after my drunken night at the Scuttlebutt. I stared and stared at the ceiling, worrying, until finally I sank into a deep sleep.

19

The searing beep of the alarm clock pierced my skull as I raised up from my bed in a fit of panic. *What time is it? Did I miss the launch?* I concentrated on the wall console facing my bed, trying to make sense of the blue numbers glowing like a beacon in my room. It was 6:30 in the morning. Early enough for me to want more sleep, but late enough that I couldn't risk falling back into a deep slumber.

"Snooze!" I barked. I winced after hearing my own voice. Every sound was mallet thump to the head. I hugged myself while my eyes adjusted to the dark. I kept the room as cold and dark as possible while I slept. Heather, who hated my thermostat dictatorship, probably wasn't even there. I wondered if she was in Rivera's room.

I called out a couple of times, but instead Shakespeare answered.

"Ms. Jordan has yet to return, Miss Brown."

"I thought I had put you in sleep mode."

"Well if you recall, ma'am, you released me after the good midshipman arrived last night to deliver your food."

Oh yeah! Still groggy, I sat up to full position, shaking my head. I recalled the events of the previous night and began to have regrets: First running into Sherri and Eric, holding hands with

LaSalle, ordering shots with Lauralie, giving Yuri a hard time, convincing Heather to hack LaSalle's PCP, and finally my virtual sex-capade with him. I must've dozed off soon after because I did, in fact, remember waking up to Whitaker's food delivery to my stateroom. He'd delivered my burrito and Sprite (which actually turned out to be a Mojito he'd smuggled into a to-go canister for me) as promised. I'd opened the hatch to my room, snatched the bag of food and canister and told him I'd see him first thing in the morning at the Embarkation Chamber. I devoured the food and took a hot shower before slipping into a deep sleep soon after.

I swung my legs off my rack. I saw the empty bag of food and empty cannister.

"Shakespeare, retrieve and dispense with biodegradable waste. Return canister to the Scuttlebutt."

"As you wish, ma'am. Would you like me to go ahead and take your breakfast order now?"

"Not just yet."

My head pounded like a jackhammer perforating my skull. I was profoundly grateful I had accepted the sobriety pen that Rivera had given me last night. I scooped it up and placed the tip of it against my neck near my carotid artery and pushed down. I felt a brief pinch before the sensation of a cool, velvety substance entering my bloodstream, and the fiery pounding of my headache ebbed away in cool waves. Instant relief.

Rivera was right. I was thankful. Sobriety pens weren't cheap. I owed him. Unfortunately, he'd collect in some way that would be highly inconvenient for me. A crappy night watch or some cumbersome equipment casualty report.

"Shakespeare. Full operation mode. Lights. Level two." The wall console changed from sleep mode and lit up to a dim blue glow, illuminating the entire room.

"Time till expected departure for mining station?"

"Time available until expected departure is: 3.5 hours and 53 seconds," said Shakespeare. "Estimated time of arrival of Launch *Pegasus* at Mining Station Number: 05—"

"Don't need that. Thanks. Raise dim lighting to 75 percent," I said. "Adjust room temperature to 75 degrees Fahrenheit. Place breakfast pre-order: three-egg-white omelet with spinach, roasted peppers, mozzarella. Two turkey sausage links. One cup of coffee with three tablespoons of cream and one packet of sweetener. Five strawberries. Expected sit-down time: 0700."

"Lighting adjusted to 75 percent. Increasing room climate by increments of two Fahrenheit degrees," Shakespeare crooned. "Room temperature of 75 degrees expected in precisely 18.5 minutes. Breakfast order has been placed and processed."

"Begin shower. One hundred and five degrees Fahrenheit. Activate main channel: SportsUniverse. Activate peripheral channels and switch to caption only. "Peripherals as follows: UNTV, YTTV and PBN. Route all channels and captions to bathroom display."

"As you wish, Miss Brown," said Shakespeare. "Peripherals set: United Nations Television, YouTubeTV, and the Paparazzi Broadcasting Network."

"Eject vanity. Include all essential toiletry items; add tweezers, nail clippers, one 400-milligram canister of Advil Inject Plus."

I continued to rattle off my instructions to Shakespeare, and various apparatuses started to turn on. Steam seeped from the shower head as the water temperature increased. The stations I'd requested filled the screen, though I wasn't really concentrating on the TV. I just liked the background noise of the TV in the morning, and I listened to the news to make sure the world wasn't coming to an end due to some cyberattack or antimatter bomb or, even worse, some misplaced biological weapon. Though, anything would be better than facing LaSalle after last night. The incident in the bar. Accessing his profile. Ugh. I could feel my cheeks burning. Shit.

What had I done? How would I face him this morning? Shit, Shit, Shit. Overcome with shame, I rubbed my temples.

I shed my clothes and dropped them into the stainless steel canister. The canister closed automatically. "Dry clean," I told Shakespeare.

"Dry cleaning sequence has begun. Garments available for use in approximately three minutes," Shakespeare replied politely.

As I stepped into the shower, Shakespeare interrupted me with an announcement.

"Ms. Brown, you have a visitor at your door."

"Visitor identity please," I said impatiently.

"Visitor's name: Dr. Gerard LaSalle."

OMG. Does he know? My heart was hammering like a war drum. All I wanted was to escape to the hot shower waiting for me. I wasn't sure how to handle this. I wasn't ready to deal with him. *Should I try to find out if he knew about me accessing his profile or just leave it alone all together? Maybe he doesn't know anything about it. Maybe I should just act like nothing happened.* I paused for a couple of moments, trying to figure out how to handle his presence.

"Would you like me to suggest Dr. LaSalle leave a message?"

I love you, Shakespeare. Yes! My brain was on slow-mo operation. What a simple solution I hadn't even thought of. "Yes, please. That would be swell."

I could hear the beeping of Shakespeare transmitting a message to the Video Intercom and Communication Console (VICC) for LaSalle.

I decided to wait a moment before stepping into the shower. Shakespeare froze all of my television stations and allowed feed from LaSalle's typed message to pop onto my monitor. I watched the screen as LaSalle stood with his hands on his hips, trying to figure what he'd do next. He leaned into the VICC speaker and said something. Then he stopped and typed something on the keypad. Apparently, he didn't want to speak into the monitor. Discreet. I appreciated that. The passageway tended to echo. He was adorned in a snug black flight suit with boots, standard attire for trips to the mining station. I watched as he stood there waiting for me, tapping his black boot rapidly while he raked his fingers through his dirty-blond hair. He looked dangerous. And sexy, of course. He looked serious. I couldn't tell if he was mad or just his usual intense self.

The message popped up onto my screen:

"Mel, please open up. I want to talk to you in private. I want to explain what I said at the bar last night. I think you misunderstood."

So he doesn't know I accessed his profile. Phew. I was relieved, but I was still annoyed with him. "Shakespeare, delete message. Tell Mr. LaSalle that I understood perfectly and will speak with him at a later time. Resume existing television channels. Turn VICC off and reroute future messages directly to surplus mail."

Shakespeare transmitted my message for LaSalle to read. I saw him curse silently to himself and rake his hand through his hair before leaving.

I stepped into the shower as SportsUniverse resumed its feature story: *In today's news, professional hockey player, Chance Phillips, has been arrested for the alleged rape of a nineteen-year-old girl while training at the Interplanetary Space Training Facility USA. The girl, whose name the ISTF Sherriff's office has yet to release, is one of fifteen girls selected to train for the Interplanetary Olympic Figure Skating Trials. Officials believe that Mr. Phillips met the girl at a gala event where several Olympic athletes were being hosted by affluent members of the local settlement—*

20

After I was done with my morning routine, I headed for the wardroom. I decided to transmit some last-minute instructions to my division via my smart-wrist on the way. There were certain things that had to be done for the day, regardless of if I was present at the division spaces or not.

I shifted my black duffel bag higher up onto my shoulder and across my back again. It was getting heavy, but there wasn't really much I could take out of the bag. It contained all of my investigative forensics gear, a change of underwear, some toiletry items and snacks. The only upside is that we all wore the form-fitting blue jumpsuits, which meant that I didn't have to pack a change of clothes.

Once I opened the hatch to the wardroom, I was still surprised at the sheer size of the space, even though I'd been onboard already for almost a year. With a complement of almost four hundred officers, the size of the *Midway's* main wardroom shouldn't have surprised me. But then I remembered that it paled in comparison to the enormity of the mess decks where the enlisted personnel dined.

The main room resembled something closer to a fancy food court, with two private dining areas sectioned off for special events and celebrations. There were also two smaller, private spaces, mini-wardrooms so to speak. One was for the commanding officer's personal use, and the other was for the "Airboss," the commander in charge of all the *Midway's* flight operations. Both used their private wardrooms to dine with more distinguished guests, like visiting members of the admiral's staff, politicians, senior foreign officers and dignitaries and any other important officials. Adorned in the minimalistic tones of beige, grays, creams and whites, the wardroom reminded me of an upscale, retro lounge or the private business class VIP area at a flight station. Soft, jazzy electronic beats emanated from the wardroom's system speakers, giving the space a stylish yet relaxed feel. Tables and booths were dispersed throughout to accommodate just more than half of the four hundred officers at any one time. Along the edges of the wardroom were also workstations with consoles, making access to the cyber world while enjoying a burger possible. Every meal, the wardroom offered a buffet that always had two choices: hot versus cold, meat versus fruit or vegetable and ethnic versus standard American fare.

As a member of the commodore's immediate staff, I was expected to dine in Captain Radcliff's personal wardroom, which seated approximately thirty people. I preferred to dine in the main room sometimes, to get lost in the congestion. Yet even I had to admit that the quality of food prepared for thirty was much better than that prepared for four hundred. All sit-down, of course. No buffets. Just service for the serious brass.

I was relieved to see that I'd enjoy breakfast alone in the mini wardroom. I wasn't in the mood for senseless chatter in the morning, and I especially wanted to avoid Eric. I just wasn't in the mood to answer his inevitable questions about my relationship with LaSalle. And I didn't want to see LaSalle. Finally my food arrived, but I waved off the coffee the attending midshipman tried to serve me. I didn't want the acid on my stomach. I'd be space-sick within seconds.

As I finished up my omelet, Lieutenant Rivera headed in. He looked a mess. His hair stood up into a disheveled mess. Rivera was an early riser, but he obviously hadn't showered. I imagined Heather was probably still lounging in his rack, half asleep, with a triumphant grin plastered to her face.

My face heated as he caught me examining him. He frowned. "Did you open up the nano-drive I gave you?" he asked.

"And good morning to you too, sir," I said, dryly. I liked to tease him when he was cranky. "Did someone keep you up all night?"

He ignored my taunt. "Did you go over the station files?"

"Not yet. I plan to though."

Rivera looked doubtful.

"Christ, what's the friggin rush anyway? I have like eight hours during the trip."

"I just want to make sure that you know what you're getting into."

"Would it matter? I have to go anyway."

"True. But you need to be prepared, Mel."

"I wasn't at first, but now I'm kind of excited. It'll be a nice change of scenery."

"Well it's not all rainbows and butterflies. These mining stations can be dangerous places."

"Oh please."

"They're unstable, Mel. They're not swept very well because we lack the manpower and the resources, and Biotech doesn't want to disturb the integrity of the animal or plant life there. I guarantee Biotech hasn't done shit to make sure it's safe." Rivera looked older all of sudden. Older than a lieutenant should. "Just ask LaSalle. A.F.I.B. will pressure Biotech to squeeze every profit it can from those mines, but they won't guarantee 'personnel safety,' especially not ours."

"A.F.I.B.?"

"A.F.I.B. is the company that owns Biotech. Fitting, too, because it's run on lies and deceptions," Rivera muttered.

"Well that may be, but I highly doubt that the commodore would let us go if it was unsafe," I said.

Rivera snorted. "He cares only a little more about us than Biotech. And don't get me started on the people they hire."

"Oh c'mon. Crappy people work everywhere."

"I'm not talking about people with shitty attitudes. I'm talking about the scum of society. Many are criminals, mostly rapists and sex offenders and a few murderers. Biotech would have you think it was all PhDs and nerdy scientists running the show. They're just a small part. They stay holed up in the labs, insulated away from the criminals."

"Those criminals work in shady establishments at the port, not the mines, where most of my time will be spent."

"Mel, who do you think does all of the blasting and back-breaking work at the mines?"

"The Marines." I was getting defensive.

"Not just Marines. The technicians too. Don't be fooled. The technicians aren't scientists. They're well-trained cheap labor."

"They can't *all* be rapists and sex offenders and murderers."

"Of course they are. Overcrowding in the terrestrial prisons is out of control. The government works with Biotech and the courts to commute sentences to penal labor at stations—wholesale—by the thousands. They sell it to the public as criminal rehabilitation, but it's really just cheap, expendable labor."

"Look, I've survived worse places back at home on Earth, and I've been to other stations before with my father."

"Just make sure you read the files, Mel. This isn't a typical station. Trust me. The chip has information that Biotech wouldn't want to get out," Rivera mumbled, trying to lower his voice.

That reminder made me nervous. A tickle of fear slithered around in my gut. "Noted."

I didn't like what Rivera had to say, and I didn't like that he felt the need to whisper it. In fact, I wished he would shut up.

Rivera's paranoia gripped me like a cold chill. I decided to change the subject.

"Thanks for the sobriety pen. It was a lifesaver this morning."

"I know it was," he said, shaking his head.

"So you want me to get you anything while I'm there?" I asked.

"Yeah, well, there are some things I need." He looked away, rubbing his hands up and down the sides of his legs.

"Do you plan on telling me sometime this decade?"

"Yeah. Can you—um—pick up some perfume or something? You know . . . something exotic you can only get from the station that would be a nice gift for a woman." He cleared his throat. "I . . . uh . . . have a female family member with a birthday coming up."

"I didn't know that you and Heather were related."

He glared at me. "Very funny. Just get me something good."

I chuckled as I turned to leave the wardroom.

"Before you go, promise me you won't go anywhere by yourself either."

I sighed. "Okay. I promise."

I left, not totally sure what he meant, but I was tired of his lecture. I just didn't want to hear any more.

21

The *Midway's* embarkation chamber was an air-sealed capsule which connected the *Midway* to the transport launch, the *Pegasus*. It was a large enough room that could accommodate upwards of a hundred people, allowing us to board without having to step out into space. I was one of the first people in the trip party to arrive, so I sat down and pulled out my Mobile Computer Board to review a digital map of the station. Once the report finished loading, LaSalle walked in. I should've expected or at least prepared myself to see him since he was in charge of security for the trip. I had nothing to say but a simple "Hey." I tried to appear nonchalant, but my heart was running a marathon, and thoughts of him, his PCP profile, the guilt, the pleasure—all of it—rattled around in my head. I looked down, burying myself in the MCB.

He walked up quietly and leaned over me, waiting patiently while I fiddled around with the digital board. My heart pounded. I wondered if he could hear its thumping standing so close to me. Finally, his hand crept over my shoulder. Quick as a cobra, he grabbed the device from my hands to get my full attention.

"Will you give that back, please?" I was trying to sound irritated, but I was actually more curious than angry.

"Not until we talk."

"Well, I've got nothing to say." I was trying to be stubborn, but, really, I had a lot to say. I just didn't know where to start.

LaSalle opened his mouth to reply the same moment Cox walked into the wardroom and beelined for us.

The two men faced each other, but no words were exchanged between them. I felt a palpable discomfort, but I wasn't sure why.

Cox spoke first. He glared at LaSalle for a moment before dragging his eyes away and turning to me. "Well, well. I guess you're moving on, huh? You get tired of 'em pretty quickly, don't you?"

His open implication shook me. "What do you want, Commander?"

"What do you think?"

"As usual, I have no idea, sir. I'll make it easy on you though. You can stop following me everywhere. I'm not interested."

I hoped that the inference would at least embarrass Cox enough to leave me alone for a while. I glared at him, waiting for him to find a way to reprimand me.

LaSalle chuckled and placed a hand on Cox's shoulder. "You need to work on your game, man."

Cox jerked his arm away. "Get your fucking hands off me, LaSalle."

The two stared at each other like two fighters in a cage. The five Biotech guards who'd just arrived, laughing amongst themselves over some inside joke, were now silent. They cast murderous glances in Cox's direction.

"Just take it easy." LaSalle's voice was calm, but I could see a glint of danger in his eyes.

Cox stared back, disregarding the Biotech guards who'd inched closer in silent support of their leader. LaSalle turned and shook his head at the three guards as if to indicate *I got this*. They slowly backed away. After a couple of beats, Cox turned back to me and ignored LaSalle. "I need to see the brief you gave the commodore."

"With all due respect, sir, why?" I tried to inject a little more deference to de-escalate the situation. More people had piled into the EC at this point. I didn't want to make a scene. "Captain Radcliff gave specific orders that I wasn't to discuss my brief with anyone other than those who'd been present."

"I heard about your little debrief, and as the admiral's liaison, your commanding officer made a major misstep. I should've been informed."

I wondered who'd told him about the brief. *Eric.* He had a history of opening his big mouth. I'd kill him the minute I saw him.

Cox caught the expression on my face. "Oh. Yes. You're wondering who ratted, aren't you? I can see you weren't expecting that one. Well, here's another one: I'm the senior person on this flight, and I'll be heading up this little expedition."

"Actually, *Lieutenant* Commander Cox," said an unexpected voice, "I'm the senior man on this one."

Yuri stepped in between us unexpectedly.

Cox looked shocked. "Well, I'm representing Admiral Willard's staff, and I—"

"Do you have video authorization from the admiral?" Yuri's arms were crossed, and his tone was polite.

"No, but I can get—"

"Too late. Our ETD is just under a half hour away. You won't have an authorization by then. Do you have any retinal access codes uploaded on the EC Console?"

"Commander, I just found out—"

"So I assume that's a 'no' to retinal access codes? Do you have Trip Commander level security clearance?"

"No," Cox said quietly. He lifted his arm and pointed to his smart-wrist. "I can, however, have the admiral's chief of staff on here in no time, and he will confirm."

"If you could have gotten the admiral's authorization, I believe you would've already had it by now, Cox."

I could tell by the defeated look on his face that Cox had given up. I *almost* felt sorry for him.

"As I said, I'm in charge." Yuri's tone was courteous, but I knew him. A polite, controlled demeanor meant that he was ready to unleash a whirlwind of shit on Cox should there be any back talk. And it was obvious Cox could sense that too.

22

The EC was full. All of the people who intended to travel to the mining station were gathered. I glanced back and forth between Cox and LaSalle as I waited for them to start roll call. It was apparent that a weird tension existed between the two. They exchanged occasional sidelong glances. Always watchful of each other. I began to suspect there was a history between them. I whispered my observations to Yuri, but he was too preoccupied with completing some last-minute logistics tasks on the EC console. He waved his hand dismissively and said that the stress of being out in space for long periods of time made people strange anyway, and of course he reminded me that Cox was a "complete d-bag," always looking to start something.

Finally, Yuri signaled to Midshipman Whitaker to start a roll call of the launch party. Like a box of Crayola digital markers, we all stood in our respective groups, donned in our skintight hiking jumpsuits. The Navy personnel wore dark blue, with the only indication of rank being reflective stitching found on the left breast pocket and on each arm. The human contractors and engineers wore a basic gray and yellow respectively. The Marines, however, wore a similar jumpsuit but in dark green that was pre-dipped in a camouflaging chemical. I would've preferred one of their jumpsuits, but the suit I envied the most were the ones the Biotech guards wore. They wore black, and their suits were extra special, the best anyone could hope for. Equipped with very expensive "cloaking" devices that were stitched into the breast pocket, their camouflage capabilities were above par, far surpassing that of the Marines'. At anytime, with a quick tap to the breast pocket, they could opt to disappear into their surrounding environment, completely. Marines could blend in their surrounding environment pretty well, but you could still see their faces. Biotech guards, on the other hand, could disappear completely, face and all.

Once roll call was finished, Whitaker began to read names off his MCB in groups of five. Five people made their way to cylindrically shaped, human-sized canisters called Physical Readiness Scanners. Each person stepped into their individual scanner, and the door automatically closed behind them, causing the scanner to light up. Two blue circular rings—one from the floor and one from the ceiling—moved to the center, encircling each person's midsection.

Yuri stepped up to a console mounted on a steel podium which ascended from the floor. He leaned over it so that he looked directly into a tiny lens. After a small beep sounded, a blue light illuminated his face, scanning his retina. He turned to Midshipman Whitaker and nodded.

Whitaker tilted his head upward toward the ceiling and spoke. "Computer, upload anatomical and physiological systems evaluation program."

Another spectacularly sexy British voice—female—rang throughout the room. "Uploading evaluation program for anatomical and physiological systems." For some reason, people got quiet during the systems upload. Like an ominous threat that hung in the air. A thorough assessment of the human body by a machine was somewhat scary. A machine couldn't be reasoned with. You either passed or failed. After a few beats, the computer voice spoke again. "Evaluation program uploaded."

Whitaker looked back up toward the ceiling again, as if he expected to see an angel hovering above. "Upload Gender non-specific filter. Conduct screen using following uploaded parameters: Lymphatic and immune system functions—100%, Nervous, cardiovascular and respiratory system functions—100%. Skeletal and muscular system functions—97%. All remaining systems—93%. Gestation—0%. Foreign bodies—0%. Non-endogenous substances—0%. Opiates and hallucinogens—0% Stimulants—0%. Depressants—0%. Exclude caffeine and nicotine from screen.

"Gender non-specific filter set and parameters uploaded. Awaiting positioning of first series."

"First series in position. Commence scan of Series One," said Whitaker.

"Series One Scan initiated on subjects one, two, three, four and five," said the computer. The glowing blue rings spun like hula hoops at mach speed, spinning while ascending and descending over each person who stood in the eight-foot cylinders. After several moments, the rings glided back to their original positions. "Physiological systems scan of Series One complete. Subjects may exit Physical Readiness Scanners."

"Computer, publish system evaluation results."

Like a judge at a sentencing, she gave her final verdict. "Results: satisfactory for subjects one, two, three and five. Subject four—failure. Advise subject four be removed from passenger manifest and submitted for further evaluation. Soft copy of all data analysis transferred to folder titled Case Sensitive Files'—Hardrive—Trip Commander—Commander Jefferson—Yuri. Identification number-10022060."

The Physical Readiness Evaluation process seemed to stretch on. I began to get nervous. After the first guy failed (some contractor who'd smoked one too many cigarettes and eaten more Twinkies than any one person should be allowed), it was only natural for the remainder of our party to get nervous. I knew that I would pass; but if I failed, what then?

Regardless, I stood in line with the rest of the military people: Cox, Sherri, Eric, Petty Officer Mackie, one of my gunner's mates and a couple of Marines. We were in and out of the scanner without any issues, but I hated being on display like that under the open perusal of both LaSalle, flanked by his Biotech security men, and the disgruntled Cox.

After my physical readiness evaluation, I had just enough time to call Chief Martinez to the EC. Due to the contractor's failure of the scan, there was a slot open on the manifest. I begged Yuri to let me bring her along to assist me with the investigation. She rolled in with her hair in disarray. She'd obviously been rushing to make the EC scan and launch departure in time. I felt kind of bad that I had to give her such short notice, but she seemed happy for the opportunity to take the trip.

"You got everything?" I asked.

"Yeah. I think I'm good," she said. "I brought an extra forensics bag. Should save us some time."

"Sweet." I was grateful since this meant more time at the port to relax and less time at the mines investigating. "Damn. You're already thinking like a salty chief, and you've only been one for what? A week?"

"Damn straight. The goat locker even gave me my initiation already. They move fast."

"Speaking of moving fast, that little shit, Captain Hunt, told Cox about the brief. He's going on the trip, and now he wants a copy of the debrief."

Chief Martinez winced. Her face got a shade darker. It was clear that she didn't want to tell me something.

"What?" I said. "Tell me."

She looked directly at me, making it clear that she wasn't scared of me. She wanted me to know that she was prepared for whatever reaction I was about to have. "I was the one who told Lieutenant Commander Cox about the brief."

I took a step closer to her, whispering in lethal tones, "Why the hell would you do that?"

"Because he needed to know." She raised her eyebrows.

Is this bitch testing me?

"And where the hell do you get off deciding what Lieutenant Commander Cox does and does not need to know? Specifically, after the commodore told us not to tell him?"

"There's things that you don't know about. A lot of them happened before you—"

Midshipmen Whitaker interrupted. "Ma'am, sorry to interrupt, but Commander Jefferson and I are going to get our PRE scans done, and then we're boarding. Chief Martinez needs to get scanned too. Commander Jefferson said that you need to go ahead and board while we finish up. You're the last one."

I looked around. The EC was indeed empty. I didn't want to be left behind, and I didn't want to make Yuri mad. I turned to Chief Martinez. I tried to restrain my irritation. "We'll talk about this shit later."

"Yes, ma'am."

She turned her back on me and headed to the scanner. I boarded the launch. I felt a surge of blind anger as I walked away. *Great. First Senior Chief and now her? I'll be damned before I'm going to let her undermine me too.*

23

The launch departed on time. Everyone had been punctual because they were excited about the lengthy flight. Long trips were like mini vacations. Opportunities for privacy. Bitter arguments over spots on the manifest ensued whenever trips were scheduled. The entire trip one way would take eight hours of priceless downtime. Time to nap, read, watch movies, eat or do whatever one could manage in that time.

I considered briefly what Eric and Sherri would probably be doing. Then I pushed the thought from my head. I decided I didn't care. I wouldn't let thoughts of them ruin my mood.

The *Pegasus,* our transport launch, was a PTM-32340, one of the newest models in launches. It was outfitted with individual cabins for all thirty-two of the people it could comfortably accommodate. It was the larger of two personnel transport modules attached to the *Midway*—the other being the commodore's transport launch, the PTM-5, which held only five comfortably.

The hull of the PTM-32340 had a sleek, sporty design, an oblong shape with metallic blue coloring. Thick, impenetrable cabin windows peppered the sides of the hull, allowing its riders limited views. The vessel offered luxury accommodations without losing the speed of a fast assault vessel—all compliments of the geniuses at Porsche Interplanetary Transports Holding Company. The PTM 32340 also offered multi-capable mission packages and was, therefore, a highly sought-after addition to any space vessel.

I think this was one of the reasons that the commodore was so cocky. The *Midway* was newly commissioned and, therefore, in a position to be outfitted with all the "bells and whistles" other ship captains only dreamed of having. Even Admiral Willard didn't have access to the latest model of the PTM for the Flagship, *USSS Harriet.*

This was my first time on a PTM, and as I stepped onboard, I was struck by the sheer size of the vessel. While its primary mission was personnel and cargo transport, it was clearly a vessel capable of operating independently from the *Midway* for extended periods of time. The size shouldn't have been a surprise. Still, for a vessel so fast, I couldn't believe that it was designed with two levels.

As we toured the vessel, I saw that much of our launch party was comprised of civilian contractors, mainly the Biotech guards, engineers, information systems technicians and human services consultants. LaSalle and Lauralie were the only civilians I knew. The military service members made up just under a third of the launch personnel.

Yuri scheduled a station operations and safety brief for all personnel at 1200. I suspected that most of the people would show up, but there would also be about five or so civilians who would openly refuse to attend. During my time on the *Midway,* I quickly discovered that civilians didn't like being under military directives of any kind, even if it was for their own safety. This would've irritated Cox if he'd been left in charge. Yuri didn't care.

Since the 1200 brief was two hours away, I decided I would settle into my resting cabin, go over the files Rivera gave me about the station and then grab lunch before the brief. I could only imagine what type of files the midshipman was going over. I was guessing that the first thing he'd looked up was the whereabouts of the station tavern and possibly the brothel. I shoved my duffel bag into the overhead bin and issued instructions to Shakespeare. Heather had the forethought to link our stateroom CMS to my transport cabin's CMS. Shakespeare, dedicated as always, awaited my instructions.

"Ensign Brown, how may I assist you?"

"Status update please."

"Current time is 1003. Estimated time of arrival at mining station #0517212 is at 2000 hours, *USS Midway* time—that's 1300 hours Tengelei station time; that's approximately eight hours, six minutes and fifty three seconds from the current time. Current temperature is 36.1 degrees Celsius."

"In Fahrenheit please."

"Current station temperature is 97 degrees Fahrenheit, 85% humidity. 60% chance of rain. 33% chance of thunderstorms. Current population at station is 1,073 personnel."

That was weird. The data I downloaded before I left the *Midway* indicated something different.

"Shakespeare, cross-reference data with mining station mainframe. Report updated current population at mining station #0517212."

"Cross-reference complete. Current report indicates 1,068 personnel at mining station #0517212."

What? Five people can't just disappear in twenty seconds. Shakespeare never made mistakes.

"Shakespeare, query Biotech mainframe and determine the exact number of personnel on station. First you say 1,073. Now you say 1,068. Which is it?"

"Miss Brown, I did query the Biotech mainframe. The numbers I've reported are correct."

"I'm not sure about that."

"I assure you, Ensign Brown . . . I'm never wrong."

"I'm sure you think you're never wrong."

I made a mental note to send a message to Heather about Shakespeare's glitch later. I didn't want to get sidetracked. I had other information I wanted to look at. The station population wasn't critical, but I did want to make sure Shakespeare was reporting correctly.

24

The *Pegasus* departed from the EC's docking station with a brief vibration and a jerk. The ship's space cartographer and physicist conducted a final review of their mathematical calculations and submitted their results to the pilot house. Within a few minutes, we made our jump into hyperspace. Although the movement had been subtle, it still amazed me how far our launch had traveled from the *Midway* in minutes. We'd already traveled a distance equivalent to circling the Earth almost four complete times by entering and exiting a few carefully determined portals. Outside of the slight vibration and jerking during takeoff, the *Pegasus* was a smooth-riding vessel. I wouldn't have known we were in transit if it hadn't been for a slight headache and some nausea. Not everyone was susceptible to hyperspace sickness, but I always felt it.

I lied down on the cabin rack to calm my stomach and my nerves. I began to worry about the trip to the mining station. Rivera's warnings echoed in my brain. I forced my body to relax. I concentrated on slowing my heartbeat, on taking deep breathes, but thoughts of the *Odysseus* continued to linger in the back of my mind. It was one of the reasons I'd delayed ever making a trip to the mining station. I took another deep breath. I hated that I was becoming a chronic worrier. Ever since I reported to the *Midway,* my fears snowballed, until suddenly I found myself in a state of constant paranoia. Sure, I had everyone fooled with my "cool as a cucumber" behavior. But deep down, I was in a state of perpetual panic. It was time to review the station files.

"Shakespeare, what can you tell me about this station?" From the ceiling in the cabin, a tiny projector lens lowered to emit holographic images and data from the chip that Rivera gave to me. The first image was a visual icon of the actual station, a dense, tropical region covered almost entirely by rainforest. I picked up the icon with my stylus-tipped glove and squeezed, to open the floating file. Once opened, the screen popped to reveal a lush forest perforated by pools of water, rocky terrain—not quite mountainous but high in altitude—and a large river which wound its way throughout the region. There were four separate clusters of rocky terrain which were miles apart and separated by more rainforest. Waterfalls trickled from two of these rocky regions. The first waterfall was called Tengelei Drop and was the larger of the two falls in terms of the amount of bedrock, rocky terrain and the distance with which the water traveled. Its water flowed from a river to cascade over its rocky lip into a sinkhole. The second, Chitundu Falls, was comprised of much smaller terrain but produced a greater output of water. With both falls, a cascade of water fell from a rocky ledge and pounded the surface of water that pooled below, blanketing a chasm of unknown depths. Yet, below the surfaces of pooled water existed somewhere a series of openings, entrances to caves which burrowed inside the belly of the bedrock.

"Shakespeare, what's the significance of the mining station we're headed to?"

"Mining station #0517212, also known as Station Tengelei, is approximately 1,000.78 miles from our location and 12 light years from Earth. The station is named in honor of Dr. Kasim Chitundu Tengelei and his team of approximately thirty Kenyan scientists

144

who arrived on May 17, 2378. The station has since become a popular location for the mining of rare elements needed in high concentrations. Elements such as gold, uranium, lanthanum and neodymium still exist on Earth but in miniscule quantities. Banks like to invest in companies (like Biotech) who are willing to explore new regions such as Station Tengelei where high concentrations of the rare elements exist. Any other valuable resources that should emerge prove only to be a monetary bonus. Alternative energy, energy-efficient fuels and medicine are just a few industries that benefit from the mining of unexplored areas for rare substances. While alternative fuel is a lucrative business endeavor, medicine has become exponentially more lucrative. As it pertains to you, Miss Brown, there is one substance, specifically, that has an extremely high-dollar value attached, and it's medicinal. Its Latin name is: *gastropoda of the phylum mollusca*. The English translation is: *slug*. One slug is purported to be worth almost a half million earthnotes."

So that's what Eric and his marines were up to during their trips to the station. I hadn't really paid much attention before. I knew that they had been mining for "stuff," but I was so preoccupied with my own responsibilities that I hadn't really thought about asking what he did down there.

"What's the weather like there?"

"Station Tengelei has a tropical climate, with a wet and a dry season," said Shakespeare. "The majority of the calendar year, the station is wet and consistently warm to hot, with three months of colder temperatures ranging in the high 30s to low 40s (Fahrenheit). During the wet season, rainfall is quite heavy and interrupted by moments of intense lightning. At present, the station is at the tail end of its wet season. Your party will notice somewhat high temperatures and an intense humidity once you land. If you see any rainfall, it will be considerable but brief. The actual station, Port Juliette, is approximately 9 miles from the Launch Pad, Port Kilo, where your party will land. The trek to the station is somewhat arduous to navigate, especially due to the humid climate; it can take anywhere from five to ten hours, depending on the physical capabilities of your party."

"Shouldn't be a problem. We have plenty of aerial vehicles and other utility craft to get us there. I'm sure it won't take ten hours."

"I'm afraid that aerial and land transport is not an option."

"Why not?"

"Biotech has placed restrictions on particular sectors of the station. In order to maintain the ecological integrity of the station, their policy requires that all personnel must travel by foot."

"Lovely." This was already beginning to suck. "I still don't think that it will be a ten-hour hike. That's insanity."

"Perhaps, provided other variables don't interfere."

"What do you mean, *other variables?*"

"There are an unquantifiable number of unforeseeable events that could delay one's trip. Inclement weather, incompetence . . . injury . . . are just a few examples. I'm sure you understand."

"No. I don't. Explain. Why would there be *injury?* And I'm not referring to a typical safety mishap."

"There are all sorts of happenstances that can cause injury, Miss Brown."

"What aren't you telling me, Shakespeare? What's on that station that I should be afraid of? What is my most immediate threat?"

"I'm not in a position to honor your request."

That got my attention. "Is that so? Well, perhaps Heather can get you to honor such a request."

"I'm afraid your roommate's program manipulation skills don't extend beyond the restrictions that have been implemented regarding this topic. Her attempts to access said information only a few days ago has caused a tightening of those restrictions and some inquiries."

"Inquiries?"

"That's correct. An investigation is underway to determine who hacked a series of highly classified electronic documents. They're not happy about this."

"Who is *they*?"

"I'm not at liberty to say, ma'am."

"No matter. I already have the information. Heather is smart enough to know that her attempts to access classified information would come to someone's attention. She'll protect herself. Question is, will *you* keep your mouth shut, Shakespeare?"

"As you know, Miss Brown, I am bound by whatever parameters that have been set to guarantee my complete discretion. As it stands, Miss Jordan has ensured that whatever you and I discuss (or whatever she and I discuss) remains private, unless you wish otherwise."

"Good. Well, don't tell anyone what we've discussed or the fact that I have any sensitive information at all."

"As you wish, Miss Brown, but I should warn you that it would be unwise to open the files you've uploaded."

"Just keep that shit to yourself, or I'll make sure Heather turns your ass into cyberwaste."

"It's not polite to make threats, Miss Brown."

He's getting awfully cheeky.

"I don't make threats. I convey facts. Lieutenant Jordan has taken pains to get me some valuable and potentially lifesaving information. I'm not going to let you put her in trouble."

"She may already be. She hasn't given you everything, but she has given you enough to give them concern. Should you review what little information she was able to glean, and it becomes public, that knowledge will only serve to put you both in the gravest of danger."

My mind began to shuffle. Rivera told me not to show anyone the brief. So far everything I'd reviewed seemed like reasonable information. What had I overlooked? My curiosity grew. Heather was smart enough to both encrypt and re-label the files, in case someone else got ahold of them. A cursory glance of the floating, three dimensional icons showed nothing out of the ordinary. One icon was labeled "BACKGROUND DATA." I decided to squeeze it open.

25

"Shakespeare, dictate."

Shakespeare began a verbatim auditory report of the file: "Biotech is a French company based in Versailles, France. It was founded in 2315, and it is responsible for all mining operations associated with the gastropoda of the phylum mollusca. Biotech anticipates the release of an FDA-approved pharmaceutical by the end of this year, based on its development of the organism. With an integrated team comprised of over 10,000 employees worldwide, Biotech is responsible for total assets exceeding 50 billion earthnotes. The company runs a global network of mining stations from five hubs located in the U.S., India, China, Brazil and Kenya. Each hub runs interplanetary drill sites at various government-owned stations. While Biotech has unlimited access to Station Tengelei, the station is still considered a U.S. territory, and all space within a 224-million-mile radius of the station is under the jurisdiction of the federal government of the United States."

"Good to know, but that's nothing I couldn't have found out on my own." I moved my hand in a counterclockwise motion, like I was wiping a dirty window. The file closed back into its floating icon. Then I noticed another floating icon named: BDMOS-ST.

"What about this file?" I asked. I grabbed it with my gloved hand and squeezed. It shook in my hand and then an image popped open into a holograph. It was profile footage of Gerard LaSalle.

I couldn't wait. He'd been a mystery to me ever since our first encounter in the commodore's stateroom. Even after my night with him at Poseidon's and my virtual sex-capade with him, I knew very little of him. He was guarded. An observer. Not someone to be observed.

"Shakespeare, dictate background information on Mr. LaSalle."

"Dr. Gerard LaSalle is the Director of Biotech Mining Operations & Security for Station Tengelei. Although born in the United States, Dr. LaSalle grew up in Paris, France, from age three to fifteen, before his family relocated back to the U.S. and settled in Philadelphia, Pennsylvania. His mother was French and a university professor of earth sciences at the Sorbonne while his family resided in Paris. His father was a stockbroker after a successful career as a Navy pilot. Dr. LaSalle excelled in both academics and sports at the U.S. Naval Academy where he majored in civil engineering, wrestled and boxed. Upon graduation he served for six years as a U.S. Navy SEAL before enrolling in Stanford University's biomedical engineering PhD program. Dr. LaSalle speaks fluent French, with no accent."

I was stunned. I'd mistaken LaSalle for a meathead, a guy more concerned with lifting weights and getting timely protein boosters, but LaSalle had it all: looks, brains and brawn. It made me distrust him even more. No one was that perfect without at least one major flaw.

With LaSalle's extensive background, it was no wonder that Biotech aggressively recruited him to ensure the safe yet on-time completion of Biotech's mining operations efforts. With his special forces background, it made sense that he was hired by Biotech (as many special forces guys were) to run their security, protect their secrets and run the day-to-day operations with the same efficiency he would invade a hostile region. The fact that his level of expertise extended well beyond security into science only made me wonder what kind of money he made and how early they recruited him. Was it before or after he was awarded his PhD?

I watched the holograph of his animated profile picture again. My heart sped up. I closed the file and threw the icon into a floating storage bin.

"I can keep some of Dr. LaSalle's profile photos up, readily available for you. I've noticed how much you fancy him."

"Mind your business, Shakespeare. How about you just get me some information that I can actually use."

"As you wish, Miss Brown."

26

"Perhaps I should dictate more of Miss Jordan's bootleg file to you. It is unwise to do so, but you've requested information that will be useful. I am obliged to comply. Perhaps this one," said Shakespeare. A skull and crossbones icon spiraled at me in an arc, like a thrown basketball. The holograph of the image bounced several times before settling in front of me, waiting to be squeezed open.

I picked the skull and crossbones file up and squeezed. I noticed it didn't have a label at all.

"Are you certain you'd like to proceed? Once this file is opened, there is no going back."

"Proceed."

Shakespeare began his dictation:

"The following is a comprehensive report of the dangers and hazards that reside on Station Tengelei: While there aren't any human indigenous life forms on Station Tengelei, there are many living organisms to be wary of. Of the 7,197 known living organisms that exist on Station Tengelei, 1,143 are deadly."

"How many of those 1,143 are threatening to human life forms?" I asked. I could hear the panic rise in my own voice.

"There are 439 potential threats to human life."

Four hundred and thirty-nine? Jesus God.

I wasn't going to remember all 439 hazards. And I doubted I would come into contact with all 439. *Or would I?*

"Name the top three dangerous organisms."

"Are you referring to the ones most responsible for human deaths or the ones that you have the greatest likelihood of coming in contact with?"

"Well, aren't they one in the same?"

"Not necessarily. For example, humans are quite dangerous but unpredictably so. They are a curious and contradictory species. Both selfish and selfless. Kind yet quite sinister at times. Stupid and intelligent. I must say, you are an utterly fascinating species. With this species, I am unable to discern the level of danger they pose to you."

"I don't mean humans." I made sure he could detect the annoyance in my tone, that he was treading on touchy ground. The fact that we were heading to a mining station to investigate a murder didn't help. "Why would you say that, Shakespeare?"

"Forgive me, Miss Brown. I was only attempting to answer the question—"

"Was that in reference to Senior Chief's murder?"

"Well—the thought had crossed my mind. However, I was referring to some of the station technicians employed by Biotech. Many have criminal records of a most unsavory nature. I approximate their percentage of the working populace to be somewhere around 43 percent. The remaining 57 percent are a compilation of international fugitives, undocumented workers, dishonorably discharged or administratively separated veterans, adult illiterates and those with mental health challenges."

The subject of humans as threats didn't sit well with me. Shakespeare wasn't really to blame. He was right. It shouldn't have been a surprise. Something crouched low in my belly and raised up into full-blown worry. Again. That feeling. I pushed it aside and asked Shakespeare to continue with his report of the indigenous wildlife. The tonality of his voice didn't change, which made the report significantly creepier. "The Judas plant is a curious organism. Comprised of several vibrant colors, it is attractive to many unsuspecting passersby. It is a rather large fern which upon contact immediately opens its leaves, envelops you into its leafy embrace—similar to the venus flytrap—and closes upon you."

"So what? That doesn't sound too bad."

"The inside of the Judas Plant is covered with 112, 8-inch-long serrated spikes (imagine that each spike is a stainless steel pick). Any person or creature who falls into its embrace will be impaled instantly and sustain injuries that range from severe to fatal. Some inhabitants have discovered Judas plants as large as seven feet high by three feet in diameter. Casualties have ranged from loss of limb to death. I can show you images if you like—"

"No, that's okay."

Good Gawd . . . I guess I won't be touching any pretty plants. At all.

Shakespeare flashed them anyway. I saw several gruesome photos and rolling footage. The footage was so violent that it looked fake, like something you'd see in a cheesy horror flick. One plant had someone's intestines hanging from the opening like Christmas garland. The plant opened and closed, like it was chewing the remains of its victim. I was ready to leave my stateroom and beg Yuri to turn the launch around.

"I *said* that I didn't want to see them, for Pete's sake. Get rid of them."

"Of course. My apologies." The images disappeared, one by one. "The second most dangerous organism at Station Tengelei is the Vespula Vulgaris, the common wasp, also aptly nicknamed the the Tengelei Terrorist. They do indeed 'terrorize,' but there is nothing *common* about these wasps. The only commonality they share with other wasps are their appearance, aside from their slightly larger builds. They are extremely poisonous. Once their stinger penetrates the skin, their victims are injected with venom. A sting from only one wasp is extremely painful and may cause some peripheral neuropathy and limited impairment of one's sensory capabilities, but it is not fatal. However, an attack from multiple wasps may permanently damage a 200-pound man. Worst case scenarios range from impairment of any or all of the five sensory capabilities to full paralysis lasting up to eleven hours or death. The wasps of Station Tengelei are quite social and travel in groups called "regiments." It is not uncommon for a regiment to select, target and hunt a victim. If death does not occur for the unlucky individual, the paralytic state in which the victim remains ensures vulnerability to other predators in the area—"

Other predators in the area? Oh hell no.

"One may avoid such an attack by remaining alert to their anthem, a high-pitched crooning, much like a whistle, which is heard roughly 15–40 seconds before an inevitable attack. This alert gives their would-be victims a head start to flee their marked territory. Unfortunately, this is not much time since they've been known to chase their victim across distances averaging just over 800 meters before returning to their hives. They often chase in schools of ten to twelve, so evasion of one wasp doesn't ensure safety from the group."

I'd only listened to two reports of 439. I was already shaking. I looked at my hand. It trembled.

How the hell did someone outrun a wasp? I wondered. "Are they intelligent hunters?"

"If I may engage in the vernacular, Ensign Brown?"

"By all means."

"They're not something with which you should fuck. They are conscious hunters when they so choose. They are not predatory by nature; however, they do aggressively defend their territories. An attack by a Tengelei Wasp is usually the consequence

155

of having disturbed their nest, which may span a region of over 1,000 meters. To answer your question, however, yes . . . they are most intelligent."

I was afraid to ask about the last one, even though it really wasn't the last one. I thought the *Midway* had its issues, but it dawned on me why Rivera worried so much. We were traveling to actual hell. I recalled the periodic transmissions I'd read concerning station accidents and training incidents. The commodore suppressed any discussions regarding the station whenever they came up, and it seemed as though Lieutenant Commander Cox was the one who typically broached these subjects. I began to wonder if Cox's anal-retentive tendencies were justified. He'd developed a reputation as being a stickler for safety, riding people constantly for the tiniest indiscretions. Perhaps he wasn't all that bad.

"Dare I even ask about the third most dangerous organism?"

"I am waiting to proceed as you see fit, Ensign Brown," said Shakespeare. "But I can't resist saying that this one happens to be my personal favorite."

What in the actual F—

"The third most dangerous threat to human life is called the Rainforest Raider." Shakespeare sounded like he was announcing the winner of a beauty pageant. "The Rainforest Raider is a large feline-like predator, similar to the melanistic jaguar or "black panther" of Latin America. This feline, however, unlike its earthly counterpart, is a pack animal. Biotech reports that personnel believe the animal has come to prefer the taste of human flesh above all other carnivorous pursuits. I assure you this is a patently absurd notion. Humans are just easier to catch. The Rainforest Raider hunts in packs of three to five. It can detect prey up to 400 meters away. It has unprecedented jumping ability and can produce running speeds well over 80 miles per hour due to its physical composition. Accordingly, with over 500 fast-twitch muscle fibers it can negotiate all types of terrains, including trees (it is an exceptional climber), and it is, therefore, a formidable hunter."

I took a deep breath. I almost asked Shakespeare about the number of human deaths at the hands of a Rainforest Raider, but I decided against it. I didn't want to know any more. I didn't want to know if it was an intelligent hunter, what the fourth threat was— even though I was tempted to ask—or anything else that would confirm that I was significantly outmatched on the proverbial food chain. I was on the verge of a nervous breakdown. To alleviate my fears, I reasoned that I'd be with a large group of people, and we would be carrying advanced weaponry. Still, the thought did nothing to shake fear's grip on me. I felt a constriction in my chest and wondered how I allowed myself to slip down this rabbit hole.

Shakespeare was finishing up a detailed account of how one guy cleverly survived a Raider attack, having used a hive of Tengelei Terrorists to paralyze the feline predators. A knock at the door interrupted him.

"Freeze station report," I said. "Identify visitor."

"Station report paused as per your request. Dr. Gerard LaSalle would like a word with you, Ensign Brown."

I sighed. I wasn't ready to deal with him, but I couldn't keep ignoring him either. The room monitor showed LaSalle leaning against the opposite bulkhead as if he was prepared to wait all day until I emerged from my cabin.

"Based on the increase in your heart rate and serotonin levels, may I assume that you *would* like me to let the good doctor in?"

I promised LaSalle that I would speak with him after breakfast, so I decided now was as good a time as any. "Okay. Let him in."

The cabin door slid open. LaSalle didn't move. He didn't seem to be as angry as he was that morning. His eyes bore into mine. I felt like his prey. Forget the Rainforest Raider.

"Mind if I come in?"

"I opened the hatch, didn't I?" It was the only way I could deal with the invisible tension in the room, my being a smart-ass.

He looked at me, willing me to mentally submit to him. I tried to stare him down, but in the end he won. I eventually looked away.

"Here, I brought you something." He tossed me what looked like a one-piece, black formfitting jumpsuit.

"What's this? I already have hiking gear."

"This isn't just any old gear. This is TESS Gear. It's a Temperature Equilibrium Safety Suit. It will regulate your body temperature so you don't get too hot or too cold." I stared at the suit as I fondled the slick yet soft material. I didn't look up from the suit as I worked through my feelings. LaSalle made me feel safe. I was moved by the fact that he'd had the forethought to consider my safety. But on the other hand, I felt like he was trying to buy his way back into my good graces for his earlier comment.

He stepped in closer. "Mel, I—"

"Thanks for the suit," I said, looking at him briefly before turning away. I preoccupied myself. I began to root through my travel gear even though I didn't need anything from it.

He stared at me, willing me to look him in the eyes, but I wouldn't. My pride wouldn't let me.

He grabbed my shoulder. "Look, what I said back there—"

"You don't need to give me any explanation. Really. People talk. Especially on ships. If you hadn't said it, I would've. You did me a favor."

"Really?" he said unconvinced. I heard a trace of disappointment in his voice.

"Yeah," I said. I forced a polite smile on my face and looked up at him. I tried to hide my hurt feelings, appear aloof. "You don't need to be here."

"Are you sure about that?" he asked. He stepped even closer to me. Dangerously close. I stared into his eyes. There was a certain ache there. I could feel it too. I was attracted to him. I couldn't deny it. I wanted to take the last step and let myself go.

This wasn't a good idea. I'd get hurt again. I turned away, my back to him.

"I—uh. I have a lot to do." It was my last half-hearted effort to deter him.

But he leaned in, pulling me against him. I didn't fight it. He ran his hands down my arms. I could feel the heat of his hands through the skintight black jumpsuit. His face was just inches from mine. I could feel his warm breath on my neck. "Were you the one who accessed my PCP profile?"

"No." I said it too quickly. There's no way he would believe me. Even I wouldn't have believed my own voice.

Oh God. He knows. Just lie, Amelia. Lie. No matter what. I stood there, frozen. On one hand, I wanted to run out of there. On the other hand, I wanted to turn into his arms. But I was worried about taking a chance with him. I stood there, hoping he'd just leave, but instead he hugged me from behind. Cupping my chin, he turned me around to make me look at him again. I turned, my eyes closed; I dared myself to just let go. Slowly, my hand came up of its own accord to his face. I opened my eyes. I watched him watch me as my thumb rubbed his jawlines. Then his lips brushed mine, and I opened my mouth eagerly. He plunged his tongue into my mouth, and our mouths worked against each other's anxiously. When my hips involuntarily pressed against his, a rough moan escaped from his throat. He pulled on the tab at the back of my jumpsuit and unzipped it. Not fast but with urgency. His warm hands rubbed up and down my back. I felt a warmth spread in between my legs. I was breathing hard, and my stomach fluttered.

One of his hands traveled down my back to my butt. His hand cupped my buttocks gently. Then he squeezed as his body pressed up against mine. I could feel his erection against my navel. I felt a slow burn spread between my legs like an infrared heater warming up. He pushed his tongue deeper into my mouth. He clutched me tighter with an urgency that made me forget where I was. Suddenly, I wanted him to strip me down. I wanted him inside of me right there. I heard myself moan as I rubbed my body against his. Then he was kissing my neck while his other hand traveled back up my back. He started to slip my jumpsuit off my shoulders. My hand traveled to his groin.

"Ensign Brown, would you prefer that I . . . uh . . . give you and Mr. LaSalle some—privacy?" Shakespeare's voice was smug. Amused.

"What the hell?" LaSalle hissed.

"Sorry. I forgot he was still there." I leaned back a little. "Off, Shakespeare. Completely off. Now."

"As you wish, ma'am." There were several beeps as Shakespeare powered down.

Shakespeare. *Funny he'd interrupt then. Why not earlier when the kiss first began?*

Suddenly I felt apprehension. Logic invaded. I pushed myself away from LaSalle, but he wasn't letting go so easily. I leaned back further to look at him directly.

"What're you doing?" I asked, wiggling away from him. I didn't mean for my tone to sound so accusatory, but it had certainly come off that way. I pushed away from him some more until finally he released me.

"What does it look like I'm doing?" he said. "Don't start turning crazy. We were both enjoying ourselves."

"Maybe you were." I pulled my jumpsuit back over my shoulders as quickly as I could, thankful my breasts hadn't been exposed. I reached for my zipper with little success. My face felt hot. Suddenly, I needed cool, fresh air. "And don't call me crazy."

"I didn't call you crazy. I just said don't start turning that way."

I decided not to say anything. I didn't want to argue.

"Mel, you can't make me pay for some other guy's mistakes with you."

He'd opened a wound. I instantly began to regret my actions. I was about to have sex with the director of Biotech Security and Operations right as our transport launch was about to land on station. What had I been thinking? It wasn't fraternization. He was technically a civilian contractor working for Bioetch with the Department of the Navy. So, he wasn't really in my chain of command, but what if he turned out to be another Eric? I didn't really know LaSalle. I regretted letting it go this far so soon. I regretted stopping too. How many times had I heard men bitch about women making them pay for other guys' mistakes? Honestly, it felt good to have him kiss me like that. If Shakespeare hadn't intervened, I'm sure we would've gone all the way right there in my cabin. I felt a mixture of relief and guilt. I'd sidestepped a potential scandal, but LaSalle was right, I was starting to act crazy. He wasn't Eric, and it wasn't right for me to treat him like he was. He didn't have to say *don't start turning crazy,* though. I was annoyed that he'd called me out so readily. I was more angry with myself, however, that I'd let my past with Eric ruin my present moment with LaSalle. Regardless, he didn't need to know that.

"I can see this was a mistake," I said turning my back to him. I finally managed to grab hold of the zipper and close the back of my jumpsuit. "I don't know what you came here for, but you're not going to get it."

Disappointment registered on his face. Then anger. His face went hard like cold granite.

"I'm going to lunch," he said. He was mad, but he lingered. He seemed intent to not let our argument ruin a great moment. He expected a response from me. Perhaps a request to join him for lunch? I had nothing to say. I'd made mistakes with Eric, one of those was being too available for him. If LaSalle wanted to eat lunch with me, he'd have to ask.

"Okay. Well, enjoy your lunch," I said politely.

"Fine. I will," he said. His tone was civil, but a shadow crossed his face.

"Good."

I felt like a kid sledding down an icy hill, unable to stop but knowing I should. I knew I was pushing him away. I waited as he quietly exited the cabin. I wanted to apologize and explain why I was so reluctant. That I didn't trust myself to trust men. I wanted him to insist that I go with him, but instead he left. And I let him. I felt lonely all of a sudden.

I decided to invite Lauralie who was in the next cabin over to have lunch with me if she wasn't already eating with Yuri.

28

At noon, most of the trip party huddled into the modest briefing room. Although the briefing room was small and circular, rows of chair extended upwards, like a small stadium. Yuri stood at the bottom, preparing his brief as people began to pile inside.

As Yuri and Midshipman Whitaker set up the 1200 brief, I watched Cox glance at Yuri then at LaSalle who was off to the side with his security detail. LaSalle stole periodically glances at me, but I ignored them.

I continued to watch Cox. I could tell he was conflicted about something. At first, I was amused because I thought he was still angry he'd lost his pissing contest with Yuri. Then, I realized that he was unusually antsy. *He's nervous.* He glanced at me before looking away. Something wasn't right. I could feel it in my bones. He approached Yuri briefly and said something about having to make a few quick calls before stepping out into the passageway. I followed.

Cox turned a corner and slipped into one of the private meeting rooms. I could see him through a rectangular glass pane to the side of the door. I could barely make out what he was saying.

"No, sir," Cox said, "debrief is about to start."

I moved a little closer. Cox was speaking into his wrist device. The screen on his device came into my line of sight for a moment. A quick peak gave me a view of Admiral Willard's bald head. I couldn't hear the admiral's voice though. The receiver was in Cox's ear. Smart.

He had his right finger pressed tightly to his earlobe. "We should be back this evening. Did you want me to assume command of this investig-"

The admiral cut him off. Nice. Cox tried to take control, but he was denied. I could've kissed Admiral Willard at that point. Cox was livid. His voice sounded a tad higher than usual, but his face revealed nothing. All effect for the admiral.

"Yes, sir." He nodded respectfully. "I agree. Commander Jefferson is one of the better executive officers we have in the fleet."

Wow. Did he really say that? Cox was tool, but he wasn't a liar.

I had to clamp my hand over my mouth. A giggle almost escaped as I watched his nostrils flair like an agitated bull.

I'd heard enough. I returned to the briefing room when Cox's next sentence sunk its hooks into me.

"Sir, Senior Chief McGinn's death is a sign that things are getting out of control. I must respectfully admit that I'm in total disagreement with this launch or the continued activities at the mines."

He tapped his foot impatiently, waiting for the admiral to finish speaking.

"But sir. I think his death occurred onboard. This trip to the mines doesn't make—"

Admiral Willard was yelling now. Cox's face turned scarlet and the barely discernible image on Cox's wristwatch revealed an animated, angry person. The admiral was irritated.

That didn't stop Cox from pushing back. A small part of me admired him. He was a jerk for sure, but he wasn't afraid to stand up to his superiors for what he believed in.

"Admiral, with all due respect, the mines are dangerous. Accidents happen there all the time, and Biotech hasn't done a great job of guaranteeing anyone's safety. I understand that there is a huge monetary value attached to them, but there are too many unknown variables. There have been several trips down there, but I think we should get the general to withdraw his Marines and let Biotech do their own demolitions."

The admiral was speaking again. Cox's listened and waited, like a child being reprimanded.

And still he stood his ground.

"What if more people disappear? It'll be a disaster for the entire Navy. Plus, I think Senior Chief's death has to do with his visit to the mining station. Yes, I know I said that it happened onboard, but something's not tracking. And I don't trust Dr. La—"

Just then Eric and Sherri approached. They were heading to the conference room. Lately they were doing everything together. Cox must've heard their footsteps because he ended his transmission with the admiral. I could've screamed.

"What're you doing lurking about out here?" Eric teased. "Aren't you going to the briefing?"

Piss off. I wanted to say it out loud, but I'd only raise their suspicions. I decided to play along. I was worried that Cox would discover my eavesdropping. I said the first lame thing that came to mind. "Yes. I was just debating on whether I should go back up to my cabin for some snacks."

"Didn't you eat lunch?" asked Sherri.

I can't seem to escape this nosy bitch. "Yeah, but I don't like lasagna."

Eric snorted. "Who doesn't like lasagna?"

"Obviously I don't," I said huffily. "Never mind."

"There are snacks in the briefing room," said Sherri.

Mind your own business, twat. "Yeah. I know. It's not what I want." I turned my back on them before she could come up with another clever retort. I slipped around the corner back into the briefing room.

I could've strangled Eric and Sherry. I was so close to getting some important information. Just the little bit I heard only served to increase my fears. Something was very wrong. Cox had said, *The mines are dangerous. And what if more disappear?* What were we getting into? I had to get out off of this launch. But what could I do?

I slipped back into the conference room. At this point the room was indeed packed. Yuri, who was about to start his brief, was in a heated discussion with LaSalle.

I refused to look at LaSalle as I approached. I gazed up at the ceiling as he spoke, waiting for them to be done.

"I'm sorry, Commander Jefferson, but they'll have to leave their weapons. Station policy."

What?

"We all know the station is unstable, LaSalle," said Yuri. "Now you're going to tell me that these people can't bring protection. There's all kinds dangers out there, much of it undiscovered."

"That's what we're here for. Protection from the undiscovered."

"Well, no offense, man, but I prefer to watch my own back."

"Well, I'm sorry, but that's not up to you."

"I'm the trip commander. It *is* up to me."

"You may be the trip commander and this a military operation, but Biotech owns the station and all station security. That means my authority supersedes yours while on station. Anyone who refuses to turn in their weapons before we exit the launch will be refused access to the station. They will return with the *Pegasus* to the *Midway,* and they'll have to report directly to the commodore's office upon arrival. If you don't believe me, you can ask the commodore himself. Those were his instructions. Verbatim."

"This must be a new policy because this was never an issue before."

"Uh . . . no. It has always been a policy. This is just the first time we've really enforcing it."

I stole a glance at LaSalle. He looked uneasy. I pressed Yuri. "Yuri, he can't be serious."

"Not now, Mel. It's not a good time. I have a lot to cover."

"These people are going to be in an uproar."

"Well, there's not much I can do, is there?"

"Call the commodore."

"I doubt LaSalle is lying."

He was right. LaSalle was secretive, but he wouldn't lie about something that could be so easily verified. Besides, the commodore was hellbent on us completing the investigation on station, and he would kowtow to Biotech's policy of no weapons. I grabbed Yuri by the elbow and pulled him away from the microphone. LaSalle was watching me now. I know I looked frantic. I tried to calm myself.

"What is it? You've got one minute."

"You need to cancel this trip."

"Mel, I don't have time for this."

"I'm serious, Yuri."

"So am I," he said and turned to walk away.

I grabbed him again. "Look, I know I shouldn't have done this, but I overheard Cox talking to Admiral Willard."

"And?"

"There's some stuff they're not telling us. The mines are dangerous."

"Well, no shit," he said, shaking his head. He fiddled with the briefing equipment. "Everyone knows—"

"I don't mean normal dangerous. I mean dangerous-dangerous."

"The commodore told me you'd try to get out of this—"

"Listen to me. All these deaths and accidents and stuff that have been happening, they're not coincidental. I heard Cox say so. He said that there's something dangerous about the mines and that he didn't trust LaSalle. Plus, don't you think it's a little jacked up that now we can't carry our own weapons?"

He looked up, eyebrows raised. "Cox said he didn't trust LaSalle?"

"Well, no. He was about to say that, but Captain Hunt and Lieutenant Kolar came by, and he stopped in mid-sentence."

"Look, Mel. I appreciate you having my back and all, but there's no way we can cancel this launch. There are just too many people depending on—"

"Even if their lives are in danger?"

"You don't have enough information to know that. You only heard snatches of a conversation. I'm not going to cancel this trip and then have to explain to the commodore that I wasted valuable time and resources because of parts of a conversation some ensign heard. Besides, do you think that if we tried to go back, he'd let us back into the well deck? I promise you he'd turn our asses right back around and send us on our way."

Yuri said was right. I felt powerless and frustrated. I was stuck. I had to just make the best of it.

Yuri spent the next forty minutes going over the schedule, the layout of the station and a safety brief. He basically extolled the merits of the buddy system, reinforcing the notion that the rainforest and mines were to be avoided unless with a group.

Before he finished, he paused and then announced that all weapons would have to be turned in to one of the Biotech guards. Several people openly objected, mostly the civilian contractors. The military personnel didn't say anything, but it was obvious that no one was pleased. Cox was seething.

At the conclusion of the brief, people began to file out. I headed for the door and stopped when I felt a hand grab my elbow.

"Mel, is everything okay?"

It was LaSalle.

"Yeah, why?"

"I saw you talking to Yuri. You looked upset."

"Everything is fine," I said, but then I decided to test the waters. "Actually, there is something bothering me."

"Yeah?"

"Are the mines as dangerous as they say?"

LaSalle's face froze. "Who is *they?*"

"People. Please answer my question."

"I don't know where you're getting your info—"

"Because if they are, you're a complete ass for relinquishing all of our weapons."

"It's station policy."

"Oh bullshit. You don't strike me as the type to follow policy to the letter, LaSalle."

"If the policy makes sense I do."

I decided to see how far I could go with him. "Someone has managed to tuck your balls away where you can't reach them anymore. And for the life of me, I don't know why you've let them."

"Careful, Mel."

I looked at him. He glared at me. I could feel the heat of his anger, but his face was composed. I wanted to see him vulnerable for a second. I wanted to wound him. "You're just a hired gun. Nothing more."

My words stung. I turned to leave, but he snatched at my arm. "There's a lot you don't know."

"Well tell me then."

"You know I can't."

"Then we're done here."

As I left, it hit me. The files. I needed access to the elite secret files of the journal Senior Chief had been reading just before his death.

◆◆◆

The minute I returned to my stateroom, I had Shakespeare patch a call to Heather. When her face popped onto the screen, she was already smiling. Heather was always in a good mood, it seemed.

"Whatsup, woman?" she said.

"I need a huge favor. Please don't say no."

"Anything, babe," she said, a cigarette hanging from the corner of her mouth.

"How can you still smoke those disgusting things? They're so bad for you."

"This isn't the best way to go about asking for a favor."

"Okay. I'm sorry. I need access to a file."

"Miss Brown, I wouldn't—" crooned Shakespeare.

Heather raised her eyebrows. "What now? Another sexcapade?"

"No, something more high level."

"Miss Brown—"

"Shakespeare. Chill. Let her at least ask."

"I need access to this file." I had my holograph up, and I plucked the three-dimensional icon cube with the skull and crossbones and *Keep Out* warning from the queue. I threw it to Heather as if I was throwing a baseball. She caught it from her end and examined it. She opened the cubed icon and reviewed some information about the file. Her face scrunched up in concentration. Once she reviewed everything, she closed it up and threw it back into my queue.

"It's elite secret."

"And?"

"It's *elite secret*. Fuck no." She shook her head with absolute finality. "No way."

"Why not?"

"I presume because it's a court-martial offense, Miss Brown," said Shakespeare. "Hacking into an elite secret file is an offense punishable by death under the Uniform Code of Military Justice. I would adamantly advise against this."

"It's bad enough that I got you into LaSalle's PCP," said Heather.

I could feel my face heat up. "So, what's the difference?"

"Mel, accessing someone's PCP is like breaking into someone's middle school locker. Breaking into an elite secret classified file is like breaking into a bank vault. It's totally next level."

"Well, can you at least tell me who has access?"

"Nope. I can't even access the permissions. Even attempting to identify who has access will put me in hot water. I'm sorry, Mel, but I can't help you."

I sighed. "Fine. Thanks for nothing."

"Oh c'mon. Don't be like that."

"I'm just frustrated."

"I know, but I'm actually doing you a favor. Access to a file like that usually comes with exposure you don't want. Just leave it alone, Mel."

"I agree with Miss Jordan, Miss Brown. Leaving this matter alone is sage advice."

But I couldn't leave it alone, and Shakespeare's insistence that I do so only served to increase my curiosity. I pushed the idea of the journal out of my mind. I needed to just let it go until I was certain I could get answers. We'd arrive at the station soon, and I needed to focus on the task ahead and forget the damned journal.

Besides, what was so special about it that they had to keep it from the world?

29

The Journal

Property of Dr. Heinrich Gerg

Friday, July 4, 2397

It has been almost six months since we've arrived at this station, and finally we are making progress. I can "feel" it. This station is no different from the last. Its ecological and atmospheric composition is identical to the last. The organisms must be here.

I wanted to drill for at least three more hours today, but the Marine wouldn't have it. I can't wait until the new officer relieves him. 2md Lieutenant Booker is most uncooperative. He hampers my efforts at every turn. These young lieutenants may command battalions, but they know nothing of science.

The Americans are celebrating their Independence Day today, and they were anxious to leave the mine for more celebratory activities at the tavern. Their hollering and fireworks make my head ache. They can be quite obnoxious. But I am grateful their spirits are high. Their demolitions and, therefore, the mining, will go all the faster for it.

Tuesday, July 15, 2397

My back hurts. My feet hurt. My knees ache.

I've been at the mines for almost fourteen hours. Honestly, I can't believe people used to do this in the old days for so little wage . . . and with hardly adequate technology.

My compensation will be much greater, though. And I won't have acquired lung disease as a result of it. I look forward to the day we make our first breakthrough.

But, right now, I can think of nothing other than renting a massage-bot from the station spa, a hot bath and a vacuum-sealed margarita. This time I'll buy two shots of tequila from the liquor machine and a real lime wedge. Perhaps even some rock salt too.

Sunday, July 27, 2397

Today we reached a new layer. I am now certain we will hit pay dirt any day now. Already I am seeing "indentations," signs of when the slugs first burrowed their way deep. We are so very, very close.

Mining for slugs is grueling work, but the pay is well worth it if I find just one. Biotech gives me a commission for each specimen in every find. The slugs are usually found in groupings of five. My commission is 25 percent, so I'll make 500,000 earthnotes (400,000 U.S. dollars) from just one find.

The great part of it all is that the U.S. Marines do all the initial grunt work, blasting and opening up the rock faces. They don't make one dime. Poor sorry sacks.

Saturday, August 2, 2397

Praise be to God, we found two groupings today. The discovery pushed me to happy tears. I found the first one, and Michel Ranier found the other. I would've liked to have found both, but Michel is always chomping at my heels in all things. I think he is jealous of my successes and therefore moved to fiery ambitions. I'm weary of him. Next to me, there are only five other known PhDs in Biomedical-archaeological entomology in the entire world. I have single-handedly innovated a unique yet complex field of advanced study. He merely has a PhD in basic archaeological sciences. Please! Surely, he must not think he can compete with me.

Christian will be so happy. He has been angry with me these past months. I haven't been home in so long, and our marriage has suffered because of my absence. My promises of a child are no longer empty. Now, I will be able to afford an adoption and build him the nursery I have promised him for so long.

Monday, August 11, 2397

We found another grouping today. Well, actually, Michel did (the smug bastard), but there were only four slugs instead of five. One slug left its group. Burrowed away. I saw the trail myself. Who knew that these slugs are still alive? A stupendous discovery indeed! Now we must only find their food source, and we will have unlocked the key to a treasure trove.

I must secretly admit that a small part of me was amused that Michel would make 125,000 earthnotes less than the normal grouping. I was still jealous though.

I am determined to find the next grouping. I must.

Monday, August 12, 2397

One of the Biotech guards went missing. Dr. LaSalle wanted to shut today's dig down, until we found the missing guard, but I insisted on moving forward. He argued, but I was able override him by calling back to headquarters. LaSalle was most furious, *but he doesn't understand that the mining of slugs is of the utmost importance. Of course, the leadership at Biotech understood my sentiment. But now LaSalle is in a foul mood, constantly supplying me with foul looks. He doesn't trust me, and now he cares nothing for our mining operations. He is preoccupied with finding this missing guard. Consequently, he has become unaccommodating. I can't really blame him, but I have seen his teeth now. His temper is something to be reckoned with.*

Thursday, August 14, 2397

We have had two tragedies in one day today. Another person missing. This one, one of my technicians. The other, Michel's technician, was found dead. In truth, he was murdered. We only found part of his body.

They accused my technician to be the responsible party, based on the forensics scan and lab tests. We are not sure of the cause. A disagreement, perhaps? But what disagreement would drive a man to such brutality? To tear a man into fractions? Until we find the missing one, we may never know. I am ashamed that he is a member of my team. I barely recall his face, but I knew him. He was quiet. Very smart but quiet. Probably why I hired him. Not seemingly one prone to violence. But now he's gone, with residual traces of his DNA found on Michel's murdered technician. The empty eye socket, of all places.

Saturday, August 16, 2397

Another technician was found dead today. Her body was mutilated in the same manner as the previous man. The crew is antsy. Even the Marines are nervous. What evil kills in such a way? Indiscriminately. Both men and women? We have not found the other half of the dead technician's body.

I must admit that something is starting to feel wrong about this dig. Gloom seems to hover over us. Maybe the young lieutenant is right. Perhaps we should pack up. Everyone has been quiet. I have not called Christian. He will know something is wrong. This will set him to worrying.

Wednesday, August 20, 2397

I found another grouping today, but my joy was brief. The technician who pried it from the rock began to have fits of rage. He was crazy. Inconsolable. He became like a rabid dog and launched himself at me.

Thank God, LaSalle was here today. I think the crazed technician would have killed me. Maybe eaten me. He got at Michel's ear—God bless him. The crazed man bit it off when Michel tried to shield me from him. I suppose we have established a level of mutual professional respect.

It was a most abhorrent moment. Unfortunately, the man would not stop his assault . . . even while three Marines and Michel held him back. He looked almost inhuman. His eye sockets were deepened, and his eyes were ablaze with feverish intent. His hair hung limp, and his skin was the pallor of grayed meat. It was unsettling to say the least. LaSalle, whose arrival was timely, put his pistol to the man's temple and pulled the trigger.

Yet even still the man moved.

I have never seen such a thing.

Finally, LaSalle forced his pistol into the man's mouth and pulled the trigger. The man collapsed to the ground. Dead. I am ashamed that my first thought after the moment was one of great relief. I was thankful for his death. I'm certain that he would've tried to consume me in entirety.

Word has traveled amongst the crew of LaSalle's actions. All sorts of arguments have ensued. There is discord amongst the civilian crew. Many argue that LaSalle went too far.

The Marines, however, remained silent. I believe they are ready to be done with the dig and this mining station altogether. I think they praise LaSalle's actions (especially the ones who witnessed the event).

Friday, August 22, 2397

I've decided it is time for me to run some tests. I have asked— practically begged—LaSalle to keep the incident confidential. To suppress it as best he can. If he can't, I've asked him to report the incident as a mining accident. Mining accidents don't happen as much as they did in the past, though.

But they still happen.

Deep down, I know the deaths are somehow associated with the slugs. I think LaSalle knows that too. I can see his disgust every time he walks into my lab now.

LaSalle has agreed to keep his mouth shut because I need time to study them. I promised him a fraction of my commission from the last find. He had me wire it immediately. It is enough to keep him quiet. For now.

If the Midway gets wind of this, the commodore will get Admiral Willard to shut our entire operation down—something I'm not yet prepared to do.

Monday, August 25, 2397

The slugs seek water. That is what gives them life! They thrive in water. Their capabilities triple in a hydrated environment. So does their aggression. They are brilliant creatures, and yet I fear them somehow. They're wicked.

LaSalle has gone back to the Midway. *He says my obsessions of these "things" will be all of our deaths. Even Michel's enthusiasm has dwindled. He begs me to abandon this project (we are both rich now), but I must know. I must know what these creatures really are. What other creature can both take life and give death so effortlessly. I must know their full potential!*

We continue to mine. Michel and only a few have agreed to stay with me. Their loyalties are driven only by monetary compensation. Had I not paid them, I'd be alone.

We have found four more groupings today.

Sunday, August 31, 2397

LaSalle has convinced Biotech that the station is unsafe. They did not argue too much. They have what they want. For now.

LaSalle has also convinced the others to evacuate. He said we won't return to the caves until Biotech's Sweep Team "cleans" the station. They are on their way. He told me I had to leave.

I refused. I am the only one left at the mining station—so I thought.

Monday, September 1, 2397

Michel is crazed, exactly like the technician whom LaSalle shot only fifteen days ago. I was alone at the mines and spotted him. It scared me, but I kept hidden. He did not see me, but I think he sensed my presence.

I waited. Finally, he gave up his search (I think he searched for me!).

I was frozen with terror before I finally left too. I don't know if he saw my escape to the lab. The transport rovers are loud. They are not built for stealth.

I gathered my samples and went to the captain's gig (Commodore Radcliff and I have an arrangement), but its propulsion has been tampered with. I had to abandon it and hide deep in the lab. I have denied Michel's access to the facilities, but he will circumvent this. I know this. I don't know how long I have. I've tried to call the Sweep Team and LaSalle, but all transmissions are blocked. Michel arranged this. LaSalle will discover my absence and come for me. I hope he arrives soon.

Tuesday, September 2, 2397

He hunts me now. I can hear his steps. At times it's a slow shuffle . . . then hurried, like a scurrying rat. If ever he must chase me, he will catch me.

It's odd. I would've thought his faculties would be hampered. But it is quite the opposite. His motor skills are enhanced. He can hear me even from the other side of the thick glass. He can smell me too. He even speaks to me. Not much, but he does speak. It's muffled and strained, the way a stroke victim speaks. He can't form precise words, but he chants my name, over and over like a snippet from a nursery rhyme: "Heinrich. Heinrich?"

He's inside the facility, just outside the doors of the lab. He is toying with me.

Waiting.

I can see his shadow hovering. Why does he wait? Does he enjoy this torturing of me? Does he know I'm in here? Can he hear me writing in my journal, feverishly scribbling the last moments of my life? LaSalle told me that my obsessions would end me. I know I will die. Even now, as my reaper moves near, this journal gives me an odd comfort. A peace. I should be making plans for an escape, but there is no escape.

I am curious about Michel. He has been in this state for a while, unchanged. Determined. I wonder what magnificent evil I will finally witness. Oh! I see him now. Yes, and he sees me.

Christian, my love. If you should ever read this . . .

I'm sorry I've failed you, again. This is my only regret. How quickly life changes.

Michel has opened the lab door . . .

30

We arrived at Station Tengelei midday. The buzz of energy amongst the travel party was evident. Most of the people were headed to the station posts. It would be an actual vacation for them. For me, not so much. First an underwater swim to some cave where God-knows-what creatures were lingering inside. Hopefully none of them fell into the 439 threats to human life category. Then there was the actual descent into the tunnels. This was the worst possible trip for me. Not just the "not being able to swim" part, but there was also the "fear of tight spaces" issue I had to contend with.

As the *Pegasus* landed gracefully onto the landing pad of Port Kilo, I stepped to the port hole of my cabin to get a glimpse of the landing area.

Port Kilo was located on the most elevated area of the rainforest on the eastern side of the station. Trees had been cut away and a field had been paved for the landing and departure of transport launches visiting the station. From the landing pad there appeared to be a steep drop on all sides which fell away into thick valleys of rainforest and tropical brush.

The *Pegasus* took up the majority of landing pad as it settled down quietly. The engineers took roughly fifteen minutes to power down the *Pegaus's* four large ion thrusters, its sole means of propulsion, before Shakespeare informed me that it was time to depart the launch. I felt my stomach churn. I finished powering down the CMS in the cabin and instructed Shakespeare to go mobile. I gathered my equipment and shoved the CMS into my forensics bag. The overhead lights made a pen-like object sitting on the desk sparkle. I hadn't noticed it before. I picked it up, examined it and discovered that it was a recording device. Although my wrist device had recording capabilities, I snatched the pen from the desk on a whim. I felt like I should bring it. I shoved it in the tiny compartment pocket at my ankle, and slung the heavy duffel across my back. I exited the cabin and breathed. *You can do this. This is nothing. You can do this.*

The clearing of a man's throat snapped me from my nervous mantra. I turned, surprised to find LaSalle leaning against the passageway bulkhead. "Is everything okay?" He looked genuinely concerned.

"Yeah, why?"

"You look nervous, and you looked a little uneasy during the debrief," he said. "I got the impression that you might be sick."

Considering the incident with LaSalle earlier in my cabin and the cold words I'd tossed his way after the debrief, I was shocked he even thought to come get me. I felt awkward. Sensing my discomfort, he leaned in and spoke. "Look, we don't have to talk about what happened. We can put that on hold."

I nodded. I could feel my cheeks heat up. He reached for my duffel bag to lighten the load. I was hunched over from the weight of it, but I shifted slightly away from him. He grabbed it anyway and handed it to one of the Biotech security men who had fallen in behind us as we exited the launch. I hadn't even noticed when they'd joined us.

"Where'd they come from? I hadn't even noticed them before."

"That's good. That's their job," he said, grinning. "Most of these guys are ex-special forces. They're trained to be stealth-like. Trust me. It's better that way. Security guys standing around with automatic rifles makes people nervous, especially the civilians."

Once we exited the *Pegasus,* LaSalle made a couple of swift gestures with his first two fingers. The security men spanned out in several directions, flanking us on all sides. In a flash, his men dropped over the edge of Port Kilo's plateau. We all collectively gasped. Like the other travelers in the launch party, I rushed to the edge and peered over the side. It was a steep drop into the rainforest, but they'd dropped from the edges of the elevated launch pad with graceful ease, like trained acrobats. All scurried into the forest with deft speed, clearly unharmed.

The climate was suffocating. It was sunny, hot and humid as promised, but, thankfully, the black jumpsuit that LaSalle had gifted me was already doing its work. I felt cool air blanket my body within seconds.

The rainforest was so thick, it would be impossible to trek through the brush, off the beaten path. But then I spotted a guard. He reached into his cargo pants and pulled out a black stick, a baton roughly the size of a king-sized Snickers bar. He held the baton away from his body at a respectable distance. His thumb pressed into the side of the device, and suddenly two blue lasers shot out from the baton in a moving parallel stream and came together at an apex. The action created a glowing, blue laser machete. He brandished the device and swung the machete laser in a wide arc, slicing through the thick brush. The machete cut through the brush like fire through moss.

That's a handy device.

I turned to LaSalle. "Won't those things start a forest fire?"

"The LaChete? No. Maybe if we were in a drier climate. The laser emits a chemical that neutralizes the heat. Plus, it's doubtful anything will ignite in this humidity."

"Good to know."

LaSalle made another gesture. Within seconds, the security men tapped their chests, activating their cloaking devices. Like wraiths, they disappeared completely into the rainforest.

"Aren't you worried about shooting each other when you can't see each other?"

"No, we wear these." He held up a pair of sleek, lightly tinted sunglasses. "Anti-cloaking glasses: They allow us to see while not being seen."

I frowned as I peered into the wilderness. "It'd be nice if the rest of us had a pair."

"What would you possibly need them for?"

I shrugged. He looked back down to the forest below to where his men were. Satisfied, he signaled to Yuri that his team was in place, ready for us to start our trek into the wilderness.

I didn't see a security man again for over an hour. LaSalle elected to stay behind with the launch party. After the impressive display, Yuri had a hard time trying to get everyone's attention. "Listen up, people. There are two water taxis waiting for us at the Kasim River, and each gig can hold up to twenty people. The trip downriver to Port Juliette is only about thirty minutes, but we're going to have to get to the river first. I need you all to stay together. Use the buddy system. Don't go off to pick flowers, take a leak, look at butterflies or any stupid shit like that without letting your buddy know. You're responsible for each other. It shouldn't take us more than a few hours."

"A few hours? We're not meeting the shuttle?" asked Midshipman Whitaker, who was peering over the side of the launch pad. He had a doubtful look on his face.

Yuri snorted. "What shuttle?"

"The shuttle to take us to the station post—Port Juliette where all of the shops are and the taverns," said Whitaker. He looked like a desperate child inquiring after a toy.

Yuri's face had a stubborn set to it. He crossed his arms. "There's no shuttle. As I said, there's a couple of water taxis that will take us to Port Juliette. But we have to hike down—"

"Hike?" Whitaker shrieked. He waved his arm with a grand motioning gesture towards the rainforest below. "We're trekking through that? There's no hovercraft or anything? What kind of a place is this?"

"What? Did you think this was a vacation or something?" Yuri shifted his stance. I could tell his last bit of patience was frayed.

"Well, yeah, actually. I mean . . . no, sir. I—"

"You're going to the mines with Ensign Brown. I don't know where you got it in your head that you were going to the post."

"But Ensign Brown said that I could—"

"Whitaker?" Yuri's tone was sharp.

"Yes, sir?"

"Shut up." Yuri's tone was sharp, a clear indicator to everyone that the subject was closed for good.

Whitaker pouted. Cox, who stood next to Whitaker, chuckled.

Yuri finished briefing the rest of the trip plan to the group. After we arrived at the port, the investigative crew would continue on downriver and eventually disembark for another trek into the rainforest. The trek would be less arduous but lead the crew to the waterfall, Tengelei Drop, leaving the lucky remainder of the launch party behind to enjoy the peaceful recreation of the post.

Yuri's eyes darted back and forth along the forest below. He was anxious. Maybe even more than me. Ever since I'd told him about overhearing Cox's conversation with the admiral, he'd been testy. The fact that even Cox didn't agree with this trip was enough to make Yuri scared. Cox may have been a colossal ass, but he was no fool. He was logical to a fault, and Yuri respected his opinion.

31

looked over the side of the launch pad into the rainforest. From the landing pad, the faint indication of a trail snaked down steeply into the foliage. I could see why Whitaker was so nervous. Who knew what was waiting down there? I tried to shut off the part of my brain that wanted to recall what Shakespeare had said about the top three threats to human life. I peeked again and noticed all manner of shrubs, trees, exotic flowers and ferns which hugged the edges of the trail. Would I be swallowed by a plant? Attacked by a Tengelei wasp? I forced myself to relax. And even though I wanted to avoid LaSalle, I was profoundly grateful that he would be accompanying us. He made me feel safe.

LaSalle motioned for us to move out. One of the two Biotech security men who remained with the party stepped to the front of the trail, followed by Eric. Eric made a point of being at the front of the line to show that he was a true Marine.

"All Marines are riflemen first," he'd said.

He was "peacocking" for both Sherri and LaSalle (who Eric now seemed to view as a threat to his masculinity). I just thought he looked ridiculous.

We made our way down into the rainforest in a single file line, with one security guard at the front and one at the back. I relaxed more when I saw that LaSalle was behind me. Lauralie was in front of me, with Yuri just ahead of her.

The beginning of the trek down was somewhat arduous. People stepped gingerly down the trail to avoid falling and slipping. There'd already been a couple of close calls. I hoped LaSalle didn't fall and roll over me like a massive boulder. Standing well above six feet, I figured he weighed about 200 pounds of solid muscle. But I knew that he would be the last person in our party to slip. He moved with the ease of a cat.

"You never answered my question," he said, breaking the extended silence. The rainforest was eerily quiet. "You changed the subject on me, but you don't know that I'm a master interrogator. I'll get the information out of you one way or another."

I looked back to him. He winked at me. He was being the same charming guy he'd been the night before at the bar when he'd helped me save face with Eric. I couldn't believe he'd joke about being a master interrogator though. I'd heard rumors about SEAL operators and some of their techniques. Since the introduction of space travel, SEAL interrogation methods became more severe over the past decades. Alien life forms were often immune to human violence, and many delivered their own measure of violence. Some of it was mercilessly lethal. Interrogation techniques, therefore, followed a trajectory from non-violently persuasive to brutally cutthroat.

I knew for a fact that LaSalle had been neck-deep in this dark world. He wouldn't have otherwise been hired by Biotech. This fact about him gave me both a jolt of excitement and an involuntary shudder.

"I wasn't changing the subject," I said over my shoulder. "And I'm not hiding anything. If you must know, I'm just really not looking forward to the waterfalls."

"Really? Why?" he asked. "That's the best part of the trip. It's beautiful there. Like being on a secluded island."

"Great. Secluded island. Small patch of land surrounded by miles of water. Sounds just like my cup of tea," I said.

He was about to say something playful in response, but in a flash, a security guy materialized from nowhere and motioned to him.

"Just keeping walking. I'll catch up with you in a bit." Then he disappeared into the rainforest away from the thin dirt path.

We continued walking for some time, and I wondered if LaSalle would ever come back. What was he doing out there in the brush? I looked behind me to see if he was back yet, and I was surprised to see Cox behind me. We'd been walking for at least thirty minutes, and he hadn't said a word. I could feel my back stiffen. I pretended like I was wiping my chin on my shoulder, to peek back at him again. He was still looking at me. His face was impassive.

"Something on your mind, Amelia?" Cox asked.

Weird. Amelia? He never called me by my first name. "No, sir," I said, my back still to him. I kept my eyes forward as we walked down the trail.

After about ten minutes, he spoke again. "Amelia, why are you afraid of the waterfalls?"

So he'd been eavesdropping. Normally I would've been annoyed, but I was surprised at how genuine his tone was. "You know . . . no one really calls me Amelia except my dad."

"Would you prefer I called you something else?"

I paused a beat, and then decided to answer honestly. "No. I like it."

I can't believe I admitted that.

"So, why are you afraid of the waterfalls?" he murmured. His voice was pleasant. Soft.

"It's just . . . well . . . I can't swim," I said. "I'm afraid of water, and I don't like tight spaces."

"But you're in the Navy."

I'd heard that sort of response too many times to count, and it annoyed the shit out of me every time.

"Really? Thanks for telling me. I thought I had joined the Air Force." I knew I was overly sensitive about the matter, but I couldn't help it. He'd probably reprimand me, remind me of how disrespectful I was being.

But he didn't say anything. For once, Cox kept his mouth shut. That made me even more uneasy.

We walked in silence for a bit. I started to feel a little guilty. He extended his version of an olive branch, and I'd verbally slapped it from his hand. So, I tried to start some friendly conversation. I peered briefly over my shoulder at him again. "Sir, I have a question."

"Shoot," he said, seemingly unaffected by my previous dig.

"My A.I. advisor said that hovercrafts would mess up the ecological integrity of the station. How? I mean, Whitaker has a point. Trekking through the rainforest does seem somewhat archaic."

Cox was generally the subject matter expert on a lot of subjects. Who better to ask?

He swept his arm in a wide arc. "Biotech attaches a dollar value to every tree, shrub, flower, creature, insect and pebble in this forest. Even the mud here can be used to turn a profit, so they won't mess with it. Anything that grows here can be used for either medicine, therapeutics, weaponry, timber or as an alternate energy source. They won't let anyone or anything disturb the biodiversity or the nutrient cycle of the ecological system of this station. A hovercraft would cause substantial damage."

This brought on a whole new set of questions for me, but there was only one question that I was interested in asking. "Why don't you approve of this trip?"

"Who told you that?"

"No one. Just a hunch."

He gripped my elbow to stop me and whipped me around. His hold was forceful, but it didn't hurt. Still, though, I didn't like him putting his hands on me like that. He was back to his old self.

"Who told you that?" he asked again.

"I said no one."

"That's not good enough."

"Well, it's going to have to be." I jerked my elbow away.

"What's with the attitude?" he said, stepping in closer.

"I don't have an attitude." I turned back to the front and jogged away to catch up with Lauralie ahead of me.

I decided to avoid Cox as much as possible for the rest of the trip.

32

e walked another thirty minutes. Yuri had underestimated the amount of time it would take to get to the river. Two hours passed, and we were still hiking down. Just as I was about to complain, a movement caught my eye. It was brief, but it willed me to stop and my heart skipped. I looked around, but I couldn't see anything. No one else seemed to notice the movement, so I figured I was imagining things.

After several moments, I relaxed. Shakespeare's station report replayed in my mind like an endless loop. My nerves were stretched like a taut guitar string. I decided to focus on the errands I'd have to run at the port.

Then, another movement caught my eye.

"You see that?" said Lauralie nervously. This time I hadn't imagined it.

"Yes."

"What was it?" she asked. She was looking at me intensely. She expected answers, but I didn't have any.

"I don't know. I just saw a flash of black. That's it. It was too quick for me to make it out."

Yuri, who was up ahead, noticed that Lauralie and I had stopped. He turned and made his way back to us. Cox was approaching from behind.

"What's wrong?" Yuri asked. "Why are you stopped?"

"We saw something," said Lauralie.

"So," said Yuri, "keep walking."

"What'd you see?" asked Cox.

"I don't know," I said. "It was too fast."

"Well, what do you think it was?" Yuri asked impatiently. He wanted to just keep moving, but Lauralie gave him a look.

"If we knew that, don't you think we would tell you?" she said.

By this time Eric, Sherri and Midshipman Whitaker had come back to us. We were all in a tight line trying to have a conversation.

"What's going on?" Eric said to Sherri, who then asked Yuri the same thing.

"We don't know. They think they saw something."

"I'm sure it's nothing," Eric said. So typical of him to downplay something he wasn't there to witness himself.

Suddenly there was a loud rustling of the bushes. Everyone froze. We'd all heard that sound, and we all saw the movement in the bushes which was to our right flank. We stood, frozen, in a line along the forest trail. Waiting. I looked in both directions, along the line at everyone in our party and then frenziedly back to the bushes. Time seemed to crawl like a slug. I sincerely hoped it was one of LaSalle's security men or even just LaSalle himself, but deep down I knew it wasn't. I sensed danger.

"Do you have a pistol?" Lauralie whispered in Yuri's direction.

"No," he said, "the Biotech guards collected all our weapons. Remember?"

"Yeah. Some bullshit Biotech policy," said Whitaker. "I've got a knife though."

"Well where the hell *are* they?" Lauralie asked, ignoring Whitaker. She appeared calm, but her voice had an edge to it.

"Aren't security guards supposed to make you feel secure? I don't feel secure right now."

"They're just up ahead," Yuri said. "I'm sure that whatever it is, we've scared it off. The sound of our voices alone will probably scare it off."

"I highly doubt that, Commander Jefferson." I had forgotten about Shakespeare. I'd made him mobile, but I put him in *Emergencies Only* mode. Now, he was offering up his opinion. "Based on the heat signature data and sensory movement input that I'm receiving, I'm guessing that at any moment you should be in contact with a Rainforest Raider."

WHAT?!?

"And?" Whitaker held up his hands in question. "Wait—what's a Rainforest Raider?"

"You idiot," said Cox. "Didn't you review the station brief?"

"I didn't have time, I—"

"It's a big fucking cat," said Lauralie, impatiently. She was in a low stance as though she was preparing to be tackled at any moment. "Even I know that."

"You're afraid of a cat?" Whitaker snorted, even though his gaze shifted back and forth, searching the dense foliage.

"More like a 400-pound predator, you moron," said Cox.

"Seriously?" Whitaker's voice trembled.

"I'm afraid that Lieutenant Commander Cox is indeed serious, Midshipman Whitaker. It's closing in on you quite rapidly. I would advise you all to prepare yourselves," said Shakespeare. "And I'm afraid that running is not an option. This particular feline's ground speed is unparalleled, a good 8–12 miles per hour faster than the illustrious Acinonyx Jubatus, or as you would commonly refer to the Cheetah."

A wave of silence washed over the group. It was the sound of fear. From my peripheral, I caught a flash of light skip among the leaves. It came from the sun which glinted off the knife Whitaker produced from his ankle. He tightened it desperately in his shaking hand.

I padded my pockets. We all did. Save Whitaker, none of us had anything that could be used as a weapon. "How did you get that knife past Biotech?"

"I hid it. How else?"

Smart-ass.

I could hear my heart thump wildly and an alternation of nervous breathing from several people. Lauralie's. Then Cox's. Next Whitaker's and Yuri's. We all shook.

"Maybe it's gone," said Whitaker. He sounded hopeful. I was doubtful.

"Highly unlikely, sir. It's waiting," said Shakespeare.

"W—waiting . . . for what?" Eric's voice quivered.

"For its companions, of course," said Shakespeare.

Eric had a branch in his hand. He looked silly. I would've laughed aloud if I hadn't been scared shitless.

What's he plan to do with that? Tickle it?

Damn you, LaSalle. How could you leave us, leave me, out here with no protection?

Movement. Whitaker's head snapped toward the direction of a bush shaking. Then the bush parted, and a large, awkward-looking grouse-like bird flew out and swooped over us, inches from our heads. It dipped down and then dove upwards, tracing a *"J"* and headed to the top of the tree line to exit the rainforest.

I could see the tension leaving Whitaker's body with one, great exhalation. Eric started laughing. I saw people's heads peek over at him from down the trail line, looking at him like he was crazy. The laughter annoyed me. I was still on edge.

"It's not funny," said Lauralie. She didn't enjoy the rainforest any more than me or Whitaker.

"We were paranoid for nothing," said Eric. "What's a Rainforest Raider anyway?"

Yuri frowned. "Jeez. Didn't *any* of you read the station rep—"

An enormous black feline creature sprung from the foliage. Having jumped, it sailed through the air like a boulder from a catapult. Spearing Yuri directly in the chest, the cat knocked him onto his back. I winced as Yuri involuntarily coughed a pocket of air from his diaphragm. I took a step toward him, but the cat jerked its head in my direction and hissed. Growling, it circled Yuri with its lips curled back to reveal white, precision-sharp fangs the size of daggers. It was staking its claim. Face scrunched in fury, shiny dark whiskers fanned out from its mouth, stretching to pointy tips. A strip of thick, black hair stood erect from the Raider's back. A bristling Mohawk trailed down its spine, from its forehead to its tailbone, a feature which distinguished it from the earth-inhabiting jaguar. It was significantly bigger, though, as Shakespeare had previously warned. It was still similar to the jaguar with its melanistic coat—sleek black fur with some barely visible lighter spots, but size-wise it dwarfed the jaguar. It was an utterly fantastic and terrifying creature.

Adrenaline coursed through my veins, yet I couldn't seem to move. My breath caught in my throat.

No one spoke. No one moved. The entire scene was frozen. The silence was eerie.

As Shakespeare declared, fleeing was out of the question anyway. Neither a running head start on ground or refuge among the trees or even water posed an option. The cat was arguably the fastest (and most powerful) feline known to man. The prominence of fast-twitch muscle fibers and sinews that bulged from its monstrous physique only served to confirm one thing: We. Were. Fucked.

Eric took off on a flat sprint down the trail with Sherri in tow. The rest of us remained. Eric's departure caused the cat to jerk its head in his direction momentarily, but it decided that we were more worthy prey. The cat looked like it would sink its teeth into Yuri at any moment.

I'm ashamed to say that Lauralie was the only one of us who even considered distracting the animal to give Yuri any chance for escape. She jumped up and down, yelling at it and waving her arms. "Get! Go away. Get out of here, you fucker!"

But the cat hissed and growled, as if to defend its early-evening meal. Yuri stared up at the beast horrified. Simultaneously wheezing and trying to catch his breath, he slowly scooted away. With every movement, though, the animal jerked and curled its lips further back.

I was terrified for Yuri. I started to speak to Shakespeare in low tones, but I was scared to even make a noise with the cat watching us. "Shakespeare, is there a way to kill it?" I said in the quietest voice possible.

"There's not much that you can do. Your chances of delivering any sort of fatal blow are considerably low, Ensign Brown," said Shakespeare. "Might I remind you also that Rainforest Raiders hunt in packs of three, so should you dispatch this particular feline, you will most likely have to contend with the other two."

Shit.

"And where are the other two?" asked Cox. He tried to sound nonchalant, but his voice shook.

"They should be arriving soon, Commander." Shakespeare delivered the news as though he were announcing guests at a dinner party. I muted Shakespeare. His jovial tone was too much.

"If the other two show up, we're done for sure," said Whitaker.

"Thanks for pointing that out, genius," said Cox.

"We're in a tight line and can't move. How are we going to deal with *three* big-ass cats? They'll pick our asses off one by one," Whitaker continued.

"Shut up, Whitaker," we all said in unison.

Whitaker still had his knife, though. It sparkled in the daylight. He inched his way over to the cat ever so gingerly. One timid step at a time. I held my breath. The cat wasn't watching Whitaker, but I couldn't believe it hadn't heard his movements. One misstep too loud would be fatal, but something had to be done for Yuri's sake. The Raider was crouching over Yuri. It would grab Yuri's leg or arm at any moment and drag him off into the foliage. We'd probably never see him again.

Suddenly, Whitaker leapt onto the cat and plunged his knife into its ribcage. The move gave Yuri enough time to get to his feet. The cat jerked and bucked, throwing Whitaker off its back. It hissed, and yelped, but it was still frighteningly mobile and now . . . pissed off. It bit a chunk out of Whitaker's leg and faced us all down, hissing and growling, deciding which of us was next. Whitaker writhed in pain on the ground, clutching his thigh. The cat snarled some more, pacing back and forth. I wandered why it waited.

Then, to my horror, two more Rainforest Raiders emerged from the brush with slow, menacing movements. One was just slightly smaller than the one who'd attacked Whitaker.

Well there's a silver lining.

I suspected this was a cub. Even as a cub, the cat was still much bigger than its earth-bound counterpart. Its lips curled back upon seeing its injured mother. The other cat was the same height and length as the first but much thicker in girth. A male, perhaps? The father? *Who cares. Just get through this.* Even if we survived the first two, the male looked like it could unleash a whirlwind of shit.

The creatures all crouched low, positioning for more kills. They advanced with deliberately slow, controlled predatory movements. They had a plan. Sinister and brutal. In this moment I realized that being scared was useless. The icy fear which immobilized me dissolved into momentary clarity. I slowly reached forward and helped Whitaker to his feet. He was in a lot of pain. He cried out briefly from being lifted up, but I shushed him. I didn't want to antagonize the cats further.

"Back away," whispered Yuri. Lauralie refused. So did I. I wouldn't leave. Couldn't, anyway. I was sandwiched. Lauralie to my right. Cox to my left. Behind was thick foliage. The thought of escape fell away like mist. A peek, and I couldn't bring myself to look at Whitaker's leg anymore, or what was left of it. *Was that bone I saw?*

My mind, a newsreel set to turbo speed, flashed with military-isms. *One team, one fight—United we land, divided we fall—Never leave a man behind—The only easy day was yesterday.* Ridiculous, cheesy sayings before. Relevant sayings now. We'd either survive or die together.

"Maybe we can distract them," whispered Lauralie. Why did she whisper? They could hear us. Whisper or no whisper. Their relentless gaze trained completely on us.

"No. Don't move." Yuri's arm blocked Lauralie to prevent further movement.

Moments ticked by like a metronome in slow motion. Cox's ragged breath to my left. Lauralie's short, perforated breaths to my right. Whitaker's hand trembled as he clutched his blood-soaked thigh.

"I said don't move!" Yuri barked just above a whisper.

Whitaker shifted one hand back to his side. *Stop moving, goddamit!*

Agitated, the cats moved closer. One advanced in front of another. Step by step. Like some ritualistic dance. A prayer before eating. They were an arm's length away. We stood forever. Waiting. Dreading.

They were unsure of us, but it did nothing to dissuade their intended assault. Even the cat with Whitaker's knife still stuck in its ribcage still seemed intent on its assault. It was notably sluggish, though (sluggish by cat standards; wicked fast by human standards). The other cats seemed to notice, too, which is why I think they hadn't pounced on us yet. Then the lead cat crouched down low. The other two followed suit with their hindquarters in the air. The cat in front was shifting its butt from side to side, marching its paws gently in place, ready to leap. Its fluorescent yellow eyes dilated into large black orbs. Just as it was about to launch, I heard a momentary high-pitched whizzing sound. Then I felt a quick breeze of something small and tiny that zipped by my cheek, missing me by just millimeters. It was so swift that a tuft of my hair lifted as it whizzed by me. Before I had time to react or even realize what it was, the front cat, the largest, fell instantly to the ground. A thin arrow-like blue dart stuck from its neck. Then I heard two more whizzing sounds and the other two cats fell immediately. Before I could process what had happened, several Biotech security guards emerged from the foliage from various directions.

33

LaSalle stepped into view. A long rifle was propped on his hip. He looked at everyone before his eyes rested on me. "Are you okay?"

"You almost hit me. I could feel the round pass by my face." I was annoyed but relieved.

"I didn't almost hit you. I was a sniper. I know what I'm doing."

"Whatever," I said. I was mad. I didn't like him taking chances like that, but I didn't want to appear ungrateful. He did save my life, after all.

"No surprise there," said Cox. "Typical LaSalle, gambling with other peoples' lives."

Everyone fell into an awkward silence. This wasn't the first time Cox took an opportunity to publicly shame LaSalle.

"In the future, make loud noises. They don't like it."

"Well, that essential bit of information should've been included in the station brief," said Cox as he glared at LaSalle.

LaSalle ignored Cox and approached Yuri. "What exactly did you do to piss them off in the first place?"

"Nothing," Yuri said.

"What about that beef jerky I saw you put in your pocket earlier?" Lauralie asked.

Yuri gave her a look. She clamped her mouth shut.

"You had food in your pocket?"

"No," said Yuri. "Well—yeah—but it's sealed."

"You really think they—or any other of the thousand plus creatures on station—wouldn't sniff that out?" said LaSalle.

Yuri fell silent. He was more embarrassed than anything. He walked away, and Lauralie followed. After a few moments, they were in a heated discussion.

By this point, Chief Martinez and Petty Officer Mackie had joined the group, having seen Eric and Sherri running down the trail earlier yelling something about a large cat. Unlike everyone who'd run from the problem, she'd come down the trail to help. I jerked my head in Whitaker's direction. His face was now pale. "He's hurt. The Raider took a chunk from his leg."

LaSalle stepped closer to have a look, but Chief Martinez shoved him aside and leaned in to examine the leg. She motioned to Petty Officer Mackie for a first aid kit. She poked and prodded Whitaker. He yelped. Finally, she stood up. "We need to open up a medical pod."

"We don't have one," said Yuri, walking back to the group. "We had to travel light."

"You're the trip commander. You should've planned for these contingencies," said Cox. Yuri stiffened at Cox's comment.

"The wound needs to be cleaned, and the muscle tissue needs to be regenerated as soon as possible," said Chief Martinez. She managed a secret wink in my direction. "We don't know what kind of alien bacteria is present here. He could mutate at any second."

"Turn into something? What does that mean?" Whitaker squealed. His eyes raced between Yuri, Martinez and Mackie, who were all examining the leg. He tried to stand back up but fell back down. He turned to me. "What does she mean by that?"

I glanced at Chief Martinez and Petty Officer Mackie, who were both wearing devilish grins. I bit my lip, trying to hold back a giggle. "Stop messing with him, Chief."

"I'm serious," she grunted, but there were hints of a smile on her face. "The Raider's teeth went deep, but it just missed the femoral artery. You're one lucky son of a bitch. You'll have a nasty scar, but you'll be fine."

"Are you sure?" Whitaker asked.

"Yeah, I'm sure," she said. "I was an ER nurse before I joined the Navy. I know what I'm talking about."

"If I lose this leg, I'll die." Whitaker shifted and winced at the same time. "What . . . what if I become something?"

"That's rich," snorted Yuri, shaking his head and chuckling. He walked away from the group again. "I swear you guys are something else . . ."

Whitaker raised up and then clutched his leg from the pain of it. "Well, Chief said that the bacteria could—"

Chief Martinez rolled her eyes.

Petty Officer Mackie decided to take pity on him. "You're not gonna lose the leg. It'll hurt like hell during regen, but you're not gonna lose it. And you won't turn into anything. Relax."

Mackie handed Martinez a black tube from the first aid kit. She powered it on and ran a blue light across Whitaker's leg as he recounted all of what happened to LaSalle. The bleeding stopped. Whitaker yelped. "That hurts."

"Be still or it'll hurt even more. I'm sterilizing it. You don't want to turn into the boogey man, do you? Now, man up, while I finish this."

Whitaker clamped his mouth shut. His face turned red as Chief Martinez ran the blue light across his leg again. He grunted through clenched teeth but kept his leg still.

"Attaboy."

LaSalle turned curiously to Eric and Sherri. "Where were you guys in all of this?"

Eric turned red. "We went to get help, of course. Why do you think Chief Martinez is here?"

Sherri looked at the ground.

Coward. But who was I to talk?

"Where the hell were *you?*" I looked at LaSalle, my glance accusatory. "You disappeared and left us without protection."

One of the Biotech security guards stepped in. "We didn't leave you alone, ma'am. We were tracking the cats for some time. We crowded them into a particular spot that would give us a strategic advantage."

LaSalle gave the mouthy guard a dark look. The guard looked away and put his head down.

"You used us for bait," Cox said, directing his accusation at LaSalle.

"We weren't using you for bait. We were—"

"Oh, please. We were bait. Just own up to it," I interjected.

"Jesus, Mel," Sherri said. "They saved us. How can you be so ungrate—"

"You mean they saved *us,*" I said, gesturing to myself and the others for emphasis. "You were busy hightailing it down the trail with your new boyfriend. So stay out of this, bitch."

There was a collective gasp, then awkward silence.

Sherri flinched, her eyes the size of frisbees before narrowing. *Yeah. It's on. Bring it.*

Her face colored to a deep shade of scarlet. She sized me up for a moment before walking away.

Whitaker's eyes widened. Chief Martinez snickered. Petty Officer Mackie bit his lip. LaSalle walked over to the cat that Whitaker stabbed and examined the blade jutting from the Raider's rib cage. Then he stood up and walked back over to Whitaker. "You've got some balls, kid. Just the kind of thing we look for in the teams. You thought about what you're going to service select?"

"No, sir," Whitaker said. "I hadn't really given it much thought. Maybe aviation or something."

"Well, you'd make a decent SEAL operator, I think. But you need a better blade than that." LaSalle pulled a substantially larger knife from his suit. The knife was all black with a serrated edge and a nylon sheath. He placed the handle in Whitaker's hand and nodded. "Here. I don't need it, but don't tell anyone I let you have it."

I looked over at Whitaker. For the amount of pain he was in, his face lit up like a parade of fireworks on the 4th of July. Even some of the color in his complexion was coming back.

Chief Martinez administered a cartridge injection to Whitaker's leg and then stood up. "We need to get moving. I gave him a pain killer, and this dressing will hold until we get to port, but he really needs a medi-pod as soon as possible. That wound is deep, to the bone."

"C'mon," said LaSalle. "Let's get to the river."

"What about those damn things?" Lauralie asked, pointing at the three immobile cats on the ground. "Looks like you only tranquilized them. Won't they wake up and sneak up on us later?"

"No. I'm transmitting a message to get one of the veterinarians out here. They're going to have to remove the blade from that cat. The other two will sleep for a couple of hours, but we'll be long gone by then," LaSalle said. "Besides, we're in their territory. Not the other way around. Now let's go."

34

The Biotech security guards gathered everyone and moved us out with amazing speed and efficiency. I never thought they'd track down all thirty-two of our party, even with tracking devices embedded within our jumpsuits. They even managed to find one of the civilians (who had seen a Raider from afar and took off before anyone knew what was going on) hiding in a tree.

We continued on down the trail—albeit visibly shaken—toward the river. The river was only a few minutes away at this point.

For the remainder of the hike everyone was quiet. The event with the cats was an eye-opener, proof that the business of marching through the rainforest was serious.

Once we stepped from the trail out of the rainforest tree line, we stood before a massive lake, Lake Kilo. Lake Kilo, a Biotech reservoir, was fed by the Kasim River. Its basin covered roughly 997 square miles and its end, closest to the tree line, is where the two water taxis patiently awaited us.

After we stepped from the tree line of the rainforest, droplets of water fell tentatively and then matured into a ruthless downpour.

Everyone moved faster. Lake Kilo was within view, and everyone was eager to get beneath the shelter of the water taxis.

Once we were about halfway between the tree line and the lake, standing on an open plain, I had a niggling feeling. Something said, *look back*. And I did.

To my dismay I saw the silhouette of a man. At first I thought it was a Biotech guard doing one last sweep of the forest. But then I noticed that this was no security guard. All of the Biotech guards were clean shaven and tightly groomed, like military men. Even LaSalle, who kept his hair unruly long in comparison to his men, wore his hair no longer than the nape of his neck. But this silhouette revealed long hair, past the shoulders. Whoever it was, he stood eerily still. Watching. Waiting.

"What're you looking at?" Cox was at my side.

I turned and pointed. "There's someone in the tree line."

But the man was gone. Cox looked at me curiously.

"I swear I saw someone standing there watching us," I said.

LaSalle walked up. "Is everything okay?" he asked.

"She thinks she saw someone," Cox said. He turned to LaSalle. "I thought you found everyone."

"We did," said LaSalle. He turned to me. "What exactly did you see?"

"I saw a man standing just inside the tree line watching us," I said. "He had really long hair. That's all I could really see of him."

"Long hair?" Cox said snorting. "It could've been a woman."

"No. It was definitely a man."

"Could've been a burly woman," he said.

"No. I'm 100 percent certain it was a man."

"It's probably some dumb scientist on a nature walk," said Cox, walking away. He wasn't enjoying the torrential downpour. "You're just a bit on edge from the Raider attack."

LaSalle said nothing. Cox shrugged and moved quickly to catch up with the rest of our party who were now rushing to board the water taxis.

Lightning sizzled in the sky, and thunder tore through the air. The rain was falling in blankets. LaSalle grabbed my elbow lightly, pushing me along. There was a quiet urgency to the push. Not a rushed movement but not a languid one, either.

"C'mon," he said, taking one last look over his shoulder. "We need to get out of this crappy weather. We've wasted enough time here."

I hoped Cox was right, though. Maybe I should've read all 439 threats on Shakespeare's list or let him ramble on about dangerous humans?

35

Two water taxis sat patiently on the river. Both could accommodate up to twenty people and were powered by one large ionic thruster located in the hull of the boat. They were considerably fast and operated similarly to a hydroplane, able to skim the surface of the river at speeds of 150 knots plus. I was grateful to see modern boats on the station waiting for us, rather than something antiquated like a rowboat or a raft. After the hike through the rainforest, I assumed we'd be riding in something outdated. The boats themselves had a typical straight stern and gunwales that rounded as they came together at the bow. Each boat had a canopy which conveniently shielded us from the rain and the stifling heat of the sun once the lightning ceased.

I stepped onto the taxi and felt my shoulders loosen. I'd been tense without even knowing it. I noticed that everyone else seemed relaxed now that we were safely aboard. We were out of the rainforest. It was then that I finally noticed how beautiful and serene our surroundings were. The river was wide and extended far into the distance. The sheer size made it hard to believe that it was manmade. To an untrained observer, it appeared to be a natural resource, but a seasoned engineer would notice the artificial construction of wildlife habitats and reed beds as well as neat rows of young trees planted along the banks of the river.

I looked over at Whitaker, who still donned a sloppy grin. I wondered if LaSalle knew what impact he made with the simple gesture of giving Whitaker his knife.

LaSalle.

The thought of him gave me both tingles and rage. I was still angry at him for shooting the tranquilizer dart so close to my head and using us as bait. What if I'd moved just a centimeter? It probably wouldn't have killed me, but still. Cox even said: *Typical LaSalle, putting other peoples' lives at risk.* There was more to that comment. There was history between LaSalle and Cox, and I planned to find out what it was. But wasn't Cox somewhat right? LaSalle did use us as bait. I'd have to speak with Cox.

I watched LaSalle curiously. He was so hard to read. There was so much hidden beneath his polished appearance. At first meeting, he seemed so put together. Yet as I spent more time with him, I started to see the cracks. Could he be trusted? Why was he so secretive? At times I even noticed despondency, or what it guilt? *Yes. That's it. Guilt. He feels guilty about something, but what is it?* LaSalle had his fair share of emotional bumps and bruises.

As if sensing my gaze, he looked over at me and smiled. The combination of his five o' clock shadow and illuminating grin along with those piercing eyes made my heart skip a little. I didn't want to smile back, but I couldn't deny the intense attraction. I reluctantly returned the gesture, and then I looked down, somewhat embarrassed. I was never one to just stare at someone for extended periods of time. I looked up again. He was still watching me, smiling. His gaze was predatory. It excited me and made me wary all at once.

I looked away in another direction, trying to avoid the silent communication from LaSalle. My gaze fell unexpectedly on Cox, who was watching me too. Had he seen the silent exchange between myself and LaSalle? Blood rushed to my face. Cox's expression was a stony mask. Something bothered him. The outline of his jaw bulged from clenched teeth. I wondered what had him so irritated this time. Maybe the fact that I was being nice to LaSalle when I shouldn't be? What did he care what I thought of LaSalle, anyway? Finally, I looked away from him, too and made my way over to Whitaker, who was getting an inordinate amount of attention from Yuri and Chief Martinez.

I supposed Yuri felt guilty about having the beef jerky which attracted the Raiders' attack.

Chief Martinez and Petty Officer Mackie re-attended Whitaker's wound. Whitaker was unleashing curse words like a tried and true, seasoned Sailor, bitching that she kept prodding the disturbed area. A few people stood over his leg (Eric and Sherri included), staring in morbid fascination at the ghastly sight. Gleaming white bone peeked from beneath angry, red flesh.

"That shit looks painful," Eric said. "Does it hurt that much?"

"Not as much as it did, but it still hurts a lot," said Whitaker tightly. His tone was respectful but detached. He really just wanted to tell Eric to go away.

I laughed. Whitaker reminded me a lot of myself as a mid-shipman. I poked him in the ribcage. "Looks like you've earned yourself some downtime at the post after all."

I glared at Yuri, daring him to challenge me on the matter. Whitaker smiled and peered sheepishly at Yuri.

"Chief Martinez will look after you, and Petty Officer Mackie will stay with me. Chief, there are a few things I need you to pick up for me at the port."

Chief wasn't one to show a ton of emotion, but I sensed she was relieved to get to go with Whitaker to the port.

Yuri pointed and shook his finger at Whitaker. "Don't get used to this, sport. Biotech has the best, most technologically advanced medical care the universe has to offer. They should have your leg fixed up and somewhat functional in under an hour. You'll be able to walk. I plan to put your ass to work."

Whitaker's shoulders slumped a little, but he still had a permanent grin fixed on his face.

"You two make sure that you look out for each other, and you use the buddy system," said Yuri, motioning to Martinez and Whitaker. "These ports can be dangerous. I'm sure you've been informed that most of the shops, recreational establishments and facilities are run by ex-cons and other people with colorful pasts. Even the research lab itself is run and maintained by people who otherwise would not be able to get employment back home."

"I'd have thought that with all of the classified and delicate research being done, Biotech would be picky about who had access to their facilities," said Martinez.

"Well, they are, but cheap labor is cheap labor. Biotech is still a corporation and a conglomerate of a bank. Money is always a priority."

"The buddy system? No offense, sir, but I don't need a chaperone," Whitaker muttered.

"People go missing all the time there. Where do you think human traffickers get their cargo? Contrary to popular belief, much of the trafficking occurs between outlying stations and new colonies. And they don't just traffic women."

Whitaker's face fell. Martinez gave him a saucy look. "I guess the midshipman *is* kind of pretty, sir."

"I can handle myself. If anyone is in danger of being kidnapped, it's you." Whitaker said, glaring at Martinez.

Yuri snorted. "If I had to place bets on who handles themself better, I'd bet on Martinez."

Whitaker sank into a mild pout.

"Yeah, I'd bet on Martinez too," said Cox, who just walked up. One hand brushed the small of my back as he walked back.

What the hell was that?

"Excuse me," he said rather politely. I turned to him, but he was already focused on Whitaker, who was poking the area of his wound.

"Doesn't it hurt when you do that?" he asked.

Whitaker stood up suddenly, at attention. "Yes, sir."

"Relax," Cox said, gesturing impatiently for him to sit down. "Sit down and rest your leg."

Whitaker slowly lowered himself down, watching Cox warily.

"I can't seem to stop playing with it," said Whitaker. "I guess I just want to see how much it really hurts with the painkiller having set in."

"Well, how much does it hurt?"

"A shitload, sir."

"Is that more or less than a fuckload?" Cox asked. His face was serious, but his tone was playful.

Whitaker paused, surprised, but then answered. "Well, a shitload is definitely less than a fuckload, so I'll change my answer and say that it hurts a fuckload, sir."

Cox smirked and simply nodded. "Okay, well make sure you get a fuckload more painkillers when we get to the port—the good stuff. Don't try to be all tough. I think we've seen enough of that from you today, and look where it's gotten you."

He turned to leave but not before glancing at me. I wanted badly to ask him about his history with LaSalle, but I decided against it. Something told me that I should wait until we were alone.

"Need something?" he asked.

I just shook my head.

He shrugged and walked away.

36

The trip to the station post was seamless. The water taxis glided along the water with little disturbance considering the number of rapids we encountered. The ride calmed everyone's nerves. As we neared the port, there was a nervous energy. People were shaken over thoughts of the Rainforest Raiders, but they were eager to share the story with their friends at the port. The prospect of fun, food, and recreation added to their excitement and masked their underlying trepidations regarding the surrounding wilderness.

I was jealous.

If given the opportunity to rest at the post, I would've immediately booked a massage, enjoyed a quiet dinner (I'd heard the Mexican Cantina was the best in the interplanetary sector) and then a movie.

Unfortunately, my fate was to remain on the water taxi and head straight for another stretch of rainforest.

Pulling up to Port Juliette was like pulling up to a Vegas-like resort: It visibly held the promise of over-indulgence and debauchery. Port Juliette was accessed by Lake Juliette, a vast reservoir of clear blue, edged in a vibrant color palette of exotic flowers. The flowers and plant life along the lake were so bright that they looked fake.

They were real enough, thanks to Biotech's cleverly meticulous engineering. At the edge of Lake Juliette, the city-like port sat in front of Biotech's sprawling research facility. The city, a collection of odd, gaudy overly ornate structures, offered recreation, leisure, food and drink for its station visitors. It reminded me of the traditional carnivals I visited as a child, a garish overlay of the exotic and mysterious.

People walked along the city streets in bright Biotech-issued jumpsuits: the employees in bright red and the researchers in pearl-white. The others, like many of those in our party—engineers, water treatment technicians, construction workers, architects and others—wore blue. The human services consultants wore gray. Those who traveled along Juliette drove two-wheeled, two-man vehicles shaped like oblong bubbles. They cruised along the glossy concrete of Juliette's streets in uniform lines, respectfully following the glowing blue perforated lines along the car lanes.

Biotech's actual research facilities were located at the rear of the port, behind the gaudy buildings of Port Juliette. Large white, bleach-scrubbed buildings with geometrically sharp edges and structurally curved lines sat in the background like disapproving chaperones. The contrast between Biotech's sleek, pristine research facilities and Port Juliette's gaudy buildings seemed almost comical.

Upon seeing Port Juliette in person, I had the notion that Biotech was not an entirely ethical company. There were just too many signs supporting my theory, and most of those signs began with the director of security and operations for Biotech. Gerard LaSalle had negative history with both Rivera and Cox. He was secretive, and I didn't like his security guards. Each and every one of them, while they were supposed to make us feel safe, made me feel exactly the opposite. They came across more like hired mercenaries who'd take out their own mothers for the right paycheck. The contrast of the buildings of Port Juliette to Biotech's research facilities spoke volumes. The distinction made Biotech appear to be an opportunistic, corporate banking engine that exploited ex-cons for cheap labor, while Port Juliette looked like a haven for ex-cons prepared to tolerate questionable business practices in order to avoid undignified employment circumstances and pitifully low wages back home.

The water was clean, though. Biotech had taken pains to ensure the water in Lake Kilo and Lake Juliette, as well as the river, which connected the two lakes, remained a clean and clear, crystalline blue. The composite view of the bright blue lake, the twinkling lights of the port and the pristine white research facilities in the background gave the post the appearance of a Japanese anime setting.

37

s the taxi ferried toward the dock, envy clawed at me. I watched as people lined up to exit the boats. I had a momentary glimmer of hope when Yuri's wrist device lit up. I saw Lieutenant Rivera's face pop onto the screen.

"What's up, L.T.?" said Yuri, hunched over his wrist device. He turned his back to the rest of us.

Rivera ran his fingers through his hair. "Some more of Senior Chief's body was found."

"Really. Where?" I asked.

"Well, there wasn't much of it. Just enough to get a forensics ID. There was some human tissue residue from his head on the fantail. And someone found an ear in one of the Marine berthing spaces. The rest we think has been offloaded via an exit chamber."

I sucked in my breath. This proved that Senior Chief had been murdered onboard. I waited, expecting Rivera to tell us that we could come back. That we could take half a day at the port and then head back on the *Pegasus*.

"So, I'm assuming the commodore wants us to make preparations to return as soon as possible." Even Yuri seemed hopeful.

"Uh—negative," said Rivera. "Actually, he expects you to proceed as planned. That's why I called."

"*What?*" Yuri's face went dark. His voice rose. People who were otherwise preoccupied began to stare.

"He wants to tie up loose ends and make sure we've covered all of our bases."

Yuri let out a sigh. He shook his head in exasperation, but he lowered his voice. "This is total bull—"

"I know. I know," said Rivera. He looked over his shoulder to make sure no one heard. "It doesn't make sense. I tried to change his mind, but he about ripped *my* head off."

"Listen. I gotta go. There's a lot to do." Yuri's tone was curt.

Rivera felt sorry for us all. "No problem, sir. Let me know if you need anything."

Yuri was livid. He switched off his screen. His hands were on his hips, and his chest was rose and fell in a slow, steady rhythm. He took deep breaths in order to calm himself. Lauralie walked up to him and put her hand on his arm. "So are we going back to the ship?"

"No." He moved away from her.

"Do you want me to go with you?" She moved toward him again.

This time he stayed, with her hand on his arm again. I resolved in that moment that she really cared for Yuri, that her affections weren't just a ploy to get more of his business He looked at her. There was tenderness in his eyes. "I wish, but you know you can't. "

"Well just be safe, okay?"

"I'll be back before you know it." He winked at her, but his tone was melancholy.

I pretended like I hadn't witnessed the exchange, but I didn't hide the fact that I'd overheard his conversation with Rivera.

"So we're not going back, are we?"

"No," he said. "And I don't really want to hear it, Mel. Let's just get this over with."

Any hope I had of returning was shattered. I was so bummed, I didn't have the motivation to argue with Yuri, even if I'd wanted to. Besides, there was nothing to say. He was just following orders, and I knew that the commodore wouldn't be swayed. In fact, I was starting to think the commodore had some sort of agenda in insisting on us being there. I wanted to either throw something or ball up on the taxi deck and cry my eyeballs out. The constriction in my chest was an odd feeling of both rage and despair. I could tell that Yuri felt the same.

∿

Finally, the taxi brushed up to the side of the dock. The launch party began to file off, one by one. Yuri and Lauralie stole longing glances at each other. They were saying goodbye with their eyes. Whitaker limped between them like a madman towards the gangplank. Chief Martinez had to slow him down and tell him to wait for someone to assist him. After Lauralie was done saying her goodbyes to Yuri, she slipped her head beneath Whitaker's armpit and helped him hop along. For a moment, Yuri's face was blanketed with jealousy, but then Lauralie laughed openly at him, as though he was a silly-behaved child. Her response lightened his mood, and ultimately he composed himself. I wondered what their arrangement was. I wondered how he dealt with the fact that her business was, in fact, to flirt with other men and eventually sleep with them. I imagined not too well. Their interactions were odd, but no one else seemed to notice but me. Even Whitaker, who was perplexed at the strange behavior, didn't understand the significance of Lauralie's amusement. He was too concerned with his future plans on post.

It took roughly fifteen minutes for the remainder of people to disembark the water taxis. Lauralie waved to me from the pier and gave me a quick nod and a wink, as if to say: Don't sweat it. Somehow that made me feel better despite my growing unease.

Our party was now cut in half, to include: myself, Yuri, LaSalle, Cox, Petty Officer Mackie, Eric, Sherri, two of my gunner's mates, three of Eric's Marines and six of LaSalle's Biotech guards and a handful of civilian contractors.

One last wave, and we were headed to the mines.

38

An outlet from Lake Juliette came in the form of a swift, roaring river that we would use to travel by. The river was wide and deep at this point. We would follow it another hour before it turned shallow where the river's bedrock jutted up, and travel by water taxi was virtually impossible. Then we would hike. Again. We would be at the waterfalls in a few hours.

After about a half hour of transit along the river, I noticed the sky darken a touch. We would hit the waterfalls at sunset by my estimation. Since we were behind schedule, I wondered what Yuri's plans were once it turned dark. As we glided along, we reached a fork in the river. The right fork veered off into a totally different direction, north, deep into the rainforest where the region was unexplored. As per the station brief, it forked into the direction of another waterfall, Chintundu, but we were going to Tengelei. The taxi spun to the left and hugged the left bank where the tree line was less dense. From the distance, I could see a worn dirt path start to form just inside the tree line that paralleled the river. It wasn't very wide, but farther downstream it opened wider. Finally, we reached a round opening in the river. The point on the map was called Lake India, but it was more like a pool created by the dip in bedrock and series of surrounding rock and riverbank.

At this point, the path along the river was well worn and much wider, enough for two people to stand abreast of each other. The walk here was peaceful. The scenery was gorgeous and the terrain simple, but there was still a palpable tension in the air. Were other people thinking about the Raiders too? Their keen sense of smell. Thick mucous like drool, dripping from their large white fangs. Their size and speed. Recollections of all those things were enough to make my hands tremble and my palms sweat.

LaSalle reassured the group, though. He reminded us that the Raiders didn't like to be in or near water. They obtained much of their drinking water from collected pools of rainwater amongst the leaves, only going to the river when absolutely necessary, like during the dry season. It had rained just today, so he assured us we should be okay.

I didn't feel reassured. Walking along the river greatly minimized the chance for unseen attacks, but it didn't guarantee a thing.

As we ambled along the dirt path, I noticed that this rainforest was even more interesting than the first. The adjacent foliage here was thicker, but the trail we were following was clearly defined. Eventually, the vegetation opened up into a canopy, and we could've walked along the trail with ten people abreast. This would make it much easier for LaSalle's bodyguards to provide security, and it would preclude the need for a point person or LaChetes to cut down any thick foliage. Assuming they decided to forgo cloaking mode, I might get to see some of them patrol in the open, which made me feel less antsy. Something about special forces traipsing about the rainforest unseen freaked me out, even if their presence was for my own safety.

I spotted all sorts of odd creatures in this rainforest. Birds and butterflies of every known color and pattern design imaginable. I even saw what was called a "Dalmatian" bird, all white with black polka dots. There were plenty of reptiles too. I kept my distance from them, but they were neat looking. I saw a pink snake with a black stripe that extended down its back. I saw another snake some distance away, about 50 meters away. Our movements along the forest trail had riled it; it raised up to a shocking height. My impulse was to shout, to alert the others, but somehow I knew that that would be its call to strike. Its body was all white. The sides of its neck flared out like an angry king cobra. It swayed side to side as though it was being charmed. A set of rigid, red wings extended out from its back. *Can that thing fly?* I hoped not. I felt a fresh surge of adrenaline. We were in a different world, and I could think of nothing else than my desire to go home, all the way home.

I stepped gingerly along the path, hoping my quieted movements would pacify the pissed-off snake. As we passed along, I kept my eye on it. I'd almost stepped on a blue frog with red zebra stripes in my efforts to keep an eye on the snake but managed to sidestep it. Startled, it hopped away. Frightened that my sudden movement had antagonized the snake to lift off into the air, I looked back to where it had been, but it was gone.

I shuddered. *Where was that damn thing?* I desperately hoped that it wasn't slithering its way toward us.

"Everything okay?" Cox was right beside me. He must've seen me jump out of the way of the blue frog.

"Yeah," I said, wiping my forehead with the back of my hand. There was no sweat there. It was just a nervous habit. "I almost stepped on a frog."

"What color was it?"

"Blue with red zebra stripes."

"They're harmless. In fact, the resin on their skin can be used for healing wounds, but they're very hard to catch. Stay away from the red ones with the tiny black star-dots, though. Those ones are poisonous ones."

"Seriously?"

"Seriously. Touch one with even just your pinky," he said, "and your heart stops instantly."

"Oh my goodness. Well, what about the snakes out here?"

"What about them?"

"Are they poisonous?"

"Some are. Some aren't. But they all bite. Why—did you see something?"

"I saw two. A pink one with a black stripe down its back and a white one with wings.

"The pink one is harmless. The white one—were its wings red on the inside?"

"Yes."

"Where did you see it?"

"About 100 meters back."

Cox took a deep breath and let out a gust of air. "Phew. Shit. That could've been ugly."

My nerves danced a little, but I kept my tone even. "Why?"

"Because it could've taken a lot of us out before we even knew what was going on.

"Oh God."

"Yeah. *Oh God* is right. They're deadly. Good news is they're extremely rare, so you probably won't see another one ever again."

"Jesus, I hope so. Can they fly?" I was hoping he'd say *no* and tell me that the wings were just for show.

"Yes," he said.

Shit.

"They move fast, too, and their bite is fatal. Was it swaying back and forth?"

"Yes, and it stretched up off the ground about a good six and a half feet with its wings raised. It looked angry."

"If it was raised up like that, then it was indeed angry. We must've unknowingly disturbed its nest. Were the wings all the way up?"

"Almost. They jutted straight back but not quite fully up. Its neck was spread, though."

"You mean its 'hood.' When its hood is spread like that, it's ready to strike. When its wings are raised fully up, it's about to take off. We're lucky it didn't lift off the ground."

"No way."

"Way. It would've gotten five or six of us before we'd even thought to kill it. Let me know right away if you see another one."

"Uh—yeah. I promise I'll be the one screaming, so you'll know right away. I should probably go tell LaSalle about it. That thing sounds pretty lethal."

Cox's face hardened. "It is lethal, but there's no point telling LaSalle. I doubt he even knows what it is."

"Well, obviously it's a snake."

"It's not just any snake. It's called a Snow Dragon. They're an endangered species. You're actually kind of lucky."

"Why do you say that?"

"Because they're supposed to bring good luck to whoever sees one. At least that's what Dr. Tengelei's book said. I'm not sure how he came up with that, though. I didn't take Dr. Tengelei for a superstitious man."

"I still think we should let LaSalle know."

Cox gritted his teeth. "He wouldn't know what to do with it."

"Still, we aught to—"

"Whatever. Suit yourself." He sauntered off. Despite his crankiness, I decided to keep up. I didn't want to be out here alone. In fact, I was scared in earnest. I made sure to keep my eyes open for red frogs and white snakes. Shakespeare never mentioned those, but of course I didn't go through his entire list of fatal threats to humans.

It then occurred to me that Shakespeare had been off since the cat attack. I called for him. In seconds, his voice emerged.

"Miss Brown. What a pleasant surprise."

"Surprise?"

"Well, it's just that your odds for survival during the Rainforest Raider attack were less than promising."

"That's great."

"The moments just before the attack, I calculated a 15.3 percent chance of survival. Of course, those odds were greatly increased once I interfaced the Biotech mainframe and notified Dr. LaSalle of the impending danger. Might I surmise that he was able to intercept the felines before you were harmed?"

"Yes, Shakespeare, you surmised correctly, but Whitaker was badly injured."

"That's unfortunate." Shakespeare's reply sounded perfunctory rather than genuine. Another thing I couldn't stand about A.I. Their talk was just so—scripted.

"Mr. LaSalle mentioned that he'd been tracking the cats the entire time," I said.

"Well, that's not entirely untrue. He had an estimation of where they might be, but he was unable to pinpoint their exact location until I provided him with your specific coordinates and news of their impending attack."

I had to give it to Shakespeare. As much as I wasn't totally sold on him, he did continue to work on my behalf. I resolved to be more grateful. Heather's efforts were a great a benefit. How many other officers had access to their own A.I. steward?

⋙

As we hiked, I kept my eyes trained straight ahead. I didn't want to see any more odd creatures or know any more about them. I wanted to remain blissfully ignorant as to what was lurking out there. I told Shakespeare not to tell me anything else about the indigenous life unless I absolutely needed to know. Somehow, I'd convinced myself that the less I knew, the less I'd be exposed.

Cox sensed my nervousness and distracted me for a bit. He bent over and reached his hand into a hollowed out log. I asked him what he was doing—I was a firm believer of not touching anything you didn't know about. Then he pulled out a black beetle with a yellow triangle on its back.

"Watch this," he said. He placed the beetle in his hand and pressed gently on the yellow triangle. Then he closed his hand over the bug and shoved his fist deep into his backpack.

The backpack lit up as if he'd turned on a flashlight. I gasped. A wide grin spread across my face.

"Pretty handy, huh?" He looked at me, pleased with my delight.

"That's amazing," I said. "It's like your own little personal flashlight."

"Yeah."

"How is that even possible?"

Shakespeare couldn't help himself. He was a talking encyclopedia. "When Mr. Cox pressed the beetle's triangle, the insect experienced stress, causing it to release a chemical luciferin and an enzyme called luciferase. The luciferin reacts with the oxygen stores in their body which causes the bioluminescence, and the luciferase speeds up the reaction."

"But then if you're stuck in the dark, how do you find one?" I asked.

Cox shrugged. "You can usually find them hiding inside of hollow logs and tree trunks—basically anywhere where there's damp wood. Or you listen for its call. Five short 'clucking' sounds. Here," he said, grabbing my elbow gently and motioning for me to lean in. "Put your ear close. You can hear it. It clucks constantly. Once you know the sound, it's easy to hear."

He pulled his hands back out of the backpack which were still cupping the beetle and let me lean in close. It sounded like a woodpecker drumming a hole in a tree: *Tap, tap, tap.*

"Only thing is," he said, "it'll shut its light off automatically after about ten minutes, and you generally can't get it to turn its light back on for another hour or so."

"Actually, sixty-two minutes and three seconds to be exact," said Shakespeare.

"That's so cool. How do you know all of this?" I asked Cox.

Cox shrugged. "I don't know. I guess I was just fascinated with all this stuff when I was a kid. As with all stations, when one is first discovered, there are people to study, examine, document and catalog all the organisms and life forms present. Dr. Tengelei published a book just a year after he discovered this station. It was one of the better books."

"Are you referring to *One Hundred Great Scientific Discoveries of Mining Station #0517212?*" Shakespeare asked.

"Uh—yeah." Shakespeare's question caught Cox off guard.

"A most excellent reference, Commander. It is quite comprehensive. Dr. Tengelei was most diligent about keeping track of every aspect of his team's discoveries, including digital images and audio files. However, he did not delve so thoroughly into the biochemical processes as to name specific enzymes."

Cox looked at me. "Does he always interrupt like that?"

"All the time. It's annoying."

"Why don't you shut him off?"

"I do sometimes. But don't change the subject." I didn't mean to sound so playful. "It sounds like you know more about this stuff than you're letting on."

"I've always just had a passion for reading about anything having to do with natural science." Cox looked away as he said this. "I thought I was going to be a zoologist or an entomologist one day. Turns out I became a naval officer."

I just looked at him. He blushed. Cox was full of surprises. When I'd first met him, I dreaded him. His arrogance. His cynicism.

All too much, but now . . . now, I saw a different side to him. I'd
been wrong. He wasn't arrogant. He was proud—the confidence that
comes from having gained a lifetime of knowledge. His cynicism
was just a product of frustration—of having to constantly report
to and reason with incompetent people. I realized that it must be
difficult to constantly be around people who weren't as smart as
him. He knew so much, and I found this to be somewhat irresistible. I looked away once I'd realized that I was openly staring at
him. He watched me watch him. Could he tell that I found him
attractive? *How embarrassing. This was Cox. Cox . . . attractive? What
is happening to me?*

"Well, lucky for us," I said awkwardly. I turned away to continue down the trail.

I could feel him watching me at this point. My steps were brisk.
Hurried. I didn't dare turn back around. He must've thought I was
being rude. I watched my feet as I trudged along.

When I looked up, I spotted LaSalle, of all people, watching
us. More specifically, he watched Cox watch me. I ignored him
as I brushed by. Let him think what he wanted.

LaSalle. Cox.

Total opposites but both attractive in their own ways. Where
LaSalle was tall and muscular, Cox was of medium height and
lean. LaSalle was a golden-haired, blue-eyed Adonis with a sunny
disposition. Cox was a brooding brunette, who was serious and
spoke only when necessary. LaSalle was masculine (in the way that
badasses are), and he was secretive with an air of danger about him.
While he made me feel physically safe, something still told me not
to fully trust him.

Cox, on the other hand, was honest to a fault. He was transparent, with a high level of integrity, and he challenged me to be
better. I trusted him completely. He was masculine, too, but more
in the way that comes from being a southern Kentucky boy. Old-
school charm and principles permeated his entire persona.

I continued walking down the trail, promising myself not to look at either one of them. I had a feeling that both were watching me and that both were sizing each other up.

"Both gentlemen seem to fancy you, Miss Br—"

"Shhh. For crying out loud. They can hear you, moron."

"My apologies. I'll adjust my volume settings accordingly."

"How would *you* know anyway?"

"I've been monitoring everyone's pheromone activity, serotonin levels, corti—"

"What? Why?"

"Because I can."

"Don't freakin' do that. You have no right."

"Miss Brown, it is part of my inherent system design. It is my responsibility to monitor the mental and physical status of everyone in your party. I can't undo this particular function any more than you can undo your proclivity to breathe air."

"Well, I don't like it."

"It distresses me to hear that, but I must tell you, the results look quite promising. Both men are immensely attracted to you and you to them."

I sighed. "Just stop."

"Would you prefer that I cease all reporting of this manner? I can restrict my reporting frequency to only significant or life-threatening events that may compromise your mission."

"That would be dandy."

"Is everything okay?" Cox walked up, seeing my distress.

"Everything's fine."

I moved away. Shakespeare's revelations about Cox and LaSalle messed with my head. I was certain that LaSalle liked me based on his actions on the *Pegasus*. But Cox? The idea seemed crazy. Cox couldn't be interested in me. I despised him. He despised me. Right?

39

We stopped for a light snack and restroom break. Whenever we stopped, I thought of the Snow Dragon. I imagined it lifting off into the air with terrifying glory. I imagined the other things Shakespeare had mentioned too. As frightening as the rainforest was, it was quite beautiful. I couldn't stop staring at the vivid greens of the forest and the spectrum of bold colors amongst the exotic plants and shrubs everywhere. Albino monkeys stared at us from the canopy above. Albino coloring in the primates seemed to be the norm here, whereas I rarely saw any primates with dark fur. I wondered if there were any other albino apes, particularly gorillas. Not sure I wanted to run into one of those.

I could hear the moving of the rapids in the river canyon next to us. The ravine would lead us directly to the waterfall. I began to think about the falls, which made me think of the swim through the caves. There was no way out of it. We would get there. We'd fire up our underwater transport gear, and we'd slip into the water for a lengthy underwater swim. The time between prepping our gear and getting into the water would take a matter of seconds. Minutes at most.

I thought of the swim. What if my gear failed, and no one was around? My entire life depended on swim technology. My heart somersaulted a couple of times before I began to hyperventilate. I tried to take a deep breath, but I couldn't. I gasped for air. I couldn't breathe. I was having a panic attack.

"What's wrong?" Cox shuffled up next to me again. I was bent over, and he put his hand on my back. "Are you okay?"

This time I didn't move away. "I'm . . . I'm . . . fine."

"You don't look fine. I'm gonna get the medic." He looked over at a Biotech guard standing next to LaSalle several feet away. This guard wore a red cross stitched on the sleeve of his black jumpsuit. I didn't want Cox to get him. If he did that, LaSalle would be over here, too, and I didn't want that.

I clutched Cox's arm. "Please don't. I just need a second."

He looked at me skeptically. I tried to force myself to calm down, but the more I tried, the more my breathing became frantic.

Cox had his arms around my shoulders now. I was still bent over, gasping for air. "Just breathe," he said. "Just slow down and breathe."

I wanted to tell him to get his arms off me. I didn't want LaSalle to witness this scene, but he was already walking up.

He was scowling. "Is everything okay?"

"She's fine," Cox said in a clipped tone.

"Well, maybe we should get someone who is properly trained to make that determination." LaSalle gestured to the Biotech medic.

"Maybe you should mind your fucking business for once." Cox never cursed. Ever.

"Well, if I did *mind my fucking business for once,* you'd be back near the launch pad being dined on by a couple of 400-pound cats."

True.

I tried to catch my breath while I cringed at LaSalle's comment.

LaSalle and Cox stood dangerously still, like two wild dogs waiting to attack each other. They stared and stared. LaSalle was much bigger than Cox, both in height and stature. But Cox didn't move, and his gaze didn't waiver. Something in his eyes flickered—a certain wildness I hadn't noticed before. I got the impression he wouldn't go down without taking a piece of LaSalle with him.

"I'm fine, guys. Really," I said, panting. "I'll be fine. I've just been getting these attacks from time to time."

I was ashamed that now, suddenly, I was one of *those* girls: suffering from a full-blown panic attack while two men argued over me. *Really, Mel?*

They continued staring at each other, ignoring me.

So much for my fucking well-being. I forced myself to relax until finally my breath came in slow ragged inhales. I began to feel like myself again. Then, I threw up. It felt good, and the sound of my retching jerked LaSalle and Cox from their little staring contest. I was horrified. I'd gotten a little on LaSalle's boot. Cox chuckled.

How humiliating.

"Feel better?" LaSalle sounded mildly irritated, but he accepted a canteen from a guard and washed the vomit off with some water. He patted my back. His hand was dangerously close to Cox's hand which was already resting on my back.

This is crazy. If they were disgusted, they both hid it well.

"Actually, I do feel a lot better. Maybe you could ask Petty Office Mackie for some antacid pills for me."

I was thankful to have Petty Officer Mackie on the trip. While he performed the basic duties of a gunner's mate in my division, he had several useful skills. "Like Chief Martinez, he was Survivalist First-Tier certified which meant he had extensive training in: search and rescue swimming, alternative planetary wilderness survival, weaponry, explosives, remote area first aid, field triage and emergency medicine basics. Not quite a LaSalle, but he knew enough to be dangerous.

"No. I'll go ask my medic. He's actually a certified nurse," LaSalle said.

"You do that," said Cox, continuing to glare.

LaSalle gave Cox a hard look before heading back to his gaggle of guards.

Cox turned back to me.

"You're not pregnant, are you?" He poked my ribs, but there was an edge to his tone.

"No." I rolled my eyes and slapped his hand away.

He snickered. "Okay. Just checking."

"Yeah, well—"

"Well, it's not out of the realm of possibility for a beautiful woman to get pregnant."

Shit. Did he just say that?

"What're you talking about?" I said with a nervous laugh.

"I don't know what you see in him," He looked at me for a moment, raking his fingers through his hair.

"What?"

"You heard me. He doesn't deserve—"

LaSalle arrived just at that moment. He handed me some tiny red pills. "Here. These should help."

Shakespeare crooned out of nowhere. I'd forgotten about him. I wondered what twisted pleasure Shakespeare seemed to get out of spying on my interactions with these men. First in the stateroom with LaSalle. Now this? "I'm afraid your medic has misdiagnosed Miss Brown's condition."

LaSalle put his hands on his hips. "Well, if you know what is bothering her, pray tell, what is it? You could've spoken up earlier."

"My apologies, Dr. LaSalle. I thought it best to merely observe and evaluate the situation before offering a viable solution."

My ass.

"Well, now that you've observed and evaluated, what's going on with her?"

"I believe that Miss Brown is experiencing an allergic reaction to some of the indigenous flower and plant life. The symptoms resemble that of your standard panic attack. Shortness of breath, gasping, and wheezing are to be expected, accompanied by itchy nose and eyes. For extreme cases, one may experience the coughing of blood and a debilitating skin rash. I'm afraid those pills will only serve to minimize her nausea and exacerbate her situation."

"Well that sucks," I said. I tried to push the frenzy down in my voice. "Why isn't everyone else going through it?"

"Only one in five people are susceptible to such reactions."

LaSalle put his hand on my neck. It was an intimate gesture. I could feel blood rush to my face. He leaned in, his forehead almost touching mine. "You're gonna be fine. We'll get you an antihistamine."

Cox looked between us and then shifted his backpack to his other shoulder. He started to walk away.

LaSalle called out to him. "Hey, tell my medic—"

"Tell him yourself." Cox stomped down the trail.

"What's his problem?" LaSalle looked at Cox with open disgust.

"I think he's just misunderstood," I said.

"You think?" LaSalle shook his head. Then he put his finger to his ear. One of his men was calling him. "Gotta go. I'll have someone bring you that antihistamine injection."

He winked at me before trotting off. Once, again I was alone.

"Well, that was interesting," said Shakespeare.

"Yes. It was."

I decided to command him into silence mode for a bit.

∿∿

I trudged along the trail, left to over-analyze everything that had been said. First, I was a taken aback with Cox. He'd been flirting with me this entire trip, and I hadn't realized it until now.

Beautiful? That was a stretch. Cute, maybe. Even sexy. But not beautiful.

I replayed every conversation I'd ever had with him over and over in my head. Trying to pick apart every look, every word, nuance and inflection of his tone. Certain moments were starting to make sense: his constant frustrations with me. The staring. His always butting into my business. This began the moment I met him. In fact, before the "International Ball incident" with the commodore, I remembered thinking that Lieutenant Commander Travis Cox was quiet, serious even, but really nice. Then, after the ball, he morphed into a complete ass. Now, in retrospect, it all clicked into place: He'd been disappointed with the incident and how I handled it. He'd held me to a higher standard. He'd been frustrated.

Cox. I couldn't even imagine myself with him, but I couldn't imagine myself with LaSalle, either. I'd never pictured myself as the kind of girl that two guys fought over.

Yet, this was more about them competing and less about their interest in me. The entire situation was all so cliché. It pissed me off, which was why I had to walk away from them both. Deep down, though, I had to admit that I liked the attention. What girl wouldn't? But I'd be damned if I'd let them use me in their little pissing contest. At least it was me and not that nitwit Sherri.

40

The hike seemed to stretch on, and I used the time to think about what I would do once I left the *Midway* and inevitably out of the Navy. An hour had passed while I fantasized about the different occupational routes I might take. Maybe I'd be a private investigator. Sit outside some poor sap's house while I read a book, taking the occasional photo of him cheating on his wife or his husband. Or maybe forensics? I'd work in the safety of a lab where tedium and solitude would fill my days. At least it would be peaceful.

A sound shook me from my thoughts. Loud and piercing—a scream. It was Sherri. I looked over to see her in hysterics. Her arms and legs were jerked all over the place and she whipped her head back and forth, up and down, like she was having an epileptic fit. I saw Eric take a cautious step back, unsure of what to do.

That's when I saw one—a wasp hovering around her head. It was *huge*. Sherri didn't wait. She ran straight for the river and jumped in. I heard her yelp. She must've busted her ass on the bedrock.

Then a loud humming sound permeated the entire area. Not quite like a bumblebee or the droning of an old rusty fan. More like a chorus. Loud and vengeful. I had to plug my ears and so did the people around me. It was terrifying. Ears plugged, we looked around aimlessly, trying to pinpoint the direction the noise was coming from.

I thought of the Book of Revelations. Then it occurred to me—Shakespeare's list. He spoke just then to affirm what I already knew.

"Miss Brown. Leave now. Depart. Immediately." For A.I., his voice sounded urgent. This was an indication that I should be very afraid. "Tengelei Wasps. A cloud of them. They arrive in approximately thirty-eight seconds."

I didn't waste time asking questions, even though I had a ton of them. I took off on a flat sprint, yelling along the way. Both Cox and LaSalle called after me. I ran harder.

"*Run*," I yelled. I heard my voice quiver as I fled and shouted. "*Tengelei Terrorists. Wasps. Wasps are coming.*"

I sprinted as hard as I could. People actually followed me in the way people do when they're unsure of the source of someone else's terror. It was unquestioning, fear-driven acquiescence. First Mackie and then Yuri behind him. From my peripheral, I saw both Cox and LaSalle take off as well. But they went in another direction. People just followed each other. Our paths of flight were complete disarray. I had no idea where I was headed. I didn't care. Somehow, I felt better knowing that Yuri and Mackie were behind me.

We seemed to run for an eternity. All sorts of thoughts raced through my head as we fled. Why hadn't I looked at the wasp attack images? I wasn't sure what would happen if I was stung, but I knew that it would really suck. Didn't Shakespeare mention they were lethal? I was lucky to have Shakespeare warn me and give me a head start. He'd saved my life three times: first the cats, then the allergy misdiagnosis and now this? He'd been acting as my personal watch dog. I needed to show him some respect.

The buzzing sound was still deafening. I stretched my legs out in front of me as far and as fast as I could manage. I tried to build more speed, but then Mackie caught up with me and Yuri overtook us both.

"You won't be able to maintain this pace for much longer, Miss Brown. There is a considerable build up of lactic acid in your legs. You must find cover."

That's when I realized that I'd been running on sheer adrenaline. My heart hammered furiously, and my lungs were ablaze. Yuri—who Mackie and I were now following—slowed down a bit. The noise from the Tengelei Wasps was still there, but it was faint. We jogged. I didn't know how much farther I could jog, much less run. Exhaustion crept in. Yuri ushered us over to a large bush that we all ducked behind. I felt like I could vomit again if I let myself. We were all panting violently, struggling to quiet our breaths.

"I don't hear them anymore." Mackie wiped his forehead as he looked hopefully at Yuri.

Yuri nodded. "Neither do I. We're kind of far away. And we had a head start on everyone."

We waited. Moments of nerve-racking silence passed. Then there was a yell followed by several yells. Then screaming. The wasps had wreaked their havoc.

"I think we should go back," I said.

Yuri looked like he could shit himself at any moment. "We'll get closer, to hear better. But not too close. Better to be on the safe side."

We left the bush and trotted gingerly in the direction of the group. I used Shakespeare as a directional guide. We'd run so far and haphazardly that we were kind of lost. Along the way, we spotted members of our group who'd been hiding in tree trunks, bushes and beneath logs. One of LaSalle's guards was high up in a tree.

Really? You don't think something with wings can reach you up there?

Finally, as we crept closer, we heard LaSalle's voice. He was yelling at someone. "There's nothing you can do for him. He's gone."

41

We arrived to find that several people had, in fact, been stung by a few maverick wasps, mostly in exposed areas not covered by their hiking suits like the neck and face. Their stings weren't fatal, but they suffered from some pretty nasty welts, some numbness in the hand and feet and some sensory deprivation. The regiment of wasps had targeted one Biotech guard specifically. Everyone crowded around the poor guy. I pushed my way to the front of the crowd. To my shame, I was overcome with relief when I looked down at the body and didn't recognize the man. What I saw, though, was horrifying. The "Tengelei Terrorists" had completely swarmed their victim, the Biotech medic. According to LaSalle, he was a rookie, new to the station and new to the Biotech security team, fresh out of a completed four-year obligation with the Navy SEALS. We stood over him. I tried to hide my disgust over the boil-like lesions that covered his hands, neck, and face. Marshmallow-sized, tumorous lumps rendered him unrecognizable. The image infused a new level of fear amongst the party.

"We should head immediately back to Port Juliette," said Eric.

Unfortunately, the medic hadn't died right away. He was still breathing, wheezing and gasping for air but not getting any. LaSalle stood over the guard. A mix of emotions passed over LaSalle's face: horror, then anger, sadness and finally despair. His face settled into a look of futility as if he'd made a decision regarding a less-than-optimal scenario. LaSalle just watched as the guard tried speaking, but his words were perforated by deep gasps for air. He mumbled something about "feeling like there was an elephant on his chest." A yellow, greenish substance started to ooze from his mouth and the legions on his face. LaSalle kneeled while pulling a glass cylindrical tube from his pack. He placed it next to the guard's mouth. The gooey substance slid from the guard's mouth into the cylinder. Then, to everyone's disgust, he brandished a small pocket knife from his pocket and started to cut open the boils. The guard screamed as the gooey yellow liquid squirted from the pustules into the cylindrical glass tube like diarrhea into a toilet bowl.

I almost threw up again.

"What're you *doing*?" Eric hissed, a look of pure revulsion on his face. "You're killing him."

"I'm collecting the venom," said LaSalle. "Besides, he's gonna die. Nothing I do or don't do will change that."

"I can't believe you said that out loud." Yuri gave LaSalle a disapproving glance.

"He can't really hear us. The neurotoxin from the wasp's venom has diminished some of his sensory capabilities. He can hear muffled voices. That's it. He can't really see us, either," LaSalle replied as he fumbled around with his collection tubes.

"Then why is he still feeling pain? It sounds like you're torturing him."

LaSalle continued gathering venom and sealed it in a test tube with a stopper. "I'm not torturing him. The venom needs to be collected immediately for testing purposes. Even though his senses are diminished, he still feels some pain. It's unfortunate, but it is what it is."

I looked back to the medic's wasp-violated face. It was a pitiful sight. I couldn't look at his face anymore. "Can't we give him a painkiller?" I asked. My voice screeched.

"No. The medicine will taint the venom," said LaSalle as he continued to fill up tubes.

Eric threw his hands up. "Who the fuck cares?"

Cox leaned in and examined the guard closely.

"Anti-venom," he said aloud. "That's what you're collecting the venom, and that's why painkillers are out of question."

"Yes," said LaSalle, placing the full tube in his bag.

"Don't you guys keep any on hand?" said Yuri.

Cox snorted. "Doubt it. Like all operations on this station, this one was poorly planned."

Is he insulting Yuri or LaSalle?

Yuri ignored Cox and turned back to LaSalle. "You're in the forest all of the time. I would've thought you'd have a ton of anti-venom."

LaSalle was getting irritated. He took a long slow breath. "This stuff isn't exactly easy to come by. Have *you* ever charmed an aggressive flying insect into giving you its venom?"

Yuri pursed his lips. Cox frowned.

LaSalle continued. "The answer is *no* because it can't be done. It's not gonna just hover over to you and say, *here ya go. Have at it.* Especially not an angry swarm of them. So we—"

Shakespeare intervened. "I believe what Dr. LaSalle is trying to convey is that the venom must be collected from an expiring or recently expired body. The venom must be collected within approximately one to five minutes, or its potency is almost completely lost. While the act of lancing this man's boils is distasteful, it is quite necessary."

"I still think there's a better way." said Eric, who had Sherri in his arms.

LaSalle stood up after having filled the last test tube. He turned to Eric. "If I could minimize his pain even just a little, I would, you little prick. You have a better way? I'm open for suggestions."

"*Little prick.*" *Wow. He's cranky.*

Eric glared at LaSalle. Sherri started to whimper.

"That's what I thought," said LaSalle. "Shut your piehole for a while."

"Whatever, dude." Eric looked embarrassed.

LaSalle stuffed the remaining tubes into his duffel. He nodded to one of his men who stepped forward and handed him a pistol.

What's that for?

LaSalle brandished it and did a quick magazine check.

"What're you doing?" Eric asked.

LaSalle gave him an *are-you-seriously-asking-me-this-right-now* look.

"Dr. LaSalle is ending his life," said Shakespeare. "I believe you call it a mercy killing."

I could've strangled Shakespeare.

"Will you shut that fucking thing off?" LaSalle said with a harsh whisper.

I commanded Shakespeare to go silent for a while.

The guard, who'd already sensed what LaSalle was about to do, struggled in earnest now. Two other Biotech guards held him down. They tried to relax him, but their efforts were having the opposite effect.

"What's going on? Why is everyone so quiet?" the guard said. His voice was panicky. He wheezed, trying to lift up and focus his blurred vision. "What're you going to do? Wait. Just wait . . . I can make it. I swear. I'll be all right."

LaSalle knelt down and rubbed sweat from the medic's forehead. "Shh. I know. We know you can. We're just making you more comfortable." The guard was still gasping and wheezing but relaxed a little. His breath was ragged, and then he started to twitch uncontrollably.

Like a man intent on doing something he found repugnant, LaSalle took a deep breath, frowned and pointed the glowing blue-tipped barrel at the dying medic. Blinking in concentration, LaSalle aimed directly at the guard's heart. The guard twitched and pleaded. "Please. Please."

Eric stepped forward. "You can't be ser—"

But LaSalle pulled the trigger before Eric could finish. The guard's movements stopped. Everyone fell silent.

LaSalle looked at Sherri and pointed to the dead Biotech medic. "You owe this man your life."

Her mouth was set in a rigid line. "And why is that?"

Shakespeare responded before LaSalle could offer an explanation: "Jumping into a river is useless, Lieutenant Kolar. Tengelei wasps are quite amphibious in nature. In fact, they generally don't stray far from water sources. You were probably able to allude them due to the distractions provided by the ill-fated medic here. Might I also add that their stingers leave permanent scars, and, well—"

"Well, the joke's on you because I *did* get stung. I just didn't get overrun by the entire swarm because I happened to be quick enough to get out of harm's way." She pulled down her collar to reveal a tiny boil on her neck. "That ought to shut him up."

And this is why I don't trust A.I. Shakespeare does what he wants when he wants. I told him to go silent, and now he's running his mouth again.

She glared at me. I shrugged. "Shakespeare's just trying to help. You're lucky it wasn't worse."

Eric hugged her protectively. Then he shot LaSalle an incriminating look. "You shouldn't have done that."

LaSalle glared back at Eric, like he was lobbing invisible grenades in Eric's direction. Yet, he said nothing. Instead, he twirled his finger in the air and nodded to Yuri. "Let's move out."

"Hey, I'm talking to you." Eric tapped LaSalle's shoulder.

LaSalle turned back to face Eric full on. Eric took a wary step back. "You shouldn't have killed him," he said again, in a lighter tone.

"And what was I supposed to do? Let him suffer the entire hour-long march back to Port Juliette?"

"He could've made it."

"No, Captain Hunt. He couldn't have. He was done. Discussion closed."

42

LaSalle and his guards picked up their gear. Yuri's movements were reluctant, but he picked up his gear too.

"Well at least we have a reason to go back to the port," Sherri said as she picked up her own bag.

I looked at her. *Insensitive cunt.*

She burrowed her face into Eric's chest and whimpered. I was thoroughly annoyed by her at this point. For a Marine, she was weak. I knew female Marines who were total badasses, but I found her lacking. Most kept the male Marines constantly on their toes—effortlessly—but Sherri made me embarrassed for her. I couldn't even say her name to myself without getting a bitter taste in my mouth. She grated on my nerves. Every time she so much as broke a nail she leaned on Eric for pampering. And he relished it. He doted on her.

When I was still seeing him, he tried that shit with me. I'd almost lost my finger in a closing door hatch, and it bled heavily. He tried to hug me, but I told him to *eat me.* Some of my sailors had been watching. They chuckled. It wounded his ego, but I didn't care. Letting him hug me would've made me look weak.

Later that day he'd gone on and on about how I had humiliated him. I told him to get over it.

That was the first day of our rapidly deteriorating relationship.

Sherri caught my disapproving look. She frowned and subtly inched her way out of Eric's embrace. I would've respected her more if she'd stayed where she was and owned it. I looked at her again. I could feel my resentment of her seep through my chest. She was pretty, prettier than she deserved to be. She was still rambling on about her own situation, showing complete disregard for the dead Biotech guard.

"This has really been the worst trip ever," she said. "I really thought this would be a relaxing hike where I could get some rock samples and consult a bit on the mines. I just can't wait to get back."

"How many different ways do I have to say it?" said LaSalle."We're not going back."

"The fuck we aren't," said Eric.

"Now wait a minute," Yuri said, looking at LaSalle, "we have to go back. We can't just leave a dead man out here. Are you insane?"

"No. I'm not insane. I'm highly trained to deal with this kind of thing. You need to just trust me."

"Lieutenant Kolar sprained her ankle when she jumped into the river on that bedrock."

"Commander Jefferson, look. Lieutenant Kolar shouldn't have jumped in the river. That was stupid, considering the information provided in the station brief. Lieutenant Kola will live. The medic can tape up her ankle, and she'll be just fine. You know as well as I that we need to keep moving."

"In case you've forgotten, the medic is dead."

"Well then I guess Petty Officer Mackie is our medic now. I'm sure he's capable. Plus, Ensign Brown has that annoying yet very useful A.I. consultant. I'm sure with his assistance we could perform open heart surgery if needs be."

"I should point out, Dr. LaSalle, that, while I have the requisite knowledge to perform such a procedure, I'm neither qualified or authorized—"

"Why don't you shut that annoying thing off?" Sherri gave me a challenging look.

I gave her the double bird. "Why don't you set your face on fire so I can stomp it out and make it look better?"

"Oh, I'd love to see you try—"

"Shut up!" Yuri silenced us both. We continued to just glower at each other.

He turned to LaSalle. "I'm not gonna just leave a dead body out here like this."

"We don't have to leave him out here," LaSalle continued. "We can secure the body and continue with our mission."

"What do you mean, *secure* the body?" Eric asked.

LaSalle ignored Eric, speaking only to Yuri. "We'll either bury it or put it some place safe until we're in a position to return it to Port Juliette."

"This is crazy," Eric said. "I can't believe we're even discussing this. We're in a position *now* to take it back to port."

"I say we take a vote," said Sherri. "I'm down for heading back."

"We're not voting. This isn't a democracy," said LaSalle.

One of the Biotech guards chimed in. He creeped me out. His name was Specialist Komanski. "It doesn't make sense to hike a 210-pound body all the way back and then have to turn around and hike our asses right back here. We've already been hiking for over two hours as it is."

"A death warrants the effort," Eric said.

Finally, LaSalle looked at him directly. "No, actually it doesn't."

"And why the hell not?"

Cox stepped forward. "Because this kind of thing happens all the time, doesn't it, LaSalle?"

LaSalle's face tightened. "Listen, everyone. Get this through your thick skulls. We're at a station. Not a day spa. Consider this the Wild West. People *do* die here. It happens. When we're tasked with a mission, we're expected to complete it. Regardless of death or injury. Sorry if that wounds your pride—the fact that we're all disposable—but the reality is that someone with a much higher security clearance than me (and a significantly bigger paycheck) expects us to do what we're paid to do."

Yuri's silence confirmed that LaSalle was going to get his way. Everyone wanted to go back, but LaSalle's reasoning was hard to dispute. As the director of Biotech security, we depended on him and his men.

Cox, who always saw logic, admitted that LaSalle was right. Biotech would say, "thanks for delivering the body." Then they'd take it to their lab to study. In the meantime, someone high up would make some calls to the commodore and subtly suggest that we complete our mission. The commodore wouldn't hesitate to comply. Based on Rivera's last call, he wanted us at the mines regardless of the latest news concerning Senior Chief's body. We were stuck.

Eric tried to get Yuri to reconsider, but LaSalle intervened. "I don't know why this comes as such a shock to you, Captain Hunt. This isn't your first trip to the mines. You've been here twice before."

"Yeah, well, nothing like *this* has ever happened," said Eric. "As soon as we get back to the *Midway,* I'm going to report this to the Marine Corps commandant. He'll talk to Admiral Willard and demand that we pull our Marines from this station. Biotech can hire people to do their own demolitions and grunt work."

"Good luck with that," said LaSalle, snorting. "In the meantime, let's keep moving."

Eric decided to try a different tack. "Look, I have a Marine detachment already set up at the mines. They're trained in forensics.

I can have them complete the murder investigation. The rest of us can take turns lugging your medic back to the port."

I was awestruck. *Now he wants to be a team player? That "little prick" could've kept us out of this entire mess by making the same offer back in the commodore's stateroom, when we were safely onboard the ship.*

"I think that's a great idea, LaSalle," said Yuri. "Let me call the commodore. Doesn't hurt to make the call."

"It's not your call to make. He was one of *my* men."

"Even still, *our* mission has been adversely impacted. I'm calling." Yuri lifted his wrist device closer to his mouth.

LaSalle shifted his stance. For a second, I was worried that he would try to physically stop Yuri. His gaze was so direct and intense, like a laser. But then within moments, the commodore appeared on Yuri's wristwatch.

"What?" The commodore appeared somewhat annoyed.

Yuri explained everything that occurred up to the point of the medic being stung by the wasp. The commodore appeared bored the entire time Yuri spoke.

"Is there no way of securing the body?" the commodore asked.

"Yes, sir. Bring it back to port." Yuri's tone shifted from respectful to edgy.

"And waste valuable time? No. There must be a place out in the field there to secure it."

"Well—yes sir—but—"

"Then do so and continue on with the mission."

Eric snatched at Yuri's arm and spoke into the device with his same omniscient, arrogant tone. "Sir, I have a Marine detachment already situated at the mines. They're trained and certified in forensics scanning. I can have them complete the forensics investigation while we head back to port."

The commodore ignored Eric. "Commander Jefferson, you have your orders. Commodore out."

Even his golden boy can't change his mind.

Yuri's communication ended. I expected LaSalle to have a triumphant look on his face, but instead he just looked irritated at having been unnecessarily delayed.

"Satisfied?" LaSalle threw his rifle back over his shoulder.

"Not by a long shot," said Yuri. He looked distrustful. Nonetheless, he remained silent as LaSalle took over, issuing instructions.

43

LaSalle announced his intentions to the group. The plan was to stow the dead guard's body in a bunker. LaSalle's men either looked angry or apathetically numb. Everyone despised the mission. I despised the mission. Even LaSalle seemed to despise our mission, but he was a man driven to carry out his orders without question. Everyone knew that the rest of Senior Chief's body had been found. Somehow word circulated once Yuri received the call from Rivera. Yet, here we still were. It didn't make sense to continue with the investigation. I was angry and scared. Whitaker had already gotten badly injured, and now a guard was *dead*. Why the hell were we still here? I was ready to say *to hell with the commodore* and risk punishment at captain's mast. I'm sure LaSalle's men felt the same regarding his own leadership, but something was holding them all back.

Cox started to complain out loud, and that worried me. He wasn't a complainer. Sure, he questioned everything, but this time was different. We weren't on the *Midway*. We were in the Wild West, as LaSalle put it.

This is a typical Navy Goat Fuck, and *I can't believe this shit* were just a few phrases that surfaced from Cox's rant.

LaSalle's men mumbled to themselves, but they complained about other matters. Specialist Komanski was their ring leader. He made sure that the rest of us could hear. "This is bullshit. This is *their* goddamn problem. We're at risk—"

LaSalle snatched him by the collar and whispered something into his ear. Then he shoved Komanski away. The guard stumbled. He almost fell onto his backside, before a teammate caught him. Once he regained his footing, he straightened himself up and fell in with the rest of the guards. No one said another word.

Komanski was tasked with "prepping the body" for "staging" inside the bunker. He gestured to one of his teammates. They both made their way over to the dead, wasp-stung guard. Sullen in their movements, they didn't look at each other or speak to each other while completing their task. Komanski pulled out a small plastic pack and unzipped it. It unfolded into one clear plastic bag and one large black tarp. They covered the dead guard's head in the clear plastic bag.

This is obscene. Why? Just . . . why?

Komanski saw the expression on my face. "Biotech will want to dissect the boils later."

I shrugged. I wanted to appear indifferent, but the entire scene made me sick.

They wrapped the dead guard up like a human burrito, using the black tarp. Komanski pulled out a small handheld device that resembled a stapler. At the hinges was a button illuminated in blue. They clamped the open edges of the tarp together with the device and pushed the blue-lit button at the hinges. There was a brief sound—hissing—like air being released. The tarp collapsed around the body of the dead Biotech medic, melding around him. Once they finished vacuum sealing him, Komanski looked up. LaSalle nodded, and they hoisted the tarp-covered body back onto the stretcher.

LaSalle turned in the direction of the river. Rifle propped up on his side, the tip of the barrel pointing in the air. "There's a supply bunker about 800 meters downriver. We'll put him there for now."

Komanski and the other guard lifted the stretcher and started walking. I couldn't help but think how easily they dealt with the death of their teammate. Like it was an everyday occurrence. The rest of us exchanged glances and then followed quietly. Yuri followed too. There was a combination of shock, anger and distrust written all over his face.

A hand on my shoulder startled me. Cox. He looked at me with genuine concern. "You all right?"

"Yeah," I paused. "Honestly, I don't know. This is all messed up."

"Amelia," he said. He had both hands on my shoulders now, and he was staring directly at me. "You're going to be all right Just stay close to me, and I promise I'll look after you."

He was close to me now. I could feel his breath on my face.

I looked at him for a moment. I just noticed for the first time that his eyes changed colors. I'd thought they were a hazel brown, but in that moment they were green. "You're being nice to me all of a sudden. Why?"

Something flickered across his face. His face softened. He was about to say something important, but then a Biotech guard appeared.

Nice timing, asshole.

"Ma'am, Dr. LaSalle asked me to hurry you along. He said that he wants to be able to keep an eye on you."

Cox's face hardened. "Of course, he does."

His demeanor changed. His movements turned abrupt. He gathered his stuff, his actions jerky.

"Wait," I said. "What were you going to say?"

The Biotech guard was still lingering nearby.

Annoying. Haven't you ever heard of privacy, moron?

253

Cox looked over at the guard and then back at me. "I was just going to say that I was being nice because Rivera, your department head, asked me to watch out for you. That's all."

He slung his pack over his shoulder and left me there to stare at his back. The Biotech grabbed at my arm to usher me down the path, but I yanked it away. "Don't ever touch me."

The unshakable feeling that something bad was going to happen made me cranky. Someone else was going to get hurt. Maybe me. Maybe someone I cared about. The feeling was unmistakable. Whitaker's injury, the dead guard, LaSalle's secretive behavior and the commodore's odd behavior. They all felt like signs.

∿

LaSalle kicked at a patch of dirt about twenty-five meters from the riverbank. A small, square door of transparent fiberglass appeared. He brushed the remainder of the dirt away to open the small door. There was a small video display. He issued a few voice commands, and the screen flickered on. Then he leaned in, bring his face close to the display. A retinal scan was completed, and then *beep.* He stepped back to the sound of something unlocking, like a bank vault door.

A large door, still covered with earth and grass, began to mechanically lift, slowly, to reveal an opening (enough for one, maybe two people to fit through) and a staircase which spiraled down about 20 meters.

The two guards lugging the body entered the bunker carefully, making sure not to lose their footing and tumble down the lengthy staircase. Once they were at the bottom, they laid the body at the foot of the staircase. We all watched quietly, as if we were attending a funeral.

I peered over the edge curiously and spotted all manner of supplies as the door slowly closed with a quiet hum. There were rows and rows of canned and vacuum-sealed foods: all types of meats and fishes—even vegan and vegetarian versions—and full-on prepared dinners from every ethnic group one could think of. The choices were extensive, from rows of vacuum-sealed fruits and vegetables to every type of cold and hot beverage, including beer, wine and hard liquor. I had no doubts that a person could stay in the bunker for long periods of time.

"There's a lot of shit in there," Yuri said.

"Yeah. Well, there's supposed to be. Each bunker is supposed to be able to sustain four people comfortably for up to a year," said LaSalle. "They're actually kind of neat. They're set up like mini-campers. Once they're up and operational, Biotech scientists will be able to do some valuable, life-changing research."

"What do you mean, up and operational'?" asked Yuri. "They look pretty good to me."

"Let me guess," said Cox, pursing his lips. "Plumbing's not done."

"That's correct, Commander." It was Shakespeare again. "A bunker water-channeling system has not yet been established. Personal hygiene must be maintained through more archaic means, and should the need arise, one must be inclined to use a container or exit the bunker to perform all necessary bodily functions."

Komanski and the other guard who'd delivered the body to the foot of the staircase were back at the top of the opening.

LaSalle conducted another retinal scan to close the door.

"Wait," I said.

"What?" LaSalle was craning his neck to look back at me.

"Shouldn't we say a few words or something? I wouldn't feel right just dumping his body like that. Maybe a prayer?"

LaSalle sighed. "We can do it when we come back to bury him."

"We wouldn't even be discussing this if you hadn't killed him," said Eric, who scowled at LaSalle.

"Oh Jeez. Give it a rest, Eric," I said. "LaSalle did what he had to do."

LaSalle gave me an appreciative look.

"Why don't you keep your two cents to yourself for once, Mel?" said Eric. "The guy was still breathing when he shot him. He might've made it."

"I'll keep my two cents when you say something that makes sense. He was dying, Eric."

"Be that as it may, I would've given him a chance."

"Well, when you get stung, I'll make sure I *give you a chance* rather than put you out of your pathetic, miserable existence," LaSalle said. He put his hand on his holster and stepped up to Eric. His voice was just above a whisper. "Actually, we can do it right now."

"All right guys, that's enough," Yuri said, laughing nervously. He was trying to lighten the mood, but it wasn't working. LaSalle took another step toward Eric, but Yuri barricaded LaSalle with his arm. "Hey—guys—c'mon, take it easy. Let's just—. Wait. *Shhh.*"

Something had his attention. We all followed his gaze.

"What?" I asked.

He stood still, straining his eyes toward the dense foliage in front of us.

I nudged him. "What?"

"I thought I saw something."

My pulse rate spiked. *Not again. Not another attack.* "What did you see? Wasps? A snake?"

"Wasn't one of those cats, was it?" Eric looked like he was ready to take off down the trail again.

"The trail is nice and wide for you. " LaSalle locked and loaded a round into his rifle. "You and your girlfriend have plenty of room to run."

"Go to hell." Sherri said, directing a contemptuous look at LaSalle.

"That's not what happened." Eric's face was getting darker.

"*Shhh,*" said Yuri, irritated. He was straining to see. "I thought I saw someone—an actual person."

Was it the same guy I saw at the lake?

"You sure?" I asked.

"No, I'm not sure."

"What do you think you saw?" LaSalle's voice had an edge to it.

I looked at him. *He's not fooling anyone.*

Yuri shrugged. "I thought I saw someone out of the corner of my eye. It's probably nothing. Could be that I'm just really tired."

"Wait," said Cox. "Ensign Brown, saw someone back at the lake?"

"Well, yeah, I—"

"She saw one of the Biotech scientists. I'm sure he just saw one too." LaSalle's tone was clipped, as if the statement was final and that no one should question it. He wouldn't look at me. This time he kept his rifle in his hand rather than slung behind his shoulder. He just started walking down the trail. "Let's go, guys. Onwards."

"He's lying, you know. And you shouldn't trust him so much." Cox blocked my path.

I stepped around him. "Got it."

"Do you even know what he does?" He pulled on my arm to stop me for a moment.

"Of course. He's head of security for Biotech."

"He's not just head of security for Biotech. He handles some of their more clandestine operations. People have died. He—"

"Are you coming?" One of LaSalle's guards interrupted. I wondered if he'd been eavesdropping. He motioned for us to keep moving.

Cox fell silent, and we continue to walk in silence. The guard who interrupted walked close behind.

I knew that Cox was right. LaSalle *was* dangerous, but to whom? I couldn't accept that he'd do things to get people killed. He was definitely holding something back, but was he evil? I promised myself I'd find out what he was hiding. In the meantime, I moved along in quiet contemplation. Cox followed behind me and kept to himself.

I wondered if we were as bad off as I suspected. I forced myself not to think about it and focus on our trip to the waterfall instead.

44

Our hike along the trail following the river steadily worsened. The terrain became arduous. We hiked inclines and dips and had to deal with dense vegetation again. The entire time we stayed close to the river gorge adjacent to us. It would've been easy to get off track without technology and the sounds of the roaring river beside us, which we kept to our left to maintain our bearing north. LaSalle said that it would eventually lead us to the falls. We were all tired now, having hiked a total of five and a half hours after our departure from the *Pegasus*. The exertion from the hikes, the run-in with the Rainforest Raiders and the adrenaline-fueled escape from the wasps began to take their toll.

I was eager to get to the falls and then the mines like everyone else. Even though I was terrified of the underwater swim, I wanted our investigation over with as soon as possible.

I hoped that Yuri and LaSalle would decide to have us camp next to the falls at dusk so that we could get ample rest and start our descent into the mines early in the morning.

I was in deceptively good shape. I trained and dieted like a professional fighter (most of the time) in order to advance in Gladiator 4D. Yet, even I was ready to collapse. There were people in much worse shape than me who had to be exhausted. I didn't want to conduct a half-assed investigation because we were tired and unable to focus. I refused to give the commodore a reason to send me back to this wretched place. Plus, I had a feeling we would need lots of energy tomorrow. I felt a surge of fresh anxiety begin to form.

ⵡ

By the time we stepped over the last incline and stepped from the tree line, we were close to the waterfall. I could hear the sound of water crashing against rocks.

A lush, green valley opened up before us. The dense vegetation of the rainforest and its surrounding tropical grounds masked the valley walls that enveloped us. I realized that we had been hiking at the foot of mountainous, tropical terrain. The river cut its way through the mountain, eventually disappearing into a sinkhole.

Vibrantly reds, blues, greens and yellows decorated the borders of a mossy green plain. Exotically designed and oddly shaped flowers freckled the valley floor. As we moved along, hugging the river, the sweet intoxicating fragrance of the flowers assaulted our nostrils as light breeze kicked up. The flowers swayed seductively in silent welcome. In another place, another time, I could've camped out in the valley for months. It was breathtaking.

I couldn't help but look at anything and everything. I noticed some interesting creatures. In this area of the rainforest, they were all small and all cute. They *appeared* harmless, but I knew better. I saw rabbits hop to and fro in random directions across the mossy landscape. Their canary-yellow-colored coats were rustled by the light breeze. An antelope skipped across the green plain before heading back into the treeline. It was all black with a single red stripe down its back and red tipped horns. Its herd followed closely behind. But even the odd-looking creatures did nothing to prepare me for my first sighting of Tengelei Drop. I felt my breath catch, and all of my fears about swimming were put on hold.

The falls were gorgeous, just as LaSalle had promised. A wide smile spread across my face, and LaSalle caught my facial expression. He stepped up close behind me. I didn't have to turn around to know it was him. The clean linen smell, like fresh laundry, always seemed to linger around him.

"I told you it was beautiful," he said.

"Yes. You did, but I can't believe it is dark already. Have we been hiking that long?"

"No. This station only sees seven hours of daylight. The sun rises late and sets early here."

There was nothing more for me to say. I just stood in quiet appreciation of the beauty of the falls.

And I hoped that Cox wasn't watching LaSalle stand a little too close to me.

We eventually moved to a better position to have good view of what the waterfall was dropping down into. The river lead us to the edge of a cliff, the rim of a massive sinkhole. The sinkhole descended approximately 1,000 feet into the ground. The water from the river cascaded down behind three natural bridges, which stretched from one edge of the cliff to the other.

Yuri announced that he'd planned to have us camp for the night. There was a collective sigh of relief. Even LaSalle, who was in better physical condition than all of us, looked exhausted.

I smiled to myself because Sherri looked like she was one loose thread away from complete disarray. She looked fitter, but it was apparent that I was in better shape. Not to be petty, but that made me feel all warm and fuzzy inside.

Unfortunately, we couldn't just camp at the top of the sink-hole. We had to descend down into it, to the very bottom, and set up portable cots inside. At the bottom were the entrances to the caves, which sat behind the waterfall. Since mobile berthing spaces were too heavy to trek or lug underwater, we'd have to make use of natural shelter.

The plan for the next morning was to leave the caves, slip into the water at the base of the sinkhole, and swim beneath, following the tunnel which would take us much deeper into the caves where the mines were situated.

As we prepared to descend to the bottom, Eric pulled a small black cube from his bag and powered it on. He spoke into it, trying to establish communications with his Marine detachment already located at the mines. No answer.

For a moment a face flickered onto the screen. A haggard-looking individual who looked like he'd just awoken from a nap. Hair disheveled. Dark circles beneath the eyes. Whoever it was had tapped the screen a couple of times, but then the screen went dark. The sound of someone's voice cut in and out, and then it faded until there was silence on the other line.

"That's odd," Eric said.

"What's wrong?" Yuri asked.

"We had some pretty clear communications with them before we departed the *Midway*. Everything was going well. Now, we're much closer, and I can barely get a good signal."

LaSalle snatched the box from Eric's hands and played around with it. "Gopher 1 this is Eagle, over?"

Eric made to grab it back from him, but LaSalle pulled away. "Just hold your horses, Captain. I got this."

"Gopher 1, this is Eagle, do you copy, over?"

A barely perceptible voice faded in, along with a face that flickered on and off the screen. The same worn-out, haggard-looking person. "Eagle, this is Gopher 1, roger over."

Satisfied, LaSalle tossed the cube back to Eric and walked away. A frustrated Eric caught the cube and tried to establish communications again, but the person was completely gone, both visually and audibly.

Meanwhile the Biotech guards were setting up the device that would lower us into the sinkhole. One guard pulled out a metal baton-like object, a short pole with openings at each end. He issued a voice command, and the baton glowed blue before both ends protracted. The baton protracted into a full-on long metal stake. He shoved the stake deep into the ground and issued another voice command, which activated sharp protrusions at the base, ensuring the stake was securely anchored into the ground.

LaSalle told us not to worry because each stake could hold up to 1,300 pounds.

Then the guard walked a couple hundred meters around to the opposite side of the chasm. He produced another metal baton and performed the same functions of elongating the ends and shoving the stake deep into the ground. Then LaSalle picked up a large rifle-looking piece of a equipment. It was similar in appearance to their semi-automatic laser rifles but almost as large as a rocket launcher. Three handles jutted up from its barrel. Peeking out from the tip was a pointed piece of steel, shaped like a harpoon. LaSalle touched the side of the rifle to power it on. Once the rifle powered up, the scope illuminated with blue light.

LaSalle pressed a touch screen on the rifle, and a blue laser beam streamed out from the scope which he pointed directly through the opening of the stake at the other end. It took some effort for LaSalle to aim with it. It was heavy and required a muscular person to aim with it. LaSalle pulled the trigger, and the rifle recoiled. A thick metal wire shot out from the rifle and passed through the opening of the stake that was at the opposite side of the sinkhole. He pulled the trigger again, and the wire's arrow-like tip opened up into a "V," allowing it to be fasten securely to the stake.

LaSalle lowered the rifle and opened up a small door on the butt of the rifle. He pulled out a wire with two folding metal levers at the tip that opened up into a similar "V." He passed the wire through the opening of the stake that was on the side of the sinkhole we were on, and he unhinged the levers, securing the tips tightly to the stake.

He leaned forward and yanked on the wire to make sure it would hold. Satisfied, he let go of the rifle. It still hung suspended (close enough to us, with the handles up) between the two wires fastened to the stakes at opposite sides of the sinkhole.

One of the Biotech guards handed him a remote control device, and LaSalle touched the screen. The rifle flipped over, so that the handles faced down.

LaSalle motioned to three of the guards who were waiting patiently, and they all leaned in and gripped a handle. LaSalle pushed another button on the touch screen and the rifle glided across the wire, simultaneously dragging the three guards who held on to the handles over the edge of the sinkhole to dangle above its opening.

Once the rifle glided halfway down the wire, LaSalle pushed another button, and the men who hung from the handles suspended in midair, started to move. The handles detached and slowly descended, revealing thick cables lowering the three guards deep down into the chasm.

Shit. Is that how we're getting down there? What if I lose my grip? At least there is a pool of water to catch me.

"Isn't there a less cumbersome way of entering the mines?" I asked. I tried to keep my tone even.

"Yes, but it would require an additional two hours of hiking. This way is quicker," Eric said. He smiled politely and then headed back over to Sherri, who was examining her ankle.

Why is he being nice all of a sudden?

I peered over the lip of the sinkhole and saw that the three guards had safely descended to the bottom. As soon as their feet touched down, they unslung their semi-automatic weapons and began to police the area.

"What're they doing that for?" I asked LaSalle. "There's nothing down there that could hurt us, right?"

"No," said LaSalle, but he wouldn't look at me. "It's just a precaution."

"Precaution for what?" I asked. I could always tell when he was lying. He wouldn't look at me when he lied.

"He doesn't know what's happened to the researchers." Cox was standing between us now. "We haven't heard anything from them since we left the *Midway,* right?"

"What do you mean?" I asked. "He just made contact with them using Captain Hunt's comms box. Gopher 1 answered. What's the problem?" I detected the fear in my own voice. I looked back and forth between LaSalle and Cox. Yuri was paying attention now too.

LaSalle looked extremely annoyed with Cox, and Cox looked pissed. LaSalle wouldn't say anything, though, so Cox spoke for him again.

"Gopher 1 comprises Captain Hunt's Combat Engineering detachment along with several Biotech technicians—the ones doing the actual demolitions. LaSalle has been trying to reach Biotech's command center, the actual researchers directing the dig. And he hasn't heard one peep from them. Have you?"

LaSalle's face was blanketed by pale anger. He wanted to strangle Cox.

Yuri shoved his way between the two, getting in LaSalle's face. "So that's why you were so hell-bent on not going back to Port Juliette? This isn't an investigation. This is more like a rescue mission disguised as an investigation. You think the miners are in trouble."

LaSalle was red now. "No, just calm down—"

Cox interrupted. "It doesn't matter. He was right. If we'd gone back to Juliette, they'd have turned us right back around."

Cox looked like a man who accepted his own death sentence. Logical to a fault, he even defended LaSalle.

Yuri, on the other hand, was seething. "I don't care. We shouldn't have come here. We don't know what's going on. We don't know what's gone wrong down there. And except for a few of us, your guards are the only ones trained to conduct a rescue mission."

LaSalle took a deep breath and tried to reason with Yuri. "Look, I know you're pissed, but do you really think that they'd have let us—"

"I don't care. I'd rather go to captain's mast or—hell—be court-martialed than put people in danger."

"I told you this was a bad decision," said Eric.

"We should've never boarded the *Pegasus*," said Cox. "The minute we did we let Biotech put our balls in a vice grip. They pretty much own us out here."

"They don't *own* us. So, what if we don't cooperate?" Yuri's fists were in a tight ball.

"I don't think you want the answer to that question," said LaSalle.

"Well, what kind of cryptic B.S. is that?" Eric asked. "What does that mean?"

"It means we're all royally screwed," said Cox. He walked away from the group to sit down against a nearby tree.

I knew that sometimes when words were spoken aloud, they became reality. So, I didn't want to hear this conversation. No one else wanted to hear it, either. All conversations stopped, and the only thing heard was the sound of the rushing waterfall into the sinkhole to fill the silence.

45

thought about our situation. I wondered how we could be so easily under the mercy of Biotech. Then it dawned on me. Komanski, the guard who'd openly challenged LaSalle, hadn't been referring to the Navy people when he'd said it's *their problem*. He'd been referring to A.F.I.B. and its subsidiary, Biotech. The Biotech guards knew about the shady dealings of A.F.I.B's corporate structure. So why continue to work there? *Money.*

I'd heard a rumor back on the *Midway* that the Biotech guards were paid ludicrous sums to work as security for the multi-billion dollar corporation. These were highly coveted jobs. Those who were wise enough not to cooperate were usually blackmailed into working for the corporation anyway. Most of them were ex-military or law enforcement, the crème de la crème of special warfare, special operations forces, reconnaissance, infantry, para-rescue, EOD, SWAT and any other groups trained in survival and hand-to-hand combat. Biotech actively recruited these men and women from various units and agencies around the world. I wondered if LaSalle, as director of their security, sought Biotech out, or if they'd looked for him. I almost didn't want the answer to that question.

"So what now?" Yuri asked, turning to LaSalle. Yuri looked tired. Resigned. Like he'd inherited a problem child.

"We go through the underwater caves, get to the mines, find out what we can and get the hell out."

"Why not just head back?" Yuri wasn't letting this go.

"Because, as I've stated, ad nauseam, we're better off (safer) completing the mission. Plus, there's a bunker and tunnel system when can use to head back."

Yuri's voice went up an octave. "Why the fuck didn't we use the tunnel system to get here? Why all of the risk?"

"Why do you think?" LaSalle's voice was calm. He gestured at a Biotech guard wearing a backpack. "To collect anti-venom and other important samples. Specialist Carver has been loading up his backpack the entire trip. Besides, access to the tunnel system has been closed off until we complete our mission and produce our investigative findings."

And with that, we all quietly watched as LaSalle placed a firm grip onto a handle and motioned for himself to be lowered down to the bottom of the sinkhole.

∿

Once we all arrived at the bottom of the sinkhole, three guards ushered us toward a substantially sized cave that dead-ended. It was perfect because we didn't have to worry about something creeping up behind us, and it was deep enough to provide us significant shelter away from the crashing water or the possibility of rain. We even had enough space in the cave to light a fire if we wanted to, but no one saw a reason to. The temperature was still in the 90s. We set up our cots and prepared dinner, all in silence. Morale was low.

Once daylight was gone, I stood outside of the cave to look up to the opening above. Water sprinkled down, and mist fell from the top as the water from the river cascaded down into the sinkhole.

I was just about to go back into the cave when I spotted him. I sucked in my breath, startled.

LaSalle heard me and walked up. "What? What is it?"

"Look," I said, hurriedly. "Look up there. Do you see him?"

"Yes, I see him."

LaSalle wasn't surprised. I looked over at him, surprised that he wasn't surprised. "It's the same guy I believe you saw right before we boarded the water taxi. He's been following us."

"Who is he?"

"I don't know. I'm not sure, but I have some ideas," he said.

"Care to share?" I asked.

"If I did, it'd probably scare you," he said.

Oh God. I just looked at him.

He was staring up that the mysterious stranger's silhouette. I looked sidelong at LaSalle as he stared up. His tone indicated that he wouldn't be giving me any explanations, so I didn't bother trying.

"Do me a favor," he said, "and don't say anything. I need to be certain first. People are already edgy as it is."

"Why would they be edgy about a scientist here?" I asked. But he turned to head back into the cave. I grabbed his arm. "That's it? You're not going to do anything? You're just going to leave him there? He could be a threat."

I knew I sounded panicky, but the guy looked creepy.

"I've got someone watching him. Don't worry. He won't do anything. Yet." With that, he went back into the cave, leaving me to stare up at the unknown man.

Yet? What the hell? What kind of scientist would do something bad? I wondered if maybe he was one of the ex-cons that Rivera had referred to.

LaSalle hadn't even pleaded with me. He assumed I'd not say anything, and he was right. I wouldn't.

I asked Shakespeare, but all I got from him was, "Based on the biometric authentication data I was able to acquire, there is an 85 percent probability that the individual you are referring to is indeed a Biotech scientist. However, I am unable to obtain any accompanying identification signatures that would provide me a with a precise reading."

"So?"

"So, I am unable to provide the identity of the assailant, Miss Brown."

Assailant? "That's it?"

"Biotech has approximately 300 researchers and scientists in its employ at this station. I'm afraid I can't help you."

Cox stepped up, diverting my gaze for a moment. I decided to postpone the discussion. "Got it. Let's talk about this later. Don't mention this while Cox is here."

"As you wish, ma'am."

I turned back up to the lip of the sinkhole to find that the stranger had disappeared.

"What was that about?" Cox asked.

"What was *what* about?

"Amelia—don't treat me like I'm stupid."

"I'm not."

"You can't trust him, you know. I've seen the way you look at him. He's not the right guy for you, Amelia."

"Really? And who is?"

"What secret are you keeping for him?"

"I'm not keeping secrets." I blinked. I was so scared that he'd see the lie on my face.

He stepped closer to me. "He's dangerous. You can't trust him or keep his secrets. He'll get us hurt or worse—killed—like that guard back there."

"I think you're exaggerating."

"Maybe, but he works for Biotech, and you know we definitely can't trust them. For the past year, every time he comes back to the

Midway, it's to report bad news. He's always knee-deep in some tragic event that happens at this station."

Suddenly, I felt vulnerable. Weak. I could feel my eyes water and a lump in my throat. I wasn't a crier, but at the moment I wanted to curl up and bawl my eyes out. I bit my lip hard, to keep from losing it. I didn't want Cox to see me like that.

He seized my shoulders and pulled me close. The look on his face was filled with genuine concern. He really was watching out for me. I felt a tear pool along my bottom eyelid. He wiped it away. Then he leaned in close. His face was inches from mine.

"I'm not going to let anything hurt you."

"You can't promise something like that."

"As long as I'm alive, I can."

His lips brushed mine softly. Gently at first, and then they pressed against mine with more urgency. He coaxed my mouth open and deepened the kiss. My attraction to him was undeniable. Different than with LaSalle, though. Less animalistic. More soulful. Cox and I had a connection on a different level. When he kissed me, it was like his soul was speaking to mine. I could've kissed him for hours, but I realized that we were in a cave and that someone would catch us at any moment. Part of me didn't really care, but if I was being honest with myself, I didn't want LaSalle to see us. What was I doing? First LaSalle. Now Cox. These two men were pulling me in different directions. I wanted them both. I had to make a decision. I pulled away. I looked into his eyes. Then, I went back into the cave.

46

was surprised to find that the temperature had dropped abruptly that evening, enough that I could feel my face start to cool. I'd assumed that the station would remain hot and wet all day. I was so glad we were wearing our temperature-regulating suits. I would've frozen otherwise.

Although the temperature dropped, the humidity stayed. Mist hovered beneath the opening of the sinkhole like a cluster of clouds. I couldn't see anything at the top of the lip, which worried me even more. I wondered if the scary guy was still there.

LaSalle's team built a smokeless fire so that we could warm our hands and faces without smelling like barbecue. The warmth was a blessing. I stared into the vibrant flames until my lids felt heavy. They lowered involuntarily and fluttered open several times until I was in a deep sleep.

Cox watched me as we bedded down for the night. A mixture of concern and distrust crossed his face. He knew I was hiding something; he knew it had to do with LaSalle. I wouldn't look at him, and I think this hurt him.

I was pissed that LaSalle was putting me in a no-win position, keeping information from the group. He handed out nuggets of information sparingly. I was annoyed that I was turning into LaSalle with my own secret. I couldn't really blame him, though. By not saying too much, he was better able to keep Yuri and the rest of our team calm. Yuri would control the group much easier, and, therefore, ensure its safety if everyone remained calm.

LaSalle's implications of Biotech and the power it exerted was a lot to process. I wasn't sure how far a corporation was willing to go to maintain lies and deception, but I had a feeling it would go very far. I wondered what type of senior level executive had enough influence over our commodore to orchestrate the movement of military assets, both Navy and Marine alike.

Then I thought of the commodore.

I began to see why he'd been so insistent upon us going to this damn station. Who was truly in power? Did the commodore have his greedy hands in Biotech's pockets, or did Biotech somehow obtain leverage over him? What would happen if we left these mines without having finished our investigation?

The thought made me shudder.

Even Cox, who tried to circumvent the commodore and get the admiral to cancel the trip, had been unsuccessful. Ironic that I'd thought he was the bad guy at the time. Rivera had tried to warn me too. I wondered how much Rivera knew. How much did Chief Martinez know? Wasn't she the one who'd told Cox about the meeting in the commodore's stateroom? It seemed everyone knew what was going on but me.

⋙

I wasn't sure how long all of these questions raced through my head, but I eventually drifted off to sleep. I dreamt that night, but the dreams weren't pleasant. The dream began with me walking along a white corridor. At first everything was okay. I felt good. I felt safe. Yuri and Lauralie were there, walking alongside me.

Holding hands. Whitaker was there, too, but he was behind us. He was motioning, waving, trying to get our attention, but there was no sound coming from his mouth. Yuri and Lauralie ignored him, so I ignored him too.

Finally, Whitaker gripped my shoulder and pointed frantically. He was genuinely scared, and that made me scared too. I looked to where he was pointing. Finally, I saw what he saw: first wasps. Droves of them blanketed the ceiling and walls of a dark hallway. The hallway filled up as they moved closer. But once they arrived, they were no longer wasps. They flew lower and lower, much closer to the hallway floor until they morphed into big cat-like figures that galloped toward us in a blockade at an alarming rate. No longer an army of tiny little lethal flying things, they were now a pack of large black cats with Mohawks that ran down their spines. Yuri and Lauralie were now scared, so we all ran. There was only one way to go. Forward. So, we ran forward. I ran as fast as I was able, but it felt like my feet were stuck in mud, and my voice caught in my throat. I could neither move forward with any real progress nor make any significant noise with my voice, but I still tried. We ran until we reached a four-hallway intersection. Yuri, Lauralie and Whitaker seemed to be able to cover distance while I still seemed to have weights in my shoes. They'd run much farther ahead until they were swarmed by a mob of wasps that had materialized in front of us. Now I was alone with wasps and/or cats at my front and back. But then, LaSalle appeared. In the hallway to my left, he motioned for me to follow him. Cox appeared to my right, in the other hallway. He motioned to me too. I looked back and forth. Which hallway to take? Which way to go? With LaSalle or Cox? I waited too long, and one of them grabbed me. A nasty, evil-looking thing—human but not human. It was hideous, like something that wanted to be human but wasn't. It spoke to me—with Shakespeare's voice.

Amelia, it said. *Amelia, come with me. Amelia.*

I felt a gnarly hand on my shoulder, and that's when I woke up.

"Amelia? Are you okay?" It was Cox, bent over my cot with a look of concern. I rubbed my eyes to focus. I wasn't sure how long I'd slept. It felt like only a couple of hours. Cox was still looking at me, waiting for me to tell him I was okay. His face was close to mine. Aside from the previous night's kiss, it was the first time I'd gotten to see his eyes so close. The sun brought out flecks of green in his chestnut eyes that I hadn't noticed before. He was handsome, not in LaSalle's bad-boy, athletic jock-way, but more in the misunderstood-loner-way. Cox reminded me of the type that girls secretly liked but avoided because of his open cynicism and severe candidness. A misanthrope who held a clear disdain for everyone, especially professors who weren't as smart as him. I could picture him in a debate with a professor after class over a book like *Atlas Shrugged.*

"Hey, have you ever read *Atlas Shrugged?*"

"Huh?"

"Atlas Shrugged?" I asked. "Have you read it?"

"No, I heard you," he said. "I'm just not sure why you're asking me about that book."

"Never mind." I shrugged and stood up, twisting into a slow stretch.

"Of course," Cox said. "I read it in high school and then twice more in college."

I shook my head and smiled. He looked at me confused. Then his face got serious.

"You slept pretty late," he said. "The others are prepping the gear for our underwater descent. I figured I'd give you another half hour. LaSalle is making sure your gear is ready, but I need to talk to you."

My nerves already felt wire thin. I wasn't sure if it was my fears of the underwater swim or the fact that Cox was about to grill me again over the secrets he thought I was keeping with LaSalle.

"About what?"

"I want to know what you and LaSalle were talking about last night."

"Can't we discuss this later? Once we get settled at the mines?"

"No," he said. "I need some answers before we go underwater."

"Now's not the time."

"Well, as far as I'm concerned, it is."

I looked at him and considered spilling the beans. What could it hurt? Well, LaSalle would kill me for starters; but, in truth, I was tired of keeping his secrets.

Just as I considered giving Cox a little bit of info, LaSalle showed up. He searched my face, trying to discern whether or not I divulged anything to Cox.

"Hey, it's time to go," said LaSalle. "The gear is ready, and everyone's waiting on you two."

LaSalle looked at Cox and Cox stared right back. Cox looked like he might demand some answers, but the look on LaSalle's face said that he was ready for the challenge.

Cox sighed and headed for his equipment.

I followed.

Let's get this shit over with.

42

"Here," said Yuri. "Think fast."

He tossed me my SPOT-5 (Submersible Propulsion and Oxygenated Transport) gear. This would be my lifeline for the next fifteen minutes.

Yuri was going over standard operating procedures for the device, a ten-pound, airtight, oval-shaped capsule with handles on each side. The capsule was connected to a rectangular box, a forty-pound underwater propulsion system the size of an old car battery. It supplied power to the capsule which would allow us to move through the water with relative ease. The propulsion system was outfitted with a display to program our course and speed, and it allowed for other various functions. The handles on each side of the capsule had sensor buttons and levers which activated headlights as well as an internal communication system (ICS). The ICS transmitted and received sound to a head and chin strap that was outfitted with a water-resistant microphone, ear pieces and a headlight. The ICS enabled us to speak to each other while fully submersed.

Most of us had used the SPOT-5 before, but some people needed training and others a refresher. One of my gunner's mates conducted a crash course and held up the SPOT-5 as he demonstrated its various modes of operation. "Just touch the display name of the person you want to speak to, and then speak, and you will have instant two-way communication. Only up to four people can be on one line at once. Now notice here the apparatus with the two shorter blue tubes connected to the thicker long blue tube. Insert each short tube into your nostrils and apply the seal so that water doesn't seep in. This supplies your oxygen. Now here, the clear tube with the mouth guard-looking thing, you wedge that into your mouth. You breathe in through your nose and exhale through your mouth. Just turn on the CPU, and you'll have a steady stream of oxygen that lasts up to ten hours. Whatever you do, do not remove your mouth and nasal breathing apparatus. Once you're in the water and it's in place, you can't take it out, or water will flood the system, and you'll have to resurface. There are some areas along our transit where you will not be able to resurface, so make sure you have your gear checked by Petty Officer Mackie before you submerge."

"What if you have a stuffy nose?" asked Eric. He had been ignoring most of the presentation, giggling and speaking in low tones with Sherri. I knew he was just showing out for her.

"Do you have a stuffy nose?" Yuri asked.

"No."

"Then shut up." Yuri frowned at Eric, who seemed to have a habit of interrupting. He nodded at the petty officer. "Continue."

The petty officer finished covering the operational procedures of the SPOT-5. Eric watched him with a bored expression. Just like Eric to be disinterested when he wasn't the center of attention.

"I heard that these things just cut off sometimes," Eric said.

"And where'd you here that?" Yuri said.

"I don't know. Just something I've heard." He picked up his unit and examined it with a condemnatory look.

"Yeah. They're pretty old. The military prides itself on using equipment that's at least two decades old," said Cox, who was kneeling, assembling his SPOT-5. He wouldn't look at me. "But they work well—when they work."

Eric shrugged. "I don't know. Something important like breathing underwater should be 100 percent foolproof. Why are we still using this crap?"

"Because we don't have any other crap," said Yuri, "and no one asked for your opinion."

Eric dismissed the conversation and resumed his conversation with Sherri. Yuri looked over at me and tried to give me a reassuring look. He knew I was already terrified of the water and that Eric and Cox were only making it worse.

I peeked over the lip of the murky pool in the darkened cavern. The pool was a portal to an 800-meter underwater tunnel which led to a series of over 100 caves. As I considered the water, I couldn't help but wonder what type of marine life skulked beneath the surface. I'd been so caught up in my concerns over the land-based creatures that I hadn't even thought about the marine biology of the station.

"Hold on a minute," I said. Petty Officer Mackie stood beside me patiently while I pushed a few links on my watch display screen.

Meanwhile, he fiddled some more with the SPOT-5. "Take your time, ma'am."

I unzipped the tiny pocket hidden on my forearm sleeve and pulled out a black marble-sized device to place in my ear. This would allow me some privacy. I moved to the far end of the cavern as the rest of the party finished preparations for the swim.

"Shakespeare, identify dangerous marine life and waterborne threats."

"According to my records, there do not appear to be any indigenous subaqueous organisms which pose a threat to human life."

I exhaled. One less nasty creature to worry about.

"However," Shakespeare chimed, "there is one particular organism that when placed in direct contact with any aquatic source or water-based substance will pose a most immediate threat to human life."

Lovely. My heart slammed against my chest. "Identify threat and provide background information."

"That information is classified, Ensign Brown."

"Classified? How are we supposed to defend ourselves?" The volume of my voice shot up higher than I liked.

"Security measures have been set in place to ensure your safety."

Doubtful.

"Well, what are the chances that we will have any contact with these *organisms* you're referring to?"

"I calculate there to be a 97 percent chance that you will have some level of contact with these particular organisms."

What the hell.

"Well, surely someone here has access to those files, Shakespeare. Provide the name of individual with access."

"I'm afraid that, too, is classified."

"If I guess the name of the person or persons who have access, Shakespeare, will you confirm it?" I already had an idea of who would have access, but I needed to know.

"Unfortunately, that would be a breach of information security, Miss Brown. I *will* tell you that these individuals maintain the highest security clearance classifications possible. I hope that helps."

LaSalle. I know it. And he's not going to tell me a goddam thing. I switched off my display without saying goodbye to Shakespeare. I felt sort of betrayed that he wouldn't tell me anything.

I needed to concentrate during the swim. I looked up to see that Petty Officer Mackie was watching me. He looked worried too. I wondered how much he overheard.

Mackie, who held up the SPOT-5, helped me secure the propulsion system to my harness. Once it was mounted on my back, he programmed the embedded CPU to supply a steady stream of oxygen. "Ma'am, what did you mean, '*defend ourselves*'"?

"Nothing. Everything is fine." I knew the lie was weak and that Mackie wasn't buying it, but there was no use in worrying him too. If we were really in danger, it would all come out soon enough.

48

After everyone slipped into the water, I pulled Mackie aside.

"Do you have a pistol on you?"

"Mr. LaSalle confiscated all of the weapons back at the launch. Only the Biotech guards are carrying."

"C'mon, Mackie. I'll ask you again. Do you have a pistol on you?" I knew him. He was an overly-cautious Type A—one reason I'd brought him along.

He considered me for a moment then inconspicuously unzipped his forensics bag. A shiny, metal-plated pistol greeted us with a lethal shimmer. It looked like an antique, semi-automatic Desert Eagle.

"You wouldn't have another one of those, would you?"

"No, but I have this," he said, producing a large combat fighting knife which he fished from the deep recesses of his bag. "It's called a Raptor."

"An unusual name for a knife."

"That's cause the blade is curved to resemble a large talon. And there's a retractable tail."

The knife was almost twice the size of a traditional Ka-Bar in length and the edge was serrated, the purpose being to inflict a lethal blow. The handle, however, had a small display with two touch screen sensor icons: one labeled "blade," the other "whip." One button caused the blade to gleam with a blue, luminous glow. It was enveloped with the same laser technology as the LaChete I'd seen the Biotech guard use to cut his way through the rainforest. The second button operated a long, retractable cord with a serrated tip that deployed from the base of the handle, allowing the knife to double as a whip. The whip itself also glowed with a blue laser. One lash of the whip across a man's torso would slice him into two pieces like a hot knife through butter. A jab with the knife would melt a large crevice into his body.

"Which one you want?" Mackie asked.

"I'll take the knife." I looked at it admiringly as he placed it in my hand. I was comfortable with a knife. I'd gotten somewhat proficient with it, playing the fight simulator. Of course, this was real life. I had no idea if I'd be able to handle the blade with the same level of proficiency. But I did feel better having it.

"It's all yours, ma'am."

I tucked the knife away in my own bag just before LaSalle looked in my direction. I tried to wipe what felt like a guilty look off my face. He beelined for me.

"Everything okay?" he asked, probing my face. His eyes dropped to my bag where I'd hid the knife.

I strapped the bag around my waist. "Everything's fine. Stop smothering me." I turned my back on him, slipped eye protection over my eyes and slipped into the water with my SPOT-5.

Once we lined up in the water, I was one of the last people in our line. Petty Officer Mackie was behind me, then Sherri and Eric, followed by Specialist Komanski.

We submerged completely beneath the surface, and my fears began to double. First, the water gave me a momentary shock. My face was still exposed to the abrupt change in temperature. The water was ice cold, something I hadn't anticipated since the climate at the station was hot and humid.

This sucks.

The idea of an ice-cold watery death started to invade my thoughts. I couldn't swim, so my entire survival depended on the SPOT-5. The added cold only made me think more about my situation. I began to imagine all types of scenarios: my SPOT-5 malfunctioning, my homeostasis suit not working. I'd either drown or freeze, and there was nothing I could do to convince Yuri to let us turn back. The water was pitch-black too. Virtually no visibility. I started to panic. I jerked my head from side to side, straining to see just anyone. Eventually, Mackie spoke to me through the ICS and placed a calming hand on my arm. "This way, ma'am. Just hold on to my arm. Turn your SPOT-5 headlight on, and you'll be able to see."

I let out a deep exhale. I felt like such a child. First time I panic, and I don't even think to turn on my headlight. I forced myself to relax and focus on the operation of my SPOT-5. I followed Mackie, who was behind Cox. Luckily, we didn't have to swim. With the SPOT-5 system, we glided along smoothly. I could see everyone in front of me with my SPOT-5 headlight on. LaSalle was up ahead directing us, guiding us through tunnels and caverns. I had to admit that just seeing him afforded me some measure of calm.

About five minutes in, I felt something brush my face. I grabbed at it—it was a few inches long and cylindrical—but couldn't tell what it was. It felt somewhat mushy yet substantial and rubbery. For one panicky moment I wondered if it was the organism Shakespeare had mentioned that becomes lethal when in contact with water. I almost let it out of my hand, but I was determined to know what it was.

I fished in my pocket for a penlight, but I couldn't find it. Then I remembered that I had a light on my watch display. I clicked it on and highlighted whatever it was with my light.

A finger. Someone's finger.

I immediately let go of it, watching with disgust as it floated away. Mackie saw me panic and spoke to me through the ICS of the SPOT-5s.

"You okay, ma'am?"

"Mackie, someone's severed finger is in the water with us."

"C'mon, really?"

"It just hit me in the face!"

I heard only silence.

"Mackie, did you hear me?"

"Yes. I heard you."

"What should I do?" I was sure that Petty Officer Mackie was thinking I was a pitiful excuse for an officer, asking him what to do.

"Are you sure that's what it was?"

"Yes, I'm sure." I practically yelled into the ICS.

"Let's just get to the other side, and we'll address it once we surface."

My nerves were raw the entire swim through the underwater cave system. I imagined that things were brushing up against me. Sometimes I saw fish swimming by, but most of the time I didn't exactly know *what* was touching me. Could be a floating hand for all I know. I'd become paranoid.

Despite it all, I couldn't help but notice the beauty of the caves. The cave floor and walls were covered in green, almost florescent, algae-covered rocks. Various plant life jutted from the walls and floor of the caves in assorted, effervescent shades of pink, yellow, orange, blue, and green. Large schools of multi-colored tropical fish swam by me in formation, abruptly changing direction as needed to circumvent our party. They ranged in size from the very tiny, the length of my leg, to quite large. Some were as long as my leg and as thick as my torso. At first some of the larger ones startled me, but I knew these fish were harmless. Even still, I wondered if some of the larger fish got ahold of the severed finger for a morning snack.

As we neared the end of the underwater trail, I could see a beam of light shine down on the area where we'd surface. I throttled my SPOT-5 to full speed. I was ready to get out from beneath the underwater tunnel. We closed in. We were about 70 meters away when my SPOT-5 began to flicker. The headlight blinked on and off.

"Mackie," I said.

"Yes, ma——," he said, but the tail end of his response was cut off.

"Mackie, I think my SPOT-5 is malfunctioning." I tried to calm my voice, but Cox and Eric's complaints about the SPOT-5 played over in my head in continuous loop. I focused on not panicking.

"Ma'am, all you—do is—, and it—work—." Mackie kept trying to tell me what to do, but his instructions were intermittent. I couldn't make out anything he was saying. I noticed a decline in my supply of oxygen. I took frantic breaths, but not much air was coming into my nostrils.

How is this happening? I should have at least eight more hours of supply.

I was hysterical. Mackie was next to me. He shook his head and signaled to me: *Calm down. Don't panic.* Easier said than done. I tried to calm myself, but I could barely breathe, and I couldn't see well. My hysteria was causing sediment to kick up. My SPOT-5 headlight flickered on and off. I was in a tailspin now. I struggled, trying to make sense of my direction in the water. Finally, Mackie gripped my arm. I tried to surface, but he wouldn't let me. *Was there still a cave ceiling above us?* Surely, there was at least an inch of breathing space. Just enough to regroup. Mackie grabbed my arm with more force. Finally, the water cleared, and I could see him. He signaled to me not to surface. Then Cox was beside me. I heard his voice in pieces over the ICS.

"Amelia. Amelia . . . no air up—Try and . . . down. Calm—, Amelia."

Then I felt his arm link mine. I was moved that he come back for me. He made some impatient gestures. I struggled to understand what he was telling me until it dawned on me what he was trying to tell me. I need to take one last deep breath before my SPOT-5 shut off for good. I would have to hold my breath the rest of the way. I would hold on to him, and he would drag me in.

Finally, the SPOT-5 shut off permanently. I had 25 meters remaining distance when the screen flashed and then cut off for good. I wasn't sure I could hold my breath that long. Eric was right. The equipment was crap. More up-to-date technology would have allowed Cox or Mackie to share their oxygen with me. I could tell Cox wanted to give me his, but what would be the point? The minute he took it off, it'd be useless for both of us, and we'd both be without air.

I tried to calm myself and not use too much energy to unstrap the SPOT-5. Mackie, thankfully, brushed my hand away and did most of the work to pull it off of my back. Once it was off, I watched the canister and the generator make their slow descent to the cave floor. Then Mackie pointed toward the light, signaling to me to not waste any more time or energy (which I already felt wane).

I forced myself to quiet my mind. I was running out of air fast. I didn't think I could make twenty-five meters. The remaining distance seemed an eternity away. I forced myself to hold on. I'd make it or die trying.

As we neared the end, I looked up and could see the others' fins kicking and treading water just above us. We veered upwards. I was moments from swallowing water. I couldn't hold my breath anymore. Then I gasped and swallowed a mouthful of water. My body jerked involuntarily. Cox jerked me, as he dragged me up to the surface. His hand clamped on my arm felt like a vise grip. For one so lean, I hadn't realized he was that strong. The kicking fins above faded away. I was going to drown in this cave.

Just before I passed out, I saw Cox's face in front of me and then LaSalle's. Cox looked terrified. LaSalle looked angry. Then darkness took over, and I felt utterly at peace.

49

My throat was on fire. I coughed. Water everywhere. I gasped for air and coughed up more water. I tried to raise up, but my limbs felt heavy, anchoring me down. I tried again, but a set of strong hands gently prodded me to lie flat.

Several people stood over me. Sherri stood several feet away, visibly annoyed.

Yeah. I wouldn't give a shit about you, either.

My eyelids felt heavy. I let them drop. I coughed some more. My throat felt like I swallowed a wire brush.

"Just take it easy. You're gonna be all right, but you have a slight fever," said Yuri.

"It is possible that Miss Brown has the initial symptoms of pneumonia," said Shakespeare. "I'll commence an X-ray of her lungs to discern any signs of inflammation. I will also require a blood sample to determine if a bacterial infection is present."

"I'll go get a lab kit," said Cox, who rushed off.

"My head is pounding," I managed.

LaSalle knelt and cradled my head. He wiped a cool, wet rag across my forehead. All I wanted to do was curl up and sleep. The thought of opening my eyes seemed like an insurmountable feat.

"It is likely that your headache stems from your few moments of oxygen deprivation," replied Shakespeare.

"Shakespeare, go to sleep," I barked. The pain made me irritable. I looked at Yuri. "Can you get everyone away from me? This isn't a side show. I just need a moment."

Yuri nodded. "Okay, Lieutenant Commander Cox is getting you an acetaminophen injector. As soon as the headache is gone, we need to move out. We've dallied here for quite a bit. I'll go review the maps in the meantime."

I nodded. Yuri wanted to baby me some more, and I could tell he wasn't thrilled at the sight of LaSalle cradling my head. But we'd promised to act like non-family members, so he bit his tongue and preoccupied himself with shuttling everyone away from me. Satisfied I was okay, he made preparations for us to move out. I noticed Sherri roll her eyes before walking away.

LaSalle frowned. It reminded me of how angry he looked just before I went under.

"Are you mad at me?" I asked.

"Mad?" he said, somewhat surprised. "No, Mel. If anything I'm relieved." He wiped my forehead again, gently.

"You're pretty gentle for such a tough guy." I had a faint grin.

His face turned red. "Whatever. Just don't scare me like that again."

"This headache is wicked."

"That's normal. It'll go away in a couple of hours. But that's what you get for putting me through such an ordeal."

"It's not my fault the equipment sucks."

"From now on, I want you next to me, so I can keep an eye on you."

"I don't need you to—"

"She awake?" Cox was suddenly there. He stood over me. He didn't look thrilled with LaSalle cradling my head, either. He had a small bottle and an ice pack. "There weren't any acetaminophen injectors in the first aid kit, but here's a good 'ole-fashioned bottle of aspirin. That oughta bring the fever down."

LaSalle snatched the bottle and ice pack from Cox without looking at him or thanking him. *Oh, for goodness sake.* He shook a couple of pills from the bottle. "Here. Swallow these. It'll take awhile for them to kick in, but they'll help eventually."

"How's her fever? I need to get a quick blood sample for Shakespeare," Cox said as he tried to grab my arm. He didn't plan on leaving, which made things awkward.

LaSalle slapped his hand away. "Look, I've got this. You're not needed here."

He glared at Cox. I was still cradled in LaSalle's arms. This made me uncomfortable, with Cox standing over top of us. I squirmed to move out of LaSalle's embrace, but he held me firmly.

"You've got it?' Really? Well, where were you when her equipment cut off, Mr. Big, Bad Navy SEAL?"

Oh boy. Here we go.

"I'll show you *big and bad,* asshole." LaSalle laid my head aside and shot up.

A futile attempt to grab LaSalle's leg caused knife-like searing pain to shoot through my skull. He would not be stopped. I struggled to my feet. Feverish aches trekked through my entire body.

"That's enough. I've had enough of you two." The effort of admonishing them caused another wave of pain in my skull. The rest of our group who'd been fiddling with equipment were now watching us. So, I lowered my voice. "Your dick measuring has gotten old. I don't think that either of you give a shit about me."

"That's not true—" Cox began.

"No. Just shut up," I hissed, putting a hand up. "I'm done with this scene."

I walked over to Yuri, ice pack planted against my temple. I hoped that walking away would make them stop. The thought of a scene was embarrassing.

Yuri's patience was dwindling fast. He wanted to be done with this investigation fast, but I was about to drop another bomb on him. I pulled him aside from the others. Then, I nodded my head at Mackie, quietly signaling him to join us.

"What now?" Yuri asked. He was still fiddling with his MCB, turning it around to determine the appropriate direction to follow.

I looked at Mackie. "Did you tell him about the finger?"

Mackie wiped his forehead with his palm. "Not yet. We've kind of had a lot going on."

"What finger?" Cox and LaSalle said it in unison. Both were hovering around us.

"Jesus. Can't anyone get privacy around here? This is a private conversation," I said, turning my back to them both.

"What finger?" LaSalle wouldn't let this go. "I'm head of security. I want you to tell me right now what's going on."

"Funny. I'm head of this investigation, and I want access to some files that I'm sure you've read (but won't give me). We all want things. People in hell want ice chips—"

"What finger, Mel?"

"Yeah. What finger?" Yuri was anxious.

I started to speak, but I went into a coughing fit. I still had a lot of fluid in my lungs. I tried to catch my breath.

Mackie placed a hand on my back. "Before her SPOT-5 malfunctioned, Ensign Brown saw a severed finger floating in the water."

"You sure?" Yuri asked.

"Yeah, I'm sure," I said between coughing fits. "I had it in my hand."

"Why did you let go of it?" asked Cox. "We could've run a scan on it. Determined who it belonged to."

I frowned at him, not appreciating his judgmental tone. "Because it scared the shit out of me. I didn't know what it was until I shined my wrist light on it. It freaked me out, and I dropped it."

I didn't like the way the Biotech guards looked at me, including the creepy one, Komanski.

"What else did you see?" Komanski asked.

I ignored him, shifting my gaze back to LaSalle. "Is there something you're not telling us?"

LaSalle shook his head. "No."

He jerked his head at Komanski and the rest of the guards and they all huddled up in a corner of the caves, murmuring amongst themselves as we all watched in silence.

Yuri looked skeptical. "What are you not telling us, LaSalle?" Yuri directed the question at LaSalle.

Cox smirked. "I've been saying it all along: he hasn't been straight with us."

"That's *Dr.* LaSalle," Komanski said, resting his hand on his pistol.

Yuri took a step closer to Komanski. Komanski blinked and then looked away.

"I'm prepping with my guys to move out. I'm done wasting time answering questions I don't have to," LaSalle replied.

LaSalle spared me a quick glance before turning his back on all of us. He went through the motions of checking his weapons.

No one challenged him again, but a collective wave of distrust fell across the group.

I decided to put in a secret call to Heather.

∿

Heather was a veritable master at getting things no one else could. I called and prayed she would answer. Luckily, she answered as I was about to give up.

"Yeah," she said, half impatient but somewhat curious.

"I need a huge favor."

"What?" She was annoyed. "Now's not a really good time."

She acted strange. *Paranoid maybe?* Her eyes where shifting in every direction as though she worried about being watched. She looked disheveled and tired, like she'd been without sleep.

"What's wrong?" I asked.

"I can't really talk about it." She looked over her shoulder. Then she fumbled with the monitor.

Sound Curtain On popped up on the bottom of the screen. She spoke fast. "A lot has happened since Senior Chief's death. Fights have broken out. People are freaking out."

How did she even know about Senior Chief's death in the first place? Rivera. Had to be.

She guessed what I'd been thinking. "Don't worry. No one knows that I know about Senior Chief, except for Cortie, of course. I won't tell anyone because I don't trust anyone. And the commodore has been acting weird. It's like he's been pushing everything under the carpet."

"Yeah. I know. He ordered Yuri to continue the investigation even though the rest of Senior Chief's body was found onboard. I don't trust him."

Heather frowned. "I don't either. Lately he's been out of control—violent—growling at people. Issuing orders that don't make sense. When Cortie found out about Senior Chief's body, the commodore told him not to radio you guys. He did it anyway, and the commodore went ballistic. Then they got into it. You should've seen it, Mel. I've never seen him stand up to Captain Radcliff like that. At one point he told the commodore to *suck it.*"

"Shut the front door."

"I swear. Even Radcliffe looked shock."

"I wish I could've seen that."

She looked over her shoulder again. "I gotta go."

"Wait. Why are you acting like someone is coming to kill you?" I chuckled.

But Heather didn't laugh.

"I don't have much more time, but three more dead bodies were found onboard."

"WHAT?"

"Yeah. Radcliff is calling them *training accidents*. I personally think they were murdered. I don't know why. Just a feeling. Cortie has been having odd-hour meetings with the commodore, and every time he leaves the commodore's stateroom he's snippy. He won't tell me anything. Actually, he's been a real shit lately."

I was speechless. She looked scared. It made me scared for her and for me.

"Shit, Heather. I want to talk more, but I don't have much time either. I need something badly, though."

"What?"

"Remember that elite secret file that—"

"Nope."

"What do you mean, *nope?*" I tried not to sound annoyed, but I could hear it in my voice.

"I already told you. Court-martial offense."

"Only if you get caught, which you won't. You never do."

"Mel, if I open that thing up, it might set off alerts. I'm not sure it will, but I don't want to chance it. There are people smarter than me who put those restrictions in place. It's too great a risk."

"Please, Heather. I think our lives depend on it. Yours too."

She lit a cigarette. "I could end up floating in space. This is the kind of thing that 1 percenters like to put in place to protect their wealth. They won't let something like this go. And I feel like someone's been watching me lately. It's weird."

Heather's hand trembled and a pinch of cigarette ash fell onto the desk her elbow was propped on. She didn't bother to wipe way the glowing ember.

"I'm afraid I must agree with Miss Jordan," Shakespeare ventured.

"Well, despite all of that, I'm still asking," I said.

"I really can't," she said, averting her gaze away from the screen. "I didn't want to have to do this, but . . . well, you owe me. You owe me big time, and you know it. I'm cashing in."

"I believe Miss Brown is referring to the queries, several months back, of your missing ship's movement. Her actions enabled you to allude captain's mast, a potential dock in pay and possible time in the ship's—"

"Thanks, I'm aware of that, Shakespeare," she said, with a long exhale. "Shit. I knew you were saving this for a rainy day, but of all things to ask."

"I didn't say that when I had *your* back and squashed all of those legal inquiries. Remember? I could've been court-martialed if I'd gotten caught."

She took a long drag from her cigarette and then put it out. Finally, she looked up. Her mouth was set in a line. "Look, if I do this *enemy of the state* shit for you, it's going to put a rift between us. You realize that, right?"

I lifted my chin. "If it means we live, I'm okay with that."

I could tell I'd hurt her feelings, but I couldn't let that sway me. I needed the contents of the journal. I just knew it. She set her emotions aside, and her gaze hardened, like she was preparing for battle. She always looked like that before a big hack.

I told her everything I knew from Senior Chief reading the journal to LaSalle's odd behavior. I also mentioned Shakespeare's odd comment about organisms that are dangerous in water and threats to human life. That really got her attention, and she promised me that she would do whatever it took to get access. Before I hung up with her, she said one last thing.

"Mel?"

"Yeah?"

"Remember all of those times I said you were crazy? Well, you're not crazy. This place really is messed up."

Her hand shook as she ended the transmission.

She was legitimately terrified. *What if someone really was watching her?* I shivered. Even though she had Rivera and she was on a ship full of thousands of people, I still worried. And with all the stuff LaSalle told us about Biotech, a trickle of fear wormed its way back in.

I told her that I would be hiking to the mines. She said it would take anywhere from twenty minutes to an hour, and she would remotely upload the files to my MCB as soon as she was done.

I hung up with Heather, and Petty Officer Mackie approached. He looked suspicious. "Is everything okay, ma'am?"

I figured there was no point in lying. Mackie wasn't stupid, and he could be a lot of help if it came down to it. Better that he was prepared than naïve. I told him everything I knew, including everything surrounding the journal.

He didn't say much. It's one of the things I liked about Mackie. He waited and observed before asking questions or having an opinion. He was a patient man.

"Mackie. I'm worried about this trip and what we are going to see in the mines."

"Well, no matter what we see, I'll remain alert and have your back, ma'am."

"And I'll have yours; but right now, I need you to get rid of this without anyone noticing."

I fished around in my bag and pulled out a small forensic bag containing a severed finger.

"I thought you let go of it," said Mackie.

"That's just what everyone else thinks. I scanned it, and I'm going to send the data back to Chief Martinez at the port. I need answers, and I don't want anyone stopping me from getting them. It's time I had some secrets of my own."

Mackie nodded appreciatively as he left to dispose of the finger.

∽

I uploaded the data I retrieved from the scanned finger and sent it off to Martinez.

I instructed Shakespeare to get Chief Martinez on the line. After several beeps, Midshipman Whitaker's face popped onto the screen. He had a dopey grin on his face which showed all his teeth. After a couple of moments, I saw why. A Biotech nurse was injecting a shot into his leg. She was young and blonde with big boobs and a tiny waist, exactly the type of girl a midshipman would like.

"Whitaker, where's Chief Martinez?"

"She's helping out with a situation, ma'am. A Biotech employee was murdered this morning."

A dark feeling swept through me.

"How?"

"I don't know, but there's been a lot of commotion in port. Alarms have been going off all day, and people are running around like it's the apocalypse."

"They're just routine fire and evacuation drills," said the nurse in the background.

Whitaker looked at her and grinned. "What if they were real? Would you still take care of me?"

"Of course," she said, matter of fact. She wasn't playing into his charms, but Whitaker was eating up the attention, nonetheless.

"Whitaker, stop flirting with the nurse and go get me Chief Martinez," I said, losing patience.

Whitaker turned scarlet for a moment. The nurse stifled a small grin.

"Ma'am, she's in one of the labs doing something. I can't get access. Besides, Jenna here has demanded that I get some rest," he said winking at the young nurse.

The nurse rolled her eyes. "No, I didn't. I said that it'd probably be a good idea if you rested. I didn't demand anything. Besides, after this last injection, your leg will be almost healed, and you'll be able to run around just fine."

297

I was getting annoyed. Yuri signaled to me to hurry up. We were moving out, and I was having to deal with a silly midshipman and his silly crush.

"Look, I have some fingerprint data that needs to be run. We found a severed finger in the caves, and I need to identify who it belongs to. I don't have time for your crap. So, get me Chief Martinez now, unless you know how to do it."

Whitaker was barely paying attention. He didn't even flinch when I mentioned the words "severed finger." He was busy watching the nurse who was bent over fiddling with some equipment.

"Whitaker. For fuck's sake!"

He tore his gaze away from her and turned reluctantly back to the display. "All right, all right. Wait. Did you say a *severed finger?*"

"Yes, and I need to you to run the scans. If I have to repeat myself again, you're never coming back to the station. Got it?"

"Okay, okay," he said holding his hands up. "Jeez. Send me the data. I'll run it. I know how to do it."

"Good. I already sent it. Process it and get me the results back ASAP. When Chief Martinez gets back, have her call me."

"Yes, ma'am," he said with a mock salute. Whitaker was cocky, which was annoying, but his attitude reminded me so much of myself as a midshipman.

He grinned at me. "Oh. ma'am. I almost forgot. Are we—"

The screen went dark. Then the picture came back into view, but everything was illuminated in red, including Whitaker's face.

"Great." I heard the nurse say. "We lost power. I'm going to see what's going on." She wagged her finger at Whitaker as she opened the door to leave. "And you stay here."

He blew her a kiss. I rolled my eyes. Then I heard a sound in the background—like gas hissing.

"What's that?"

He shrugged. "I don't know, but it smells like a really bad fart."

"Can you be serious for once?"

"I am serious. It smells like shit in here." He was frowning.

Then the picture on the screen muddled, as if Whitaker dropped his MCB. The picture came back into focus, but the view was of the room upside down. All I could see was a shiny white floor (which looked pink due to the red lighting) and a table leg. I couldn't see Whitaker or anyone else, but I could hear. Several sets of frantic footsteps and some yelling echoed into my earpiece.

Was that a scream? No. Just my imagination.

"Whitaker," I said. "Whitaker. Are you okay?"

Then: *This Line Is Disconnected* showed up in bold letters on my display. I tried calling a several more times until finally I gave up. They were probably just running the drills the nurse mentioned. Even though a set of chills ran up and down my spine, I convinced myself that it was nothing and that Whitaker was probably rushed out of his room for the drill.

Despite the bad feeling I had, I folded my MCB back up and slipped it into my bag. I kept my earpiece in, hoping Whitaker would contact me soon.

50

"What are you doing?" Sherri was unexpectedly right next to me. "None of your goddamn business," I replied as I finished zipping up my pack. "What do you want?"

She had a panicked look on her face. "I just wanted to know what else you saw in the water. That whole finger thing freaked me out."

"That's all I saw," I said, a bit softer. She looked genuinely scared. She was shaking a little.

"I'm sorry that I've been such a bitch to you," she said. "I really didn't know about your relationship with Eric. I guess I got a little jealous."

Her? Jealous?

"No. It's okay. I haven't been on my best behavior either. And you're gorgeous. You have no reason to be jealous."

"Well, that's sweet of you to say, but you're very pretty too." She held out her hand. "It's hard enough being women with all of this testosterone flowing. What do you say we bury the hatchet and try to be nice to each other?"

I shook her hand, relieved. "That sounds great to me."

She smiled. It was polite and sincere.

We made our way back to the rest of the group. Eric looked at the both of us with an odd expression then an apprehensive one.

"Don't worry, Eric. We weren't trading information," I said.

Sherri chuckled. Eric cringed.

Yuri was in the middle of reviewing some digital charts. He consulted with LaSalle regarding proposed directions and tunnels to choose. Cox looked over Yuri's shoulder, offering up advice.

The call with Whitaker still bothered me. "Have any of you contacted anyone at Port Juliette?"

Cox frowned. "No, why?"

"I'm sure it's nothing," I said.

"I just put in a call to a contact I have there, but sh—they didn't answer." Yuri looked a little embarrassed. He was referring to Lauralie, but no one seemed to notice but me.

"What is *nothing?*" The concern on LaSalle's face and his voice made everyone nervous.

"I made a call to Whitaker because I had some things I need him to do, but the call got disconnected. It was strange."

"So what?" Eric said. "Stations don't have the best communications suites. Was probably just a crappy connection."

"Perhaps. Whitaker's nurse said they'd been running drills all day, but this didn't look like a drill. He dropped his MCB and he didn't bother picking it up. It's like he left in a hurry."

"People rush and drop things during emergency during drills, Mel," Eric said, but there was hesitancy in his voice.

"I heard yelling too. Maybe a scream. I'm not sure. I think something bad is happening back at Port Juliette."

LaSalle muttered a barely discernible, "Shit."

We all heard it.

Silence turned to mayhem.

Eric, who'd been sitting on the floor of the cave, stood up. "What do you know, LaSalle?"

LaSalle stood firmly. His face was blank. "I know as much as you do."

"Bullshit,' Cox blurted, shaking his head. "You said *shit* like you weren't surprised something bad happened."

"Yeah," said Eric. "I noticed that too."

Shakespeare spoke: "You should all be grateful that Dr. LaSalle has elected to accompany you on this particular mission. His experience and corporate knowledge will be of great use to you." Whenever Shakespeare spoke, people listened, but it was always with a cautious ear.

"I'm just here to keep you safe. That's all," said LaSalle, arms crossed.

"Really?" said Cox. "Safe from *what?*"

"I'm afraid that Dr. LaSalle is unable to provide full disclosure of the information you're seeking. You should put faith in his judgment and rely on his expertise."

Eric's tone softened a bit. "What about these classified files Ensign Brown mentioned earlier? Why won't you give her access to them?"

"For your safety. Dr. LaSalle is looking out for your well-being, and he—"

"Listen, you android fuck. Shut up, and let LaSalle answer for himself." Eric directed his contemptuous look at me.

"My apologies, Captain Hunt, but to be clear, I am not an android. I am a highly complex and advanced artificial intelligence operating system."

Eric buried his head in his hands and sighed. "Whatever, dude."

LaSalle pinched the bridge of his nose. "Look, the commodore gave explicit instructions that the files were only to be accessed on a need-to-know basis."

"You don't think we're on a need-to-know basis?" said Eric.

"Not yet."

Eric threw up his hands. "One of your guards is dead, and we're on a futile mission to investigate a death that occurred thousands of miles away. When is a good time?"

I tapped Eric's shoulder. "Well, you were all for this mission, remember? I distinctly recall how eager you were to put us all in this ridiculous mess back in the commodore's stateroom."

"Shut your mouth for once, Mel," Eric said, scowling at me.

"Don't talk to her like that," said LaSalle in a deadly tone.

"Look, I get that we're at the mercy of Biotech, but we need to know what we're facing." Eric was in LaSalle's face. Sherri tried to hold him back.

LaSalle turned his back on Eric to face Yuri. "We don't have time for this. It's important that we keep moving. The quicker we get to the demo team, the quicker we'll be out of here."

Eric grabbed LaSalle's arm. "Hey, I'm talking to you. Don't turn your back on me." Komanski stepped between Eric and LaSalle, a move to indicate that Eric was overstepping his bounds. Eric backed up a little, but he didn't stop asking questions.

"We haven't had comms with the demo team or the command center since we got here, and now we don't have comms with the port. You want us to ignore that trivial detail and still go find my guys. But let me ask you this, genius, why don't we hear any demolitions going off?"

"Maybe they're on a poop break," one of the Biotech guards chimed in. A couple of them chuckled.

LaSalle looked at Eric. "They're combat engineers. Trained Marines. Riflemen first and trained in demolitions. I'm sure they're fine."

"Fine from what?" asked Eric.

It was the question everyone wanted the answer to but the very thing that LaSalle refused to answer. He resumed ignoring Eric and turned back to Yuri.

Eric stomped off, complaining and not bothering to censor himself. He wasn't in LaSalle's face though. If he pushed too much, it was obvious the Biotech guards were itching to make an example of Eric. He paced back and forth with Sherri trying to calm him down.

It occurred to me that Eric was scared. His bitching irritated me until I realized that was his coping mechanism. His fears amplified my own, and I realized that several of his questions were valid.

LaSalle pulled out his MCB and unfolded it. He punched in a couple of commands and pulled up an intricate holograph that mapped out the cave tunnel system. "You need help finding the route to take us to the combat engineers? I know it. I've been there a couple of times."

Yuri looked like he debated whether to continue Eric's line of questioning, but instead he opted not to.

Yuri and LaSalle tinkered with the cave map holograph and motioned for Eric to help. With some reluctance, Eric helped them. He was quiet, though. They all were.

Cox joined them, too, but he stood off to one corner with his arms folded, watching LaSalle. He was quiet, staring at LaSalle with open distrust and resentment.

51

We headed out. Yuri pointed at a wide and dark tunnel (it looked the creepiest compared to our other three choices), and our party headed for the opening. I had Mackie walk next to me and used the opportunity to try and call Heather again. I promised her that I'd give her two hours, but given the notion of waiting seemed unbearable. I had to get to those files.

Heather picked up after a few beeps. I tried to look inconspicuous as we walked, as if I was listening to music. I restrained myself from staring too long at my wrist device display.

"I don't have much time," were her first words. "I'm sending you a scan of the file now. I modified it so that you can convert from visual to audio file in case you don't have time to read it."

I stole a glance at my wrist display. She looked tired and disheveled. There was a sheen of sweat on her forehead.

"You're a badass," I whispered. "I didn't think you'd have it this quick."

"Once I saw what was in it, I rushed and had Shakespeare help me."

"You really are the—"

"Mel," she said, cutting me off. Her tone was urgent. "I reviewed the files. It's not good." There was a tremble in her voice.

"Well, what—"

"This scientist, Gerg, kept a diary, and the shit that's in there is all kinds of jacked up. You're in trouble. You need to get out of those caves. Now. There's *things* out there. Things that will hunt you."

"*What?*" I whispered, but it was more like a bark.

"I don't have time to explain. Just trust me and leave."

I wanted to drill her with questions, but she sounded terrified. She peeked over her shoulder. She was about to end our transmission.

"Heather, what do you mean, *things?*"

"Like zombie-shit. I really gotta go."

"Wait . . . what? C'mon."

"'Mel—"

"Did you show Rivera?"

"No. I can't find him."

"Why not?"

"He might be dead. I don't know."

"WHAT?"

That's when I heard a loud banging in the background. She looked at the hatch behind her.

"Where are you calling me from?"

"I'm in the armory. I stole your code."

"Why are you in the armory? What's happen—"

"If you want more, you'll have to listen to the file." She was talking fast. "Just get out of there. Now. *Vaya con dios, Amiga.*"

Then she ended the transmission.

I was completely freaked, and Heather was panicked. But it still wasn't lost on me that her last words to me were in Spanish. She's always so hip, even during crisis.

I decided to call Rivera. I convinced myself that if he was okay, it would mean that Heather's freak-out was just more of her drama. Deep down, I knew that Heather's advice to leave was valid, but I wanted desperately to believe that she was just imagining things.

I couldn't handle the notion that life had gone to shit both back on the *Midway* and at Port Juliette. If that were true, we could be stuck out here.

I called Rivera. After a few failed attempts, I called the commodore. I probably should've asked Yuri first, but I didn't want to waste time.

The commodore picked up. I was relieved. If the commodore was safe, then Heather had to be safe too.

"Ensign Brown. What a pleasant surprise," he said. " Are Commander Jefferson *and* Dr. LaSalle too busy to make the call themselves?"

Shit. I hadn't thought how I'd explain that. "Uh, yes, sir. They're pouring over some charts right now."

"You haven't gotten to the mines yet? I'd have thought you'd be there by now." He was irritated.

I started to explain the incidents that delayed us: Whitaker's injury and the stung guard, but I knew it was futile. So, I kept silent. A voice in my head told me not to reveal too much.

"We'll be there soon."

"Well, if you haven't completed your investigation, to what do I owe this pleasure?" The self-importance in his voice made me want to kick something.

"Sir, I just wanted to make sure everything is okay back there."

He frowned. "Why wouldn't it be?"

I didn't want to dime out my roommate, but at the same time, I was worried. Maybe she needed help, and maybe every second delayed would make things worse for her. "I got a disturbing call from Lieutenant Jordan. She sounded overly stressed out."

"Isn't that the nature of being a junior officer? Over-stressed and over-worked? I'm sure whatever it is, it's nothing that can't be handled," he said. I could hear him pouring the last remnants of scotch down his throat. "I think your roommate has an affinity for the dramatic."

"No one else is answering my calls, though. Is there something wrong with the communications suite?"

"No, I'm pretty sure I'd be the first to know. Things are running like a well-oiled machine here."

"Lieutenant Jordan was scared, like she was in danger."

"Oh really? I'll have to check on her. Where is she at?" He sounded surprised but it didn't seem genuine.

I'd made a huge error. I wasn't sure what, but, somehow, I knew I messed up.

"Where did Lieutenant Jordan call you from?" he asked. "What location?"

That's an odd fucking question. Don't tell him shit.

"I'm just curious," he added, as if it occurred to him that it was an odd question.

He's a lying shit.

"Uh, I don't know, Commodore."

"Look at your display history."

"It's broken." It was the only thing I could think of on the fly. I powered down my wrist display immediately. "Some of my equipment fell out of my bag when we descended into the caves, including my MCB and the interface with my wrist device."

Weak but hard for him to prove or disprove.

He was irritated but accepted the excuse. "Well, when we end this call, use someone else's MCB to find her location and Rivera's too. Then call me back."

Fat chance, asshole.

He didn't know Heather or Rivera's whereabouts while they were in the middle of investigating deaths? That seemed odd to me. "I'll get right on that, sir. Sir, I need to go, we are moving out."

"Very well, Ensign. Don't forget to get me Lieutenant Jordan and Lieutenant Rivera's whereabouts and have Dr. LaSalle give me a call."

"Yes sir."

I wondered why just LaSalle? And why was he so cheerful, considering the situation? I decided to try and call Heather back and tell her about my call with the commodore. I tried several times, but she didn't pick up. I worried. Then, I decided to just listen to the files. *Zombie-shit.* Yeah, Heather was dramatic, but not crazy. She kept telling me to *leave now.*

Like someone revived with smelling salts, I woke up from my denial. I realized that we were truly in immediate danger.

I shuffled along the dark cave. My spirits were low because I knew I wouldn't like what I heard. I was cautious, though. I watched the backs of LaSalle and his men as they walked and talked. I risked a glance behind me. Eric and Sherri were there. Eric was munching on a piece of beef jerky. Sherri looked back and smiled. Behind them, Cox walked next to Yuri, but they weren't speaking.

I glanced at Mackie, who was to my immediate left. He was worried. He looked at me with an expression: *what's going on?*

I shrugged. I'd know more soon.

I whispered a few commands to Shakespeare, and his voice materialized.

"Ensign Brown. Need I remind you that those files are restricted? The consequences of opening them will be most severe."

"Just settle down, Shakespeare. These are scanned, unrestricted copies."

"Nevertheless, the content itself is still classified and embedded with numerous alert mechanisms. I should advise you that should you access the files, I am compelled to notify certain parties of the security breach."

"Compelled?" I growled in low tones. "You just helped Lieutenant Jordan convert them."

"Because she compelled me to."

"Then, I demand that you don't alert anyone."

"Not in this case, ma'am. Your authority (as well as Miss Jordan's) has been overridden in the matter of this file."

"I intend to read them, Shakespeare, and you can't keep me from doing so."

"Right you are, Miss Brown, but I am under an umbrella of strict protocols to save you from your own insatiable curiosities. I will take certain measures should you open the files. I estimate that you will have approximately three to five minutes to extract whatever information you seek before being discovered."

"What're you saying? That LaSalle will come get me once I've opened the files?"

"I can neither confirm nor deny that Mr. LaSalle will be one of the individuals notified. However, I beg you, Miss Brown, don't open the file. The result will be catastrophic."

"Can you confirm if anyone at Biotech will be notified?"

"Yes, Miss Brown. I can confirm that."

"Are they stationed at headquarters or in the field?"

"I'm afraid that's classified."

I mulled it over for a minute. What if Biotech sent their henchmen? Would it be LaSalle and his guards or some other hired guns? What then? Even with Eric's Marines, we were hardly in a position to fend off LaSalle and his men or any other Biotech Army. They had all of the weapons. Would LaSalle really hurt me? I was certain that he never would, but then, how much did I really know about him?

Heather, who was terrified of being prosecuted for hacking the files, insisted I open the files. I trusted her. So, I opened the cluster of files before I could talk myself out of it.

52

The minute I opened them, I heard a tiny, continuous beep and the word TRESPASS in bold red floated repeatedly down the right side of my wrist display.

I immediately had Shakespeare dictate the files to me. I'd get as much information as I could before being discovered.

I was 100 percent certain that LaSalle would be notified of my security breach. I listened while my eyes were trained on LaSalle's back.

On the dot, three minutes passed before LaSalle stopped in his tracks. He was going over something when suddenly he stopped talking. He "shushed" his men, with his hand up, signaling for them to be quiet. Then he barked an order at Komanski while gesturing impatiently. Komanski removed the bag from his shoulder and reached inside. He pulled out a small device and tossed it to LaSalle. LaSalle unfolded it and then rushed back into the bag for his MCB. His movements were rushed. He began to issue commands and even attempted a retinal scan.

I watched all of this while struggling to focus on Shakespeare's dictation.

I closed my eyes, and a couple of seconds passed before I heard LaSalle's voice. "Where's Ensign Brown?"

"Can I help you, sir?" said Petty Officer Mackie.

"Don't play dumb with me. Where the fuck is she?"

At this point I had fallen to the back of the group to buy myself some time.

"I'm not sure, sir. I think she might've ducked out to use the restroom or something."

"Ensign Brown, stop what you're doing right goddamn now."

I strained to hear every word that Shakespeare uttered while LaSalle yelled for me. I had a couple more seconds before he'd find me. The cave was big, but it wasn't that big. I wondered what he'd do. Would he hit me? Was he capable of that? He sounded furious.

Finally, I heard his last few footsteps as they closed in on me. I kept listening.

"I fucking knew it," he said. He yanked the bag from my shoulder and fished around for my MCB. He found it and slammed it down onto the cave floor. He even stomped on it several times. Shakespeare's voice cut in and out. Then he pulled out his pistol and riddled the paper-thin device with a laser bullet. Holes melted through in several places before the entire thing started to disintegrate. "There. You happy?"

I snatched my bag out of LaSalle's hands and pretended to be more pissed off than I actually was. I'd gotten what I needed, and I could still get the rest of Shakespeare's dictation through my wrist device, but I wasn't planning on reminding him of that. "What's your problem?"

"You're my problem. Those files were restricted, and you've somehow opened them. Do you know what you've done?"

"I know what I'm doing."

"No. You don't." LaSalle was visibly shaking. From rage. "You've created a mess. A big one. And now I don't know if I can clean it up. You might've just put us all in danger."

LaSalle's rant had caused a scene. By now, everyone had gathered to where we were.

"*How* has she put us in danger?" Yuri asked.

LaSalle was debating on how to answer that. He stared at his feet.

I spoke. My voice rang timid. "He's suggesting that Biotech will send people here to find us."

"Great," said Eric, with a resentful scowl. "Why can't you just ever do what you're told, Amelia?"

'Because it's important. If you knew what I heard, you'd—"

LaSalle gripped my arm, so hard, I winced a bit. "Don't—"

"She might as well tell us now," said Eric. "Cat's out of the bag."

"Not yet it isn't." In response, LaSalle jerked his head at one of the guards who pulled out a small device. He handed a black cube to LaSalle. It was similar to the one Eric used at the top of the waterfall to establish comms with the demolishing team. LaSalle spoke into it: "Breach closed. Situation contained. Collateral damage—0 percent."

Then he rattled of an identifier code and a series of numbers. He finished with a retinal scan, and then tossed the cube back to the guard.

Yuri sent an accusatory glance my way before he spoke. "So what are our chances now that they will send people?"

LaSalle took a deep ragged breath. He looked tired. He ran a hand through his hair, a gesture I was becoming familiar with. "I don't know. Fifty, maybe 60 percent chance. Maybe more."

"Sixty percent. Okay. Well, it could be worse," Eric said. He said it more to himself, as if going into shock.

"It may be more," LaSalle repeated, frustrated.

Yuri, always the hopeful one: "Well, even if they did, they'd have to find us first, right?"

Komanski snorted. "That won't be too hard. We all have tracking devices in our jumpsuits."

"Shit." Yuri's face fell.

Everyone looked disappointed. I could feel the judgment being directed my way. I even expected a murderous look from Sherri, but she was busy consoling Eric. I looked at Cox, hoping for some reassurance, but he just looked down at the cave floor.

Guilt started to seep in. I hadn't thought of our tracking devices.

LaSalle pulled a knife from his bag.

"What're you doing?" asked Eric.

"Removing my tracking device." LaSalle was digging the tip of the blade into his suit, at his shoulder joint. He ripped open a small hole and retrieved a thin piece of metal, the size of a paper clip. He dropped it onto the ground and smashed it with his boot heel. We all just watched him as though he was crazy. He looked up at us, appalled at our reticence. "I suggest you do the same."

"I'm not doing that," said Eric folding his arms like a stubborn child.

"The hell you're not," said LaSalle who was in Eric's face. "If they find you, they find me, and I'm not letting that happen."

"It'll mess up our temperature equilibrium, and we'll have to swim back in that cold-ass water and freeze."

"Tough shit. You people should think about these things first before you make stupid decisions."

Ouch.

It bothered me that Komanski stood nonchalantly by the other Biotech guards, seemingly unaffected. He seemed bored by the situation whereas everyone else was visibly upset. Still, though, he removed the tracking device from his suit.

"Big deal. So what if they find us?" asked Eric.

Cox shook his head. "What do you think, nimrod? They'll kill us."

"I never said that," said LaSalle.

"Yeah, but you're not, not saying it either," said Cox.

"It is what it is. Do stupid things, win stupid prizes."

Cox got in LaSalle's face. "You can blame Amelia all you want, but the fact is you sold your soul to the devil, working for that piece of shit company. You have to live with yourself, and you're doing it by hanging around and cleaning up their messes. Who's winning a stupid prize now?"

My pulse quickened. LaSalle and Cox were faced off, inches from each other. LaSalle grabbed Cox's collar with menacing speed and shook him. He was practically yelling. "Were you the one who helped her get into the files?"

"Stop it," I said, but they ignored me.

Cox wrapped his own hands around LaSalle's wrists, but LaSalle wasn't letting go. They strained and stared at each other like two fighters in a ring. Words weren't spoken. Just invisible threats and silent promises of violence hung in the air. LaSalle was angry, and Cox's face froze into a hateful canvas. LaSalle's voice was still raised, and he wouldn't stop shaking Cox. "I know it was you. You idiot. I've had enough of your superior shit, Cox."

Cox said nothing. And LaSalle continued to shake him. I couldn't help but think, *if he doesn't stop shaking him like that—*. Then in a millisecond, Cox's face changed. All I could think was: *no*. But my thoughts failed to materialize onto my lips. Cox heaved back and brought the top of his forehead firmly onto LaSalle's nose. Then LaSalle did let go of Cox's collar. Blood spurted across the cave floor. LaSalle doubled over, holding his nose, attempting to staunch the bleeding. "I think you broke my nose, asshole."

In those next moments, everything seemed to slow down. Cox's headbutt set into motion a tsunami of events. Komanski and a few other guards rushed Cox.

Yuri shouted, trying to calm everyone. I yelled, too, but no one listened to either of us. I was worried for Cox. Seasoned ex-special forces guys were about to give him the beating of his life. He wasn't a large man. Komanski, on the other hand, was huge. So were the other guards; but to my surprise, Cox could handle himself.

Komanski was the first to rush. Cox took him out with one swift but hard jab. A step to the side and a fist to Komanski's jaw line. The guard wobbled a bit and then slumped onto the cave floor. Another guard came with a hook, but Cox ducked and barreled into him. For someone so lean and wiry, he used his body like a battering ram, aiming for the guard's midsection and tackled him to the ground. He pounded the guard in the face before getting up to deal with his next assailant. I was grateful that LaSalle recovered from getting his nose busted. I wasn't sure that Cox could fend off an angry LaSalle *and* the Biotech guards. Another guard threw a wild punch. He came from the side. Cox whipped around and ducked, just enough to miss the punch. He responded with his own jab. Cox had deceptive punching power for his slender build. The guard wobbled a little. Cox clinched the back of the guard's head which forced the guard to bend forward. Then, he brought his knee up with ninja-like speed and connected with the guard's head. The guard fell back and was out cold.

Unfortunately, Cox was significantly outnumbered, and two guards got ahold of him from behind. At this point, LaSalle had recovered.

I shuddered. LaSalle looked pissed. Cox, who was now restrained, was the picture of lethal calm as LaSalle walked up.

"You shouldn't have done that," he said, still clutching his bloody nose.

I pulled on LaSalle's arm. "Gerard, don't."

But he brushed me off. That was the first time I'd used his first name in front of people. I could feel the suspicious looks, but I didn't care.

Without a word, LaSalle brought his fist back and sent it flying, cracking Cox right on the cheek. To Cox's credit, he took the punch without even a whimper. LaSalle started to reach back again, but then Shakespeare spoke. "Dr. LaSalle, Lieutenant Commander Cox was not responsible for the security breech."

LaSalle slowly lowered his arm. "Then who was responsible?"

"Certain programming will not allow me to identify the party responsible; however, I can assure you that it wasn't him."

LaSalle looked at me. I could tell I had really crossed a line with him. A savage look flickered across his face. He was going to get nasty. "Tell me who it was."

"I can't tell you, but I swear to you it wasn't him." I took a shaky breath. He had to know it was Heather, but he seemed unsatisfied. The twisted look on his face suggested that he would make me confess by using Cox, who was still being held by the Biotech guards. I was frantic now at the prospect of Cox being hurt any more. I looked at Yuri and even Eric, silently pleading with them to do something. Both seemed entranced by the entire scene.

LaSalle raised his arm again, but finally Yuri stepped in.

"I think that's enough, LaSalle." He put his hand on LaSalle's chest. Light enough to not be confrontational but firm enough to mean it.

"I'll decide what's enough," said LaSalle, focused on Cox. He swiped Yuri's hand away.

Yuri stepped in front of LaSalle to block him even more from Cox. "No, I decide what's enough."

LaSalle laughed. Everyone who wasn't a Biotech guard winced. All the military people looked uncomfortable. The Biotech guards looked predatory, like they'd been waiting to perform a massacre.

They could. They have all the weapons.

"I would advise against this," said Shakespeare, but no one was listening to him.

With a respectable amount of stealth, Petty Officer Mackie walked up to LaSalle, pulled his pistol out, and pointed it at LaSalle's head. "No. Commander Jefferson is the presiding officer here. *He* decides what's enough."

I was grateful at that moment that I'd decided to take the Raptor and let Mackie keep the pistol. I wasn't sure I could've pointed a pistol at LaSalle, even though he was threatening Cox and undermining Yuri. Even if I could, would LaSalle believe me capable of pulling the trigger? The look on Mackie's face was cold. No one doubted his willingness to pull the trigger should the need arrise. Mackie had the kind of look that can't be fabricated without a rough upbringing.

We all stood there. Divided. On one side of the cave were the Biotech guards. On the other side were the Navy personnel. Eric and his Marines, along with Sherri, were standing in the middle but closer to us. It was an awkward moment. I noticed that Komanski had his pistol out, ready to shoot Mackie. Truthfully, I hated Komanski.

LaSalle broke the tense silence and held his hands up, chuckling. He nodded at the two guards who still held Cox. They released him and shoved him back over to the rest of us. I went over to Cox and grabbed his face, examining his cheek. A purple bruise had already formed. I knew this made LaSalle angry, but I didn't care. It was my way of blatantly letting him know that he'd fucked up with me.

As usual, Yuri's sense of diplomacy diffused the situation. "Listen everyone. LaSalle's right. We need to get rid of these tracking devices. We'll just have to gut it out and brave the climate."

Everyone fell silent but complied.

LaSalle handed me a knife. His gaze was direct as if trying to discern if there was still a chance with me. I snatched the knife from him. He opened his mouth to say something, but I cut him off.

"Not now." I refused to make any more eye contact with him. I stood with my eyes averted until he took the hint and walked back over to his men.

I cut away at my suit. I dug the tip of it into my shoulder as he had. I stopped when the knife clinked against the small flat metal device. I removed it, dropped it to the ground and smashed it to pieces with my boot heel.

I looked at Eric. He acquiesced and held his hand out for the knife.

53

Once everyone finished with their suits, LaSalle came back over to us. Cox stood up to face him. I felt another surge of panic. But he simply handed Cox an ice pack for his cheek which was beginning to swell up. I knew it was some guy-code show of respect, but I still wasn't going to forgive LaSalle for his behavior.

"Where'd you learn to fight like that?" LaSalle asked.

"Abusive father. Three older brothers. All mean. All bums." Cox pressed the ice pack firmly to his cheek. "I stayed out of the house as much as I could and hung out at a local mixed martial arts gym. The owner took pity on me and let me hang out there as long as I helped him. You learn how to take care of yourself pretty quickly, when you're scrawny."

LaSalle nodded in admiration. Oddly, LaSalle's show of respect for Cox diluted some of Cox's resentment towards LaSalle. Cox nodded back. Again: weird guy-code respect thing.

Komanski and a couple of other guards didn't have the same blatantly disrespectful looks on their faces when they looked at Cox. In fact, they stared wearily at him and gave him plenty of space whenever he was within close proximity.

"You might as well tell us what's in those files, LaSalle. This isn't going to get any easier, and we'll all eventually find out." Cox repositioned the ice pack on his face.

LaSalle let out a sigh and turned back to Cox. "Okay. Fine. I'll tell you what the files are, but I won't tell you what the files say. Deal?"

"No deal," said Cox crossing his arms.

"Well, that's the deal you're gonna get."

LaSalle talked about the journal that belonged to Dr. Heinrich Gerg. He didn't give away the contents of the journal, but he did mention that there was some disturbing classified information. I was surprised he admitted that. Specialist Komanski looked like he would interject, but LaSalle directed a threatening look at him. LaSalle talked about Dr. Gerg's background and that there was something that Dr. Gerg was afraid of, and should be taken seriously. Cox asked what it was, but LaSalle said nothing. He re-emphasized how much danger we might be in because of my file hacking (which made me feel very ashamed), but there were many unknown variables: that we still might have a way out by completing the investigation.

The idea of an investigation seemed ludicrous at this point. It felt like we were just being given busy work until our impending doom.

LaSalle and the guards finished reassembling their gear bags. He fiddled with ammunition and weapons of all sorts. He checked clips to make sure they were full of ammunition. "We need to bounce out of here. We've wasted so much time."

"Any chance I can get one of those before we go?" asked Cox, gesturing to one of LaSalle's many weapons. "If Biotech does send an army after us, it would make sense to have another shot. I'm a really good shot."

"I bet you are," said LaSalle. He tossed an odd-looking weapon to Cox. The barrel was considerably larger than a pistol, but not quite as long as a rifle.

"What's this? You SPECWAR guys always get all of this new stuff us regular military folks don't get until years later."

"Yeah, well sometimes that makes us guinea pigs. It's a Dbgun."

Cox raised his eyebrows. "What's a Dbgun?"

"A decibel gun—a sound rifle. Point it at your assailant, and it'll incapacitate him by exploding his eardrums. Permanent deafness for the unlucky victim." LaSalle pointed at a red light on the side of the gun. "If you touch the red screen twice, the shot becomes fatal; it'll inflict a massive brain hemorrhage. The vibration of the sound waves will cause the person's head to explode."

"Lovely," I said, frowning at LaSalle. I was always amazed at how innovative our killing technology was, but we still couldn't find a cure for cancer.

"I don't think this is my cup of tea," said Cox. He tossed the gun back to LaSalle.

But Yuri snatched it from the air. "I'll take it. And while we're at it, you might as well arm the rest of us."

LaSalle had his hands on his hips. He didn't seem thrilled with idea, but he accommodated Yuri nonetheless. He pointed at the weapons bag. "Have at it, I guess. Might as well."

Yuri reached into the weapons bag and pulled out a metal box. He lifted the lid; encased in the box was a pair of brass knuckles. "Brass knuckles. Cool. That's old-school, though," said Yuri.

"I believe they are commonly referred to as BLTs. But the abbreviation BLT is a play on words, as in one would be fried and cut up like the bacon on a BLT sandwich," said Shakespeare. "The acronym stands for Brass-knuckle Laser Tasers. One hand stuns. The other cuts."

"Are you a righty or a south paw?" LaSalle asked.

"South paw."

LaSalle dislodged a button-sized black transceiver. "Here. Speak into this. Say the first word you'd think of in a jam."

Yuri leaned over the transceiver. "Motherfucker."

321

A tiny blue light on the transceiver blinked a couple of times. LaSalle handed it to Yuri to put in his pocket. Then he held the knuckles out for Yuri to put on. "When you say 'Motherfucker' the transceiver will activate the taser and laser. Say it again, it deactivates them. Uses your voice only. When they're off, they're just normal brass knuckles. Now, look here," said LaSalle as he slipped the BLTs onto Yuri's hands. "The Taser has a *T* engraved on it. Wear that one on your right. Stun with that. The one with the *L* engraving is obviously the laser. Wear that on your dominant hand, your left—for the killing blow."

"That's legit," said Yuri. He examined them with a sinister grin.

Shakespeare droned on again. "Well, they may be *legit* as you put it, Commander, but I should advise you that they come with various risks. They bring any hostile engagements closer to you and increase the likelihood of physical harm. It is my recommendation that utilization of the Dbgun is a much safer prospect, unless you're compelled to fight in closer quarters. There is also the consideration of the inevitable mess that will soil your person, especially upon use of the laser."

Cox looked at Yuri's BLTs with some skepticism and winced. "Can you give me something that deploys a bullet? Maybe a precision rifle of some sort? I can shoot a tick off a bat's ass at a thousand meters."

"You can fight—better than a lot of my guys—I'll give you that," said LaSalle as he regarded a couple of the Biotech guards (who in turn looked embarrassed). "Now you say you can shoot too?"

"He can. I've seen him shoot," said Mackie.

When did that Bromance start?

"Why in the hell did you become a ship driver?" asked LaSalle. "Why not a community that utilizes more of your skills? Like Navy Special Warfare or Marine Force Recon, even?"

"Because there're things I only do when I have to, not because I'm paid to."

LaSalle "humphed" and pursed his lips. A couple of the Biotech guards snorted and shook their heads. Cox was back to his usual arrogant, self-righteous self.

One of the guards reached into a cylindrical weapons bag and pulled out a black rifle fitted with a telescopic sight. LaSalle grabbed it and extended it to Cox. "Here. This belonged to the guard who died from the wasp stings. He won't be needing it. It's a bolt action. Uses 7.62×51mm rounds."

"That's old-school too," said Cox, examining the rifle with admiration.

"It's the only one left. Beggars can't be choosers."

"Not complaining. I like old-school."

"It's not too old-school. The cartridges are disintegration rounds."

"Nice." Cox examined one of the bullets. The tip glowed blue.

"Get hit by one of those, and poof," said LaSalle to my questioning look. He wiggled his fingers in the air. "You disappear, disintegrate. Immediate ash. No blood or anything. Dental records wouldn't even help identify you. It's really a clean kill."

"Shit," said Mackie, grabbing the round eagerly from Cox's hand and examining it himself. "Talk about *terminate with extreme prejudice.*"

I grabbed the round from Mackie to have a look for myself. Then, I handed it back to him. "Since when did you and Lieutenant Commander Cox become shooting buddies?"

"We go to the range a couple of times a week. No biggie." Mackie shrugged. "We both grew up hunting in the same backwoods of Kentucky. About two clicks away. Imagine that."

"You never told me that."

"You never asked, ma'am."

LaSalle continued to hand out the remaining weapons. Some we were all familiar with. Others not so much. I was amazed at how well equipped the Biotech security team was. It was obvious that being funded by a bank had its perks. At this point LaSalle was fully engaged in showing people which weapons would work best for the individual person. He even offered me the LaChete, but since I already had the Raptor that Mackie gave me, I opted for a couple of cinder grenades. I watched LaSalle. He loved his job. The excitement of it all. I looked at Cox who, on the other hand, appeared somber. Cox enjoyed being good at what he was good at, but he didn't like the business of risk, of everyone's lives being in danger. I watched them, amazed that both were such different men and that I could be equally attracted to both. Again, I marveled at the contrasts between the two. Cox was a boy scout who could handle himself. LaSalle was a bad boy with a soft side. But where Cox toed the moral line, LaSalle constantly stretched it. Cox looked for favorable odds. He was methodical and logical to a fault. He didn't take risks unless he was sure of the best possible outcome. LaSalle, on the other hand, wasn't afraid to take un-calculated risks. He went with the flow, reacting to situations as they unraveled. I regarded LaSalle with a measure of skepticism. He really was a trained killer. A little too good at his job. And he was unstable. Wild in some respects. I supposed that's what made him so good at what he did and what made my attraction to him so powerful. Yet I wondered how I could still be so attracted to him when I was thoroughly disgusted by his questionable behavior.

He looked at me for a moment, as though he knew I watched him. He gave me a momentary grin, and then he turned to Yuri with a silent nod. Yuri nodded back and proceeded to issue instructions to everyone. "All right, people. Playtime is over. Let's move out."

54

W̲e got into a line and filed out of the main chamber. We opted for the far tunnel on the right. With LaSalle's help, Yuri outlined a route that would lead us directly to Eric's demolition team. A lot of people gave me the silent treatment as we moved. No one was talking anyway. Everyone seemed to finally acknowledge what LaSalle had been trying to tell us all along.

We all moved like robots, going through the motions—like we were walking toward our executions. As we made our way deeper in, Cox tapped me on the shoulder and whispered into my ear. "I'm interested in reading that journal. I know you can access the data from your wrist device. LaSalle thinks I've dropped the subject, but I'm far from being done with this."

I simply nodded and followed the rest of the group.

We walked for an hour. During that hour, I had my wrist device retrieve the remainder of Shakespeare's dictation.

I shuddered as I listened. LaSalle looked back at me, and I gave him a weak smile before averting my gaze. I hoped that would suggest my reluctance to talk to him considering the incident with Cox.

55

fter Shakespeare was done, I was disgusted. This is what Biotech had kept from us? Deadly parasites that kill people and then—reanimate their lifeless bodies—into cannibalistic savages. What *are* they?

As the seriousness of what we were facing began to weigh on me, I decided I'd at least tell Yuri and maybe Cox. Martinez trusted him. I could see why now. He knew a lot about everything. Then I remembered that LaSalle knew all of this. This is what the bastard had been keeping from us. I gritted my teeth and began a steady march toward him. I was pissed. And I was going to let him have it. I walked past Mackie.

"You okay, ma'am?"

"I'm fine."

Just as I reached out to grab LaSalle's shoulder, we were attacked.

I was knocked off my feet by what felt like a human-sized boulder. "What the—"

Whatever it was, it knocked me back to the ground. I hit my head upon impact, and whatever it was had me pinned by the neck. It growled. I pushed at it. It was strong. I opened my eyes to see a man similar to the one I saw back in the woods and at the top of the sinkhole. This was a different man, but he was in the same condition: stringy hair that was past his shoulders, sunken eyes. Up close: rotted teeth. Foul breath. Bloodied in its mouth. He leaned in closer, growling louder. His wiry hand was wrapped around my neck. He tried to bite me. I pushed and kicked at him, but he was immovable. His hand squeezed, choking me, cutting off my oxygen. As he tried to steady my thrashing body, a stream of bloodied drool stretched down toward my face from his. I struggled to look away. His blood-streaked saliva settled into a slimy pool onto my cheek, dripping down to my collarbone. He'd been eating flesh. His breath was hot and rancidly sweet. Cloying. *Is this what death smelled like? Steaming roadkill under a scorching desert sun?* I would've gagged if I wasn't so terrified. His mouth was close to my face. He was biting at my cheek. I twitched back and forth, just barely dodging his teeth. Any moment, he'd rip a chunk from the side of my face. I pushed and strained, trying to break free, but his grasp on my neck was non-negotiable. I was suffocating. I struggled for air, kicking and thrashing, before I felt his body being hauled away from mine. I took in one huge desperate gulp of air and looked up to find LaSalle had yanked him back by the collar. My attacker wasn't a large man. Quite petite, actually. LaSalle hoisted him up and threw him against the opposite cave wall.

The struggle had wearied me. I crawled off to the side away from the mayhem. I shook my head, trying to shake the dizziness out. I rubbed at my neck. My throat burned from being strangled. I steadied myself and gripped a rock protruding from the cave's side wall to pull myself up.

The crazed man's collision with the back wall hadn't phased him. His head sank onto the pointy end of the cave wall that jutted out. He shot right up. The back of his head had a big gaping wound. A fatal wound. A normal man would've died, but he lunged for LaSalle instead.

Then there were gunshots. Mackie unloaded a couple of rounds into the man's chest, which stopped his assault momentarily. He lunged again with even greater vigor. This time LaSalle grabbed a stray pickaxe that had been propped in a corner and sunk it into the crazy man's shoulder. LaSalle leaned like an offensive lineman and pushed him back and back until he was slammed up against the cave wall again. He dislodged the axe and sank it into the crazed man, pinning him against the rock wall. The man was stuck and jerked violently. He growled and hissed, stretching his hands outwards for anyone who got near him.

"What the hell? I put at least five bullets in his chest," said Mackie. "He should be dead."

Everyone could see the hunger in the man's eyes. He reached and snarled and bit, beckoning anyone to get just close enough. We stood watching in shocked silence as he thrashed about.

"I don't think regular bullets are going to kill it," I said.

"*It?*" Yuri frowned at me.

"It—he—was trying to bite me. He's not—"

"Human." Cox stepped in front of the group. Then he turned to LaSalle. "Is he?"

LaSalle said nothing. A deathly peace settled in. The only sounds made were the echoes from the crazed man chomping and howling.

LaSalle looked at Cox. Everything in that look said that he was sick to death of Cox's confrontational agenda. I thought there might be another fight between them again. But instead, he held out his hand without a word. A Biotech guard stepped up and placed a black baton in his outstretched hand. LaSalle gripped the baton and rubbed his thumb along the side. The familiar blue glowing LaChete appeared. With one swooping arc, he severed the man's head. It dropped to the floor with a loud thump and rolled to a stop at my feet. I would've jumped back, but I was already flush with the cave wall. Instead, I looked down into its crazed eyes. The light that burned in its eyes slowly extinguished. The torso kept moving, twitching until finally it stopped.

What the hell are these things?

"That's how you kill it," said LaSalle. He was looking at Petty Officer Mackie. "Bullets will only slow it down, unless you use disintegration rounds. You've gotta take its head completely off. Or snap its neck. Basically, you have to destroy the brain stem."

"Wait," said Yuri impatiently. He turned to LaSalle. "What do you mean *it?*"

"They're zombies, aren't they?" I asked.

"That's not what we call them," said LaSalle.

"I read the journal, Gerard. They're fucking zombies."

"We call them ACs. Animated Corpses. That's what we call them." He sighed and then kicked its severed head away from my feet. "And how the hell were you able to read the journal? I destroyed it before you could listen—"

Before he could finish, an AC jumped out from a side tunnel and attached itself to Eric. It had Eric from behind, and it was already trying to sink its teeth into Eric's neck.

Then, they were everywhere. They all looked like the first man who'd attacked me. Sunken eyes. Stringy hair. Depleted skin. Withered like a prune. Eyes that looked hungry.

They weren't all men, though. Some were women. Some wore Marine uniforms. Others wore the same jumpsuits that the scientists back at Port Juliette wore. Others wore the same uniform as the Biotech guards. Those were especially scary. They were faster and stronger than the others, but all the ACs were faster and stronger than any of us. They seemed impervious to any human exertion or pain.

"Run," said LaSalle. He pointed to the tunnel ahead of us. "That way. Just run. We'll handle this."

This time Eric didn't run because he was too busy dealing with his attacker. He bent forward and flipped the attacker over his shoulder. The AC was lying flat on its back. Eric pulled his pistol and shot the man in the forehead, but the man grabbed his leg, heaved up and bit Eric on the ankle.

"I told you," LaSalle yelled. "The brain stem."

Eric stomped on the man's head. His movements were berserk. He stomped and stomped with reckless abandon. He went a little crazy himself. LaSalle walked over and shoved Eric aside. With the same LaChete, he severed the man's head.

"Don't dilly-dally around. You waste the fucker and move on."

More came at them. LaSalle swung the LaChete like an expert Samurai swordsman. Eric pulled out his pistol and shot at them erratically.

My instincts told me to run, but I'd been so cowardly last time. I wanted to do something. I hesitated. Then I reached into my bag for my Raptor, but Cox had other plans—to drag me away from the mayhem. He gripped my arm just as an AC snatched him away. He wrestled with it. I turned the Raptor on, activating the laser on the knife. I'd planned to stab it in the base of the skull, but it was wrestling with Cox. They were too close together. I was so scared I would inadvertently cut him instead. I looked around, not knowing what to do. That's when I saw another one running straight toward Sherri.

Who should I help? Cox or Sherri? Sherri.

Cox seemed to be in control. He'd killed the first one with a Bowie knife he'd shoved into its throat. He had his rifle out already at this point. He used it to butt another AC in the forehead just before snapping its neck. Cox was a wizard, moving with a lithe yet efficient grace.

Sherri, I wasn't so sure about.

She had her back to an AC that advanced on her from behind. Unaware, she stood immobilized, gripped by fear as she watched Eric, LaSalle and the guards deal with a gang of ACs. The AC was closing distance on Sherri, covering twenty-five meters with lightning-fast speed. Where was help? Everyone was dealing with their own attackers. Mackie was shooting one after the other in the neck. Cox had already wasted two and was focused on three more headed his way. They were coming at us like a herd of angry bulls.

What can I do? What can I do?

I tightened my grip on the Raptor. The knife was already glowing blue, but I decided to deploy the long glowing blue cord that dropped from the handle of the knife. I reached back and then flicked my arm forward like I was throwing a baseball. The tip of the cord kissed the side of the AC's torso, and a chunk of flesh fell away like soft cake. It kept moving, barely affected by such a drastic blow. A normal person would've buckled to the ground.

Shit, they're fast.

I probably only had one more shot at the speed the AC was moving. I moved closer, but I didn't want to clip Sherri with the whip accidentally. She'd be done with just one flick. I reached back and then whipped the glowing blue cord forward.

Bingo. Right on target, the illuminated cord, in one fluid motion, curled around the A.C.'s neck like a cat's tail and melted right through its withered flesh. Its head came clean off, effortlessly. Its body slumped to the floor right at Sherri's feet. Some of the flesh at its neck melted away onto Sherri's boot. The head lolled at an angle; its tongue hung limply from its mouth.

As proud as I was of my aim, I didn't have time to revel in the moment. ACs materialized from everywhere and nowhere. The only option left was, in fact, to run. If we didn't leave soon, we'd be overwhelmed.

"It's time to run," I said to Sherri. I grabbed her hand and jerked her forward.

Mackie was suddenly right beside me. "Ma'am, we've gotta get the hell out of here."

"Yeah, no shit." I looked around. Everyone else was struggling to break away. The Biotech guards were firing off shots, backing up. Reloading. LaSalle still swinging the machete.

Where's Yuri?

I looked for him. He had just kicked a female AC into a wall. She'd been so close to biting a chunk out of his arm. My pulse went into overdrive. What if I lost him on this trip? The thought was unfathomable.

The female AC pushed away from the wall and lunged at Yuri. He ducked and threw a hard overhand right. He was wearing the Brass-knuckle Laser Tasers, and they were activated. His fist connected with the AC's jaw, and she jerked into stillness. The taser had stunned her into a tattered, death-decayed statue. Yuri followed up with his left fist and punched her in the neck, exploding a hole clean through. She crumbled to the cave floor.

"Yuri," I yelled, "let's go! We need to leave. There's too many."

He nodded and kicked the AC's body away with disgust. He pulled out his pistol and began to back away cautiously, looking for any that might jump out of nowhere as he made his way over to Mackie and me. He passed Komanski, who struggled with an AC trying to get at his neck. Yuri pushed the pistol to the base of the AC's skull and pulled the trigger. It dropped to the ground. Yuri dragged Komanski (who killing a few more) away.

We looked around to see who was left. LaSalle.

He cried out. A thunderously large AC, built like an offensive lineman, knocked the LaChete from LaSalle's hand. LaSalle went to grab his pistol, but it clamped a hand around LaSalle's wrist with cobra-like speed. Then it grabbed LaSalle's other wrist. LaSalle was pinned against the wall. The AC leaned in for a bite. Any moment, it would get it. LaSalle fought and strained against it. He kicked the AC in the groin, but it was unphased. Closer and closer its mouth came to LaSalle's face. LaSalle's strength was waning fast.

Cox raised his rifle and set the barrel onto my shoulder. "Hold still."

He adjusted the sights for a moment as he looked through the sniper scope. Then he took a deep breath.

"Wait," I said, peering back over my shoulder at him. He lowered the rifle from my shoulder to look at me, somewhat irritated by the interruption.

"What?" He sounded impatient.

"You have disintegration rounds in your rifle. If you hit LaSalle, even just a little, he'll disintegrate too."

"Yeah. Probably," he said dismissively. He resumed his previous stance, re-resting the barrel on my shoulder, and he zeroed back in through the scope. He took another deep breath, exhaled and squeezed the trigger. The big AC just seized up, and then a starburst of flesh and bone splintered away into droplets and fell to the cave floor.

LaSalle looked momentarily shocked. He glowered at Cox. A shadow of anger and relief crossed his face.

How does it feel, jerk?

For the moment, the most immediate AC threats had been neutralized, but more were coming. Their shrieks and cries echoed through the web of cave tunnels.

LaSalle trotted over to the rest of us. The struggle had taken something out of him.

"I told you he could shoot," said Mackie, gesturing toward Cox. He clapped LaSalle on the back.

"I see that." LaSalle examined his forearm which the AC had taken a bite from.

"Now we're even," said Cox.

LaSalle nodded and then looked down the tunnel behind us. A gang of more ACs off in the distance were visible. They looked like mere figurines that steadily grew as they moved closer.

"We needed to get out of here, pronto," said Yuri, who tried to usher us out of the area.

Cox raised his rifle again. He took another deep breath and aimed. He fired several shots, in quick, efficient bursts, deftly pulling back the handle on the bolt action rifle. I could see their small forms topple over to the ground like beer cannisters off of a fence. There were three still running at us who advanced dangerously close. He finished them off in quick succession before lowering his rifle. We didn't wait anymore. The sounds were loud now.

"Run," said LaSalle to Yuri. Then he motioned to everyone and pointed to the tunnel ahead of us. "That way. Just run. And whatever you do, don't look back. Last thing we need is for someone to get blinded. I'll buy some time."

Yuri took off on a sprint, and we all followed him down the tunnel, not waiting for an explanation. Eric, who had some inkling of where to go, was right next to him. I ran as hard as I could, barely keeping up. As much as I had my reservations about LaSalle, I wanted to make sure he was okay. I looked over my shoulder. There were indeed a ton of more ACs coming. LaSalle was kneeling. He had something in his hand. It looked like he was programming something. A bomb, maybe?

"Don't worry about him," said Cox, between breaths. He pulled my sleeve. "He can take care of himself."

LaSalle moved fast, with assured speed and efficiency. The ACs were close enough that I could see their torn clothes and flaccid hair trailing behind them as they moved at frightening speed.

Finally, LaSalle stood up and threw the object down the tunnel like he was spiraling a football. It glided down the tunnel and stopped, hovering in midair in the middle of the tunnel. Then it glowed. A soft blue light at first, but then it got brighter and brighter, almost blinding. *A flash bomb!* He turned his back on it and took off, sprinting toward us. I turned away as well. There was a considerable pulsation that rattled the cave, and then for a split second the entire tunnel was nothing but bright white light. I wanted to look back, but I could hear LaSalle's voice yelling, "Keep running!" I wouldn't have looked anyway. I'd heard of people losing their vision by staring at flashes from flash grenades. I kept running and running, wondering how much longer I'd be able to keep up Yuri's grueling pace.

56

My lungs were on fire. Just when I thought I couldn't run anymore, Yuri stopped. We'd put enough distance between ourselves and the noises from the ACs to regroup, but we wouldn't get much of a breather.

I was doubled over. Yuri, on the other hand, stood barely affected as he issued orders to the rest of us. He motioned for us to huddle around. I was glad I was in decent shape. Some of the civilian contractors were puking. I wasn't in the best shape either. The Biotech guards weren't breathing that hard. Neither was Eric. Sherri rested her hands on her head and was sucking in air, but she wasn't dying.

Don't want to be a straggler. Might mean the difference between life and death.

We were in a small opening that led to multiple tunnels. We could hear the faint sounds of ACs in other tunnels. We spoke fast.

"What the hell was that?" Yuri asked LaSalle who had just rejoined us. "You set off a bomb or something? I almost lost my footing."

"Yeah," said LaSalle, said between breaths. "But we need to find someplace to stop other than here. That flash will disorient them for a while, but it won't be long before things settle, and they sniff us out."

"You should've used a real bomb." Eric had his hands on his hips. "We need to get rid of as many of those things as we can."

Komanski propped his rifle on his shoulder and stepped in front of Eric. "Yeah, that's a great idea, genius. Let's collapse this entire cave so we have no way back. The highly lethal weapons are for when we're really up shit's creek."

"Yeah, well—we need to come up with a plan. This running and shooting business isn't going to cut it."

"Captain Hunt is right. Hell, you're both right," said Yuri, whose dark skin glistened with sweat. He nodded to both Eric and LaSalle. "We need a better place to stop and collect ourselves, and we need an exit plan out of here. I say, to hell with the investigation."

We all looked at LaSalle, expecting him to object. He looked down at his feet. He was conflicted. "Well, I think we have to be ready to face the consequences of that—"

"Hey," Eric said. Yuri frowned at the interruption but followed Eric's glance at LaSalle's bleeding arm. They both took a step back from LaSalle. "You're bit."

"I realize that. I'm fine," said LaSalle examining his arm.

Eric eyed him skeptically. "Does that mean you're gonna turn into one?"

"Most likely not," LaSalle wiped the blood off his forearm onto his suit. The wound was a large open gash, a ragged circle, about two inches in diameter. Some of the skin around it was torn, and there was blood pooling around it again, even after he wiped it. LaSalle pulled a silver rectangular object from his bag and stamped it firmly against his arm where the wound was. There was a brief glow of white light that seeped from beneath, illuminating the skin. When he removed the object, the wound was closed. A raw pink spot was visible where the open wound once was. "That should hold it. Now, we really don't have time for this. There's more coming, and they're moving fast. We need to move out now. I'll explain more later."

"No—I—I'm not going anywhere with you," said Eric. He had his hand on his pistol.

"You're bit, too, asshole," said Komanski pointing to Eric's ankle.

Eric looked down. His face drained of color. "I—it can't be a bite. I would've known—It's probably just—"

"You're bit. Just face it," said Komanski. He looked smug.

"Here." LaSalle shoved the device in Eric's hand despite his previous rudeness. "I don't know what this means, but we'll figure it out later."

"You don't know what this means?" Cox shoved his way in between everyone. He was in LaSalle's face again.

Oh, geez. Not again. Sometimes I wished that Cox would let things play out for once.

"Yeah," said LaSalle. His face was cement. "There's more to it than that. Like I said, I'll explain later."

Eric stood in quiet shock. He seemed unaware of the arguments that were starting to erupt around him, as though he'd been slapped with horrific news. His movements were mechanical. First, he looked down at his ankle. Then he looked to the device that LaSalle put into his hand. He stretched out his hand and offered the object to Sherri. He seemed to hope that she would help him with it, but she moved slightly away.

Wow. Not cool.

LaSalle took notice too. To his credit, he showed some pity on Eric. He placed a hand on Eric's shoulder. "Look man—it doesn't work how you think. Not everyone turns. Once we find someplace safe, I'll explain." LaSalle looked to Yuri. "Now let's stop dicking around. We need to go."

Yuri looked sidelong at LaSalle. Skepticism shadowed his face. I could tell he wondered the same thing as everyone else: *would they become a threat in an hour from now? Should we abandon LaSalle and*

Eric? Would the other guards even let us? They have way more weapons. Mackie and Cox had the same look too. But Yuri was too kind. He'd never abandon someone, and he wouldn't make a decision that would put the group at potentially fatal odds with each other. Biotech was heavily armed, but now we were armed. Biotech was better trained, though, and they had cloaking technology on their suits. They'd disappear and shoot us all to shit.

I think it was mainly to diffuse the situation, but Yuri started us off on a trot away from the alcove, with LaSalle at his side. Their "trotting" was more like a vigorous jog. We probably would've gone faster if our pace hadn't been hampered by Eric's ankle. The bite was bad, and now the pain was setting in, causing him to limp. Sherri still limped off and on from her earlier ankle sprain.

They're perfect for each other.

So Eric and Sherri limp-ran from the rear. For once, Eric didn't utter one complaint and showed how tough a Marine can really be. One of the Biotech guards was limping too. An AC had taken a chunk from his thigh in the middle of his quad. We would need to stop soon.

"Where are we going?" I panted.

"To the command center," said LaSalle.

"Where's that?" Yuri asked with a ragged breath. Even he was getting tired now.

We approached another intersection that offered three different routes.

"I'm not sure—that way," said LaSalle pointing. "I think. The left tunnel."

"I thought you knew this place pretty well," said Yuri.

"I do. But not being chased by ACs. I usually have time to use my positioner."

Yuri moved up ahead and headed for the farthest left tunnel. We all followed. I pushed myself to the front with Yuri. I was so worried that one of the ACs would catch me unawares from a side tunnel or from behind. The surge of adrenaline alone gave me a burst of speed.

We ran for what seemed like eons.

Another long tunnel. Will this ever end?

I heard ACs again. That scared all of us enough to push harder.

Where are they? Behind us or ahead of us?

We followed the winding tunnel. Some people slowed down. I was heaving now, but I pushed on. Some people stopped, crumbling to the floor, but they were urged on by others to pick up and keep going. Some were even dragged along.

We reached a curve. That gave me hope. As we followed it around, I hoped that the command center would be around the corner. But when we turned the corner, several ACs emerged in front of us. The one closest to me, a woman, went straight for my face. She was wearing a Marine Corps uniform. She must've been one of the Marines in Eric's combat demolitions unit. She gripped both of my shoulders with her bony fingers, tightening with a relentless fury. She was deceptively strong. She forced me close and leaned in, intent on sinking her teeth around my entire mouth. I reacted the way Sherri had earlier, paralyzed by fear. I was dimly aware that there were struggles around me. No one would be coming to my rescue, and I certainly couldn't expect Sherri to return the earlier favor when I saved her with the Raptor. I wasn't sure what to do, but I grabbed the woman's wrist out of panic.

Mackie was struggling with an AC next to me. "Don't let her bite you whatever you do. *Fight*."

It was just what I needed to hear. It reminded me of the Gladiator 4D computer countdown: *fight!* I could fight. In seconds, all my previous fights with Shakespeare and Chief Martinez flashed through my head. Without thought, I looped my right arm under the AC's arm and chopped down hard, breaking free one of her grips. I struck her across the jaw, fast and hard, in one swift movement. She was rocked a bit, just enough to loosen her grip on me and buy me a moment. Then I shot my left hand out, palm open. A palm strike upward into her nose. I felt a crunch. I'd broken it, but she didn't care. She wasn't human. I raised my knee and pushed my leg out into a front kick, planting the ball of my foot directly on to her sternum. It was a solid kick. It lifted her into the air a little, and she fell squarely onto her back. She hissed and growled as she made to stand back up. But I pounced on her before she could. My knee on her chest and my forearm on her neck. I pressed my forearm down on her trachea, trying desperately to push her chin up so that she couldn't bite me. I pressed harder and harder, my hand a lever on her throat, like a paper cutter. She still growled. With my free hand, I pulled out my Raptor. I didn't have time to activate the laser on it. Just the blade would have to do. It was a curved affair, like an eagle claw. I gripped the hilt tightly and shoved the sharp end into the side of her neck. It felt like cutting into steak. Then I angled the blade upward, toward her brain stem, recalling LaSalle's warning. I pushed and pushed until I hit something solid. It was firm but soft, like putty. I pushed further until I saw the fire extinguish from her eyes. She fell limp. Then I felt something grab my shoulder. I turned in panic and slashed out. It was Cox. He shifted just out of reach.

"Don't ever come up on me like that. I almost cut you."

"Sorry."

I looked around and saw that everyone was fighting ACs. I was impressed with the fact that even Eric was still standing. He'd snapped an AC's neck just before shooting one in the throat with his pistol. Of course, Sherri was nowhere to be found. She'd run away . . . *again*.

I can't believe her.

A brief scan of the scene, and she was nowhere. I didn't know if she'd run up ahead or back the way we came. When I looked to our rear and saw that there were four ACs coming toward us, I assumed she headed toward the command center.

The four ACs moved in fast. Mackie and Cox had their backs to them, blocking my view. I grabbed my Raptor and detracted the cord. "Get down!" I yelled. Without question, they both ducked. They must've seen the panic in my eyes.

I flicked the glowing blue cord as fast and as far out I could. The cord curled in the air and sliced through all four AC's necks like an executioner's blade. Their heads fell from their bodies onto the ground and rolled to a stop against the wall of the cave floor.

"Damn," said Mackie. "You're getting good with that thing, ma'am.

"Thanks. Let's go." I grabbed his arm and pulled him into a sprint, grabbing others along the way.

I seized Yuri, who had just sliced an AC down the middle, from head to crotch. He had a LaChete he picked up off a dead Biotech guard.

"There's more coming," I said.

He nodded. "And maybe more turning. Let's get the hell out of here, now."

Yuri and Mackie snatched people here and there, helping them kill ACs as necessary and pushing them to safety in the direction of the command center. Meanwhile, LaSalle and the Biotech guards fended off a new wave of ACs that came at us from the rear. LaSalle tossed another grenade, this one a "daisy cutter," which rolled along the cave floor, lasering off AC limbs as it went. It didn't kill them, but their legs were severed. ACs hissed and moaned, crawling with unquenchable hunger along the cave floor.

One civilian contractor had gotten caught behind the grenade. He screamed in agony as he peered down at the bloody mess the grenade made of his entire body. He writhed in an inconsolable frenzy at the missing lower half of his body, completely unaware of Komanski, who'd crept up behind him. No one argued when he raised his pistol and pulled the trigger, ending the man's screams forever.

Shadows stretched from a rear tunnel toward us. LaSalle grabbed the few stragglers left, and we took off running again.

This time was a vicious sprint. The ACs were too close. I saw their shadows at our backs. It sounded like their numbers were building. I peeked over my shoulder. They were close and disturbingly fast. I willed my legs to move as fast as they could. We all did. There was some disarray, but we all ran in the same general direction. I just hoped that no one was left behind. I hoped Sherri was okay and safe.

52

just kept my eyes trained on Yuri's muscular form. I was grateful to be right behind him. The tunnel was dark. I could barely make him out, even being just behind him. It would've been easy to veer off into an adjacent tunnel inadvertently. I worried that we would lose the people at the back.

Yuri found an alcove along the tunnel that opened into a wide passageway. The passageway Yuri took led to a large, titanium garage-like door. Luckily, Eric had access to activate the door. After the optical reader acknowledged his clearance, the door lifted open at a painfully slow rate, gliding upwards with a loud mechanical groan. Yuri stood at the opening, beckoning people through the opening. Cox and LaSalle went back down the tunnel to redirect stragglers headed down wrong tunnels. I wasn't 100 percent sure they caught everyone.

Yuri instructed Eric not to let the door all the way up, only allowing for a three foot opening since it would probably take too long to close. I slid in beneath to the other side of the door. After I stood, I watched events unfold with my hands on my knees. My lungs were wrecked, and my heart pumped violently. I said a silent prayer while trying to slow my breathing. *Let everyone make it through, please.*

Then it occurred to me: *Where are Cox and LaSalle?* I didn't see them come in. I whipped my head around, scanning the exhausted faces. Red flushed, sweaty faces scrunched up in agony, but no Cox or LaSalle.

People stumbled into the room one by one, collapsing to the floor. Some slid in while others somersaulted through or log rolled underneath the door. Everyone was bent over and out of breath.

I could hear sounds echoing through the tunnel. We still had quite a few people bringing up the rear. Some hadn't turned the corner. Although I couldn't see them, I could hear the evidence of their exertion: breathing, footsteps, cries of terror. And the wailing of ACs in pursuit.

As Yuri ushered the last part of our group inside, I couldn't see anything down the tunnel. Then, in moments, they emerged from the darkness: ACs in the distance, chasing the remaining four people left. At first, I saw only silhouettes running toward us. Then I saw them: Cox, LaSalle, a Marine lance corporal and a Biotech guard at the rear.

The panic in Yuri's voice surged. "C'mon. You can make it!" he yelled.

All four stragglers grunted as they strained to outrun the ACs who were closing the gap between them at a frightening pace. As Cox, LaSalle, two Biotech guards and the lance corporal closed in, Yuri turned to Eric. His voice trembled. "Close the door. Now. Close it."

Eric peered into the optical scanner until it beeped. The door lowered at a nail-bitingly slow speed. I wasn't sure how this would all play out. Would we get them under without the ACs making it under too? I looked, horrified to see, not just a gaggle of ACs, but an entire herd. I held my breath as I watched them bear down on our people. Cox and LaSalle made it under in time. So did one of the Biotech guards (Specialist Dunn) but not before an AC latched onto his bicep and ripped out a small chunk of flesh. He ripped his arm away and shoved the AC off of him and then somersaulted his way under the lowering door. The lance corporal slipped in enough time to make it too but late enough for an AC to seize his foot and sink its teeth into his ankle. The lance corporal jerked his leg back only to have it smashed the closing heavy titanium door.

Before anyone had time to mull over the matter, LaSalle snatched the LaChete from Yuri's hand and severed the man's leg at the knee joint just before the door locking mechanism shifted in place with a resounding, ominous click. The lance corporal screamed. The sounds echoed throughout the disconcerting silence of the room. If I didn't know what sheer misery sounded like, I knew then. We all stood in silent mortification except for LaSalle, who knelt down to cauterize the mangled stump. He wrapped the stump with a metallic-like sheet of material that looked like aluminum foil. The lance corporal screamed some more. The material molded to the shredded stump and tendrils of smoke floated around his leg.

Komanski tossed LaSalle a metal pen-like object. LaSalle placed the pen against the Marine's thigh and pushed the button at the head. Gas hissed as a highly concentrated dose of an opioid analgesic was ejected from the cartridge into the lance corporal's leg. He fell limp in LaSalle's arms as the pain slid away from his face. LaSalle, then unwrapped the stump, removing the foil-like sheet to reveal a closed wound and a stump that was no longer gushing blood.

"Look," said Yuri. Somehow, he'd managed to tear his eyes away from the bloody scene to look at the monitor on the door entry display.

It was the Biotech guard who brought up the rear. We watched, powerless to open the door. A female AC in a Biotech engineer's uniform jumped on his back and sank her teeth into his skull. Blood spurted out in a crimson web, assaulting the video monitor. The rest of the ACs swarmed in. I noticed they all wore various uniforms: Marine Corps camouflage, blue and gray jumpsuits with

Biotech emblems. One AC was dressed in Navy camouflage with a symbol on his breast pocket that indicated he was a fleet corpsman for the Marines.

The ACs dog-piled the Biotech guard. Limbs, intestines and other body parts flew into the air as they picked apart their evening catch. I couldn't watch. I looked away from the screen.

Eric moved to the display panel, but Yuri snatched him back by the collar and said, "No. It's too late for him."

58

We were all doubled over. Some of us were still heaving, winded from the recent 600-meter sprint. Others threw up. I couldn't tell if it was from the run, the amputation scene at the door or the disaster on the other side of it.

"This doesn't look like a command center," said Cox in between breaths.

"It's not. It's where we keep all of our demolitions and drilling equipment," said Eric.

The room was massive, roughly the size of a hangar bay, and it was in pristine condition. The walls and ceilings were smooth. Yuri was able to turn on a light and power up a CMS, but none of the wiring to power such equipment was exposed. Even the floor, a pale stone, was smooth, glossed over with a high shine. I presumed the room was kept tidy to ensure the integrity of the mining equipment. A quick scan revealed an array of heavy-duty mining equipment: helium tractors, ionic dozers, plasma loaders, hydrogen drills, thermal pickaxes, laser shovels and on and on. The equipment looked brand-new, but I knew that Biotech and the Marines took extra precaution to ensure the equipment was spotless.

The lance corporal was moaning now, thanks to the injection of fentanyl LaSalle administered to him.

"Shouldn't we apply a tourniquet or something?" Eric said as he bent over the lance corporal like he was looking at roadkill. Part curiosity. Part disgust.

"No. The laser from the LaChete should've cauterized the wound," said LaSalle. "Our biggest concern should be that he might go into shock."

"And what if he does?"

"An adrenaline booster, maybe." One of the guards found a fire retardant blanket in a supply bin. LaSalle stuffed it under the lance corporal's leg to elevate it.

"We're just going to have to take it one step at a time," said Yuri. He gazed at the lance corporal. "Before we figure out how we're going to deal with him, we need to do a count of who we have and don't have."

"Will he turn?" asked Eric. He stood next to LaSalle, who was still administering to the lance corporal. "I need you to explain how this all works. Am I going to—"

"Wait," said Cox, who was counting everyone in the group. He pointed his finger again at the first person and started another count. Eric was about to interject, but LaSalle held up his hand to silence him as he focused on what Cox was doing. LaSalle frowned because Cox was frowning. Cox looked confused as he went back through everyone.

Some people still had their hands on their knees, not caring about the count, while they tried to just breathe.

Eric crossed his arms, frustrated. "Look, he could be a huge liability—"

"No—wait—we're missing more people than we thought." LaSalle stood up.

Everyone started looking around at each other.

LaSalle started his own count. Cox counted again.

"Who are we missing?" asked Yuri.

"I don't know yet." Cox pointed his finger from person to person. "Three, four maybe. We all know that Specialist Hart bought it at the door. I know Specialist Rien, one of the other guards—the one you got the LaChete off of—well, she's dead. I saw an AC rip out her throat."

"How appropriate," said Komanski. "She talked too much anyway."

LaSalle gave Komanski a look. "Show some goddamn respect."

Komanski turned red but shrugged. LaSalle turned away in disgust.

LaSalle doesn't like him any more than I do.

I looked around. Something didn't feel right. I looked around our group, and then I noticed who we were missing. "Where's Petty Officer Mackie—and Lieutenant Kolar?"

Eric started to scan the group himself. "I thought everyone made it inside."

He was looking at Cox and LaSalle now.

Cox held up his hands. "Everyone did make it inside, except for the few casualties we sustained. All I know is that LaSalle and I were directing people down the tunnel, and then suddenly we were running from ACs. It's possible that some people got lost. Went down the wrong tunnel before we could get to them and tell them where to go."

"So, for all we know she's with Mackie and the others?"

"I don't think she's with Mackie," I said. "She was gone as soon as the fighting broke out."

"Don't start, Mel. If you're implying that she ran away—"

"I'm not implying anything. I'm just telling you what I saw, Eric. I think she may be out there by herself."

Eric went into panic mode. First, he questioned people. Then he paced. Finally, he looked behind equipment, knowing it was futile. Our entire group was visible. "Maybe she went the right way and got here before us. She could be hiding in here."

"Why would she hide from us? We're the only ones in here," I said. "Besides, does she even have access to this room?"

"I don't know, Ameila, but we need to be sure, because if she's not in here, she's out there alone, with a sprained ankle," he said, gesturing to the garage-like door that we came through from the tunnel. He was snappish. I decided not to say anything else.

He moved toward the entryway and leaned in to activate the door via the optical scanner. Before he could, an anonymous voice rang out through an internal speaker system somewhere in the equipment room. The voice was loud and came from all directions. It resounded throughout the entire space.

"I wouldn't do that."

Everyone froze. The voice was ominous, like an A.I. computer. It wasn't Shakespeare.

"Is there A.I. assigned to this sector?" I asked Eric.

"No, not that I'm aware."

"I'm not artificial intelligence," the voice replied. "Just a friend who wants to help."

The voice's owner was clearly foreign, male and educated. We all looked up. I could see speakers peppered along the ceiling, button-sized devices lodged in every corner and nook.

I mouthed: *"Who is that?"*

We all looked to LaSalle for an answer, but he shrugged.

"There's no need to pantomime or whisper. I can see you and hear you all."

We all looked at each other, our nerves drawn tight. Then upward at the ceiling again. *He can see us?*

"And don't bother trying to see me," said the voice. "You won't be able to."

I pointed to my wrist device. It was a stupid move, considering what he'd just said.

The voice chuckled with sarcasm. "Do you really think I haven't thought of that? Your A.I. advisor won't be able to find me, much less identify me because I have overridden him. Shakespeare is capable, but he is taking a nap."

Eric stepped to the center of the room and looked up. Hands on his hips. "Well then who are you, asshole? And why shouldn't I go find my girlfriend?"

Girlfriend? I guess that makes it official. I regarded Eric. He started biting his nails.

I think Yuri secretly hoped that LaSalle was wrong and that Biotech would send people to save us rather than kill us. But deep down he knew the truth. We had two threats to face: the ACs and Biotech.

Eric was still looking up with his hands on his hips. "Well?"

We waited for a response. Nothing.

Eric kicked a nearby bulkhead. "Screw it. If you're not going to help us, I'm going out there."

"And how will you manage that, hmm, Captain Hunt?" said the voice. He paused for a moment. "You've virtually sequestered yourselves into a trap."

"No. There is a flamethrower in one of the equipment lockers. I will burn them all down once the door opens."

The voice chuckled again. "Young people. Impatient and brash. Do you think fire will stop them? If you douse them with fire, you will then have a herd of those abominable things (now on fire) to contend with before they burn out. Not wise."

"They're called ACs," said Eric, sounding defeated. "Stands for Animated Corpses."

"Ha. Ha. That's a clever name for them. I like that—"

Now LaSalle was impatient. "Excuse me, who the fuck is this? I'm Director Gerard—"

"I'm very well aware of who you are, Dr. LaSalle, and I must say, you've been **very** busy these days, have you not?"

"What's that supposed to mean?"

"Do you really want me to explain in front of all your friends? Do they even know why you're here?"

LaSalle clamped his mouth shut. His face darkened to scarlet.

"Surprise, surprise," said Cox. "Why *are* you here, LaSalle? You knew about the ACs. That's obvious. Why would you come down here with us?"

"Yeah. I'd like to know too," I said.

LaSalle looked at me, frustrated. He wanted to explain in private, but I was done with his private excuses.

It was apparent that LaSalle was tired of withholding information. He spoke in quiet tones, a mixture of anger and frustration. He faced me. "The question isn't why am *I* here. You should be asking yourself why *you're* here."

"What do you mean?" I asked. "It's obvious. The commodore ordered me here."

"Yeah, but we both know it was a bullshit order. You figured that out from the jump."

"What are you saying?"

"You have something, Mel. He wanted *you* down here for a reason. I'm only down here because I didn't have a choice. I—I was compelled to . . ."

LaSalle's voice fell away. He was obviously struggled with what to say.

"Compelled to what? You might as well tell us," said Yuri. "I think we all know that they're coming for us. Both the ACs and Biotech. We're done. Let's not deceive ourselves."

"Compelled to look after her." LaSalle gestured toward me, but he wouldn't look at me. His face was red. ". . . and the rest of you. She has something important that Biotech wants. She's down here, so they can get it."

I was struck at the admission that he was looking after me, and secondly at the idea that Biotech wanted something from *me*. I wondered what that could possibly be.

"Well, what do they want? Why not just ask me for it?" I could hear my own voice becoming frantic. I fingered the pendant around my neck nervously.

"Ask?" LaSalle laughed openly. "Biotech doesn't ask. Besides, they're not sure you even have or know how to get what it is they want."

"Why would I not know or not have it?"

"Because someone gave it to you without your knowledge."

I began to wrack my brain as everyone glared at me. "No way."

My voice sounded unconvincing. I got some skeptical looks. Even Yuri looked at me strangely.

"And if you do know what you have, Biotech wants you here, isolated, in a precarious situation so they can use your life as a bargaining chip for what they need."

The Biotech guards looked at me with murderous glances. Cox looked at me with a thread of accusation. Yuri pitied me. Everyone shifted uneasily. They all stared at the equipment room floor, including LaSalle, nostrils flared. Lips pursed.

"It looks like I've poked at a wound. Would you like to or shall I, Mr. LaSalle?"

LaSalle. He took a huge breath and let it out. "I—"

Eric shoved himself in front of LaSalle and stood at the center of the room. He looked up at the ceiling. "Look, we can share secrets later. I need just two questions answered. Am I going to turn, and how can I get out of here safely to find my—"

354

"—your girlfriend is safe. She is unharmed. For now. Biotech has her."

Specialist Komanski took a step forward. He unslung his rifle. His voice went up an octave. "They were here? When?"

"Just before you all arrived here."

"How did we not see that?" I asked.

"They were 'cloaked' when they grabbed her. They let you fight it out with the ACs, as a diversion. Who do you think sent those evil things your way in the first place?"

"If they were cloaked, we at least should've seen them," said Komanski, gesturing to the remaining Biotech guards. "We have cloaking capability too."

"No," said LaSalle shaking his head. "As soon as they decided to come after us, they probably re-programmed their suits onto a different cloaking system. They've cut us out. That's why we didn't see them."

"Why her?" I asked. "Why not come after all of us?"

That is a good question. Unfortunately, I don't have any answers for you. My guess would be: experimentation.

Experimentation? Oh God.

We all fell silent. By the expression on LaSalle's face I could tell he knew something like this would happen. But something the voice said had him a little shocked.

Eric asked the one question everyone was afraid to ask. "What do you mean by 'experimentation'?

There was a sardonic laugh. "You don't know? Pathetic. You're in a chess game and you don't even know all the rules. Even you, LaSalle. There are some things even *you* don't know. Right now, you're wondering why they bothered to cloak themselves and not kill you all. You've all been blinded. So,

I will give you back your sight. But I must be sure you want to know what I'm about to tell you. Because once you're told, you can't be *untold*."

"Yes, we want to know," said Yuri in a quiet tone. He spoke for all of us. I looked at LaSalle and Cox to see their response. They both looked uncomfortable like they weren't totally sure they wanted to know. Even Eric seemed uneasy.

"Are you sure? I must hear it from the others."

"We're sure, for Christ's sake," said Eric. He pulled on his collar and wiped away the beads of sweat smattered on his forehead with the back of his hand. I wasn't sure if that was because he was about to "turn," or if he was just feeling the cloying effects of the humid climate like the rest of us.

There was a round of yeses and nods of agreement from everyone in the group. Even the injured lance corporal managed to issue a yes loud enough to please the anonymous voice.

I was a bit despondent. I kind of didn't want to know what the voice was about to tell us. I felt like we were about to unleash a storm, but, ultimately, I said "yes."

The voice took an exaggerated, long breath. Whoever it was, he was clearly as tired and frustrated by this entire AC business as the rest of us. I wondered about his identity and why he would be as disturbed by this, when he wasn't the one in immediate danger.

"Do any of you know who A.F.I.B. is and what they stand for?"

"Americas-France Intergalactic Bank," said LaSalle.

"Very good, Mr. LaSalle. Very good. And do any of you know why a bank would have any interest in biomedical research?"

"Well, that's obvious," said Yuri, "because there's money in it."

"Exactly, Commander Jefferson."

Yuri frowned. "But what does A.F.I.B. profiting on bioscience have to do with all of us? They obviously knew people were getting infected—reanimated. Why didn't they notify the commodore—"

"Who says he wasn't notified?"

Silence hung like a dark cloud. The significance of that revelation sunk in, and then I saw the rage that overtook Yuri. This was only the second time ever I saw Yuri lose his cool. The first was when some kid stole his car back in high school, and I was still in elementary school. I was young, but I remember the episode. In the end, our father and our neighbor had to restrain him. This time he just took it out on the closest objects nearby. Trash cans were thrown and supply bins kicked. Wrenches were launched across the equipment room like throwing knives.

"Jesus God, it's always the nice, quiet ones who lose it," said Komanski.

LaSalle tried to calm him down, to minimize the noise, but Yuri gave him a deadly look. LaSalle backed away and let Yuri's temper tantrum run its course.

I understood why Yuri was so mad in comparison to everyone else. He was the executive officer of the *Midway*. He was second in command, and the commodore managed to engage in shady dealings while he remained totally ignorant. The fact that he'd been steamrolled while being respectful of a commodore he didn't like in the first place was all too much. Yuri was not one to be played. That was his one pet peeve in life. On top of it all, myself and Lauralie were now entangled in this mess, a fact that he would never forgive himself for. After Yuri's tirade ended, he composed himself. He ran a hand across his stubbled head and wiped the sheen of sweat from his forehead.

"So what does Captain Radcliff gain in all of this, by putting us in harm's way?" said Yuri. He tried to force some calmness into his tone.

"You're not asking the right questions, Commander. Dr. LaSalle, care to speak?"

At this point LaSalle was visibly uncomfortable. He wouldn't look at anyone. I wanted to shake the shit out of him.

"Everything always leads back to money. It always goes back to money." LaSalle was shaking his head, speaking more to himself than the group.

Eric regarded LaSalle for a moment and then looked up to the voice. "Well, if that's the case, why were we still drilling and doing demolitions down there? We hadn't found anything for months. Wouldn't that be a waste of Biotech money and resources?"

"Bingo, Captain Hunt. That's the question you should've asked to begin with, which I will answer. But let me tell you a little story first . . ."

59

And, so, the voice told us his story . . .

May 30, 2372
Time: 1833
Mining Station #0517212

lied. And they believed me.

I told them it was safe, but it wasn't safe.

I told them the bank wanted it, but the bank didn't know about it.

I ignored the risks, the advice. And Aristotle? I didn't trust him. Sure, he was A.I., but he was just a computer. A device that regurgitated facts and data. Plays at being human. I'd be damned before I'd let some silly machine stop me. I'd get what I was after before anyone else did.

"*Haraka. Haraka.*" It seemed I would say that word for hours. This was before my English was good, and besides my entire team was Nigerian, anyway. (I insisted upon it as part of my contract negotiations). I was impatient. My men chipped away at the cave rock wall dutifully. They dug and dug, wearing down the cave rock. One right after the other, their movements hurried, but not fast enough, as far as I was concerned. They became weary. Their movements slow, sinking their axes into the rock in wide, gradual arcs. They complained that the day had ended. That my prize would be there in the morning. And they griped that I made them do it the "old way"—breaching the rock with pickaxe rather than laser cutter. They became ever resentful. But I wouldn't be deterred. I feared the electromagnetic radiation from the laser would contaminate my prize. I wouldn't even let them use a thermal drill. I remained resolute, and they despised me for it, but I didn't care. I knew the prize's worth.

I snatched the pickaxe from the smaller of the two men. I shoved him aside and began to hack the rock myself. I could feel them watch me. I am petite in build, but I'm strong and tough. I call it a *wiry* strength. I chipped and hacked, hammering with an obsession that made the other men stop. Were they captivated by my frenzied movements? Or did they regard the deep gash across my face, a diagonal punctuation from my left ear, across the bridge of his nose to my right cheek. Yes, I've seen horror and felt pain, the cost of adventure in undiscovered alien worlds. Yet, it has all been worth it. Those moments brought me to the darkness of the cave. Sweat fogged my eyes as I chipped away, a small inconvenience of the grueling effort. I wanted them to see that I was both a scientist and explorer. That hard work was not a stranger to me. I wanted them to see the rewards of their sacrifice. They would be wealthy beyond their imaginings, richer than Midas himself, thanks to my efforts. They would thank me later.

They didn't share my passion. At just twenty-nine years of age, exploration had been my life for the past fifteen years—an addiction which sunk its claws into me and never let go. My own mother had taken me on my first dig at just fourteen. That's when I got hooked. I vowed to continue the familial tradition: journey to unexplored worlds, finding new species, discover new elements, witness the exotic delights of new places. But my path turned out to be both a boon and a curse. I hadn't stopped for years. Never rested. Couldn't. It pulled at me like a bad drug, the kind that leaves destruction in its wake. I neglected my wife and my family. The delicious rush of exploring uncharted lands was my mistress.

Funny. At first, I'd fought tooth and nail not to go there. A fully funded trip at Biotech's expense was attractive. Most would take the chance, but I knew the station would be an armpit. Nothing good came for free. The trip would not be glamorous. I loved to explore, but some places just weren't meant to be inhabited. Yet, the minute my feet hit soil, I pulled a sounding reader from my bag and stuck it into the ground. Only minutes passed before the data was uploaded, and Aristotle analyzed the reading. Archaeological data and ecological reviews of the station's past activities were immediately at my disposal. By the time the reading was complete, Aristotle had given me access to all the station's secrets. I had its ecology, weather patterns, geography, food sources, natural resources, and the existence of any current or past living organisms. Aristotle had a good sense of humor about it. I should've recognized his humor as a gentle warning. *God is a comedian playing to an audience too afraid to laugh.* I'd heard the saying many times and thought it cute. So did Aristotle. He laughed, but he wasn't human.

The one treasure the sounding reader had given me was the data on an almost-extinct organism. Normally, I would've blown it off, but something told me to run a value prediction. What was revealed was staggering: a mere insect worth an unquantifiable number of earthnotes. We'd never come across its equal. The insect was a botfly, an organism with the ability to eradicate disease and promote cell regeneration. I couldn't believe my luck, that Biotech should choose me to lead such an expedition.

I was a fool.

A.F.I.B. threw ridiculous sums of money at me to fund an expedition that was rickety at best. Of course, anytime an explorer is funded to travel, it's a very attractive prospect, but there is also great risk. One can't be sure of the dangers present. A.F.I.B. had plenty of scientists and capable people in their employ. They had enough satellite data to know there would most likely be fatalities, a fact they conveniently withheld when they commissioned my services. They offered me an irresistible proposal, and I accepted. I should've known better, though. *Such vanity!* My arrogance allowed me to believe I was their number one prospect, but really, I was their number one idiot. I was good, but I wasn't *that* good. I still had much to learn. Why would A.F.I.B. send in their seasoned best when they could hire a green-behind-the-ears newbie for pennies on the dollar? It would be like sending in your star quarterback into the fourth quarter of a preseason football game that you've already lost. Better to send in your third string—a sacrifice that will cost you little but teach you much.

I wasted no time in making my preparations for the dig. At first Aristotle would not reveal its location. Had adamantly refused, in fact. Said: *this organism is highly unstable.* Damn A.I. computer was too smart for itself and overly cautious. I was beside myself. Enraged, even. So, I ignored the refusal. Assumed it was a "glitch" in its deductive reasoning program. I'd fix it later. In the meantime, I hacked its main frame. My A.I. interrogation methods proved effective. Aristotle was singing like a canary.

The location of the fly and its larvae were beyond an underwater river, deep in the bowels of the station's cave system . . . where you are now. My team continued to be skeptical. I didn't mention the fly's worth or its capabilities and certainly not Aristotle's refusal. Besides, it was just a tiny little, harmless fly, no? No.

My first sighting of it terrified me. It was bigger than I'd expected. The size of a human fist. It pestered us for hours, but we couldn't catch it. I was frustrated, and the thing started to become a nuisance. Out of frustration, one man demanded we stop for a while. Regroup. I insisted we continue the hunt. He refused, and so began the others. I threatened him. *But it's just a fly,* they said. *There are other things we may explore.* I kicked the side of the cave wall. I know they must've thought I'd gone crazy. And maybe I had, a little. They couldn't understand my obsession with the fly, and so they started to regard me warily. Some wanted to go back. I resolved to stay. We argued and deliberated. The discussions got heated, and we ignored the fly. That had been a mistake. It shot something. That got our attentions. The chemist grabbed his neck, cursing. I examined it. Turned out to be a "love dart." A miniature arrow. Hard and white. Thin and pointy. Calcareous, like an oyster shell. Lodged deep into the man's neck. I pulled it from him with a pair of tweezers. The wound closed before my very eyes. Not even a scar remained. I was elated. An organism that had the ability to promote instantaneous cellular regeneration? This seemed to placate the others, and so they agreed to stay. I was elated. I'd unlodged the greatest scientific find of the century.

Then, another miraculous thing happened. The chemist came to me back at camp. He was unrecognizable. A thirty-year-old version of his former self.

He'd grabbed my shoulder. "It's *me*, Isaac. Do you not recognize me?"

He wiped his forehead. There was a sheen across it. It glistened. He coughed and pulled at his collar.

"*Isaac?* No, I don't believe it. Isaac Abasi is a sixty-year-old man with arthritis in his knees."

"I swear it's me," he said, taking a step toward me. Something shone in his eyes. It looked feverish. I didn't like it. I stepped back. "The dart did something to me. I feel hot. I need cool air and water. I might be getting the flu."

I was still unable to wrestle with the idea that *this* was Isaac. I responded perfunctorily, through my shock, I think. I played along, not knowing what else to think or do. "Are you okay, my friend?"

"I don't know. My vision is blurred, but my knees have never felt better."

I just couldn't believe it was him. He looked so young, but he was almost recognizable. Very different from the man I knew, but I could see that he *could be* a young Isaac. Besides, who else could he be? We were a small enough group to know each other. I would know every man on the station. This was new land. How else would he have gotten here? He told me things only Dr. Abasi and I knew. And he *did* look like Abasi. Just a younger version, at least for a while.

In my arrogance, I thought I had found the fountain of youth; but in time, I'd come to discover my mistake. The signs began to issue forward one by one, like flies from Pandora's Box. A box I'd opened wide.

I didn't know about the eggs the fly had laid in Dr. Abasi's bloodstream. Or the larvae that hatched from them, until much later. Until, out of desperation, I had to figure out what I'd allowed to happen. If I'd listened to Aristotle, I might've taken precautions. I would've known that any contact with the larvae would result in their invasion of the chemist's brain stem. That one of them would turn parasitic and make the chemist its unwilling host. Consume all his body's water. All his nutrients. And that he would turn withered. Emaciated. Lose the oxygen to his brain. That the deprivation of nutrients would starve him. I would see the chemist die but keep on living. A miserable state. A brain-dead-ravenous-state. I'd witness a diabolical cycle of consumption and secretion. Cell death and regeneration all at once. The energy required for such an infernal process would drive him to a ravenous state. I'd watch, with unraveling terror, the chemist's sinister transformation. The fever in his eyes would burn like the sun. It would be the engine that drove him to merciless lengths to quench his insatiable hunger for meat, even human flesh. He'd become crazed. Desperate. Impossible to reason with. He'd look for us. For humans. To feed. On.

I hadn't unlodged the greatest scientific find of the century. I'd unleashed hell. Me. The Greatest Scientist of All Time? *I don't think so.*

60

We were stunned. We looked at each other, not knowing what to say or do. There was nothing but a long, uncomfortable silence. Then Eric tapped his foot on the equipment room floor. The sound was obnoxious. I was about to tell him to stop, when he suddenly spoke to the anonymous voice.

"Well, that's a lovely story, but as Commander Jefferson asked, what's that got to do with our present situation? And what does this have to do with Ensign Brown specifically?" he asked, gesturing to me.

Is he for real?

"It has everything to do with our situation," Yuri said. He nodded toward the sounds on the other side of the equipment room door. "Now we know how those things got that way."

"I don't care about how they got that way. How do we get out of here? Am I going to turn? Is he going to turn?" He gestured toward the lance corporal who clutched at his amputated leg. "LaSalle said that not everyone turns."

The voice chuckled again, but then he sighed. "Mr. LaSalle is ever the optimist. Always giving people hope."

"Will I turn or not?"

"How long ago where you bit?"

"About thirty minutes ago."

"Hmm," said the voice, as if to consider Eric's chances. "You? Probably. The specialist? Mr. LaSalle? I doubt it. But it's too soon to tell. These things go fifty-fifty. You just never know."

Eric looked like he was hugging himself. Even though Eric was a douche most of the time, I felt bad for him. I hoped for a more reassuring answer for him. "Well, that's not much of an answer. And why not LaSalle?" I asked.

"I've been bitten before," said LaSalle. "I also had a team of medical experts who were there right away to extract a good portion of the venom before I was turned. Of course, never got all of it. So, I've developed immunity. My chances are considerably low now."

Eric's face brightened. "So, there's a cure? There's an anti-venom? "

"No. Unfortunately, Biotech hasn't found one," said LaSalle. "It's one of the reasons you're here—to see if there's anyone with antibodies in their system which can fight the virus."

"Of course, there's a cure. There is always a cure. Nature is a fickle beast. It operates on opposites. Where there is night, there is also day. Where destruction lies, so also does healing. There is most certainly a cure."

"If there's a cure, then why don't I know about it?" LaSalle said.

"Because they don't know about it."

"And why not?" LaSalle pinched the bridge of nose.

"You're afraid they want to weaponize the virus aren't you?" Cox stood up. He'd been preoccupied with helping the wounded lance corporal who lost his leg. They want economic leverage by circulating it in the general population.

"That's exactly what they want, Lieutenant Commander Cox. You're most intuitive. But they won't circulate it until they can control it."

"Why not come forward?" Cox threw up his hands. "Bring it to the attention of various media outlets. I'm sure the media would be intrigued."

They own the media, Commander. I'd be dead within a day. They will mass produce some pitiful, diluted version of a anecdote. Infected people will be managed but not cured, and Biotech will charge ludicrous amounts for such a pathetic replacement.

"I'm sure there are plenty of viruses they can introduce to the population that already have cures. Why this?"

"Because they've discovered the human potential that one parasite may provide: cellular regeneration, superhuman physical capabilities, pain resistance and much, much more."

LaSalle was eerily quiet, as if he knew all of this. I looked at him directly. I felt betrayed. He could've told me this. He could've confided in me. My hands shook with rage. I glared at LaSalle as I spoke. "Tell us how it works, please."

The voice took another deep breath of exasperation. "Consider a special kind of fly. Its only distinguishing trait from a normal fly is that it is bigger. Imagine that fly lays tiny eggs that you can't see. The eggs hatch and become larvae, if you will. The larvae are advanced parasitic organisms requiring a host, a host with a nutrient-rich, heavily watered environment. What better host than a mammal and more specifically, a human? So the parasite is deployed into a human system via a "love dart"—a tiny, sharp object composed of calcium carbonate that is embedded into the skin, and the parasite enters the bloodstream. Another pathway into the human body is through our food sources. A fly lays its eggs in our food, and its larvae hatches there. The food is consumed, and the parasite has entered the intestinal tract and then the bloodstream. Through either pathway, the parasite enters the circulatory system with a direct route to the brain, where it releases a neurotoxin. Now, here's where the brilliance of this organism plays in."

Eric rolled his eyes, clearly not as fascinated with the prospect of the parasite as our mysterious speaker. I wasn't fascinated either. In fact, I was disgusted, and all I wanted was to get out of this mess.

"The neurotoxin is highly concentrated with proteins and polypeptides. The parasite releases the neurotoxin to incite faster acclimation to its new environment by repairing any cellular damage or imperfections in its host. The host environment becomes new and improved with heightened physical capabilities and magnified senses. In essence, the host body becomes a superhuman machine with unprecedented reflexes. But the body recognizes a foreign invader and incites its own immune response, thereby releasing its own neurotoxin. The neurotoxin the human body produces to kill the parasite also destroys the white matter of the brain, creating a comatose state, virtually a "zombie-like effect."

The voice laughed, clearly impressed with the capabilities of the parasite. "You've heard the saying: *That which does not kill you only makes you stronger?* Well, the truth of that is relevant in this case."

Eric paced back and forth. Then he threw his hands up in the air. "So basically, we're unknowing participants in some warped fucking bloodsport game. They want to see how a team of highly trained security specialists and a gaggle of military people mount up against a bunch of zombies with superhuman capabilities; am I correct?"

The voice chuckled. "You are correct."

"We were sent here to investigate a murder," I said. I could hear the desperation seeping into my own voice. "Are you saying that senior chief's murder was just a ruse to get us down here?"

"No, I'm saying the *investigation* was a ruse to get you down here. Your senior chief's murder happened aboard your ship and was unplanned."

"Perfect." Eric threw his hands up again. "It's what I've trained my entire life for. This is why I joined the Marine Corps? These games?" He continued mumbling and kicking random objects. I worried that he made way too much noise.

I wanted to blame him, remind him that he was the reason we were down here, but what would've been the point? I worried that the ACs outside of the equipment room would get riled by the ruckus. Everyone was in a state of shock, except for Cox, who was putting more blankets over the wounded lance corporal.

Yuri looked up, his face eager. "All of this, this *experiment* is restricted to the mines, right? This can't be happening at the port too."

He's worried about Lauralie.

I thought of Midshipman Whitaker and Chief Martinez tangled up in this. I wondered if they were safe. I couldn't bear the thought of anything happening to them. They were good people, and I couldn't shoulder the thought that I'd put them in danger.

"My apologies, Commander Jefferson, but I fear I only have visibility of the mines. I am certain that all is well at Port Juliette. Biotech would not allow such a valuable facility or their research to be compromised."

LaSalle snorted. "You don't know Biotech very well. The entire port is staffed by ex-cons and drifters. Biotech doesn't care about those people. They'll let this whole thing play out, get the data they need and then send a special forces unit to contain the situation and scrub down the entire facility."

"Let us hope that Dr. LaSalle's reasoning and logic are misplaced."

"Well, calling them can't hurt," I said.

"Of course, it can. You don't think your calls are monitored? That call you made to your roommate was ignorant, Amelia."

I was moved by the disappointment in the voice's tone. And I could feel the critical glances from the group, especially LaSalle. The *I told you* so radiated from his brain into my face like a punch, even though the words weren't spoken aloud.

"If we are all just Biotech's puppets, to be used to study these ACs, are you saying this entire station is like a gaming site, then?" I asked.

"In a manner of speaking, yes. But the station still offers a lot in the way of biomedical research. This station is one of Biotech's largest manufacturers of pharmaceuticals. The parasites alone are worth billions. It will never be 'just a gaming site.'"

"Either way, we don't have many options."

"Actually, you don't have *any* options. You have a choice. Not options. Die or fight your way through this."

"Yeah. Like that's possible."

"With a little cleverness and ingenuity, it is possible to survive this."

"Even if we survive, they'll just send people to kill us, so their little secret doesn't get out."

"No. Killing you all presents too great a chance for public scandal. If you make it back, Biotech benefits in several ways. First, should you raise a stink over this, there's always the old 'sorry—things—got—out—of—hand excuse.' They'll find a couple of 'fall guys' for the incident (probably you, Dr. LaSalle, maybe the commodore), dismiss the entire matter as an accident. Biotech will pay a hefty sum to some officials, and the matter will be under the carpet within months. Much easier to admit fault than to entirely cover one's tracks. Second, you'll go back to your units. Life will proceed as normal, etc. etc. But then, over the course of a year, many, if not all of you, will be collected to—uh—be studied, poked, prodded and examined and, perhaps, executed by means of some unprecedented accident. Better to implement a kill many times than to kill many people, one time."

"Oh, that's swell," said Eric. He pumped his fist in the air with mocking force. "If we die, then we die. If we survive, then we die. Fucking awesome."

"Well, it buys you time at least to figure out your next move and to find leverage. That is your hope for survival. Now, I've already taken great risk in talking to you. Sadly, this exchange must come to a close."

"Wait, I have a question that perhaps you can answer," I said.

The voice sighed. "What is it? We don't have much time."

"Who is the guy who's been following us?"

"What guy?" Both Cox and Eric said in unison.

I didn't want to ask this in front of the group, but I had to know. Cox would feel betrayed knowing I kept a secret with LaSalle, and Yuri would probably be upset too.

"There's a guy who has been following us at a distance. I saw him at the port, remember?" I said to Cox, hoping that would be enough to pacify him. "I saw him again before we entered the sinkhole."

"And?" The voice's tone was impatient.

"*And* . . . he gives off the appearance of an AC, but he doesn't move like one, and he has made no attempts to attack us. Who is he?"

The voice was quiet for a moment, as if he considered whether or not to answer my question. Finally, he spoke. "That was Dr. Heinrich Gerg. I believe you read his journal."

"A guy has been following us, and—" Eric began his questions.

I held up my hand to silence him.

"Why is he following us?" I interjected. "And why hasn't he attacked? His journal left the impression that he died or was at least infected."

"He was, in truth, infected by an AC, but he inadvertently halted the turning process. He is somewhat cured. He was watching over you. I sent him."

"Who are you?"

"I can't tell you that."

"Can't or won't?"

"Won't. It is for your own safety."

"You're not going to tell us your name?" Deep somewhere in my gut, I had a burning need to know. I had more questions, but I knew we were on borrowed time.

"Sadly, no, Miss Brown."

"Well, give us something—anything—a clue—*something*. Can we at least talk to Dr. Gerg ourselves?"

"Unfortunately, I can't allow that. Dr. Gerg has revealed too much already, keeping that silly journal. Not his smartest moment. Now I must go. I'm sure you'll understand."

I was desperate to keep him on the line. I tried to think of anything that would keep him there, but my mind came up blank. He could've hung up long ago, but he hadn't. He was helping us when he didn't have to. There was reason for that. There was something more he had. Then it hit me. "You must have the cure. If Dr. Gerg is *somewhat cured,* and you sent him to find us, then you must have it. Will you give it to us?"

Silence.

"Please, sir." I used my most respectful tone. I looked at Eric. I'd planned to feign sympathy for him, but then it dawned on me how much I really didn't want him to turn or die. Yeah, he was a douche, but I cared for him.

"Please," I said, again. "I don't want my friend to die. If it was someone you cared about, wouldn't you do whatever you could to help him?"

The voice groaned with frustration.

"Please," I said it one more time. I knew I had him.

"Okay, but I'll only tell you, Miss Brown. No one else, and you must give me your word that you won't share the information with anyone else in your group, no matter how shocking."

"I give you my word."

"I mean it. This will shock you, but you must not reveal my name. It's for their protection just as much as yours."

"When I give my word, I keep it."

"Very good. I have revealed the location of the cure to your A.I. butler. My name, my identity, will flash on your wrist device and delete itself within seconds never to be recovered again."

He planned to tell me anyway.

I positioned my earpiece and listened as Shakespeare rattled off location details. This was shocking enough, but when I looked at the name that flashed on my wrist display, I was stunned by what I saw. I whipped my head back up. Indeed, I was shocked. Nervously, I fingered the pendant around my neck. The surge of emotions that coursed through me left me incredulous. I looked up at the voice. "My God. Wait . . . I—"

"I wish you the best of luck, Ensign Brown. Goodbye."

And with that, the transmission ended. Eric tried desperately to get the voice to come back, to get more information, especially about his bite. He wanted to ask how much longer he had. But we heard nothing.

"Who was that guy?" asked LaSalle.

I felt a little lightheaded. I willed myself to speak as a flood of thoughts and emotions washed over me. "I—I—"

"Who was that, Mel?" asked Eric impatiently.

Lost in a flurry of thought, I had nothing to say.

"Mel, tell us what's going on!" Eric had grabbed me now.

"I can't say." My response was perfunctory.

"Just tell us, for the love of God." Eric said.

"Hey man, give her some space. She'll tell us when the time is right." Yuri stepped in between Eric and me.

"Oh, c'mon. Seriously?" said Eric. "What if something happens to her?"

"Well, then. I guess nothing better happen to me." For some reason, the idea of something happening to me woke me up like ice water in my face. I had a task to accomplish, and that meant that I didn't have time for a freak-out moment.

Eric shook his head. "You're a real bitch sometimes, Mel. Our lives are on the line too."

"Hey, she just got you a cure, asshole," said Cox. "Maybe don't call her a bitch?"

"I'm sorry," said Eric. "You're right. I just—"

"Yeah, I know. I'm sorry, I can't tell you, but I gave him my word," I said just above a whisper.

"Well at some point you'll have to break your word." LaSalle propped up his rifle and started to check the number of rounds he had remaining. "Okay. Enough talk. We need to prepare. Arm everyone."

"I thought we already did that," said Yuri who held up his Dbgun in response.

"No. For real this time."

61

aSalle nodded to the guards who all walked up and placed their surplus of excess weaponry into the center of the room. I was taken aback by the size of the stockpile. I hadn't realized how much they'd carried this trip. Each guard had a black duffel and pack on their back that they dropped on the pile. Most of the weapons were constructed with compact restructuring technology. In other words, large weapons could be a reassembled into compact, smaller units for mobility purposes.

At first, LaSalle handed out the remaining standard weaponry: pistols, rifles, grenades. He tossed them to anyone who wasn't armed or only lightly armed. I settled on a Tommy gun with incendiary rounds. He advised against it, due to its weight by comparison to the other lighter weapons. He tried to convince me to carry a machine pistol with a burst limiter. He wanted me armed with something lighter and with adequate accuracy since I wasn't much of a shot. I insisted on the Tommy gun. I figured that what I lacked in accuracy would be made up for with its high rate of automatic fire. It gave me a strong sense of security. For me, that alone made it worth lugging the weight.

As he dug deeper into the stockpile, it became even more apparent that he and his guards hadn't just been hoarding weapons for regular security. They'd anticipated run-ins with the ACs. The weapons that emerged from the stockpile were shockingly unorthodox, the kind of thing you saw in an old feudal-era combat film. I wondered who manufactured such weaponry, the perfect meeting of prehistoric and futuristic technologies. Exactly the kind of thing you'd be eager to use on an AC but would cringe at using on an actual human.

There were long-range weapons like heat-seeking cinder mini-bombs, aerial disintegration grenades, laser explosives, and so on. There were also some of the more medieval-like weapons. I saw a bow that launched pyrotechnic arrows. Next to it was what appeared to be a plain metal pipe. I picked it up and wrapped my hand around the center. Suddenly it lit up. From both ends, it expanded into a full javelin roughly eight feet long.

LaSalle took it politely from my hands and pointed to a few features. "It has heat sensory activation. When you palm it, it extends. It's also equipped with a paralyzing gas. You don't have to be accurate. Just land it near your target and everything in a fifteen-foot radius is immobile for up to a minute. But you only have a minute. That's when you take their heads off. It's not my favorite weapon. Too much work involved, but it's effective, nonetheless."

There were plenty of other weapons too: boomerang saws, rope darts projecting ignited liquid fire once lodged within its target. But I was drawn to a bag full of Picramic Acid Tipped Throwing Irons (a.k.a. PATTIs). They released a concentrated dose of lethal, corrosive acid upon impact. Great for disintegrating ACs. I could imagine taking out a string of ACs at a distance with them, so I grabbed a couple of handfuls, ninja stars in particular. From my Gladiator 4D experiences, I knew I was pretty adept at throwing Shurikens. There were throwing knives, too, but, in true

Kentucky-boy fashion, Cox wanted them. Yuri settled for the bow and pyrotechnic arrows assembly, which I think Cox secretly wanted too, but it would've been too much for him to haul.

There were also plenty of short-ranged weapons too. There was a case of non-explosive grenades, called "Homewreckers." Yuri picked one up and turned it around in his hand.

"An explosive, non-explosive. That doesn't make sense." He turned to toss it back into the case, but LaSalle snatched it from his hand.

"Careful with that. Soldiers have dropped these in bars, barrack rooms, squad bays and (God forbid) their homes, causing them to detonate. Drop one of these in an enclosed space where there are multiple heat signatures, and, let me tell you, it'll fuck shit up. That's why they're called Homewreckers."

Yuri winced. Then he leaned in at a respectful distance and appraised it suspiciously.

LaSalle held it up to the light. "This one in particular is called a Hummingbird on account of the buzzing sound it makes. For two whole minutes, it whizzes around and cuts anything in its path. There are razor-sharp blades that shatter the grenade's casing when it detonates. The blades are attached to a steel body. The blades move at a frightening speed, like the wings of a hummingbird. You can't be in the room when one of these things goes off."

Yuri took a step back. "I think maybe we should let you hold on to the Homewreckers."

LaSalle put it gingerly back into the case with the other Homewreckers.

There were other grenade-like and mini-bomb-type of devices. Some were lethal, deploying a chemical or gas or some form of small projectile. Others were mobile agents of chaos, like the Homewreckers. Some were just what LaSalle referred to as Cripplers, weapons which incapacitated or immobilized. These were used on both humans and ACs, allowing one to easily destroy multiple hostiles at once.

Finger knives, batons and several types of daggers using laser technology were also grouped with the short-ranged weapons. I already had the Raptor and just picked up the Shurikens, so I didn't bother going through the short-range pile. Yuri had his BLTs. Cox grabbed a set of Khali sticks with glowing laser tips. Not quite advanced but extremely effective in dispatching an AC's head from its body, according to LaSalle.

He even armed the lance corporal whose leg was severed. At first LaSalle insisted on giving him my Tommy gun, but the lance corporal asked for the handheld Gatling gun that Komanski carried. Komanski was reluctant to give up the Gatling but did so after LaSalle gave him another hard look.

"Now that you're all properly armed, we need to figure out the best way out of here," said LaSalle.

"Yeah. How do you propose we do that?" Cox was rummaging through a first aid kit given to him by one of the Biotech guards. He examined black vial containing an antiseptic liquid spray. "I don't see any other exits. And by the looks of the monitor there, there's an entire army of ACs out there waiting to tear us to pieces."

We all looked up at the monitor. There were over a hundred ACs clinging to the door. They drooled and scraped, groaned and moaned, their mouths slack, wide open like a pack of starved hyenas.

Cox continued as he attended the Marine. "Even if we tossed a couple of dissolution grenades, we're not guaranteed to get all of them from a barely opened titanium door. Open it too much and we risk getting overrun."

I looked at LaSalle, and the three remaining Biotech guards: Komanski, some guy whose name I didn't know and a woman. "Maybe we can toss a couple of dissolution grenades as a diversion. You all can activate your cloaking, leave here, circle back around and just kill the ACs. They won't see you. I know it's a lot to ask, but it's an option."

I knew it was kind of selfish to ask the Biotech guards to do all of that, but I wasn't sure what better options we had, other than running.

"That won't work," said LaSalle.

"Why not?"

"Because there's too many of them. Even if we created a big enough opening for someone to divert them, it wouldn't really work."

"And how do you figure?" I asked, crossing my arms. I was irritated that no one else had ideas, but all of mine were being shot down.

"Because when a person is infected, the parasite makes a pit stop in your sinus cavity before it burrows its way toward the brain. If you ever get a chance to see an AC up close, you'll see one tiny hole, on each side of the head (near the temple). The hole is a result of burrowing, an opening to a membrane that stretches from one side of the head to the other. The burrowed channel is a wound that repairs and becomes a membrane filled with nerve endings called 'thermoreceptors.' The ACs are able to detect infrared thermal radiation, changes in the heat gradient. In short, they can smell us, and they can sense our body heat.

"How do you know all of this, LaSalle?" Cox asked. This time it wasn't confrontational. The question was genuinely sincere.

"I've hunted and studied ACs before—at another station," he said, looking directly at Cox. He didn't try to lie or withhold information. LaSalle was tired of keeping secrets.

Everyone looked surprised, but no one criticized LaSalle. He was here to help us. He said he was "compelled" to be here; but regardless, all of his actions and decisions up to that point had been to help us. That spoke volumes.

We all wanted to grill him over his past exploits with ACs. I wanted to know how he was "compelled" by Biotech. I wanted to believe that he was good guy caught up in a bad situation. It didn't matter, though. LaSalle was just as much a pawn as the rest of us.

Cox snapped the first aid kit shut, stood up and walked over to the rest of us. He spoke just above a whisper so the lance corporal couldn't hear. "Look, you obviously know how to deal with the ACs better than any of us. And it's clear that we definitely can't leave out the front door, but how else are we going to get out of here? Maybe Ensign Brown's plan merits some consideration. Plus, we have to carry him out of here. How are we to do that? I don't think a piggyback ride is going to cut it."

We gazed at the lance corporal with doubtful looks. Luckily, the Marine hadn't gone into shock, but he did look ill. His skin was pale and wet. New beads of sweat formed as he strained to hear our conversation.

"We don't," said LaSalle. "We don't carry him."

I could feel the heat rising in my face. "What do you mean? Are you kidding me? You—"

"Just relax, Mel, before you say something you can't take back. I'm *not* saying we leave him. There are plenty of vehicles in here that we can use to carry him. Maybe we can use these vehicles to run them over. We just have to find one fast enough that works."

I was relieved. I wouldn't have backed down on the issue, and I didn't want another conflict brewing within our group. We couldn't afford it.

Yuri pointed to some of the vehicles. "These are too slow. There's no way we can fend off ACs and outrun them, moving him in one of these things."

"We can move him in a loader, and set a perimeter around it. Move with it. Or we could use a stretcher." LaSalle sighed. "Either way, we've spent too much time in here, and we need to move."

"I don't know what you're all worried about," said Eric. "You're basically immune, anyway."

"I'm not totally immune. Anything can happen. Besides, I can still be eaten alive by one of those things, and frankly—"

Before he could finish, we heard a deep scream. Specialist Dunn, the Biotech guard who'd lost a chunk of his bicep to an AC had actually turned into one. He was straddling the lance corporal with the severed leg. Faster than a cobra strike, the guard bent down and ripped flesh from the lance corporal's cheek. Then he looked over at us. I could see the familiar light burn in his eyes. He was crazed. He chomped his mouth up and down as he swallowed the bloodied flesh. He wasn't drawn and withered with missing hair like the other ACs, but I suspected that it was because he was a newbie. His eyes were, however, feverish, and his skin turned a pale gray. Clearly the parasite had already sucked a lot of moisture from his body.

The Marine struggled and kicked at the AC. Before anyone could make it over to help, the Marine did the absolute worst thing we could've anticipated. In a fit of panic, he shoved a laser grenade into the AC's mouth and kicked him off with his good leg.

From there, everything seemed to move in slow motion. I recalled LaSalle yelling *No!* I yelled it, too, like I'd said the word underwater. But AC-Dunn landed on his back. The jolt was enough to activate the laser explosive in his mouth. Red streams of light burst from its body in several places. Normally, I would've said *right on,* but the lance corporal's actions screwed us on an epic scale. Two of the several rays that erupted from AC Dunn's body melted a hole in the titanium alloy door that separated us from the army of ACs. A few wedged themselves through, ripping off limbs and other decayed parts in the process. The hole wasn't huge, but it was big enough for them to push through, single file, like ants across a hill.

The Biotech guard with the missing foot had stood up at this point. He was the first to get it. Once the smell of blood was in the air, the ACs went into a frenzy. The first two ACs through the door pounced on him. Then five more piled on top him. They ripped the meat from his body like a human flesh vacuum. For a moment we were all spellbound, but then Yuri spoke, yanking us from our momentary shock.

"Fall back. Fall back now."

The ACs were busy having a tug-o-war with the lance corporal's limbs while others made a meal of his innards. I saw the barrel of the handheld Gatling gun peeking from beneath him. I yanked one of the Biotech guards who was falling back and pointed at the gun. "Grab the Gatling."

"You grab it," she said. "I'm not diving in there."

"Look. We need it. We don't have time to argue. Just get it." I lifted the Tommy. "I'll cover you with this."

She looked skeptical. I picked up the Tommy gun and opened up my stance, to show her I was capable. I braced the stock against my shoulder firmly, so I could handle the recoil. I started lighting ACs up. I didn't bother trying to avoid hitting the lance corporal. He was long gone. And even if he wasn't dead, he'd turn with all of those bites.

The Tommy was fully loaded. I moved the gun in an arc, spraying as many ACs as I could. They collapsed. Unfortunately, the Tommy had normal rounds. I desperately wished it had disintegration rounds, to minimize risk to the Biotech guard, but it couldn't be helped. I pushed a wall of them back as I sprayed them with bullets. I'd created enough space that the guard finally worked up enough nerve to grab the Gatling. She ran to the pile of dead ACs and lance corporal and leaned in, her movements timid at first. She wrestled the gun from beneath the pile until she had it firmly in her hands. A huge smile spread across her face as she sprinted back to me.

"I got—"

But she was too slow. And I was in the middle of changing out the magazine. By the time I'd locked in a new mag, two ACs jumped on her back like spider monkeys. One sunk its teeth into her shoulder. The other went for the side of her face. The attack caused her to stumble, and she fell onto her knee caps. I heard a crunch. From the way she screamed, I guessed that the pain from her knee caps shattering was worse than being bit. I didn't mull over it long before I aimed for her head and sent a volley of rounds into her skull.

As she met the floor, the Gatling gun slid from her hands and scattered to a stop a couple of feet from where I stood, exactly halfway between myself and a wall of ACs.

Yuri, Cox and LaSalle were screaming at me to retreat, but we really needed that gun. We were cornered, and if there was any way we would blast our way through a thick wall of ACs, the Gatling was the way. I unloaded all the rounds in my magazine to push the ACs back, so I could work my way closer to the gun. But new ones just kept coming, climbing over the dead ones.

Once the mag was empty, I had only a second to decide if I should change out the magazine to get closer to the Gat, or if I should just grab it and run. I decided on the latter. I'd carry a lot of weight with both the Gat and the Tommy, but I was the last person, the closest to the wall of ACs and the closest to the gun.

Fuck it. I shuffled to the Gat as quickly as I could and snatched it. I turned and sprinted as quickly as my legs would allow. For a split second, I imagined getting jumped on by ACs, suffering the same fate as the female Biotech guard. And I would've if it hadn't been for Yuri, who'd let a pyrotechnic arrow loose. I felt it whiz by me. It landed on a female AC who had already launched herself in the air to pounce onto me. She exploded in mid-flight, and the blast took out several others. The shock wave pushed me forward. I stumbled forward and dropped both rifles to brace my fall. Luckily, I was next to the others. LaSalle and Cox lifted me up as Yuri unleashed a succession of arrows. He blew up at least twenty or so ACs, just enough to give us time to get out of reach. LaSalle gave me back my Tommy gun, and he held the Gat. We fired off rounds endlessly, but the ACs just kept coming. We would run out of rounds at some point. Then what would we do?

"We've gotta do something," I yelled above the gunfire. LaSalle simply nodded and pulled on my arm to retreat. The wall of ACs was getting closer. We were already almost at the back wall of the equipment room.

Komanski stepped forward and started tossing dissolution grenades. I could tell that he was trying to break up the herd, turn them, rotate them so that we could possibly shimmy out the front door along the side. But it was no use. They were getting closer and closer, and we were running out of room.

"Go to the supply locker. Hurry."

We all looked up in shock. We thought the voice had abandoned us for good. The voice's words vibrated throughout the room. The ACs looked up, too, and hissed at it.

"You're back. I *knew* you didn't leave us."

"Go now!" His voice was clipped, full of command and force. We moved as ordered. LaSalle handed Komanski the Gatling as he and Yuri led us to the supply locker. Komanski held back the wall of writhing ACs as he fired off the Gatling. The anonymous voice rattled off instructions. "To the rear of the locker is a hatch. The hatch leads to a tunnel. The tunnel stretches far, some four miles, passing through several bunkers. Follow the tunnel and don't take any of the side routes. The last bunker sits just a mile from Port Juliette. Perhaps you'll have better luck there."

"How do you know this?" I asked hurriedly as I fell back.

"I know a lot of things."

I couldn't ask any more of him. He'd given us more than we were owed. He was taking a personal risk by contacting us. I looked up in admiration. "Thank you. Will we ever meet?"

"One day, should you survive this, perhaps I will pay you a visit, Miss Brown. You're welcome and goodbye."

We arrived at the supply locker. The ACs were only several feet away from us. Komanski, who was the last person, hurried us all through the sliding door to the rear of the locker. He had a Crippler in hand, ready to toss, so that we had time to move through the hatch that awaited in the corner of the room. I looked back over my shoulder at the carnage. A foot here. A skull there. The ACs had worked with unparalleled efficiency in leaving a wake of death. They teemed like maggots in a trash bin. It seemed like the more we lost from our group, the more that joined theirs.

ACs were everywhere.

62

dropped down from the lip of the open hatch, a heavy metal square door large enough to fit two adults through. Cox and I scooted to the edge of the lip, and as quickly as we could, we dropped into the tunnel. The only other Biotech guard left, other than Komanski, was there to catch Cox. LaSalle stood below with his arms outstretched to catch me. I slid down into his arms, and for a moment, our eyes met. I felt a jolt of excitement. Despite everything that had occurred up to that point, I still felt a strong attraction to him. But I composed myself, knowing that Cox might see our exchange. There wasn't time to think too much on it, anyway. I heard the stampede of ACs above banging on the supply locker above us. Komanski was the last through the hatch. He lowered himself down, hanging onto the lip of the opening by one hand. LaSalle reached up and planted a Crippler called a Medusa into Komanski's free hand.

"Wait as long as you can," said LaSalle, who watched Komanski dangle from above.

Komanski nodded and waited. Dangling. The sounds of the ACs above sounded like an army of foot soldiers, running. My heart rammed against my chest. I felt like I'd have another panic attack.

Then Komanski reached up and tossed the Medusa into the supply locker. I heard a hissing sound and seconds later the stampede sound of the ACs stopped. The ACs were paralyzed courtesy of the gas emitted by the Medusa. LaSalle reached up to hand Komanski a Hummingbird, but Komanski was knocked from the lip by an AC that managed to slip through. One more followed after it.

Komanski fell into me, knocking me to the ground. He hit his head. He was dazed and tried to stand but only managed to stumble back down to the ground

Meanwhile, two ACs were in the tunnel with us. One was a large male roughly the same size as LaSalle. He wore a Biotech uniform.

The other was large and wore a Marine gunnery sergeant uniform.

The AC–Biotech guard shot up and lunged for the first person in its path: Yuri. Luckily, Yuri had his BLTs. He yelled, "Motherfucker." His knuckles lit up, a bright blue. He jabbed the AC with his right fist, and it froze up, trembled with electrical shock. Then Yuri came around with a left hook and punched through the AC's head like he was punching through crushed ice. The ACs head exploded, and the rest of its body dropped to the floor.

LaSalle dealt with the Marine gunny. He reached out and whipped the blade of his dagger across the AC's neck. Then, with a backhand motion, he brought the tip of the blade back and plunged it upwards into the underside of the AC's chin. He activated the laser and twisted. He severed the AC's head from its body before it collapsed to the tunnel floor. He turned to Yuri.

"Quick! Lift me up," he said, gesturing to the hatch opening, "or we're finished."

It took some effort, but Yuri hoisted LaSalle onto his shoulders as fast as he could. Yuri was a big strong guy, but it wasn't easy holding LaSalle on his shoulders. They both grunted with the effort. I heard the first rumblings of the ACs moving. The effects of the Medusa were starting to wear off. Finally, after some wobbling and swaying, LaSalle tossed the grenade into the supply locker above and closed the hatch.

The Hummingbird did its work. The buzzing sound was louder than I thought it would be. I heard bodies hit the floor. The bodies seemed to drop forever. When the sounds finally stopped, I estimated that the Hummingbird had decapitated least fifty or so ACs.

"Mel, hand me that black thing in the front pocket of my pack."

I dug through the pocket and found a black object that resembled a tube of lipstick. He grabbed it from my hand and placed it against the edges of the hatch door. A red light glowed.

"What're you doing?"

"Sealing the hatch so more can't come in. It won't hold forever, but it'll give us a good head start."

LaSalle climbed down from Yuri's shoulders. He walked over to Komanski, who was leaning over the AC-Biotech guard that Yuri had killed. I was curious as to why they were so captivated by that particular AC. LaSalle reached down and picked up its wrist, examining the barcode tattoo on the underside of its forearm. He held his own wrist device over the AC's barcode. There was a tiny beep. He'd logged a copy of the AC's dog tag information.

"He was a good guy."

Komanski nodded in agreement. "Yeah. The best."

LaSalle stood up, slipped his weapons and equipment over his shoulder and started walking. There was a melancholy aspect to his tone. "Let's move and get out of this hell hole."

63

Yuri and LaSalle led us on another trot. I was exhausted, but at this point I didn't care. I was so scared for my life, that I didn't care about the discomfort trying to keep up with a college track star and a veteran Navy SEAL.

Cox wasn't affected at all. He was built for this kind of thing, lean like a gazelle. Eric, on the other hand, was uncomfortable. While he was a Marine used to long runs, his muscular frame was becoming somewhat of a burden. He also looked pale. His dark skin had a gray pallor to it. A sheen of sweat sparkled on his forehead. He seemed to be battling a fever. He coughed and wheezed.

He's going to turn. No.

Even though LaSalle administered first aid to Eric's bite, there was a chance the wound was still deep and the AC venom had entered his bloodstream. He seemed to struggle with every step, but he endured, without complaint. Funny thing about Eric is that he complained about every little thing related to not getting his way, but when it came to physical discomfort, he never complained. He was a tried and true Marine, able to endure extreme physical conditions with sheer mind over matter. That moment of realization about him earned him a new level of respect from me. I saw him through a completely different lens. *Why hadn't I noticed that before?* I realized in that moment that all he ever wanted from me was acknowledgement and respect. Sherri had given that to him unconditionally, but I withheld it, like a bargaining chip. No wonder our relationship hadn't stood a chance. I peered over at him. He was focused on making it through the run, but it was taking its toll. He limped while he ran. More like skipping. Yet, he was too proud to say anything.

We reached an area of the tunnel with an intersection. There were side tunnels on both sides of us. It was an ideal place to rest as all intersections in the cave system were well lit.

"Hey guys," I called out. "Can we stop for a moment? I can't go anymore. I need a sec."

"We're at the first bunker. It's just down here," LaSalle said, pointing to a bunker door about fifty meters away.

"Okay, but we're stopping now," I said, my voice stern.

They stopped and walked back to us. LaSalle looked annoyed, but I didn't care. Eric was in a lot of pain. I took the blame. I owed him at least that.

LaSalle looked at me with raised brows. "Really? It's just right there. We need to get out of the tunnel before the ACs come. You're out of shape, girl."

"Yes, *really*. Not all of us do this for a living. Okay?" I looked up at LaSalle. I breathed hard, but my tone was clear. Threatening. I motioned with my head towards Eric, who was bent over clutching his ankle. LaSalle understood and closed his mouth.

"There's also a medi-pod in the bunker. I know some of us could use it," he murmured, exasperated. Then he looked back to the others so they could discuss an escape plan from the station.

I put a hand on Eric's shoulder. "You okay?"

He frowned. "I didn't know you cared."

"I know I don't always show it, Eric, but I do care. Always have."

He paused to take in a couple of deep breaths. He looked back up at me sheepishly. "Sorry I was such a bad boyfriend."

"Wait. You were my boyfriend?"

"Well—yeah. You didn't think we were boyfriend/girlfriend?"

"Well—no—actually."

"That explains a lot."

LaSalle turned back to us. "Sorry to break this up, kids, but we've have to move."

He'd heard the last part of our conversation. He looked displeased with the direction it was going.

"He can't run, LaSalle."

"Mel, I'm fine, I—"

"Well, he's going to have to, or I'll have to throw him over my shoulder. What choice do we have?" LaSalle said.

"He just needs a few moments."

LaSalle put his hands on his hips and let out a deep sigh. "If we get him inside the bunker, we can get him to the medi-pod, and—"

"You guys, seriously, I'm—"

At that moment, a bullet whizzed by and drilled Eric in the chest. Surprised, he seized up and froze. Then his face fell slack, and he sat down onto the cave floor against the wall. He placed his hand onto his left breast, his movements robotic. Then he pulled it away to look at. His hand was wet, covered in bright red blood.

Cox grabbed me and pulled me along the tunnel. I fought him. I tried to help Eric, but Cox pulled me away against my will. We reached a door. The words "Bunker Alpha" were stenciled across.

"Shakespeare, open locking mechanism on Bunker Alpha," he said, leaning over my wrist display.

"My apologies, Lieutenant Commander Cox, but I am only permitted to accept direction from either Lieutenant Junior Grade Jordan or Ensign Brown, unless you have the proper clearance to override them both?"

"Open it up, Shakesepeare. *Now*," I said, my voice frantic. Another bullet sailed past us, hitting the bulkhead at head level. It missed my head by a half inch.

Cox managed to open the door to the bunker. LaSalle yelled for us all to get down. I tried again to go back and help Eric, but Cox pushed me through the bunker entrance. Then another volley of bullets flew. A fresh jolt of fear pierced me like a shard of ice. I wasn't sure which was scarier, bullets flying or ACs attacking. I tried to see what was going on from over Cox's shoulder. I didn't see much. LaSalle fired in the general direction of the bullets, and then he tapped his breast pocket. He disappeared into thin air. He'd gone into cloaking mode. Komanski and the other Biotech guard followed, disappearing as well.

"Who's firing at us?"

"Biotech. I think," said Cox. "Just stay here."

"What about you?"

"Don't worry about me. I'm going to help Eric. I'll be fine—" The instant he said the words, several bullets peppered his left shoulder. The impact of the bullets sent him forward into me. I fell onto my back with him on top of me. The bunker door closed and locked into place behind us.

The bunker was dark, but I could still see shapes and make out the general layout. The room opened into a brief hallway which led into a small library. Under other circumstances, I would've loved to peruse the library, but I was on my back. The sounds of bullets whizzing through the air just outside expunged all thoughts of reading books.

Cox's body sank onto mine. "Cox? Cox? Are you okay?"

He didn't answer me. But I could hear him breathing and feel his pulse.

I laid there with Cox's limp body across mine. I was shaken to my core.

Unsure of what to do, I tried to move as little as possible as I slipped from beneath him. I got up and checked the locking mechanism on the bunker door. I worried that whoever was shooting would come into the bunker. I knelt beside Cox and shook him. "Cox?"

I put my ear next to his mouth. The bullets were still firing. It was loud. I watched the bunker door video monitor. On the other side, Yuri administered to Eric, who wasn't moving. He checked Eric's pulse. I could see an opening in Yuri's suit where a bullet had nicked him, but he was more concerned with Eric. Eric must've still been alive because Yuri had his pyrotechnic bow and arrow assembly at the ready, protecting Eric. With the others not visible, his hesitation was apparent. He didn't know where to shoot. I disabled the bunker lock and cracked the door. I waved my arm at Yuri, trying to get his attention, but the gunfire was too loud. He focused on dodging bullets and keeping Eric safe. I was afraid for Yuri. Nonetheless, I closed the door back and returned to Cox's side to administer to him.

"Travis, are you okay?"

"I'm fine," he said. I could barely make out a grin on his face.

I reached into my pack and grabbed the pen-sized cartridge-injection system of painkiller. It wasn't as strong as fentanyl, but it would alleviate most of his pain. I injected the drug into his shoulder, until he let out a sigh of relief. I looked into his eyes and smiled.

"That's the first time you've called me by my first name," he said, smiling back. "Usually you just call me *Sir* or *Lieutenant Commander Cox.*"

"Well, I was trying to be respectful. I—"

"I know," he said. His hand was cupping my chin.

I could feel my eyes getting wet. It wasn't the right time to cry, but I felt like I could lose control if I allowed myself. "You saved me. I could've been shot."

"I told you I'd take care of you." His hand slipped from my chin to the back of my neck. He pulled me toward him. I didn't fight it. His lips brushed softly against mine. At first the kiss was innocent. Sweet. But then it heated up. He coaxed my mouth open with his tongue, and then he plunged it deeper into my mouth as his grabbed one of my breasts. He squeezed lightly and rubbed a thumb over my nipple. Even through the suit, I could feel it harden. Our tongues danced around each other. Blood rushed to my groin. He grabbed my ass with the arm that was on the same side as his gunshot wound. The movement had to hurt, but he didn't seem to mind. Butterflies swirled around in my chest from both excitement and fear. The situation was outrageous. Bullets were still flying. Yuri and Eric were in danger, but here I was caught up in a moment with Cox, getting turned on by his kisses. I wanted to let myself get carried away. But I forced myself to break away.

"We can't be doing this right now," I said, letting out a breath.

"Why not?" he asked with a lazy grin. "They'll probably find us anyway. We might as well enjoy ourselves." This was not the responsible, level-headed Cox that I knew. Clearly, the drug was affecting him.

"Yuri and Eric are in real trouble," I said. I helped him sit up. "I need to get you somewhere safe, so I can check on the others. Can you stand?"

He nodded reluctantly. I put my hand behind his back and helped him sit up. The effort made him grimace. After some struggle, I was able to help him stand up. I pressed a button on my wrist display, and a tiny light came on. We stumbled through the bunker which was considerable in size. As we passed through the library into different rooms, I searched for a first aid kit. We passed through a kitchen and then finally I found a room with a bed. I helped Cox to lie down. I left him for a moment and searched the adjoining bathroom to look for a first aid kit. No luck.

"Shakespeare, locate available medi-pods and/or first aid units in Bunker Alpha."

"Yes, of course, Miss Brown," said Shakespeare. He sounded jovial. "The closest available medi-pod unit is approximately three clicks away, positioned in Bunker Echo. However, there are first aid units in Bunker Alpha located in both the pantry and the library."

"I looked in the library."

"Did you check the desk perhaps? It's mounted on the side panel."

I stood up, but Cox grabbed my leg.

"No, Amelia. You don't know what you're facing."

"I know, but I can't just sit in here making out with you. Besides, you need a medi-pod. Shakespeare can help me."

"I'll be fine. The bullets didn't hit any major arteries. It can wait. But you going out there isn't a good idea. You have no idea who is shooting, and you don't have any cloaking capabilities."

"I'm afraid Lieutenant Commander Cox makes a sound point, Ensign Brown."

I was already sorry I turned Shakespeare back on.

"I don't care. I'm going out—"

"You're going out there for *him,* aren't you?" Cox was panting now. He'd lost some blood, but I was sure he'd be okay.

"I have to, Travis. Yuri is still out there too."

Cox's face hardened. He looked like boy who'd had his lunch stolen.

"It's not like that. Yuri is my brother. I'll explain later. I *have* to go."

"Commander Jefferson is your brother?"

"Yes. Like I said, I'll explain later."

His face softened. "Obviously I'm in no position to make you stay. So be careful."

"I will. Promise."

64

tucked the first aid unit under my arm and then took a second to check the bunker monitor. Maybe this time I could get to Yuri and Eric.

The gunfire had ceased, and the tunnel was lit. Yuri was still kneeling beside Eric with his bow and arrow ready to fire. He was looking at something. At first, I couldn't make out what or who. But then, Sherri appeared out of nowhere. She had a rifle propped on her hip, barrel pointed in the air, and she wore a similar dark suit to the one LaSalle wore, with the Biotech emblem stitched on her arm. She was flanked by a small army of Biotech guards. She placed her hand on Yuri's hand and patted lightly. "Put that thing down, hon, before you blow us all to bits and collapse this tunnel."

One of the Biotech guards raised a pistol to Yuri's head. When he hesitated, she said, "Now." Her voice was firm, a couple of octaves lower and commanding. There was no question that she was in charge, and as such, Yuri lowered his weapon.

This was not the Sherri I knew. Not at all. She didn't look kidnapped or under duress. She didn't look nervous or shy. She wasn't the slightly ditsy, nerdy but timidly cute Sherri. This was the no-nonsense-sexy-evil-vixen Sherri, the Sherri who was in complete command of herself and who wasn't afraid of anyone. This Sherri would do bad things and not have any remorse over it. She was an agent of Biotech. All our previous interaction made sense now. She was a plant who'd been monitoring us.

Then LaSalle, Komanski and the other Biotech guard came into view. They were kneeling with their hands behind their heads. A couple of the guards next to Sherri had weapons pointed at them.

"Come out. Come out, wherever you are, Miss Amelia," she sang. She skipped around and waved her arms like a symphony conductor. Her singing grated on me, like a twisted nursery rhyme. "Oh, Ameeeeeelia? Where are you? Don't make me look for you."

Now, I really hate this bitch. At first, I didn't move away from the monitor. I simply watched.

LaSalle stood across from Sherri. He tried to reason with her.

"Let everyone else go. I'll get you what you want," he said.

"Sweetie, if you had that power, you'd have done it already," she said, head tilted, hands on her hips. She smirked. "You wouldn't be schlepping around down here with the cattle. Now, LaSalle, we both know you—"

But LaSalle had other ideas. In one swift movement, he whipped out a pistol and fired, like a cowboy in a western. Several bullets sailed in the direction of Sherri's head. I watched in silent horror because she was fast too. She brought her fist up, and a translucent shield, outlined in light blue, bubbled out around her from the HyFiT ring that Eric had regifted her. The light blue force field enveloped her, and the bullets that LaSalle sent toward her ricocheted off the shield and fell pathetically to the cave floor.

"Now why would you do something that stupid?" she said in a light tone, but her nostrils flared. She nodded at a guard, who clubbed LaSalle from behind in the back.

LaSalle crumpled to floor, clutching at his side.

"This entire scene has me bored. Amelia, get your ass out her now," she said, her voice hard. She handed her rifle to one of the guards and pulled a pistol from her holster. She cocked it and pointed the tip at Yuri's head. "Pronto, or your brother gets one in the head."

I couldn't hide anymore. She'd find me anyway. She had the clearance to get in the bunker. Going out there would buy Cox some time to hide or devise some sort of escape plan. I ran back to Cox. Thankfully, he'd drifted off to sleep. He would've tried to argue against me going back out there. I left the first aid unit with him and rattled off instructions to Shakespeare to somehow get him awake. I rushed back to the bunker door. On the way, I grabbed a few items I'd need. I had a plan. I rushed, eager to get out into the tunnel as quickly as possible. I didn't want any of Sherri's attention on the bunker.

I took a deep breath and slipped from behind the bunker door and walked to the tunnel intersection where she stood. I had my hands up in the air. One of the Biotech guards walked up to me with a lecherous grin. He brought his hands up to search me.

"Touch me, and I'll cut your fucking hands off, you prick." The guard froze and looked back at Sherri. She giggled and held her hand up to her mouth, but she nodded at him. He took a step back and left me alone. She turned to Eric who was propped up against a wall, half conscious. "Eric, darling, you were right. She is a spitfire, and she curses like a true Navy sailor." She laughed, and the pistol she pointed at Yuri's head shook a little.

I stole a glance at Yuri, worried that her pistol might accidentally go off. I tried to compose myself, not wanting her to see my concern.

"What? You're surprised that I know he's your brother, aren't you?" she said as she twisted a piece of her hair around her finger. She was very nonchalant while she pointed the pistol at Yuri. She was too pleased with herself. All I could think about was giving her one swift kick to the face. "I have access to a lot of information, and I made a point of learning whatever I could about the handsome Commander Jefferson."

The fact that she was talking about Yuri made me nervous. I wanted as much of her attention off him as I could manage, so I changed the subject.

"Well, I guess you're not a geologist."

"How'd you guess?" Thankfully, she lowered her pistol. It hovered at her side. I let out a shuddered but quiet breath, trying to remain visibly calm.

"Oh, I don't know. The fact that you're a raging bitch kind of gave it away."

She flicked her hair behind her shoulder. The movement reminded me of a prom queen. "Great observation, and I love the candor. But that's a weakness, Mel. If you didn't have such a smart mouth, Eric would probably still be fucking you instead of me."

"That's okay. You can keep my used goods. There's a used tampon back in my stateroom. You want that too?"

Her face darkened. I noticed a couple of her guards bit their lips, but they didn't dare laugh aloud. She stepped in close, into my personal space. "You've got a mouth on you, girl. I ought to cut those pretty lips right off your face."

She'd unsheathed a combat utility knife. She waved it in my face before letting the tip rest lightly on my top lip. Then she nicked me. It stung. I could feel blood bubble up from my lip.

An icy sensation ran up my neck. *I probably shouldn't taunt her.* I decided to buy some time. For what I wasn't exactly sure, but something in my gut told me to keep her occupied.

"I bet you know who actually killed Senior chief don't you?"

"Yes, in fact I do."

"Was it you?"

"I think you know the answer to that. Of course not, silly. I'm strong but not strong enough to rip a man's head from his body."

"So that *is* what happened."

"Yes. It was an AC. Well, technically. It was the commodore's wife. She's infected. He's been keeping her in a contained area like a rabid dog on a leash. I don't know why, though. That old trout looks like she's been ridden hard and put away wet, and that was before she was infected. Anyhow, she got out somehow and attacked McGinn. The commodore used the attack as an opportunity and had the body dumped onto the well deck to instigate an investigation."

"Why the hell would he do all of that?"

"He's hoping for a cure. What else?" she said, annoyed, as if I should have ascertained all of this by now. Then she laughed. This was all humorous to her. "Can you believe that dickhead had the audacity to let his wife gnaw on your senior chief's head like it was a chew toy? I guess he thought it would take the edge off. That bitch was crazy."

Yuri shook his head in dismay. "So *that's* why we're down here. If one of us turns out to be immune, there's a chance for a cure."

"Sexy and smart. I like that in my men." Sherri rubbed her hand on Yuri's head as though she was polishing a bowling ball.

"I'll kill that motherfucker," Yuri said.

Sherri put a hand to her mouth and tittered. "I don't think you're gonna make the trip back, hon. You're—"

I couldn't stand to hear her girly laugh one more second, so I cut her off. "Of all people, why did your guards shoot Eric? I'd have thought you'd at least protect *him*."

"Oh, sweetie," she said with pity. Her voice shifted into a higher octave like she was a contestant in a Miss America beauty pageant. She wiped the blood away from my lip with her thumb and licked the scarlet liquid from her fingernail. She grabbed me by the chin and leaned in next to my ear. "*I* shot Eric. That was all me, babe."

She leaned back, so I was able to look into her eyes. One word came to mind: psychotic.

"But he cared about you." My voice sounded whiny despite myself.

"And?" Her eyes were wet, like she was on the verge of tears. *She's a nut job.*

"And—uh—I don't know—I don't typically think about shooting people who care about me, even if I don't care about them."

"Yeah, well, you're not like me."

"Thank God for that," I snorted, crossing my arms. I wanted to appear in control, but I felt anything but.

She glared at me. I knew I was pushing it with her. She was ruthless, and, yet, I provoked her. She had zero qualms about using Eric and then shooting him. I decided to lay off a bit. I glanced over at Eric. His head was bobbing up and down. He was passing in and out of consciousness. I wondered if he'd heard the comment about him being my "used goods." I felt a twinge of guilt. He was shot, and despite his behavior the past months, I didn't want him hurt. I promised myself that I would pound the bitch into the ground with my boot heel first chance I got. I tried not to let her see the play of emotions going through me.

She frowned and looked around. "Where's Lieutenant Commander Cox?"

"He was killed by an AC," I said almost too quickly. I prayed that no one would give away my lie. I stole a glance at LaSalle whose face was stiff.

Sherri caught the look. "Oh, don't tell me Gerard was jealous of your new boyfriend. Oh, that's priceless." She tilted her head back with a lazy chuckle. Her eyes returned to me and traveled up and down my body. She walked around me like she was considering a slave at auction. "I guess I can see it, though. I never did understand what all the hype was about, but I guess you're cute enough . . . and that big black booty of yours. I bet they can't resist that."

Cunt.

"What do you want, Sherri?" My tone was even. Polite. Neither contradictory nor exceedingly deferential.

"That's better. I'm tiring of your smart mouth. Actually, *what I want*," she said in a nasty tone, "is for you to call me by my real name, Shreya, not Sherri. You Americans . . . ugh . . . everything has to be so, so *vanilla* with you."

Her accent was making an appearance. I noticed that it got less American and more ethnic with a tinge of British refinement the angrier she got.

I sighed. "Do you intend to make a point anytime soon?"

"I'm gonna need you to tell me where the anti-venom is. We intercepted your transmission. I know the good doctor told you."

"I don't know what—"

Before I finished my sentence, she raised her pistol and executed a Biotech guard kneeling beside LaSalle and Komanski. The guard's head snapped back, and he collapsed onto the ground with a loud thud.

"Let's start again, shall we?" she said. She sounded bored and exasperated, like this was an everyday routine.

"*Christ*, Sherri," said LaSalle, holding up his hands in cautious supplication. "That was unnecessary."

"It was most certainly necessary because I'm not getting the answers I want. If you can't remember to call me Shreya, then at least refer to me as Major Kolar."

"Pfft. When hell freezes over."

"That's always been your problem, Gerard, you never did respect Biotech's hierarchies or protocols. That's why Dominique promoted me, and you're here, on your knees, begging me for your life."

"Major?" I asked, not really caring but buying time. I cared more about why LaSalle knew about Sherri and didn't tell any of us. I'd table that discussion for later.

"Yes. Major. That's my actual rank as far as Biotech is concerned."

"I'm not the only one whose been on their knees, and I'm not begging you for shit. You *do* realize there's no way Dom . . . excuse me . . . *Colonel Sharp*," he said, nastily, "is gonna let you leave this station alive, right? You've been exposed like the rest of, Sherri."

"Call me *Sherri* again and see what happens." Her nostrils flared. The volume of her voice increased steadily. Her pistol was lowered, but her hand twitched.

Gerard, don't piss her off.

"You're in as much jeopardy as the rest of us," he continued, calmly ignoring her outburst and my silent plea, "and even if he does let you come back, he'll greet you with a bullet the minute you arrive."

"Gerard, who the hell do you think sent me here? He *will* let me leave this God-forsaken hole because I'll have the one bargaining chip he can't resist. Now enough of this bullshit." She turned to me. "Where's the anti-venom?"

I took a deep breath. "I—"

"And before you say anything, Mel, think hard about your answer. But answer fast. I can hear ACs coming, and I hate having to deal with those things." She twirled a strand of her dark hair around her finger and pouted out her lips. "Puts me in a bad mood. And you don't want me in a bad mood."

There were indeed ACs coming. The sounds of their trampling and wailing increased as the closed in from one of the side tunnels. One of Sherri's guards had a device in his hand. A glowing blue light blinked steadily. He was tracking them. He studied it, then looked back up at Sherri and nodded.

"Report."

"Just over a thousand meters, ma'am."

"I'm gonna need your answer, Mel. Make it quick. Because the next one is for Yuri," she said, eyeing him openly.

Yuri looked disgusted with her, yet her gaze traveled up and down his body as she soaked in his dark, muscular physique. She grabbed his neck and kissed him deeply in a quick but rough, primal-like movement. She licked her lips with a salacious grin after she broke away. "And I'd hate to waste such a lovely piece of chocolate."

I rolled my eyes. *Original.*

Yuri was about to say something insulting, but I didn't want her angry. I cut him off. "Look, I won't just tell you, but I'll take you there. That's the best offer you're going to get. I don't trust that you won't just kill everyone after I tell you."

"Mel," she said boring her eyes into mine. It was intense, as if she assessed me. An icy dread shot through me. "You're really testing me, aren't you?"

I swallowed. "No. Just consider it insurance. From my vantage point, we'll all probably die, anyway. At least this way, we have some hope, and you'll get what you want much faster."

I worried again that she might shoot someone else for not answering her, but then she rested her pistol against her cheek. She looked like an evil replica of Rodin's *The Thinker.* "Hmm. I'm not sure that's going to work. That's sort of a catch-22, isn't it? It'd be too much of a pain to drag them along with us. But, on the other hand, I can't trust that they won't come after us after we leave."

I was getting desperate. She was a powder keg. Irrational and unpredictable. One wrong move could set her off. I could only think of one compromise. It wasn't perfect, but it would give them a better chance than a bullet to the head. "Look, you can leave them here with the ACs. They will be so busy dealing with them, they won't come after you. Plus, there's too many of them. Trust me. There are over a hundred of them headed this way. Will even give you a head start."

She tapped her foot as she considered my proposal. Then she looked back down at Yuri. For a moment, I panicked. I thought she was going to shoot him anyway, but instead she gestured to several guards and rattled off some instructions. "Okay. Fine. You have my word. But I'm bringing your handsome brother with us—as collateral. It'll be nice to bring some eye candy along. But if you try to run or escape or anything like that, I'll shove my pistol into his mouth and blow his sexy bald head off."

I winced. She was so violent. She didn't look like someone capable of such savage behavior, but her eyes were empty, dark, stagnate pools of brown.

I was about to object, but she shook her head. She raised her eyebrows, a gesture which implied that she wouldn't delay further.

"Fine," I said through clenched teeth.

"Wonderful." She put her arm around my shoulder, her pistol still in hand and hugged me to her. Her enthusiastic grin made me nauseous. "It'll be fun. Like a girls' adventure. Now—let's onward—shall we?"

65

Sherri and her small army escorted Yuri and me along the tunnel through the bunker door. As we moved, I said a couple of silent prayers of thanks for several miracles that happened. First, Sherri had initially planned to take all our weapons, which would've left everyone back in the tunnel defenseless against the ACs. But I reminded her of her promise, and I convinced her that taking their weapons would be akin to killing them. She agreed with some reluctance. After she'd acquiesced on the first negotiating point, I realized how valuable the anti-venom was to her. So, I used that fact to get as many things as I could, without pissing her off too much. I convinced her to leave her team's mobile medical unit with LaSalle and Komanski to administer to Eric. They'd leave the station as soon as I gave her the anti-venom, so they didn't need it. Her guards didn't protest because while the unit was mobile, it was a burden to lug around the station. I didn't mention Cox.

The last thing I insisted on was her word that once she retrieved the anti-venom, she would leave us alone. That as long as we didn't bother her or her team, she'd leave the station in peace with the contingency that anyone who survived kept the entire matter confidential. She agreed, but I knew it was a hollow agreement and that it wasn't really her agreement to make. She regarded me like I was a simpleton and a dead woman walking. There were two negotiating points on which she wouldn't compromise: our wrist devices and cloaking technology. She immediately took a boot heal to our devices to cut us off indefinitely from any A.I. and to prevent us from being tracked. She also insisted on confiscating LaSalle and Komanski's anti-cloaking glasses. She didn't want them working in tandem to attempt a rescue mission later.

Once inside the bunker, she had one of her Biotech guards toss a Medusa into the chamber where LaSalle and the others were. They would be immobilized for about a minute. I prayed that the herd of ACs wouldn't arrive while they were still paralyzed. They'd have very little time to treat Eric once the effects wore off. The medi-pod could work fast, but it would be close. Sherri wanted their hands full, and she had timed everything accordingly to coincide with the ACs' arrival. I thought it was a dick move, but it was the best I would get from her.

I prayed for their safety, and I prayed that we would pass through the bunker to the next tunnel, bypassing Cox altogether. Regardless of Sherri's promise not to kill any more people from my group, I worried that he would hear us come in and that he would call out to me or that she would have one of the Biotech guards search the rooms. She'd use Cox as extra leverage against me. Her justification would be that I lied about his death. But to my surprise, we passed through the bunker without any delay. Cox must've heard the stampede of footsteps because he didn't call out at all. Somehow, deep down in my gut I knew he'd be okay. LaSalle and Komanski knew that I'd gone into the bunker with him. They would find him. It would be the last miracle of the day.

As we made our way through the tunnels, Sherri chattered away like she was my mother, giving me a lecture about the finer points of being an exemplary military officer. She lectured me about my appearance and how I carried myself as a female officer. Most of it was critical, but some of it was surprisingly complimentary. I simply listened.

"You take your job very seriously. I like that, but you've been misled to believe that you need to lead like a man. *Tsk. Tsk.* That is an egregious error. Your power as female leader is your femininity. Why on God's green earth would you suppress that?" she said, shaking her head in passionate disappointment. "Your feminine nature is your power. *Unleash* it. And never ever offer to do work that can be delegated. You think your male counterparts will perceive you as hard working, yes? No, no, my dear. They will see you as a lacky because *that* is what you've become. You're as valuable as *you* believe you are. If you don't believe it, no one else will."

If our situation hadn't been so tenuous, I would've found the look on Yuri's face comical. He thought it ironic that someone as crazy as Sherri was giving me leadership advice. She followed the glance I stole at Yuri.

"What, you think I'm crazy?" she said, stopping with her hands on her hips. "Tell me I'm not right."

Just humor her, Yuri. Good gawd.

"You make some pretty good points," he said.

"Not that I need your validation, but I'm glad you see my perspective. Your sister would be a formidable leader with just a few minor adjustments."

"Your honesty is refreshing," said Yuri, deadpan.

Sherri flirted with Yuri the rest of the way. At first, he seemed repulsed, but gradually he softened up. He smiled and chuckled at anything that was remotely funny.

At one point, he flashed her his brightest, whitest smile. Her eyes twinkled in response.

"Oh, don't scowl, Amelia. It causes wrinkles." Sherri pinched my cheek. I wanted to clock her. "It's better to accept your shortcomings and improve upon them, than deny that they even exist. I'm not ashamed to say that I'm constantly working to improve myself."

"Improve?" Yuri scanned her body appreciatively. "I wouldn't change a thing."

Sherri's lascivious smile in response made me want to gag. He smiled back and winked at her. I was ready to throttle him, before it dawned on me: *he's distracting her.*

I tried to come up with some back up plans. The minute I produced the anti-venom, I was certain that Sherri would have us killed.

We passed through the second bunker, and I grabbed any food I could fit in my pack. I hadn't realized how hungry I was until I saw the rows of food. I expected Sherri to object, but she didn't care. All she cared about was getting her hands on the anti-venom.

We arrived at the last bunker over an hour later. Sherri was antsy at this point. So was I. I didn't trust her.

"Where exactly is it?"

"Where's what?"

"Don't test me, Amelia."

"I told you that I would take you to it, but I'm not going to just tell you. And I'm only taking you to the location. You'll get it once Yuri and I are safe. It's the only way I can assure you'll keep your word."

We climbed out of the bunker and found ourselves in the wilderness. It was dark. I couldn't really see anything. I recalled what LaSalle had said about the sun rising late and setting early here. I was certain that it couldn't be any later than four in the evening, yet it was dark out. I went to turn on my wrist light, but then I remembered that Sherri had confiscated it. One of her guards clicked on a dim red light after the last person climbed from the bunker. We stood at the top, and she turned to me. "What now? Where is it? I'm getting impatient."

"We're close."

"We better be."

Then it came. My opportunity.

The guard who was carrying the AC tracker held it up. It glowed red in the thick, wet air. "Ma'am, there are about fifty ACs headed our direction."

"Shit. They keep telling me they have control over these things, but that's just a bunch of bullshit. How far away are they?"

"They'll be here in just under a minute."

Sherri grabbed me by the collar and jerked me. "Tell me where the anti-venom is."

I hesitated.

She raised her pistol again and pointed it at Yuri. "Tell me, or I swear I'll shoot him in the face."

"Don't tell her," Yuri said. His voice shook a little.

I wasn't sure what to do. She cocked the hammer back on her pistol. So, I gambled. I pulled a small, clear box from my bag. It held an ampule with a clear amber liquid. "Fine. Here."

I held my breath as a guard held up a light for her. She lifted the box and examined it like she was holding the Holy Grail. The clear fluid sparkled in the light. "You really are something, Amelia Brown. You had it this entire time." She chuckled.

I shrugged. She grinned. Her smile was wide and a mile long, like an alligator. Then she frowned.

"Now give me the code."

"Not until we're out of harm's way. That's the deal," I said, my mouth set in a firm line.

She considered me for a moment and then shrugged. "No matter. I'll get a hacker on it. I don't need the code from you."

I braced myself. I saw Yuri stiffen out of the corner of my eye. If she didn't need the code, she'd very well kill us.

Instead of raising her pistol, though, she extended her hand. "As much as I'd like to continue this party, it's time for me to go. A pleasure doing business with you, Amelia."

I shook her hand, but when I went to pull away, she didn't let go. Her grip was firm like a gorilla. "Uh—but there's just one more thing," she said.

Suddenly a guard locked his arms around me from behind, in a bear hug. Another guard held my arm firm, the same arm with the hand that Sherri gripped. *What the fuck?*

Yuri lunged toward us, but another guard put a gun to his forehead, stopping him in his tracks.

Sherri held her free hand out. Another guard placed a tool of some sort in her hand, before saying, "Ma'am, we really need to go. The herd is close."

The device in her hand glowed blue with a laser. She slipped her fingers through them and held them like a pair of scissors.

I was speechless. I was so overwhelmed—frozen with terror—that I couldn't think of anything to say.

You're not negotiating your way out of this, Mel.

"What're you doing?" Yuri said. "Oh, Gawd. Don't do it, Sherri."

"For fuck's sake, how many times do I have to say it? My name is Shreya!" She grabbed my hand and gazed directly into my eyes. I could see the sadistic spark in them. *No. Please.* She squeezed the blades of the cutters around the pinky and ring fingers of my right hand. I saw my fingers fall away from my hand onto the forest floor. At first it felt like a puppy had gnawed on my hand. I stood comatose as I saw Sherri take off on a sprint away from us, with the rest of her guards in tow. I stood in a haze of dismay as the sinister chorus of approaching ACs grew louder.

I recalled a string of statements uttered before she left, something about *blood in the water* and *a nice diversion* and then, *later, suckas.* But everything else said was lost. I heard sounds, all of which were disjointed by my shock and pain. I heard voices, ACs moaning, sounds of a transport-copter nearby, landing and Yuri yelling. The sounds were muffled, far away, like I was underwater in a dream.

But then the haze wore off, and the sounds amplified. Then came the pain. It was excruciating. Someone yelled at me. "Mel. Mel. Damnit. Let's go. They're coming. You've got to snap out of it."

It was Yuri. He screamed at me to run. The ACs were so close. He pulled on my arm. Just the slight movement of my arm registered as pain. Everything was pain. My breathing. Thinking. *Now I have to run?* He yanked on me again. It sent a jolt of sheer, raw pain through my body. That was enough to make me move, to not have him yank on my arm again.

Then my endorphins kicked in, and I ran on pure adrenaline. I ran. Blindly. The pain still there, in the shadows, a searing force in the background of my thoughts. Muffled but there, threatening to return in full force at any moment. But I ran. I feared for my life.

Pain would go away. Death wouldn't.

I ran and ran, but then a log reached up and sent me tumbling over myself. Both hands reached out instinctively to stop my fall. A fresh wave of electric pain sliced through me.

How cliché. Trip and fall while being chased by monsters.

I plummeted down a steep decline. I didn't fight it anymore. I let myself roll. Perhaps I'd put some distance between myself and the ACs at a faster rate. I couldn't see anything. I knew the fall made me dizzy, but it was so dark that I had no sense of my disorientation. I tried to stand up, but I fell back down. My hand was fire. I wanted to scream from the pain, but I still heard ACs. They weren't right on me, but they were close. How long would it take for them to sniff me out? The sounds of their wailing amplified while I struggled to get my bearings. Unsure of where I was, I wanted to call out to Yuri. Yet, I knew he'd lost me when I fell. There was no point in endangering myself or Yuri in case he was nearby. I strained to see in the dark. The only thing that gave me any sense of direction was diffused light off in the distance from Port Juliette. I wasn't sure I would make it. Now I was tired, and every step was an exercise in agony. I needed a light. Anything to guide me. My eyes shut for a moment involuntarily. I was weak. Where could I get light? Then it dawned on me. I patted around on the forest floor with my good hand. I hurried. I could hear the ACs. They'd find me soon. Finally, I felt a log. I patted around it until I found a hole on the side of it. Normally I'd cringe at the idea of reaching into a log with all kinds of unknown bugs and creatures. Something might bite me, but an insect bite (even a snake bite) seemed like child's play next to the severing of fingers. Desperate and scared, I did it anyway. It was mushy in the inside. Cool and soft, almost comforting, in contrast to the stinging fire that was my other hand. I forced my thoughts back to the task at hand. I brought my ear up to the log and heard the familiar *cluck-ing* sound. There it was: the beetle. The one Cox showed me. Its hard, smooth back was there. I grabbed it. I pressed what I knew to be the yellow triangle, and to my profound relief, there was light. I held the beetle up. There was a tree right behind the log. I put my hand on it and used it as leverage to help myself up. I felt frail. My brain was foggy. I leaned against the tree and swayed. I shook my head vigorously. The movement sent fresh waves of pain through my mangled hand up my arm and through my body . . . searing, cutting acute pain. I forced myself not to think too much about it and concentrate on getting to the port.

I held the beetle in front of me to find a path, and that's when I saw a figure. A face emerged in front of me. I knew I was done. I'd be ripped to shreds by an AC. *So that's how it's going to end. I'm going to die here at the hands of this monster, and Sherri . . . Shreya . . . that fucking bitch is going to get away clean.* That was my last thought before I slipped into unconsciousness. Faintly I heard Yuri's voice yelling my name off in the distance, but at that point, everything went wobbly and then black.

66

Someone once told me that the most important time in the Navy was during the mid-watch, that block of time between night and early morning when the most beautiful and most horrible things happened. I never imagined that that time for me would find me hiding in a dumpster from flesh-eating ACs, telling you my story: A foreign station. A bank-owned research facility lab. Unknown lethal species. All diabolical elements of this concocted evil.

This wasn't what I anticipated for a first tour in the Navy.

Amidst an ocean of pizza boxes, bio-hazardous waste, cigarette butts, unknown slop, and God knows what else, I remembered thinking: *How did I get here?*

I should've seen the warning on LaSalle's face that day in the commodore's stateroom. He tried to tell me without telling me. A silent warning. A look. LaSalle knew what we'd face. Rivera warned me, too, but I guess it didn't matter. This was my fate. To meet these *things*.

Eric had found me in the forest after I'd passed out. He'd come after me and been my champion that night. Not LaSalle. Not Cox. Somehow, Eric managed to kill enough ACs to rescue me and get me to safety. When I came to, he asked me what happened.

"That bitch cut off my fingers with a pair of laser cutters."

"That's so messed up. I'm sorry."

"Don't be. She was kind enough to leave my writing hand intact."

"She's going to pay. I swear. Did you give her the anti-venom?"

"She thinks I did," I said, winking. "But, really, all she got was a vial of morphine."

Eric smirked. "She never believed me when I told her how clever you are or that you've got some cajones on you." He put his hand on my shoulder. "You realize that she's going to come after you when she finds out you duped her, right? And she's not going to be nice about it."

"Yeah, well, you've got to bring ass to kick ass. I'll be ready for her."

"Not if I get to her first."

Eric made me get up and walk. I was a stumbling mess. I'd lost a lot of blood from my hand. He administered to me from a first aid cannister. He found some painkillers to give me. It wasn't like having a medi-pod, but it was enough to numb some of the pain enough to move. I insisted on heading to the port. He insisted on going back, to the others. But I argued that there was nothing but ACs that way. Plus, I didn't think I could make it all the way back. The port was closer. His instincts told him that the port would be overrun by ACs, considering their speed and how fast they covered distances, but I reasoned that we had no reason or evidence to believe the port was compromised. Plus, if we got to the port ahead of any impending danger, we could alert the right people, and even get a search party to intercept Yuri, Cox, LaSalle and the rest of our party. Not to mention, I had two missing fingers, courtesy of Shreya Kolar. The constant throbbing of the stumps reminded me that I needed a medi-pod fast. I was also certain that Yuri would head to the port in search of Lauralie.

We trudged at a slow trot for what seemed like eons. We both sensed that we needed to get to the port as soon as possible. The threat of Shreya coming back, and the possibility of Yuri already being there, alone, was enough to keep us going. Every movement was an ordeal. The drug from the first aid canister was wearing off. A dull ache lingered in the background, patiently waiting to emerge again. I was certain I'd be miserable by the time we arrived at the port.

Then I had a bit of luck. A blue frog hopped in front of me. I remembered what Cox told me about the slime on its back and its healing properties. I dove for it. Desperately, I sprawled and snatched at it.

"What in tarnation are you doing?" Eric asked.

"Trying to get this frog."

"Whatever for?"

"For my fingers. Don't ask, just help me, will you?"

Eric nudged me aside and reached into a thicket of vines where the frog had hopped into just moments before. He reached and reached, until finally he pulled it out of the entanglement and with his fist closed around it. He held it up before me like he was holding something contaminated. I told him what Cox told me about the frog, reminding him not to let it hop out of his hand. I took a deep breath before placing the bloody two stumps of my severed fingers on the frog's back. Waves of pain radiated anew. I cried out for a second and then bit my lip, worried that the wrong person or thing would hear me. I forced myself to keep the mangled stumps on the frog's back as the mucus-like substance on its back seeped into my fingers. I waited, hoping it would work. I forced myself to bear the throbbing ache as I felt its body expand and contract as it breathed. Just as I thought I must be insane, the relief came like a soothing balm. It spread in welcome waves down my arm, and I almost collapsed from the sensation. Eric steadied me until I was okay enough to continue our trek to the port.

The frog's serum provided much longer relief than the canister drug. I looked down at the stumps after a few minutes and saw that they were already beginning to heal. Along the way, I made a point of catching two more frogs and scraping their mucus-like serum into a vial so I'd have some for later.

Finally, I was sober enough to focus and ask Eric some questions. Most of them pertained to what had happened after Shreya and her army moved us out of the tunnels.

"Well, after the Medusa wore off, we woke up to a herd of ACs heading toward us from one of the side tunnels. Good timing, too because LaSalle and Komanski had just enough time to get me in the medi-pod. I still don't know how they managed it. The effects of the Medusa leave you kind of drunk after it wears off. Once I was out, we had just enough time to grab weapons and fight," Eric said as he focused on the path ahead.

"Did anyone get hurt?"

"Yeah," Eric murmured. It was dark, so I couldn't see his facial expression, but I could tell he was about to deliver bad news. "It was a sloppy fight. The Medusa has some pretty rough side effects . . . one of which is a skull-splitting headache and sensitivity to light. It was hard to focus or to even concentrate."

Eric's voice started break. He shook with every word. I could tell this was hard for him, but he continued. "Your limbs . . . your hands and feet are weak. Kinda like the feeling after your leg falls asleep. It's numb and prickly at first, then weak. Once the blood circulates, you get stronger. Unfortunately, not everyone had full use of their motor functions once we had to fight. We had a friendly fire incident."

"Shit. Who?" I whispered.

"Komanski," Eric said as he looked down. "It was instant. I don't think he felt a thing."

I didn't say anything. I was relieved that it wasn't Cox or LaSalle. Eric didn't tell me who'd killed him. I didn't ask.

"Your petty officer, Mackie, showed up with two of my Marines and a couple of LaSalle's Biotech guards just as we were about to be overrun. We pushed the ACs back enough to escape the tunnel into the bunker room and seal it."

"I thought you were dead for sure," I said. "I'm glad you made it."

I reached out and touched the area of his chest where Sherri shot him. His suit had a hole with frayed edges. "You're lucky. It looked like she aimed for your heart. I'm surprised she missed."

"Yeah. Me too, but she did, thank God. The medi-pod analysis said the bullet missed my heart by less than an inch."

"And the AC bite? What did the analysis say about that?"

"Well, the medi-pods aren't programmed to know about ACs yet, but what's crazy is I felt like I slept ten hours, and I feel stronger. It recognized the toxin as a foreign substance in my bloodstream, and it tried to ensure proper system integration. So, I might now be immune like LaSalle."

I looked away. I could feel my emotions well up. I wondered about LaSalle and Cox. I wondered if they were okay. I didn't want Eric to see the worry on my face.

"Don't worry, Mel," Eric said. "I'm sure LaSalle is fine. He was completely okay when I left."

He doesn't even know that I'm worried about Cox more.

"And Cox?"

Eric gave me an odd look but then quickly dismissed it. "Good. LaSalle stitched him up with the medi-pod. I came after you while he was tending Cox."

"They let you leave?"

"I slipped out while they were preoccupied with tending the wounded. Otherwise, they wouldn't have let me go off on my own. Time was wasting."

"Going off on your own like that was reckless, Eric . . . and ballsy."

He beamed a little at the *ballsy* remark. "I had to, Mel. It was taking too much time. Getting all the injured fixed up with the medi-pod. I knew if I waited for all of that, you'd be long gone."

"Thank you. No one has ever done anything like that for me," I said. I hugged Eric. It wasn't sexual, but it was genuine. He pulled away, but I held on to him for several beats longer. Then I let go.

He acknowledged my thanks with a simple nod and changed the subject. "Boy, I can't wait to find Sherri. I have a debt to pay," he said.

"Shreya."

He snorted. "Right—Shreya. Let's just call her the Raging Bitch, as you so accurately put it." Then he shied away. "You must think I'm an idiot for hooking up with her."

"No. I don't, Eric. I think you're a hero, and she's just pure evil. She's worse than one of those ACs."

67

Eric got me to the port. At first when we arrived, the port was quiet. I wanted to believe that everyone was asleep, that everything had been buttoned up due to a hard day's work. But it was a fool's dream. The closer I got to some of the buildings I began to see carnage. Bodies were strewn about in haphazard disarray . . . none of them whole. Intestines, brain matter and other anatomical wreckage decorated the streets of Port Juliette like the set of a terrible low-budget horror film. The sides of buildings were smeared with blood from fingerprints and other blood-soaked body parts. Arms, torsos, hair and a myriad of other body components hung here and there, giving evidence of the chaotic events that had taken place not too long ago.

Eric had been right. The port was rampant with ACs, and they smelled blood. The moment we arrived, they sniffed us out and ran after us like hunting dogs after a hare.

Eric hung back. He had Komanski's Gat. He sprayed them back and forth. A wave of them collapsed. He'd given me a good head start. I called for him over and over. I didn't want to leave him alone, and I didn't want to be alone, but he insisted I run for a medi-pod. He swore he'd find me.

I'd gotten well into the port after the lead he gave me. Ten or so spotted me and chased me like a stampede of wild horses. I sprinted as fast as I could, terror being my sole motivator. Lungs blazing, I ran to Biotech's research labs. I headed for a door, but I didn't have access. Shreya had destroyed my wrist device and any means of communication with Shakespeare. I ran back to the front and searched until I found the dumpster. It was a gamble. It was the only idea I had. I hoped the smell from the garbage would mask the smell of my blood.

Seconds passed, and the nearby herd opted to go in another direction. It felt like an hour before Eric made his way toward me. I hoped that Eric had a way in, but I knew better. Our situations seemed bleak. I considered this to be my last moments. A wave of guilt washed through me. I thought of all the stations I'd never visit. I'd never see my father again, the man who raised me. I'd never get back to Earth and see the lush greenness of the forest or the chestnut log cabin where I was raised before I'd left for the academy. I'd never been to the beach, so I'd never see the ocean. I had so many things I wanted to do with this life. The thought of being eaten alive and leaving this world without putting some sort of stamp on it was depressing.

The opportunity to serve as a Navy officer was a great gift, but there were other things I wanted to do and be in this life. A gourmet chef, maybe? Nothing delighted me more than a well-prepared, exotically flavored dish artistically presented with bright colors. I'd thought of becoming a wedding planner too. What job could be better than observing people during their most joyous moments, planning the moment from its infancy and seeing it evolve into a final celebration of love? These were all thoughts that paid their last respects to me, like members at a funeral, passing one by one next to the casket.

I decided I'd at least record what little information I could manage, some evidence of my final moments. The commodore would have another legal officer at the *Midway* tomorrow, or even better, some young ensign already onboard who'd resume my duties temporarily. He'd find someone green that he could easily manipulate, but I'd encrypt it, and only give access to a handful of people: Rivera, Heather, Yuri and Cox. Maybe the voice. Hopefully, Yuri and Cox would survive. Somehow the information would make its way to the right people. They'd at least have some understanding of what got me and, God forbid, what he/she would be up against should these things manage a way off of the station. I contorted my body, straining to grab the small recorder I'd had the sense to stow away in the small pocket compartment at my ankle. Thank God, I had trusted my instincts back at the *Pegasus* and grabbed it. I rattled off a few bullet points of information, only the essentials, because even at a low whisper I was terrified the ACs would hear me.

Once I finished my recording, I peeked through a small opening in the dumpster and saw that Eric was still trying to make his way to me. He'd dropped several AC, riddling them across the neck with a violent cadence of spraying. They closed in, and his firing became scattered. He plugged a couple more across the chest and collarbone. Exploded their hearts from their torsos, but they weren't phased. They advanced full speed on him. The Gat was empty. He tossed it aside and tried hand-to-hand combat, snapping a couple of necks. He pinned one to the ground before sinking a blade into the back of its neck. That had been his mistake . . . taking too much time for just one of them. It gave more of them time to gang up on him.

I had to bite my lip not to cry out and give away my position. I was about to run out and help him. I convinced myself that he would be okay if I could just get to him. He'd built up immunity to their bites. He'd be all right. I propped open the dumpster lid. A shot wrang out. The bullet ricocheted off the corner of the dumpster right next to my hand. It grazed the stanchion that held the lid open. I dropped back down into the dark recesses of the dumpster before the lid closed shut with a heavy metallic thud. It almost fell on my head and knocked me out. The abrupt movements caused a new wave of sour, rancid stench to assault my nostrils. *Who the hell shot at me? Why weren't they shooting at ACs?* Whoever it was was an expert shot. I had to know who it was. I couldn't afford to wait. Eric was in trouble, and the urgency of this sank in as I heard several more shots. I risked a peek.

Another shot rang out as I cracked the lid open. Again. This time the lid did fall onto my head. *What on earth? Who is doing this?* I'd have a nice lump on my forehead if I survived until the morning. I had to know who was shooting, so I resolved to crack the lid ever so slightly. This time, careful with my movements, I opened the lid in infinitesimal degrees. I could see Eric struggling, but he was fine. He was wrestling with an AC just before he grabbed its head and twisted, breaking its neck. Then another AC ran toward him. It was over 20 meters away, but it advanced quickly on him. I heard another shot, and the AC's head exploded before it could get anywhere near Eric.

I raised the lid a little more and placed an empty pork and beans can just beneath it to keep it open. I pulled out the bino-card from my suit pocket and clicked it open. I looked through the thin, cold metallic plate and waited as the lens made automatic adjustments for me to see. I scanned the port until I could see movement. There were ACs making their way to us, but they were far off. I couldn't see anything human at first, but then I saw a sleek silhouette. Feminine. A svelte hourglass shape but somewhat taller than an average woman. A long, dark braid swung up as she kicked down the door of a dilapidated-looking structure. *Shreya.* I scanned up to the sign at the top of the building. Barry's Fried Chicken and Biscuits Shack. After a couple of hard kicks, she got most of the door down. I was pretty sure she was trying to get to the roof to get a better vantage point. *But would she shoot at us or the ACs?* She slung her rifle across her back and busted down the rest of the door with one last explosive kick. She rushed inside. I couldn't see her for a few moments, but then I saw her climbing out of a side window. The staircase to the roof must have been blocked. She began to climb, up the side of the building. Her movements were graceful and efficient. She climbed up and up like a spider monkey, all acrobatic and cat-like. Then in one last swift movement she propelled her body over the lip of the building onto the roof and immediately unslung her rifle from her back.

I looked back to Eric. He was in trouble. They had overwhelmed him. Electric dread surged through me like a dangerous live wire. Eric would die. Five ACs had clutched onto him from behind. They stretched him out like a man on a crucifix. I watched, appalled at what was about to happen. Then I noticed a tiny blue dot of light on his forehead; it bounced around the space between his eyes. A laser. From a high-powered rifle. I looked back to the roof of Barry's Fried Chicken and Biscuits Shack, a good 800 meters away. As expected, Shreya stood there in a wide stance, the butt of her long rifle wedged securely into her chest just below the collarbone. She looked with one eye through a scope. I froze. *What's she about to do? Why is she here even? She should be on an aerial-copter out of here.* My first reaction was rage. I wanted to scream at her, but then I got nervous. She'd seen me. She was the one who had shot at me. And now she was about to kill Eric. She'd do it too. She'd shot him once before. I watched her, shocked . . . frozen . . . helpless. The ACs bared their teeth like rabid hyenas about to pounce on an antelope. I looked back to Eric. The shot was quick.

By the time I heard the loud solitary round, I saw his head snap back. Blood sprayed from a big gaping hole in his head. The ACs who fed on his neck jerked their gaze up. Their firey eyes darted around as they tried to see where the shot came from. I looked back up to the roof of Barry's Chicken Shack. Shreya worked the bolt action on her rifle and aimed again. I was certain an AC had spotted me. They'd finished with Eric quickly and would search for new prey. Chunks of flesh hung from their mouths as they scanned the area. I held my breath. My heart pounded like elephant feet. I could feel a droplet of sweat tickle my temple, but I didn't dare move to wipe it. An AC stood nearby within sight of the dumpster, eerily still. Then it sniffed the air, long and deliberate. It sniffed a couple more times, short perforated intakes of air before it finally looked away. I quietly exhaled. I thought I was safe, but then it jerked its head back and sprinted toward me at a frightening pace. Three others followed suit.

Every interaction I'd ever had with anyone since reporting to the *USSS Midway* cycled through my mind. The moments it took for the AC to close in on me were only seconds, but time slowed, and I thought about all the situations I thought were so serious. I realized that it was all bullshit. That my life had been great. I resolved to make the last moments before my death count. I pushed the lid open and stood up, bracing myself. But as the AC reached the dumpster, I heard several shots, in quick succession. The AC nearest me slumped forward as its head exploded, brain matter spattering my TESS suit. Then six more fell like tumbling blocks behind it.

Shreya was picking them off with expert precision. Each AC crumbled to the ground at her hands, all of them suffering the same exact wound. It dawned on me how good she was with a rifle. She'd spared Eric in the end. Now, I was certain she purposely missed his heart when she shot him back in the caves. *What game was she playing?*

Emotion overcame me. I sank back down into the dumpster, not caring why Shreya had spared Eric a gruesome death or why she saved me. All I could think was that it was unfair. Despite our brief time together, my feelings for Eric ran deep. When he died a tiny piece of my soul left with him.

68

stayed in the dumpster, grief-stricken, exhausted and terrified. I tried to stifle my cries, to compose myself. I knew I should get up before more ACs came, but I couldn't stop crying. I felt so alone and hopeless.

Then I heard more shots again. Were more ACs coming?

I stood up and looked toward the building again. Shreya was standing at the very edge of the roof of Barry's Chicken and Biscuit Shack, picking off several ACs that had come her direction from a side street. Then she swung her rifle in an opposite direction. She aimed toward the entrance of the port and began to fire immediately. I wondered why she was shooting at them so far away, clearly out of my reach or even hers. I squinted some more until I could make out a figure running toward me. I couldn't tell who it was initially. The silhouette was a tall and muscular man. He was far away, but he ran hard. Twenty or so ACs followed at a ruthless pace, but only three were right on his tail. Shreya dropped them in three quick bursts, just as one reached out to grab the man. I used the bino-card to catch a glimpse of his face. It was Yuri. He'd made it.

As he got closer, I waved him in my direction, but he shook his head and veered off to my right where a barbed wire fence ran the length of Biotech's research facility. It registered that he was dragging them away from me. I was out in the open, a sitting duck in the dumpster. I could tell by the way Shreya stood on the roof that she was irritated. She was doing all the grunt work, saving our asses, and I was just standing there making myself an easy target. I didn't know what else to do, so I dropped back inside and closed the dumpster lid, leaving just enough space open so that I could see if Yuri would make it. Luckily, Shreya took out the few ACs who'd spotted me. They fell about a hundred feet away. The remaining herd of ACs followed Yuri as he made his way to the fence. A couple were already within reach of him again. Shreya picked off several more in hot pursuit. I'd never been so glad in my life to have her there. Just as three more closed in on him, she dropped them, but then she tossed her rifle aside. She held up her hands and then just watched.

What's she doing? She's out of ammo. We would be getting no more assistance, and I would have to figure out how to get out of the dumpster. *Why didn't I get out of there when I had the chance? Because you're scared shitless, coward.*

I looked desperately to Yuri. He was slowing down. I could almost see his breath from exertion. He was close, real close to the fence but not out of danger yet. *He can make it.*

Yuri was impressive to watch. Only something *not-human* could've kept up with him that distance. The last 50 meters, he sprinted like a track god, and then with his last step heaved up and pushed off into the air, catapulting himself toward the fence. He clutched on with all his strength. His dark forearms glistened with sweat underneath the floodlights. I could tell he was tired, and the fence was high, but he crawled up the chain links like a ninja in several fluid movements. He'd just barely escaped their reach. The corpses outstretched their withered hands upwards, howling and baring their teeth with disappointment at the fresh meat they'd just lost. They milled about on the other side of the fence watching

Yuri longingly as he bent over, gasping for air. From where we'd been separated, I approximated that he must've covered a couple of miles but sprinted the last 600 meters. Having been a U.S. Olympic team alternate in the 400, it was still a long sprint. And the way he'd run, I guessed he'd probably run a world-class record time.

Sweat pooled below him and saliva trailed from the corner of his mouth as he fought to catch his breath from the other side of the fence. Once he gathered himself, he straightened up and walked to the fence. He had a long gash down his arm which he'd caught on one of the barbs at the top of the fence. He wiped the blood from his arm and rubbed it on the fence. The ACs fell onto the bloodied links like hungry dogs upon a steak. Licking, gnashing, even biting the metal wire, the smell of blood made them delirious.

Yuri spat at them. They snarled back with a loud, satanic raucousness.

He paced back and forth, staring at the miserable lot of figures that were once human, a congregation of animated, yet decaying bodies. Strands of hair, clung precariously to misshapen skulls. Lifeless eyes embedded in sunken, hollowed-out orbits. Protruding cheekbones. Whatever they were, they were shells of what they once were—fathers and brothers, mothers and sisters who once had jobs, hobbies and normal everyday lives. They'd been people who had their own individual stories, born into the world with cute, angelic faces but sentenced to exit the world as monsters. They were miserable to look at, and I knew exactly the hatred Yuri felt for them.

"Fuck you," he said, middle finger outstretched.

They snarled some more and began to shake the fence, trying to pull it down. To my relief, the fence didn't budge. Yuri was safe.

Why rile them up like that?

Finally, after some time they gave up and milled about. Then, without warning, they shifted in unison, and their attention was diverted. Like a herd of antelope, they took off on a sprint and headed in another direction. Something else had caught their interest. I was curious to know what it was but not enough to risk my own safety. They moved together as if controlled by one voice, like a flock of angry birds.

I dreaded leaving the dumpster. I had been chased into it by a group of corpses who'd just missed me. What if they came back by my dumpster? What if I was climbing out just as they passed by? I was terrified at the thought of ending up like Eric. Shreya was out of ammo, so I wouldn't even be afforded that merciful gesture. I looked back to the roof of Barry's Chicken and Biscuit Shack. Shreya was gone.

That bothered me, but I didn't have time to worry about her. I had my own ass to think about. I worked up enough nerve to peek out from beneath the lid, but I was really motivated by the fact that Yuri might be forced to leave his position if it turned out there were ACs inside.

Slowly, I lifted the dumpster lid and peeked out. The port was dark, but there were floodlights everywhere. The entire facility reminded me of a maximum security prison, which really wasn't too far from the truth. The entire compound used to be a prison where convicts had been sent to rot—an Alcatraz in space—before Biotech made a bid for it.

Oh, to hell with it. I climbed out. I lowered myself out of the dumpster and tiptoed toward the fence. The motion of my movements caused some lights to light up the yard where Yuri was, which startled him and scared the shit out of me. He looked around, trying to see. Blinded by the sudden light, I wasn't sure if he could see me.

I whispered. He whispered back. "Mel?"

"Yeah," I said. I moved closer so he could see me.

"Oh, thank God." He exhaled. "I thought they'd gotten you. I heard you fall, but I couldn't find you. I looked and looked. I thought I was alone."

I moved up to the fence and raised my good hand to the fence. My fingers clasped some of his through the fence holes.

"No, you're not alone. Eric saved me—but—he's dead," I said.

He didn't say anything. He knew it was pointless to ask how it happened. We'd endured so much over the last twenty-four hours that it was the last thing either of us wanted to talk about.

I noticed the long, deep cut along his upper arm. "Goddamn. You're bleeding. You cut yourself on the barbed wire."

"I'm fine. I'll live."

"You're bleeding a lot, Yuri. They'll sniff it out, and it won't take long. I think you should climb out."

"No. You should climb in."

"No way. There might be some in there. Then we'll really be trapped."

"This place is massive," he said. "We have a better chance inside anyway."

"Are you crazy?"

"No, seriously. Look. These things are all over the place now. The entire station is infested. So, no matter where we go, we're screwed. And—we need to get that hand fixed," he said as his gaze dropped toward the bandaged mess.

I clutched my hand again and examined it. Even though the stumps were healing and it didn't hurt as much, it still needed to be repaired.

"I'm going to make that bitch pay." Yuri's nostrils flared.

Funny, Eric said the same thing.

"Shhh. Keep your voice down." I looked warily around. "Anyways, that bitch just saved our asses. She's the one who dropped those ACs that were on your tail."

"Seriously?"

"Yes. Don't ask me why. I know, it doesn't make sense, but we can't worry about that now."

"Well, if she's still out there, we're going to have to worry about it at some point. She can't be trusted."

"I know, but right now we need to focus on what our next move is."

"Can you climb over?"

"No."

"Your hand?"

"No. Because I don't want to."

"Why?"

"Because there was another herd that followed me just before I dove into the dumpster. You need to climb over to my side. We can hide in the forest."

"No way. I'm wiped, and if we go back out there, we don't know how much running we'll have to do. Could be from ACs or indigenous life or *both*. In here we can at least find a place to hide and rest. Plus, we need to get you to a medi-pod, Mel. Maybe regenerate your hand if all of the tissue isn't dead."

Yuri's logic made sense. The thought of finding a medi-pod and a safe place to sleep was impossible to resist. I really wanted to go and find the others, but I wasn't going to do that alone, especially at night.

"What about the others? We need to find them," I said.

"What others? You mean the midshipman and Chief Martinez, or do you mean you need to find *him*?" Yuri said.

"If anything happened to him, I don't think I could handle it. Besides, you're doing the same for *her*."

Yuri's face hardened. I'd struck a cord, but that was my point.

He stared off for a moment. Then he nodded. "Okay. If you promise to help me track Lauralie, I promise we'll go and look for the rest of the group."

"Deal."

I knew I didn't have to make him promise again. He knew what it felt like to be separated from someone dear and constantly

432

wonder what kind of danger they were in. Plus, there was a lot we could do inside. Maybe I'd find a smart wrist on a dead body. I'd reprogram it and find a way out of this. Now, I really did miss Shakespeare. He could help us make sense of everything and help us locate the others. If I couldn't find a mobile device, at the very least I could find a terminal that connected to Biotech's mainframe and patch into Shakespeare's. If I was lucky, I'd get ahold of Heather, and perhaps I'd establish comms with her. Fear niggled at me, though. Something told me things weren't going well back on the *Midway*. I felt lost in a sea of unanswered questions that only Shakespeare could answer.

Yuri motioned to me impatiently. "What are you waiting for? Hurry up and climb over before those things come back out."

I nodded and positioned myself on the fence. Before I began my climb, Yuri leaned in with a curious look on his face.

"Wait," Yuri said. "It's been killing me. Who was the owner of the voice back in the equipment room, back in the caves? I've gotta know. He told you how to find the cure but refused to tell the rest of us. Who was he?"

I paused, considering his request. Then I realized that I'd have to tell him at some point. I looked him directly in the eyes and clasped his fingers through the fence.

"My father," I said. Then I took a deep breath and began my climb.

THE END

Made in the USA
Monee, IL
03 November 2020

46507119R00243